UNHOLY LOVES

UNHOLY LOVES

A BELLE EPOQUE MYSTERY

Lisa Appignanesi

McArthur & Company

Toronto

First published in Canada in 2005 by
McArthur & Company
322 King St., West, Suite 402
Toronto, Ontario
M5V 1J2
www.mcarthur-co.com

Library and Archives Canada Cataloguing in Publication

Appignanesi, Lisa

   Unholy loves / Lisa Appignanesi.

ISBN 1-55278-501-7

   I. Title.

PS8551.P656U5 2005   C813'.54   C2005-903712-1

Cover Design: Mad Dog Design Connection
Book Composition: Michael P.M. Callaghan
Printed in Canada by: Webcom

The publisher would like to acknowledge the financial support of the
Government of Canada through the Book Publishing Industry Development
Program (BPIDP) and the Canada Council for our publishing activities. The
publisher further wishes to acknowledge the financial support of the Ontario
Arts Council for our publishing program.

10 9 8 7 6 5 4 3 2 1

PART ONE

HOME GROUND

1

PART TWO

DEAD WOMAN RUNNING

85

PART THREE

SUBTERRANEAN

157

PART FOUR

SACRED ENDS

263

PART ONE

HOME GROUND

_ 1 _

Under a sullen sky of unbroken grey, the train chugged and hooted its way through the last of Paris. Marguerite de Landois adjusted her hat and her spirits and sat back with a sigh into upholstered seats. They emitted a slight odour of damp wool.

A maze of ramshackle streets and dilapidated houses gave way to rubble strewn fields, to huts with roofs of card and rag, to abandoned coaches converted into hovels. The gleaming express engine built to race into the new twentieth century picked up pace and sped through the waste-land where the city's most recent and poorest inhabitants had set up the rickety shelters they were forced to call home. A lone, hunched child in a threadbare jacket watched the train's steaming passage and lifted a hand in a desultory wave. Wishing the world otherwise, Marguerite waved back.

The city merged into flat countryside, the mud brown of ploughed, winter fields broken only by lines of poplars. They were traveling south-west across the plain which moved towards the centre of France, the rus-tic Black Valley the great Georges Sand had urged her stallion through, the fertile banks of the Loire and its neighbouring rivers, amongst them the little Loir, on whose banks Marguerite had roamed.

Snow started to fall. A dense flurry of flakes to mark the new year. They thickened the air into a swirling whiteness, coated the earth in soft dazzle. Trees donned fresh cloaks as light as rabbit fur only to shed them once more when snow fizzled into rain.

The pastoral idyll of *la douce France* was all around them. Valleys of vine, orchards and meadows of what in summer would be plenty bor-dered a river that meandered between willows and poplars. Cattle grazed, cocks crowed, white peasant houses grew out of the gentle roll of lime-stone fields. Here and there a graceful tower reached for the sky or tumbled amidst medieval ruins.

Past the ancient, glove-making town of Vendome, past the dome of the massive Abbey which housed Christ's tear, an old horse trudged along the road beside the track. He dragged a rickety farm cart slowly behind him. A cluster of walled buildings appeared, turned in on themselves. A cloister. An elaborately wimpled woman, book of hours in hand, appeared on a path, then merged with the wall to disappear forever into some secret interior.

It became increasingly difficult to remember that Paris existed. Paris with its glitter and bustle. Paris which was one vast construction site, a banner to speed and modernity and progress. Paris with its giant girders, new underground trains and great miraculous tunnels boring through earth and under water. Paris with its noise and engineering miracles and new bridges. Its soon-to-be-opened Universal Exhibition—an array of soaring, extravagant, national structures all to be connected by the miracle of an electrically propelled pavement to the future. Paris with its anarchists and rowdy demonstrators demanding a just republic or fomenting a return to a Catholic nation where the army was strong and outsiders ousted. Paris, with its stark contrasts and contradictions. Paris, capital of dazzle and elegance and misery.

And here, in this countryside, tucked into its winter sleep, there seemed to be nothing at all except a cloister and an old horse pulling a rickety cart along a dirt road. And two hatted men huddled on a seat, oblivious to the passing train and the changing times.

Plus, she reminded herself, one husband, who had called her to his side for inexplicable reasons.

Marguerite de Landois felt the crinkle of the letter she had placed in her pocket this morning in the library of her house in the Faubourg Saint-Germain. She pulled it out to make sure yesterday's reading hadn't been imagined.

She was a woman of a certain age, to use the phrase a generation of novelists had coined gently to imply that a woman was past her prime. She rather liked to apply it to herself. Her 'certain age' was all of thirty-three. She was tall and a little too slender for buxom times and she moved with great agility, even when she was seated. She had light hair of a golden sheen, pulled back with a number of combs and piled high, though now hidden by her wide-brimmed hat with its trim of fur. Her cheekbones were evident, her mouth generous enough to diminish the hauteur of nose and brow. Her wide, yellow-flecked eyes looked out at the world with a passionate directness and a not always fashionable intelligence tinged with spirited humour. An envious world fought for entry to her celebrated salon where the great, the good and the not so very good mingled with politicians, writers and artists. Those who saw her more than once usually thought her beautiful and grew enamoured of her understated elegance.

This expressed itself today in the long, unbroken line of her checked skirt, the fine lace frill of her high-collared blouse, the perfect cut and ingenious darts at shoulder, sleeve and waist of her soft woolen jacket.

As Marguerite reread the letter from her husband, there was a bemused expression on her face. No, there was no turning back. Incomprehensible though it might be, Olivier had definitely ordered her to the chateau which, these days, he largely inhabited without her.

Her travelling companion met her eyes and gave her the ghost of a smile before returning her whole attention to some invisible point on the other side of the rain-spattered windows. In her blue sailor suit with its midi collar and the toque of a hat that did nothing to hide the pale aureole of hair, Martine Branquart looked younger than her seventeen years, a mere wisp of a girl still startled by the harsh realities of a world she had been flung into with too much suddenness. Marguerite's heart went out to her.

Suddenly she was glad of Olivier's summons. Being in the Loir region would allow her to help the girl more directly. She was pleased that she had managed to negotiate some time off for Martine from her employers to take her along.

Martine had first come to see her at home in the Faubourg about two week ago, just before Christmas. She had been brought by Marguerite's great aunt, Madame de Verney, a redoubtable woman whose face had begun to resemble a whalebone corset, the eyes bulging out above the lines of sunken cheeks. The old woman's stories had a way of meandering and leaping sideways into tangents, so that it took some time for Marguerite to discover that Martine was an orphan linked to Madame de Verney by Martine's long-dead grandmother, who had acted as her great aunt's dress-maker years back when she still lived in the country. And that Martine, who had been in service in Paris for some eighteen months (though she had been educated to better things), had remembered the connection and cleverly come to Madame de Verney to seek help.

She feared that her sister, Yvette, who had been in service in the village of Troo on the banks of the Loir, had disappeared. This fear had become fact when her sister hadn't even responded to the sacrosanct season's greetings. Marguerite, given her contacts with the police—a word Madame de Verney spat out with a mixture of furious disdain and rampant curiosity—should certainly be able to find her.

How the old woman, who now rarely left the gilded comforts of her Second Empire chairs, had heard of Marguerite's involvement with the death of Olympe Fabre, let alone with Chief Inspector Emile Durand, she had no idea. Though news did have a way of travelling with the speed of lightning, or at least the speed of tongues, in the Paris circles she frequented. And it was true, that since her dear friend, the journalist Rafael Norton had returned to Boston, her best hours had been spent with the Chief Inspector who increasingly called on her whenever a case he was investigating for the *Judiciare* involved a member of the *beau monde* she was better placed to understand than he was.

In fact, Marguerite reminded herself as she stared out into the empty countryside, it was only the Chief Inspector who had bemoaned her sudden departure for the country. He had been able to discover nothing about the missing Yvette from distant colleagues in the Loir *Sureté*. Regional and metropolitan branches of the police rarely managed to work together, he pointed out to her on the telephone, a caustic edge to his voice. But he had threatened he might come after Marguerite to discuss a delicate and quite different matter.

As the train drew close to their destination, Marguerite wondered once more what could have made Olivier demand her instant presence at La Rochambert. In the eight or so years of their increasingly amicable separation, they had rarely broken an agreed-upon routine: a summer month together in the Loir valleys that had shaped her childhood, and a winter month in the stately Paris *hotel particulier* she now inhabited. And ten months of unquestioning independence. The arrangement had made their marriage a dual triumph—by providing the form his Catholicism demanded and the freedom from each other they both desired.

Divorce, given his family, had never been an option, never mind its rising numbers in this new electric world. Olivier's code was secret liberty and public restraint: never to be confused with secret vice and public virtue. For the good of the community, marriage was indissoluble; the family, cornerstone of society, sacred. Marguerite, as emancipated as she might be, was, like it or not, the wife of the Comte de Landois and must behave accordingly. The word 'separation' was never one he used. They merely kept to their discrete lives.

Yet Olivier had called her to his side now. Expressed urgency. Could his health have taken a turn again after the problems of this summer, when he had told her he would prefer to be on his own after a very few days? He was no longer a young man. He had hurtled past the mid-fifties mark.

With no warning, the train lurched and bumped to a screeching halt. Everyone was flung from seats to floor. Cases crashed from racks. Umbrellas and hats rolled. Baskets tumbled, their contents spilling out like restless souls. Screams and shrieks filled the air.

An eerie stillness followed the eruption of noise. It was made up of shock and unspoken questions and a testing of limbs. Images of severed bodies and broken-backed engines hurtled through Marguerite's mind together with hundreds of recent newspaper accounts of railway madness: engineers driven to hacking frenzies by the labour of feeding the beast's ravenous maul; passengers' nerves destroyed by the sheer speed of the racing demon; lovelorn women hurling themselves from moving cars; travellers in trances unable to remember who they were or metamorphosing into monstrous doubles. Ever more democratic in its reach, the railway fled through the country creating a hundred new ills alongside its benefits.

Marguerite pulled herself up, made sure that her little maid, Jeanne, and Martine were unhurt and rushed from the compartment to see if help was needed elsewhere.

Outside, despite commotion, the carriages were all upright. Toward the front of the train, a crowd of men had gathered near the smoking brute of an engine. Vapour curled in the cold air making everything hazy. A brisk wind carried it to the east across a flatness of field and tugged at top hats and caps and coattails. All heads were turned in the same direction: something just under the train held their attention.

A dog barked with a wild yap. Packed mud clung to her feet and the braided trim of her long emerald skirt. Now that she was closer, she could see uniformed railway staff bent over the track on all fours. A body was being pulled from the rails, whether dead or unconscious, she couldn't yet tell. She shuddered. All around her there were shouts and cries, distorted by the wind. An engineer was screaming over and over for all to hear that he had pulled the brake, had tried to stop in time, but the gloom of the light, the speed, everything had combined to stop him

A conductor emerged to bar Marguerite's way.

'Non, non, Madame. It's nothing. Just an obstacle on the track. Not for a lady's eyes. We're sorry for any discomfort. We'll be off again soon enough.' He was deferential, polite, but he was also firm.

The obstacle, Marguerite noted, had to be carried off on the shoulders of three men. Even at her distance she could see, as the body was laid on the ground, that the splay of the limbs, the position of the head, didn't bode well. In fact the 'nothing' that had occurred and brought the train to a screeching halt was reminiscent of nothing so much as death.

'Let me through, Monsieur. I'm the Comtesse de Landois. I have medical training. I'll be able to help.' She asserted rank and walked past the conductor now, not waiting for permission. Her claim to expertise was only a slight exaggeration after all those months of lectures at the Salpetrière and the Hôtel-Dieu, where she had sat with two other women amidst a horde of men.

But there was no help to be had for the man in the mud-splattered suit. The body was mangled. The legs, she could now see, dangled and must be all but severed at the knees—as though he had flung himself too far across the track. While voices barked conflicting orders, she pulled off a glove and felt for a pulse at neck and wrist. There was none.

A less than clean blanket had been fetched from somewhere and the men spread it out beside the man's body and turned him over onto his back. He was a large figure. Heavy in his inertness. The jowly, pock-marked cheeks had colour, though only that of weak tea, but the lips she was about to put her mirror to were ashen. She stopped mid-gesture as her gaze moved up his face. One of the man's eyes had been torn from its socket, leaving the face a grotesque shell.

Her stomach heaved and she felt her mask of composure crumbling. She forced her gaze downward. Faces were always the worst. Poor man. Who was he? What fate had led him to fling himself onto the tracks? It looked as though the ravenous birds had already got at him. Strange that. So soon. There didn't seem to be very much blood where the train had hit him either.

A cry—like that of a frightened animal—erupted just behind her, distracting her from the dead man. She veered round to see Martine Branquart toppling to the ground. She hadn't noticed that the girl had followed her.

The conductor caught her just in time.

'Women,' he muttered. 'I told her not to . . . '

He swallowed his words as Marguerite administered two quick slaps to the girl's translucent cheeks. She had no smelling salts to hand.

Blue eyes fluttered open, misty with confusion.

'Hold her firmly, Monsieur. She's in my charge. Let's get her back on the train.'

'You, too, Madame. We're about to head off, now.'

'Yes. There's little we can do for the man. You've called for help?'

'We'll send some back for him when we reach the station.'

The conductor settled them into their compartment, and the train soon after began to move. Aghast, Jeanne, her fluttery little maid, poured coffee from an intact thermos flask and forced it upon Martine.

'I'm sorry, Madame. So sorry for making a nuisance of myself,' Martine murmured to Maguerite. 'I . . . I thought I saw . . .' She shook her head, as though clearing her thoughts. 'I was thinking of Yvette. Like the girl in the story I was reading.' Her face was paler than the dead man's. 'Under the train.'

'You mustn't have such dark thoughts, Martine.'

The girl closed her eyes abruptly.

'We'll find your sister. I know we will.'

Martine gave no murmur of assent.

The taut face, pent-up, was like a child's again, but somehow less innocent now with those blue eyes shuttered more tightly than a house willfully closed to the world.

There were things Martine wasn't telling her. Marguerite remembered that until last year the girl had always lived in the region.

'Did you recognize the man, Martine? You must tell me.'

The eyes flew open. The girl passed a tongue over dry lips. 'No, no. No, Madame. Well, yes. At first I thought I did,' she shivered. 'But it was just an impression. A wrong one. Because he was so big and ugly.'

Marguerite let it go. The train had picked up speed. She patted the girl's long-fingered, expressive hand. Olympe's hands had been like that. Nervous in their expressiveness. Is that what had made her take Martine up with such alacrity? Was Martine an echo of Olympe, another frightened girl troubled by a sister? Or perhaps Marguerite had reached an age that made her want to prevent this young woman from making the mistakes she herself had?

'You'll tell me later, Martine,' Marguerite soothed. 'Later. We have lots of time.'

'He didn't have time, Madame.' Martine's tongue tripped up her words. 'Time's not on our side.'

_ 2 _

La Rochambert rose from a bumpy turn of the road like a graceful and reclusive old friend, too distant from the world to be overly affected by it, yet prepared to shelter and warm the fraught and the weary. Perched on its green hillside, the small, turreted château's sparkling whiteness was emphasized by the dark tiles of its roof and the gathering dusk. The plump roundness of the east and west towers, the mansard windows with their carved mullions and the bell tower above the portico all smiled at Marguerite with the sweetness of childhood. Where the road dipped and turned again, the row of acacias her father had planted and the gentle slopes of an adjoining meadow came into view. Another turn and the five windows of the far wing appeared, to its side the terraced gardens which eventually led to fields and a chestnut copse and another twist of the river.

For a moment as the carriage rattled over a rut, she forgot the dead man on the track and the anxious young woman at her side. She was thrust back into a childhood unencumbered by thick skirts or propriety. Daddy's girl, she raced through fields and woods, a free creature delighting in the surprises nature brought. She followed her father everywhere in those years—on visits to greenhouse or stables or coach house, on hunting and fishing expeditions on both the Loir and the Braye, to meetings with overseer and gamekeeper and even to long drawing sessions in the library, where her father guided her hand to shape leaves and flowers, tree frogs and beetles and ants of a dozen descriptions.

The fall from grace had come when she had had to don long, encumbering skirts like the mother she had never really known. Life changed ineradicably. To be a woman was something she had had to learn step by newly-shoed step in delicate heeled slippers or laced boots. Even now, she sometimes experienced it all as a masquerade.

Years on, it still troubled her that her father, so enlightened in other ways, had handed her over at sixteen to her great aunt in Paris. She was the very same aunt who had brought her Martine. He had handed Marguerite over in order to have her married off to the first respectable bidder whose fortune could be stretched to save the old family seat. What else, in the end, were women for? Olivier's family title was altogether respectable if more recent—since it had been in Napoleon's gift—than her own, and his fortune stretched easily enough to encompass the upkeep of La Rochambert.

Marguerite stared out the carriage window at a landscape that was achingly familiar even in its winter shroud. It told her that her description of the past wasn't altogether fair. She had been infatuated with Olivier at first—his experience, his intelligence, his dignity, the fine lines which gave his features such depth. She had been drawn by his bright silk cravattes and brocaded dandy's waistcoats, sights that dazzled far more than a bird of tropical plumage spotted amidst the sparrows of the valleys.

Back then, Olivier, most urbane of men, had hardly been interested in the old provincial estate. Now, he was as wedded to it as her father had ever been. Though all the finances in the world couldn't stretch to secure the paternal estate in the family for the longer term. Olivier and she had singularly failed to produce the necessary heir.

Despite her father's best intentions, time played its tricks and turns more mysteriously than any mountebank.

With something of a delayed reaction, Marguerite trembled. Death was hardly the advance welcoming party she might have hoped for in returning to La Rochambert.

The fire in the south salon blazed and crackled, giving old mirrors a golden life, warming the ancient, faded tapestry on the far wall in which women reclined on flower-strewn fields. Outside, through the tall glazed doors, the winter terraces were graced with only a few shrubby evergreens and a hedge of summer-fragrant boxwood. Everything was the same,

Marguerite noted, but subtly, indecipherably different. She felt this increasingly each time she came. The difference had nothing to do with new furnishings.

She shifted her gaze to the portrait above the fireplace and tacitly greeted the mother she could barely remember outside this frame. Her pictorial stand-in reigned in the statuesque majesty of glistening burgundy folds and finely coiled hair. Except for the stance, the current coincidence of age and perhaps the curve and sweep of arm and figure, there was little to evoke Marguerite either in feature or colouring.

She turned to Olivier, who paced the length and breadth of the room and had been doing nothing else for a good five minutes. He might have wanted her to arrive in a hurry. But he didn't yet seem to have his words prepared for her. Nor was there any sign of illness.

He was a tall man, still trim, though heavier now around the jowls. His shoulders had an arrogant set. His nose was proud, his shock of well-trimmed hair greying at the temples and in one daring stripe which swept back from his brow and looked as if it might have been painted, were it not that the shade so closely matched his moustache. He had taken to wearing the tweeds of an English country gentleman rather than the fine worsted suits of his Paris wardrobe. They gave him a diffident, casual air, which belied the man she knew, who could be exacting and punctilious.

The once passionate hatred she had felt for Olivier had long ebbed. What was left, she decided, was a naturalist's tolerance, mingled with a curiosity about the sheer variety of specimens the world presented. There was also a kind of loyal affection: they had both, after all, had to make accommodations. The loyalty was coloured by a muted hue of fear. Olivier was a scorpion whose tail might strike out at any moment. She knew that too well. The handsome, if thickening, features would offer no warning.

He had finally stopped pacing and was waiting for a servant she didn't recognize to deposit the tray, light the lamps, pour the tea, offer the pastries in the precise manner Olivier designated. Her father had never managed as much. Even the two golden retrievers who lay by the fire were impeccably trained to keep their panting presence discreet.

The changes the room sported were subtle ones. The chairs had been recovered in a pleasing blue-grey stripe. A walnut clock that chimed the hour stood against the far wall. The array of mounted beetles had gone, to be replaced by a selection of watercolours which might even have been English. She couldn't fault anything. Olivier was a man of order and taste even if his didn't extend to the new art with its sinuous, curving lines and bright post-impressionist colours.

At last, the niceties over, he spoke.

'You're wondering why I had you rush here?'

'I am, Olivier. I am.'

She tempered her impatience with a smile.

'It's difficult for me to explain.'

'I see that.'

'Perhaps I should start from the beginning.'

She nodded encouragement.

'Paul and I were planning on a morning's fishing. The day after Christmas'

'Paul?'

'Of course, you haven't yet met. Paul Villemardi. He's a sculptor. Well he started off as a stonemason. But talented. Very. I've set him up in two of the outhouses. He's creating some work for the garden. Where was I?'

'You were going fishing.'

'Yes, yes. Well, we got to the river. I don't know if you know that stretch. Just past the island, where there's a turn and the bank gets steeper. About a kilometre or two along from here. Towards Montoire.'

'Yes.'

'Well, we saw this basket.'

'A basket?'

'Yes. Not very large, nor very small. A wicker fruit basket, perhaps. The kind the peasant women bring their fruit to market in. But inside there were no fruit. There was a baby.'

Marguerite swallowed hard and muffled a cry. Olivier's face beneath the burnish the outdoor life had given his cheeks grew pale and he looked away. There was a sudden shifty air about him.

'A baby? A dead baby?'

He moved towards the window so that his face was hidden to her.

'We thought it was dead. It looked dead. We almost left it there. But when we got home, Madame Solange—Armand, her boy, was with us and had run ahead—came rushing out and she took the baby. Took it in to the fire. And while we were waiting for the curé and wondering quite what to do, we heard this, well this squeal really. It wasn't dead. The poor little blighter wasn't dead.'

'What a relief. A boy, then?'

He nodded. He started pacing again and Marguerite had to press him. 'What did you do?'

'Madame Solange thought we should take him to the Blessed Sisters. You know, the convent just outside Blois. There's one of those wooden slots in the outside wall for depositing babies. Unwanted infants. So I rode over towards Blois with Paul. We found the convent all right. The place was deserted. We stared at the old wall with its creeping moss. We located the turning cradle. I opened it and tried to peer through. All I could see was a path and a hedge and some graves. Not a single living soul. And I couldn't bring myself to do it. Couldn't leave the babe. He was watching me, you know. With those eyes of his wide open. As if he knew. He could tell. There was something other-worldly about that gaze. Pleading and chastizing at once. Anyhow, the curé thought it was right that we had brought him back. He hadn't liked the idea of the convent. He said our finding the babe was meant. Christmas and all that.'

He paused. Marguerite stared at him.

'I omitted to tell you. Madame Solange had somehow managed to round up a wet nurse, a large, plump, young woman from near Lavardin. And within a day, the child had revived a little. It was miraculous really. He didn't cry. Not at all. He just watched us. And moved his tiny hands. He wanted to live. He must have wanted very much to live. To live here. With us.'

Olivier made a delicate, aimless motion with his long fingers, then bunched them into a fist, as if he had trapped something.

'He held on to me. To my finger. So I couldn't just push this living bundle through a hole in the wall, like some bit of refuse. Abandon him. I began to agree that if I had found the babe, it was because I had been fated to.'

'Fated?'

'I thought of Moses.'

'I don't understand.'

'You know. He was found in the rushes.'

'You see yourself as the Pharaoh's daughter.'

'Not quite.' His lips curled into a faint scowl. 'It's as if I've been given a mission.'

'What has fate ordered you to do, if it isn't to turn the infant over to the good sisters?'

'That's why I asked you to come.'

'Oh?'

'Yes. I'd like to keep him.'

The statement came at her like a bolting horse. She needed to leap out of its way. Yet she could see that an abandoned child needed to be rescued.

'I want us to adopt him.'

'Adopt him?'

That addition knocked her sideways. Took all the wind out of her.

Olivier was staring at her, waiting for a response.

'I don't quite know what to say.'

'No. Of course. I understand. You'll have to think about it. Because he would be yours, too. We would be a family. A proper family.'

He gave the word an aura of ancestors and blood lines and social place. She could feel an iron gate coming down with a clang in front of her. There was another behind and two at either side. There was no escape.

Olivier's eyes burned his will into hers. Nothing would deter him from his path. She could feel it.

His expression reminded her of the occasion when his secret life had stood revealed and blazing between them—a fire that had run away with itself and threatened to burn them in its passage, but that he was proudly powerless or unwilling to stop.

They were in the hands of destiny.

Marguerite baulked. She had always baulked at fate's dictates.

'It's a rather large proposition.'

'Yes, I know. But important. The boy would grow up here, of course. You could still spend a portion of your time in Paris. I would come there more too, if what I have in mind transpires.'

'But surely it's too soon to make any kind of decision. Why, the child's parents may be weeping somewhere. Or even if he was abandoned, the mother might still change her mind.'

Olivier shrugged.

'And I'd have to know.' There was a tremor in her voice and she worked to still it. 'Are you taking any steps to find out how the child found his way into the river? Who his mother was? Or his father? There will have been a father somewhere, Olivier. Unless the angelus has murmured otherwise to you.'

The last had come beneath her breath and without her volition, but he had heard her. A flash of casual brutality edged his features. Olivier had always had the easily-irritated humour of a man who had known little but conquest and ease.

'There's no need for either sacrilege or sarcasm, Marguerite. If we had our own children, it would be different.'

She had deserved the cut, but for some reason she couldn't stop herself even now. 'They, too, would have had need of a father, as well as a mother. There was a man on the tracks, Olivier. A dead man,' she suddenly added.

'I'm interested in the living, Marguerite. Not the dead.' Olivier's pale blue eyes turned to steel. He moved his attention to the window.

She didn't altogether know what made her so resistant to his plans. In the ordinary course of things, she would have leapt to protect an innocent child from the stigma of illegitimacy, the hardship of over-crowded orphanages. But here, now, all she felt was suspicion. Olivier had something in mind, something which didn't smell right to her. She had to find out the truth.

The dead man preoccupied her too. Could he have some relationship to the abandoned child? It was probably a wild leap, occasioned by a sense that normally so little happened in La Rochambert that wasn't related to fields or animals. Yet here in quick succession were two events, monstrous enough to disturb the flow of the seasons.

Olivier was absorbed by some activity in the gardens. Marguerite moved closer to the window.

A stout, caped and white-aproned woman was pushing an ancient baby carriage along the stone path. In the falling light, it took a moment for

Marguerite to recognize it as her own. The thin, spoked wheels, smaller in front and larger in back, the pale, metallic boat-shaped body. She had last used it to keep her kittens in, safe from the foxes who prowled by night. She must have been six or seven then. How she had loved those blind kittens, especially the tiniest one, with a white smudge on his inky forehead. His mother had chosen to neglect it and Marguerite fed it with a dropper.

'Shall we have her bring the foundling in?' she asked.

'Yes. It's far too cold out there for him. I don't know what the woman is thinking. You can't trust these wet nurses. Children are always dying in their purported care.'

He went to the mantle, pulled the bell cord and turned back to her, the fretfulness still in his face.

'All this is laudable, Olivier.' She carried on their prior exchange as if there had been no interruption. 'But I will want to make enquiries. The infant might have been kidnapped, lost in some way, not just abandoned. Someone somewhere may be pining for him, searching. Have you contacted the police?'

Olivier shrugged. 'Monsieur le Curé did all that.'

'To no avail, I take it.'

'I've heard nothing. But feel free to make enquiries, if it passes the time for you. I'm in no great hurry. You're a woman. You can turn your ear to kitchen gossip in any number of houses. My own hunch is if the infant was left, it's because his mother wanted to leave him. Wanted him dead. Infanticide. Which is a crime, so she's never turned up. Never will. I've saved him. Given him new life. That makes me his father. His father in life.'

Marguerite watched him with something like amazement. This was such an unexpected passion of Olivier's that she felt she needed to shake herself back into a version of normality.

'Yes, kitchen gossip, you're right. It's a good place to start.' She was about to ask him if any staff had left of late when the door opened and a man burst in without a warning knock.

'I spied you at the window. I was hoping . . .'

The speaker stopped as he noticed Marguerite's presence. He was a young man of middle height with the strong build of a peasant, but with none of the manner. He wore his light brown hair slightly long, like a poet, and raked it back to reveal a high brow. His soft, pursed lips were redder than a woman's against skin that wore an indoor pallor. His jacket was of coarse wool, his collar slightly frayed, yet all worn with an air which shouted insouciance rather than penury. He took in Marguerite with a candor that earlier in her life would have brought a vivid flush to her cheek. Shyness battled with assertion in his speech.

'I'm sorry. I didn't know you had visitors.' He bowed in Marguerite's direction.

'My wife, Marguerite de Landois. Paul Villemardi.'

The man extended his bow.

'You'll take tea with us, Monsieur Villemardi? Olivier has told me of your work here.'

'I have also been explaining about the infant.'

'So you haven't given him a name yet?' Marguerite asked.

The two men looked at each other.

'I wanted to consult with you first. Of course.'

'Of course.'

Another maid she didn't know came into the room with a newly heaped tray. The girl simpered a little as she stepped in front of Villemardi. Was it this poetic young man who was responsible for the recent turnover in staff?

'Did you find what you wanted at the quarry?' Olivier asked.

'In part. Some of the slabs had too much red resin. Some were fine. We can start on that bust now. Did Olivier explain, Madame?'

Marguerite was rather taken aback by the casual use of her husband's first name by this young man.

'No, no. I hadn't.' Olivier intervened. 'Monsieur Villemardi is doing a bust of me, Marguerite. Several works, in fact.'

'Oh?'

'Yes.' Villemardi paused, then, with a provocative look in her direction, lowered his voice and raced on. 'I learned something rather shocking on my way back here.'

'Really?' Olivier's interest was all simulated.

'There was a suicide. On the tracks.'

Olivier interrupted. 'Marguerite's already mentioned it. Who was it?'

'That's just it. No one seems to know. Some despairing tramp, from the sound of it.'

'Inebriated, no doubt.' Oliver was callous in his contempt. 'Mistook the tracks for a bed.'

Marguerite interrupted. 'There can be reasons, apart from drink, for not getting on with life, Olivier.'

Paul Villemardi's velvet-brown eyes met hers.

'It's odd, isn't it, that no one has identified him. You know how everyone knows everyone around here.'

'He might have travelled in from elsewhere.'

'A pilgrim,' Olivier offered with new interest. 'Yes. Perhaps he was doing the pilgrim's route. From Montoire. On his way to Tours.'

'A despairing pilgrim, then. Evidently our dear Curé's benediction did nothing for his mood. That won't please our local saint.'

'Your sarcasm is inappropriate, Paul.'

Marguerite looked from one man to the other. It was the first time she had heard Olivier take an interest in pilgrims, let alone in the local site. He had never been a pious man. Quite the contrary.

'I'll see if I can find out more about him tomorrow,' she said to cut the tension that now pervaded the room. 'I need to look up some people near Montoire.'

'What on earth for, Marguerite? Who?'

She arched an eyebrow. 'It's for Mlle Branquart, Olivier. I told you. The young woman who's come with me.'

Olivier picked up the poker and jabbed at a log.

'She's from the region.' Marguerite looked at Paul Villemardi who was raking the poetic tousle of hair back from his face again. He might know something. She rushed on. 'She's fretting about her sister. She has answered none of her letters for some five months. Nor has the family where she was in service. The poor girl is distraught. I promised I'd look into it.'

'She's probably gone off with a man.' Villemardi laughed. 'She may be only too glad to leave a snooping sister behind.'

'I don't think so. No, I really don't think so.'

'Well, you'll tell me where you're going, Marguerite. You are not, I stress, not, to get involved in any unseemly activity here.'

'Unseemly? Really Olivier. You exaggerate.'

'I don't want to hear news of any of your escapades from the wrong quarters.'

'Then, I shall tell you everything in great detail before I undertake any.'

Her irony was light, but her heart sank. Nothing had changed. Out of sight might mean out of mind, but once she was in his proximity, Olivier grew invasive. He wanted to know exactly where she was and what she was up to at every minute, and that it didn't have a negative impact on the family name. It was the stifling contradiction of his tyrannical need for possession and his distaste for her which had contributed to the unhappiness she didn't like to remember.

Villemardi was playing with a cigarette box he had taken from the table. 'Olivier will explain why the need for discretion matters above all else, Madame. If he hasn't already.'

'That's quite enough, Paul.' The rebuke came with the sting of a lash. But the presence at the door softened Olivier's face. He leapt up to usher in the wet nurse.

Despite the cold, the woman glowed with some inner fire which made her cheeks and forehead damply pink. There was a robust heaviness to her movements. Around her neck on a ribbon she wore what looked like an amulet, in the shape of a naked child. She held the swaddled bundle of the live babe comfortably in her arms.

'He's asleep, Monsieur.' She curtsied in Marguerite's direction.

'That's alright, Celeste, we'll be very quiet. Madame wanted to see him.'

Marguerite stood. The wet nurse came towards her and with a single smooth gesture deposited the bundle in her unprepared arms.

Long, dark lashes shadowed porcelain smooth cheeks. The button nose crinkled as if taking in a new scent. His own was moist and milky.

Marguerite cradled the baby to her. Its small face burrowed close, nuzzled her bosom. Something like regret tugged at her. It made her sit down and position the child a little less intimately in her lap.

Olivier hovered over her. A glance revealed a face she didn't recognize. Was it pride she read there? As if she and the babe together had been transformed into prize possessions, a holy pair that he had magicked from the air. Or a tableau he had just purchased from a favourite dealer.

'Beautiful, isn't he?' His voice was preening. His lips were slightly wet. 'I was led to him, you know. I felt it.'

She passed the child to him.

He held him up at an arm's distance but with a kind of rapture which encased the two of them in an impermeable capsule.

It came to her, like the ominous fluttering of a crow's wings, that some deep, enigmatic bond had grown between him and the child. Some potent magic. As if the chance finding of the babe had turned Olivier into a saviour, allowed him to see himself as such. Yes, in the mirror of the infant's innocent eyes, he was good, a hero, indeed a paragon. The potency of that illusion of goodness would be difficult to battle, even if she were to find the child's blood parents.

Paul Villemardi was shifting from foot to foot, his shoulders hunched. The man seemed even more uncomfortable than she was in the presence of Olivier's intense communion.

Marguerite moved towards the table and poured out more tea. She addressed Villemardi softly. 'Did you by any chance hear anything on your journey about women who had suddenly left the area, Monsieur, or about lost or abandoned children?'

It took Villemardi a moment to rouse himself from his absorption and recognize that the question was directed at him.

'Women . . . No, no. But then I didn't think to ask.' His gaze flew a little fearfully towards Olivier.

A knock at the door followed by Martine's entry stopped him from saying any more.

The young woman looked around the room with the timid awkwardness of a child forced into adult company. Olivier's expression of goodness metamorphosed into one of cold assessment, followed by barely veiled contempt. Villemardi's all-but professional appraisal of a possible model was hardly better. Marguerite's introductions did nothing to ease matters. She had wanted Martine to meet everyone, to feel at home. But after a few stilted moments, the girl fled, pleading tiredness and correspondence to catch up on. Was it the time in service that made her so incapable of conversation?

'I don't know why you brought her here, Marguerite. You're always picking up waifs and strays. I thought you would have learned by now.' Olivier's complaint came almost before Martine had shut the door.

Marguerite stared pointedly at the babe the wet nurse was now holding and arched an eyebrow. She didn't bother to reply.

_ 3 _

The kitchen at La Rochambert was a large, rectangular, vaulted room in the basement of the house, directly below the principal dining room. Rows of copper pots and pans glistened on the whitewashed stone walls. Game and curing hams hung from ceiling beams at one far end. The centre of the space was dominated by a double row of ovens and a vast *bain Marie*. These were flanked on two sides by long, solid tables of unpolished oak, at one of which two kitchen maids, despite the early hour, were already peeling and chopping vegetables and fruit for the day's soups and tarts. Arched windows looked out on kitchen gardens. Beneath them stood sinks and a stretch of marble-topped counter which gave way to rows of preserves, jars of dried mushrooms of all shapes and sizes, and a giant cold store, fed by ice kept in the nearby underground cistern.

Marguerite was perched on a stool by a table next to the bread oven from which Madame Solange had just extracted a brioche and an assortment of crusty rolls. Two of these quickly found themselves on Marguerite's plate and with a hunger reminiscent of her childhood, she heaped plum jam onto them and let Madame Solange pour scalding milk into her bowl of coffee. She had come down to the kitchen early, knowing that the housekeeper would be here sipping her café-au-lait before giving the staff their instructions for the day.

She was a placid woman with plump cheeks and a fan of wrinkles around her mouth. But when she tied her capacious white apron over her severe grey dress, she looked not so very different from the young kitchen maid Marguerite had first met. Later, she had become cook and had married Henri, the gamekeeper, and Armand had come along, as stout and smiling as his mother. More recently, Madame Solange had taken on stature and learned to purse her lips into severity. She had moved out of the kitchen to oversee the smooth running of the household. But she still kept an eye on matters culinary. Olivier liked his table just so.

'How have you been keeping, Madame Solange? And the family?' Marguerite asked.

'Not so bad, Madame. Monsieur le Comte keeps us busy. Particularly of late.'

'Oh?' Marguerite left the question in her voice low key. She knew better than to try and press the loyal Madame Solange. Whatever came out would have to come unwittingly.

'Of course, what with the foundling. And with Monsieur Villemardi here . . . I imagine the sculptor likes his food?' Marguerite offered.

'That, too,' Madame Solange said with no particular change of tone, though the sudden plunge of the knife into the brioche she now sliced alerted Marguerite to some unhappiness.

The woman lowered her voice, so that it was inaudible to anyone else in the kitchen and rushed on. 'And we've had our share of visitors. All these new contacts of Monsieur's from Vendome and Blois and Montoire, the whole region. They sit over the lunch table and discuss matters for hours. Wages and schools and farming and the church. The new curé comes frequently, too.'

'A new curé?'

'Yes, Père Benoit. But perhaps you didn't know. Old Père Philippe died . . . when was it, over a year ago must be. Now we have this new man.'

'You don't like him?'

Madame Solange stiffened and averted her gaze. 'I didn't say that, did I? No. no. Far be it from me . . . I just miss Père Philippe. You know how it is. This new man is young, cuts quite a figure. He appreciates Monsieur le Comte's hospitality. And his cellar.' She stopped herself, then raced on. 'Yes, forgive me for saying it.' She crossed herself hurriedly. 'But he does like a good bottle. So do the others. Monsieur is always discussing the neighbouring vineyards. He's not so interested in the cattle now. But you know that.'

Olivier had put down a substantial cellar in the years he had spent at La Rochambert and had developed something of a passion for inspecting the vintages of the valley.

'It wouldn't surprise me if next year Monsieur decided to give another hillside to vines.'

'Our Cheverny I trust. It's excellent. But everything else is running smoothly? You've had no problems with suppliers or staff?'

'Has Monsieur been complaining?'

'Oh no . . . It's just that . . . Marguerite made a vague gesture and looked out at the kitchen garden. Only the rosemary sprouted as glossy and green as ever in the dull cold.

'It's true. Two of the maids left and one of the coachmen. This summer, one after another. I don't know much about the coachman, but one of the girls was from near Château du Loir, the other further away, from Blois. You probably didn't notice them when you were last here, Madame. Silly little chits. One of them had been here under a year, the other just over. And I can tell you they both had good mouths on them. Not shy, no. No respect, this generation of girls. I had trouble replacing them.'

Madame Solange shook her head with an air of despair. 'Yes, one of them wanted a place in Paris, the other decided she just wanted a change or maybe it was to be closer to her brother. Something like that. I think Monsieur Villemardi gave her a lift to her new post.' She paused significantly, then, when Marguerite didn't comment, rushed on. 'He was going to visit his family who's from that area.'

'You have the girls' new addresses, I imagine, Madame Solange.'

'Only for one of the girls.' The woman's face grew canny. Eyebrows arched. She lowered her voice. 'So you think as I do, Madame?'

Marguerite didn't answer.

'About the baby, I mean. Poor little mite. He could be one of the girls. Why not? The timing is possible and they were forward enough. Little hussies. Even with my Henri. It would have to be the one who stayed in the region, though. A stupid idea putting a child in the river like that. He could have died of cold. Probably what she intended. If one of the Messieurs didn't find him, then good riddance to the little blighter. It would be altogether in character. These girls always get away with murder, if there's no mistress in the house . . .' She clapped her hands over her mouth. 'I'm sorry Madame, I didn't mean . . . You know me.'

'It's all right,' Marguerite smiled.

Candid eyes sought out Marguerite's face. 'I wish Madame were here more. That's the only reason I let my words run away with me. And I don't think it's right to keep that infant here. I don't. And don't go getting soft on him. You never know what kind of blood he might be carrying. We don't want any degenerates here. Like that tramp who threw himself on the track.'

'No, no. Of course not.' Marguerite patted the older woman's hand and suddenly had an image of the dead man's dangling limbs cloaked in woolen trousers. Was he a tramp? The clothes were dirty, but the quality . . . she shook herself.

It didn't surprise her that Solange already had distinct ideas about the railway death. Nor that notions of degeneracy were table talk in the kitchens of the provinces. The church had made enough of a play about the double doom of alcohol and syphilis. Not that what she had against keeping the babe had anything to do with all that.

Throughout the night, a parade of weeping women had invaded her dreams. So many bereft Madonnas, trapped by poverty or social norms, none really wanting to give up a child or have a stranger take her place. She had to find out.

A distraught girl closer to home was on her conscience, too.

'There's something else I wanted to ask you about, Madame Solange. Do you know of the Tellier family in Troo?'

'Tellier? It rings some kind of bell, Madame. Let me think. Tellier . . . Tellier. From Tours, aren't they? Merchants. Yes. I don't know that they spend all that much time around here. But maybe . . . She screwed up her face as if her nose had caught a whiff of a bad smell. 'No, no. I'll ask my husband. His brother works that way.'

'So you haven't by any chance come across a girl called Yvette Branquart in the area?'

'Yvette Branquart . . .' Madame Solange reflected. 'Is she related to that young Martine you brought with you?'

Madame Solange missed little. But there was no more information she could provide. She promised, however, to keep her ears open.

In the growing bustle of the kitchen, there would be a lot to listen to.

The light peering through the heavy curtains of her small sitting room wore the dull, dirty grey of an old sewer rag. She looked out the window at the sullen landscape and turned to her desk. It was still too early to head off with Martine. She would write to the Chief Inspector in response to the letter he had sent her as a New Year greeting while she was still in Paris. She reread it as ammunition against gloom.

> *My dearest lady,* he opened with great courtesy, and continued with a flourish, *I wanted to thank you on this first day of our new century for all the favours you have shown me in the last and I very much trust will continue to do so. Your help in our various exploits has been of great value not only to my humble self, but if they were only to know it, to all law-abiding citizens of France. You have a clear, cool mind enhanced by a very feminine intuition. You see through both cant and convention. You are not afraid to strip the veils of hypocrisy and dissimulation to confront the tawdry mortal beneath. For all this, I am grateful to you.*
>
> *Your servant into the 20th century,*
> *Emile Durand.*

Marguerite imagined the sturdy, barrel-chested man bowing deeply and smiled. For all his occasional pomposity, his rigorous attention to form, she valued the Chief Inspector's friendship above many older ones. He was reliable and astute and the kind of proud Republican she too rarely met in her own circles. He was also—with Rafael gone—in a strange way, her remaining link to Olympe and the terrible tragedy of her one-time protégée's untimely death.

Yes, Rafael had returned to America, for good this time it seemed. Rafael with his passionate features, his quick grace and fiery enthusiasms. How she missed him.

But there was nothing for it.

Marguerite slipped into her bedroom. The lawn blouse she had asked for was freshly ironed, the petticoat and striped grey travelling suit laid out. Jeanne, her maid, was waiting to tend to her morning toilette. Marguerite indulged herself and let her mind go back to Raf.

It wasn't so much that Raf had fallen out with her as that he had fallen out with France as a whole. She had been there at the start of his love affair with her country. She could do little to prevent its end. Their passion, which had turned into the most interesting of amorous friend-ships, had now dwindled into an erratic exchange of letters. The whole sorry business of Olympe had taken its toll on them both. Her young friend's drowning had made Marguerite feel like some bereft Queen of the Night whose child had been stolen away by malevolent forces. For Raf, it had been even worse. He felt in some sense responsible for those forces.

On top of that, the latest abysmal installment in the Dreyfus affair had turned him against the country he had begun to call his second home. It was hardly surprising. The scandal had turned husbands against wives, polarized families, ranged Republicans against the military and ordinary people against a church which had grown narrowly political and patriotic, as if God could only be a Frenchman of one particular sort.

The stitching up of Dreyfus's pardon, after the fragile, victimized man had been given the choice which was no choice at all of accepting his guilt and being returned to his family, or battling for his innocence from prison, so sickened Raphael that by the end of September, he had determined to return to America.

Life seemed to be so much simpler in America. Virtue there was a dis-tinct and nameable possibility. There were so few shades and textures between good and bad that she feared no French woman she could name, Joan of Arc apart, and perhaps not even she, would qualify for the side of those angels. Or indeed the devils that virtue spawned.

She only heard Jeanne's request that she stand at her second bidding. She let the girl adjust her corset. Could this garment which so forcefully threw her bosom forward and her hips back also act as a bulwark against maudlin thoughts? Marguerite laughed at herself soundlessly, helped the girl to hook and pull and tie and at last arrange the slim skirts' fluted hips and back.

She had had to wait until the ripe age of thirty to experience long-ing in its true romantic sense. She supposed it was an emotion that sat better on the young. But she had never been a Madame Bovary, hadn't spent her girlhood amongst nuns with copper crosses dangling from their necks, sweet-faced women who taught one how to swoon on one's knees in expectation of a heavenly husband, a holy lover, an eternal mar-riage.

Nor had she, at the appropriate age, had rapturous encounters with Paul and Virginie in balmy, exotic climes, or indeed with Walter Scott in dramatic highlands. The most romantic tome in her father's library was probably Rousseau's treatise on education, *Emile*. She had been reared on Aristotle and Plato, on the Encyclopaedists and the natural scientists, with their fine distinctions and their insistence on observation. Nature, science and the published proceedings of the Botanic Society had been her girlhood romance.

The novelists had come with her marriage and the ones she read most ardently had an analytic cast of mind. They taught her that choices weren't always and altogether one's own to make, that happiness might be a fugi-tive moment most enjoyed in anticipation or memory.

Yet here she was, immersed in mourning the passing of a love she had always known would have to pass.

Rationalists, too, bore a burden of unreason, she told her reflection in the sloping cheval glass.

When she returned to her sitting room, she found Olivier bending over her desk, blatantly reading her letters.

'You left this quite open to all eyes, Marguerite.' He didn't blink. 'I gather you're rather proud of the "feminine intuition" this Durand com-pliments you on.'

She glared at him.

'Are you going to use it now to discover the identity of the dead man for us? The staff are awash with ideas. I fear they may drown in the bilge.'

Marguerite snatched Durand's letter away from him. She hated his scoffing.

'In fact, Olivier,' she said coldly, 'I was rather planning to unleash my cool, clear mind on the secrets of your foundling's parentage. But if you would rather I concentrated on the dead man, I shall be happy to oblige. You, in return, will keep your eyes well away from my correspondence.'

'You know that these policemen are nothing more than criminals in uniform, Marguerite. Remember the heritage they share with the notorious Vidocq. No better than spies and stoolpigeons, all of them. As crooked as the people they're after. Even worse than the Bohemian rabble you've taken up with in Paris. I don't know what you can be thinking of.'

'That's enough, Olivier. Quite enough.'

Anger suffused her face. With a great effort she controlled it. She had made the vow years ago. She wouldn't allow herself to be baited by Olivier. Actions, with him, worked far better than words. With the latter, he always triumphed.

She took a deep breath. 'We've had eighty years of policing since Vidocq, Olivier. And Chief Inspector Durand has less in common with him than he probably does with one of our Republican Deputies. At the moment, you're the one who's being a spy.'

He stared at her as if she had said something utterly astonishing, then averted his eyes and adjusted the silk scarf he wore bunched around his neck.

'Yes. Of course. You're right,' He smiled with sudden contrition. 'It was unforgivable of me to succumb to the temptation of the letter. I really came in to ask you whether you'd like to stroll down to Paul's studio with me and have a look at his work.'

At the side door closest to the outhouses, they found the footman talking to a uniformed constable. The latter was insisting that he had been told in the village that a Monsieur Villemardi lived here. The footman was shaking his head in adamant negation

'Leave it to me, Georges,' Olivier intervened.

As if to disprove every malign word he had uttered to Marguerite, he addressed the Constable with charming politeness. 'How can I help you?'

The man, who stood a head shorter than him, instantly bowed and removed his cap to display a tuft of reddish hair two shades brighter than his lustrous moustache.

Ten minutes later Paul Villemardi had been summoned and they were all gathered in the small drawing room, listening to the constable.

'You see, Monsieur, the suicide may have carried no identification, but in his jacket pocket we found two items. One, a woman's embroidered handkerchief, with the initials A.S. The second a card, embossed with the name 'Villemardi Fils, Stonemasons'.

Paul Villemardi's velvet eyes twinkled. 'And so you think, Constable, that this man had already selected a funerary monument to adorn his grave?'

'We think, Monsieur, that you may be able to identify him.'

'But, Constable, if you stop to read the card, you'll see that the address given on it is in the town of Château du Loir, not La Rochambert. Château is where you will find my honoured father who runs the business and may therefore be able to help you rather better than I can.'

'Which is what the footman said to me. Without wishing to be disrespectful, Monsieur le Comte,' he bowed towards Olivier, 'I said to him that a colleague was on his way to Château du Loir. He would concentrate on Père and I on Fils.'

'I shall come with you, if you like, Monsieur Villemardi,' Marguerite offered, but Olivier cut her off before she could finish.

'That is not possible, Marguerite,' He was as stern as a father disciplining a child. 'I will accompany Paul.'

Seeing her face, he lightened his tone. 'With his artist's eye, Paul will be able to give you a detailed summary on our return.'

Not trusting her voice, Marguerite nodded a stiff goodbye to the men. She had other plans for the day in any event, plans Olivier would hardly approve in any greater measure.

_ 4 _

The wind whipped through the carriage. The trees lining the river road shook and swayed like old men attacked by palsy. The sky was a sullen mass of darkening grey.

Marguerite shot a reassuring glance at Martine. As they approached the village of Troo, the girl had moved closer and closer to the edge of her seat. She was like a bundle of exposed nerves. She jumped when Marguerite began to speak.

'Why don't we ask Georges to pull up by the River Inn? We can walk up towards the Tellier house. A walk will do us both good.' Marguerite was a great believer in the health-giving properties of exercise for young women. Mental health in particular. Had she had her way, she would have ordered Martine onto a bicycle and a regime of two miles a day before lunch.

Martine nodded, her lips too tight for speech.

'And Georges can make a few inquiries at the Inn. Someone there may have information about Yvette.'

'I should go with him,' Martine burst out.

'No, it's best you come with me. The family will be more inclined to speak to Yvette's sister than to a total stranger. And we need the walk.'

The girl seemed about to protest. Her eyes beneath the blue woolen hat were wide with what Marguerite could only interpret as fear. It was as if she had already decided her sister was dead and confrontation with her employers would confirm the fact against all her hopes.

Outside it was so cold, the air cracked and whistled. The stairs cut into the crag were steep, the road unpaved. The houses huddled into the rock-face like the Neolithic caves out of which some of them had grown. In the fields around here, Marguerite remembered, there were menhirs and stones with odd carvings. Her father had been fascinated by the troglodyte dwellings, the flints and arrowheads that had been found in them. So had she, back then when she felt there was an adventure to the world growing older and older as it bounded into the future.

Now Marguerite felt the ancient village had grown less hospitable, whether it was the discomfort of not being clogged and trousered as she had been in the old childhood days beside her father, or simply the silence around them which had an unnatural, hostile edge. She could feel the villagers pausing in their activity to watch their passage from behind small, shrouded windows and barred doors.

Beyond the church square, they took a narrow winding path of pebble and mud. With no warning, a noise burst upon the quiet like an explosion of gunfire at an execution. Both of them stopped in their tracks and stared at each other. With a shrug, Marguerite moved on to where the road twisted.

The scene which confronted her brought an admonishing shout to her lips. A group of boys stood in front of a house well set back from its neighbours and surrounded by a stone wall. The boys wore thick ragged pullovers or dingy jackets and had hobnailed boots or clogs on their feet. These clattered loudly as they moved. A pile of stones and smooth pebbles lay heaped in front of them—ammunition for battle. At a command from their leader, they aimed the stones at the wall or over it. Their shouts came in raucous unison, like a hail of bullets. The echo off the rock-face amplified their noise, turning it into a tumult. The boys faces were contorted in spite. The words they yelled were not ones she would want to repeat in any company.

'What on earth are you up to?' Marguerite confronted them with all the dignity of her rank and age.

They stared at her, leers and nastiness still ripe on their features.

'Nothing,' the leader brazened it out. 'We're playing.'

He couldn't have been more than eight or nine.

'Playing?'

'Yes, we're aiming at the wall.'

'And at the witch who lives there,' a tiny voice piped up.

'A witch?'

'A bad witch. She never comes out. She just sends her wicked servants to catch us and eat us up.'

'Yes,' another voice intervened. 'A huge black witch. She eats babies. Hides them away then eats them, bit by bit.'

Marguerite noticed that this small huddled shape was in fact a girl in trousers. 'Babies?' Marguerite queried. 'Have any gone missing?'

'See, see. There she is.' The child jumped up and down in great excitement, pointing at a high window. One of them launched a stone which scaled the wall and fell with a thud on invisible ground.

There was indeed a shape at the window. It floated behind a gauzy curtain and to Marguerite's consternation, conformed to the children's description. The figure appeared ominously dark and with a tangled frazzle of hair.

'Away with you. Away.' A door in the wall scraped open. A gnarled old man showed his face. 'Away, I tell you.' He shook a fist at the children, threw a stone back in their direction.

The little girl set up a howl. Marguerite didn't think she'd suffered a direct hit. She didn't have time to check, because now the old man was staring at her with small, malevolent eyes that seemed older than the hills, eyeing Martine, too, who huddled behind her.

'And you. What do you want? Are they sending the duchesses after us now? This is a Republic isn't it? A free Republic. Liberty. Equality. We'll have to wait a thousand years for the Fraternity.' He made a high, shrill sound, like a cackle and aimed a gob of spit at the ground. It fell not far from Marguerite's skirts.

Before she could respond, the door clattered shut. She could hear a key turning this time. The children took up their shouting again, but it had grown half-hearted.

'Time to head home,' Marguerite silenced them. 'Or find something else to play at.'

As she watched the children meander off, poking and prodding each other with casual cruelty, aiming the occasional stone, she thought for a moment about Olivier's foundling. To parent a child was no simple matter.

She shook the thought away. This wasn't her business for the moment. There was Martine's sister to see to first.

'Are you still here?' The gnarled old man clattered the door open again and stared at her as if she had spoken out loud. 'What are you after, eh?'

'Nothing, Monsieur. Nothing. I was trying to stop the children. I'm looking for the Tellier House. Have I arrived?'

'Arrived? Arrived in heaven?' He grumbled some incomprehensible oath, then pointed a bony finger to the right, described a sinuous line, and slammed the door with a clang.

Above her in the distance, Marguerite saw the curtain move once more. Behind it, a shadowy figure raised a hand. The gesture could have been either rage or supplication.

A shiver ran through her which had nothing to do with the chill wind.

Up the hill and round the crest to the right, they finally found the Tellier House. It was a substantial residence, solid and square and self-important, with its own imposing stretch of grounds, an iron gate and a row of chestnuts—one of those houses which the affluent provincial bourgeoisie inhabited.

Martine stared at the gate as if it might absorb her, swallow up her vital essence in return for her sister's sudden apparition. Marguerite had seen that look before during a séance she had once attended out of curiosity. Yes. It was the expression on the face of a young woman who was hoping for word from her dead fiancé. It was exactly with that look of a supplicant, mouth vulnerable, cheeks pale and, one could feel it, bitten from within, that the woman gazed at the impassive medium lost in her real or enacted trance. Like that woman, all Martine's energy seemed now to have gone out of her. Its only residue was contained in the springy aureole of her pale blonde hair.

Marguerite laced a supporting arm through the girl's and gave the front gate a vehement prod. It opened easily enough and they strode up the tree-lined path. For a moment, she imagined herself as a girl raised to other aspirations, as the Branquart sisters had been, and suddenly thrust into service in a house like this—a house where the provincial mistress would probably be far more vigilant and exacting than Marguerite could ever be. She felt a cage of servitude closing round her, a constriction in breath and movement which was difficult to shrug off. Someone was always watching, measuring, judging. There was no escape. Destitution was round the corner. Yet flight felt like an imperative.

She held on to Martine more tightly.

The three floors of the stuccoed house had even rows of windows, large at the bottom, smaller at the top, all similarly shuttered. She waited for Martine to catch her breath, then let the heavy knocker fall several times. When no response came, she tried again.

At last the door inched open. A sturdy middle-aged woman with leathery skin and pale eyes poked her head through the crack. She was wearing a servant's bonnet and an apron stained in what might be blood or wine.

'There's no one available,' she declared before Marguerite could utter a word. 'Madame has gone to Tours. She won't be back for days, maybe weeks. Who knows. They never tell me.'

Before the door could shut in her face, Marguerite pushed it open and wedged herself in.

'A moment please, Madame, there's something I'd like to ask. I'm certain you can help me just as well as Madame Tellier.'

The woman let out a sound which was neither negation nor acquiescence.

'May I?'

Marguerite walked into a sombre, high-ceilinged hall, crowded with so much heavy furniture that for a second she had the impression she had stumbled into a warehouse. Near the stairwell, patchily illuminated from above by a stained glass window, hung dark oils of men in some unplaceable uniform covered in braid. She could feel Martine cowering in the shadows just behind her.

The servant's none too friendly attention was all on Marguerite.

'I'm Madame de Landois from La Rochambert. I trust you'll tell Madame Tellier I called on her while I was in the area. I'm trying to find news of Yvette Branquart who was, perhaps still is, in service with you.'

'Yvette! Yvette Branquart? What do you want with her? The strumpet's gone, isn't she.' A broad, gap-toothed grin burst on her face. 'And good riddance to her, too. You won't be wanting to hire her, Madame, I can tell you. Madame Molineuf can find you much better. Much better.'

'I shall remember that, Madame Molineuf. But do you know where Mademoiselle Yvette went? She's come into an inheritance,' Marguerite lied.

Calculation lit up the woman's eyes. Before she could say anymore, a thick voice came from below stairs.

'Who're you gabbling to?'

'Quiet. Watch your manners. There's a lady here. She's looking for Yvette. You remember her? Of course, you remember.'

A man appeared from the dark depths of the hall. He was broad-shouldered, with a round, rubbery face and bushy eyebrows, and walked with feet splayed outwards. It took Marguerite a moment to understand that despite his alarming size, he was not much more than a tow-headed boy.

'Yvette?' he turned a simpleton's grin on her. 'Yvette who went away. Yvette went to the doctor and went away . . .' His broad face turned into a moon of sadness. He performed the steps of what looked like a dance, then leered. 'Went away. Let's all pray.'

'What are you mumbling about? That's enough from you. My son sometimes get a little excited, Madame.'

'Which doctor does he mean?'

'Oh, I doubt he means anything. Did he say doctor?'

'Dr. Labrousse. The new doctor. Yvette and the new doctor. Doctor mockt'er.' The lumbering youth laughed. It was an odd, cheerless sound.

'And where can I find him?'

He said nothing. He seemed to have forgotten she was there.

'Near the Maladrerie perhaps?' Marguerite thought unhappily of the old leper house. But surely that had long since been abandoned.

There was still no response, so she repeated her question to his mother, who grumbled.

'At Montoire. At the hospital. Or in his *cabinet*. But don't say we . . .'

A crashing noise from the main staircase of the house put a stop to all conversation. Madame Molineuf and her son stared upwards.

A man appeared to block the top of the staircase. Leaning heavily on a stick, he loomed like a ruined tower, ready to topple at any moment and crush anyone and anything in his path. Vast, burly, unshaven, with a tumble of unkempt, greasy, grey-white hair, his skin was riddled with boils. The features repelled and frightened. The expression on his face was one of uncontrolled rage.

'Idiots!' He bellowed. 'What's all this noise? You fools. Flea bags. Rotting lumps of stinking flesh. Can't a man sleep? I told you to let me sleep.' Bushy eyebrows all but met across the man's bony nose in a colossal frown. His dark, inchoate glare floated down and behind Marguerite towards where Martine had been standing half-hidden.

The girl let out a scream and raced out the still partly open door.

The man's roar turned into a whooping laugh. He turned and with his stick pounding his passage, he made his way back up the stairs.

Madame Molineuf shrugged. 'You'd better go. The master's not at his best today. Out of here.'

Before she could say anything more, Marguerite found herself through the door. She turned back, half hoping to catch another glimpse of the monstrous man.

Instead she saw Madame Molineuf's son, doing a strange, excited little dance again, loping up the stairs behind his master.

She had wanted to ask about the woman the children called the witch. Too late now. She would have to come back. She would certainly have to come back if she was going to get a clearer notion of what had sent Yvette Branquart running to the doctor. Though it wasn't all that hard to deduce. Monsieur Tellier had the appearance of a more than brutal master.

_ 5 _

Martine was waiting for Marguerite in the carriage. She was watching Georges polish the bronze lamps—watching, but not seeing. Her hands trembled uncontrollably.

'A vile man, Martine. I'm not surprised he scared you. Lucky your sister left. We shall go to Montoire and see if we can have a talk with this doctor. He may be able to give us some clues about her whereabouts. You shall also have to tell me a little more about her, so that together we can try and work out what she might have done. Where she might have gone next.'

Martine stared straight ahead at the gleaming wood and whorled upholstery of the carriage. She nodded without replying.

As the horses moved into a rhythmic trot, Marguerite noticed a large black carriage turn off the main road and move up into the village. At the window sat a heavy woman in an elaborate, plumed hat. Carefully fashioned empire curls protruded onto a face that was too old to sport them. The woman's expression had an oddness which pricked at Marguerite's nerves. It was as if the separate planes of her face moved with no knowledge of each other. There was both blatant curiosity and disapproval about Marguerite's elegant vehicle and its presence in Troo. The door of the carriage sported a whirling gold T.

Tellier, Marguerite guessed. So Madame Tellier was back. She would go and see her tomorrow, perhaps leaving the frightened Martine behind. The woman would certainly be able to tell her things, and from the eyes she had leveled at Marguerite, it was clear that she had enough social snobbery to welcome a visit from the Comtesse de Landois.

As their carriage bumped along the road, Marguerite chatted to Martine, attempting various strategies which might bring the girl out a little. Perhaps it was the sight of the ogre of a man that had spurred it, but she found herself reminiscing about her own childhood, engaging on stories her father had told her about the area.

Her father had hardly been a garrulous sort, and much of their communication had been soundless. But now and again, when his old war wound ached and made him limp, he would recount details of the march of the German armies through the region at the end of 1870. The woods would grow hostile with the enemy's gunfire.

Marguerite thought she could still recall the rattattat of guns in the woods, though she wasn't certain. She would have been three at the time. What she was sure she remembered was the sight of crippled men, their wounds tied up in bloody rags, limping on sticks and crutches through a city street. One man, in particular, a red bandana oozing round his forehead, his face gaunt, his eyes like a frightened animal's, vast and crazed, came again and again into her childhood thoughts. He was the one she would see when her father talked. She would also see bodies falling, blood colouring the ground.

Or she would look up to the sky and see the charismatic politician, Leon Gambetta, floating past in a balloon bound for Tours, where he would rally his countrymen to fresh assaults against the invaders.

At first the brave French had beaten back the Germans at Orleans. Then came the defeats, one following the other. The Germans had even taken La Rochambert. They had occupied the château and made it their own for several weeks before moving on. That was in December and January. A bitterly cold January when her mother and father and the small child she had been had gone to stay with the mill owner down river. Her mother was already ailing. There was little to eat and they had all been constantly hungry. Her mother had never properly recovered.

'So your mother died when you were very young. Like mine?' These were the first words Martine had spoken since she had run from the Tellier house.

Marguerite took up the cue.

'Yes. It's hard isn't it? It must have been doubly hard for you and your sister, with your father already gone.'

Martine nodded. 'We had to go to our Aunt's then. She was kind, but she wasn't Maman. I can still see Maman so clearly. She had a little mole next to her eye and a kind face. So kind. And she always told us we were the best, the best thing in her life. But then her life went.'

The tears started to flow down the girl's cheeks. Marguerite squeezed her gloved hand. 'But you remember her. That's good. So good. You can bring her back whenever you like. I don't remember mine. I was too young. But my father continued to worship her. And through him, I think I had a little sense of her.'

'Lucky that you had your father. I don't remember mine at all. Nor does Yvette. When we were little we would play this game where we closed our eyes very tight and tried to imagine Papa. Yvette was better at it.'

'Was she?'

'Yes.' Martine sighed. 'She's better at everything.'

'I find that hard to believe.'

'It's true. Really.' A shy smile suddenly illuminated Martine's face. 'When we were little, she was even better at hiding. She could hide for hours and I wouldn't be able to find her until she leapt out and 'boo-ed' at me.'

'Do you think that's what she's doing now? Hiding. Waiting for you to come into sight so that she can scare you with a "Boo?"'

Marguerite put the question playfully, but the girl darted a fierce look at her. 'So you noticed. When we walked up the path to the house. You noticed that I thought Yvette might leap out. She didn't. But it's all my fault.'

The tears filled her eyes again.

'What's your fault? How can it be your fault?'

'It's my fault that she went to that terrible house. My fault that she's gone now.'

Marguerite waited. At last. At last the girl was telling her something that might be useful. Telling her a little of the truth she had been so certain Martine was hiding.

'Yes, yes. You see . . .' The girl's distress was so palpable that Marguerite wrapped an arm round her shoulder.

'It was me. I was working in that house.'

'What?'

'Yes. It was my post first of all. But I couldn't stand it. Couldn't stand that horror. Even now, when he appeared I couldn't stop myself running. So Yvette took it on. They paid well. And when I said I couldn't anymore . . .' Her voice trailed off.

Marguerite prodded her. 'How long were you with the Telliers?'

'Two weeks, maybe three, but it felt like an eternity. Then Yvette came to visit. She had a posting in Paris which was about to start. I hadn't wanted to go to Paris. I wasn't brave enough. I'm never brave enough. But Yvette did everything . . .' The sobs overwhelmed her.

Marguerite tried to make sense of what she'd heard. Martine felt responsible for her sister's disappearance. Perhaps she even felt guilty enough to believe that her sister was now paying her back for the wrong she had done her by depriving her of a job in Paris.

'And did Yvette hold it all against you? Did she feel you'd deprived her of a better post?'

'Ah no, Madame. Non.' The sobs stopped. Martine was scandalized. 'Yvette isn't like that. No. She didn't mind being at the Tellier's. Not at first. Not in her letters, in any case. The old master was away a lot, I think . . .' She stopped herself and stared out the carriage window.

This time Marguerite didn't interrupt. Martine was looking out at a particularly pretty little château that belonged to the Marquis de Conflans and rested on the crest of a hill above a stretch of field. In the nearer distance, a train chugged along an open span of track.

Suddenly the girl gripped her arm with her long, gloved fingers. 'When I saw the dead man, for a moment, I don't know what it was . . . I thought, it's him. Yvette has killed him. Killed the old master. She hated him so much she's killed him. That's why she's had to vanish. Vanish even from me. And it's all my fault. Because I wouldn't stay. Because I'm weak and stupid.'

'Do you think she'd be able to do that?' Marguerite asked softly.

Martine paused, her eyes wide, before protesting adamantly. 'No, no. Of course not. It's just my stupid imagination. It's just that I always used to wish he'd die.'

'But Yvette is brave, you said.'

'Oh yes. Very brave. She has a special kind of power. From somewhere. From God, maybe. She's always had it.'

Marguerite considered her. She was about to ask more about a bravery that even lent itself to the possibility of murder, when she saw that the girl had receded into herself. She let it rest. More questions about where Yvette might have gone were now better delayed. They had already been through the neighbours in Vendome and the few family friends. Martine had written to all of them even before coming to see Marguerite and none of them had heard anything from Yvette since the summer. Now, until she actually managed to confront Madame Tellier, the doctor was their only lead.

A regional centre, Montoire was a busy little town, self-important despite its ugliness. It sported a large market square, punctuated by rows of plane trees as regular as stunted columns, a freshly painted *Mairie*, and a non-descript church Marguerite remembered visiting only once for the wedding of some hunting friends of her father's. In the distance, from the main square, the ruins of the old castle built to protect the pilgrimage site loomed. In the murky light they trembled and served as a reminder that the town did have a past, even if it largely lay on the other side of the river. The great poet Ronsard had once presided over the ancient Priory of Saint-Gilles and its tiny Romanesque chapel huddled like a family of moles at the edge of the river.

The doctor's old, timbered house lay at the very end of an ordinary dirt road which led to the town hospital. There was little to distinguish his premises from others, except the polished brass plaque which proudly advertised his profession.

She let the knocker fall heavily onto the door. There was no answer. Martine, who had decided to come along with her, peered through a window, then jumped back.

'What is it, Martine?'

'Nothing. Nothing. I thought . . . I thought I saw a skeleton. Look Madame, there's a sign. It says the doctor won't be back until after two.'

'That's a nuisance. I can't believe we've come all this way to find no one in at all.'

She looked round her impatiently and noticed a wagon in the drive next to the house. The horse was still tethered to the ramshackle cart which was filled with blankets and burlap sacs. If the doctor's wagon was here, he couldn't be far.

To her left, a field stretched, gloomy in its winter barrenness. Beyond the house and the long, thin garden stood a line of trees. Only now did it come to her that the house gave onto the river.

'Martine,' she called back to the girl. 'Why don't you wait for me in the carriage. I just want to have a look down here.'

The river was high, swollen with winter rain. It rushed along in a swirl of grey as sombre as the sky and disappeared into the cold mist. How far could a basket stay upright in that current she suddenly wondered. It would be easy enough to bend over just here, say, and place a child in the river, but surely the basket would be tossed upside down well before it reached the vicinity of La Rochambert. And even if the infant had been belted in, it would be a miracle if he wasn't drowned.

She turned and let her eyes rove across the undulating flatness of the roughly ridged field. Only now did she see that two men, half hidden by a row of poplars, were bending over what looked like a rickety table. Odd time for a picnic.

No sooner had that thought moved through her mind, than her nerves set up ajangling. There was a body on the table. It was unmistakable, despite the low cloud.

An unmoving body splayed on an unsteady table in the midst of a winter field which stretched and stretched to disappear in haze and fog.

She picked her way across hardened mud as best she could to get a closer look.

Clothes had been pulled back to reveal a naked man. From her distance, the skin had a grey tinge more sallow than the grimy light.

The taller man had his back to her. His silhouette now bent to lift something from a brown leather bag at his side. She half expected the second man to shout at her from where he stood at the opposite side of the table. But he hadn't noticed her in the haze.

Both men were intent on the cadaver in front of them and she now understood, as she watched their movements, that the unresisting body was being carved up, expertly it would seem from the swift, certain thrust of the taller man, and the dropping of parts into separate pouches.

From behind her she heard the soft fall of feet on earth and she veered round. No one. She wished the cold river mist away. But it persisted, together with an eerie sense that she was being watched. Then, as she turned once more to the chilling spectacle, she felt as much as saw the flash from the corner of her eye, then another and another. A smell of burnt sulphur filled the air.

Marguerite turned back toward the doctor's house. The front door gave way unexpectedly to a mere twist of a knob. Marguerite let herself into a narrow hallway which abutted on the consulting room.

A desk dominated the space. To its side stood an examining table and a screen. The wall was hung with medical diagrams—an entire skeleton, which is what Martine must have seen, though she hadn't mentioned that its parts were named: a leg; the liver and surrounding vessels. Judging by the sheen of everything, the practice was new, at least to the area, but the doctor was not without some means.

She read the titles on a variety of tomes in the small bookcase as she waited. *Dictionary of Differential Diagnosis. The Memoirs of a Country Doctor*, a range of scientific titles and journals, amongst them *Le Progrès Médical.* The doctor had a scientific bent and evidently struggled to keep up with his reading, despite what she imagined must be arduous hours.

She was just taking in the box of neatly folded bandages, gleaming instruments, the washing bowls, the range of stethoscopes, the diploma from the ancient and high-ranking medical school at Montpelier, when she noticed a sheet of paper on the desk. It must have been left in haste. The top line read 'Report on Cadavre'.

She heard a step behind her and sat back abruptly.

'I'm sorry to keep you waiting. I'm afraid I had . . . certain duties to perform today. How can I be of assistance, Madame?'

His words held a greater politeness than his taut, impatient presence. Marguerite took in a tall man, probably not much older than herself. He had sparse black hair and a narrow face that might have been carved out of stone, so steep were its planes. It abutted in a dark close-cropped, professorial beard trimmed in evident haste. Through it his lips shone a fleshy pink. His clothes were not of the best quality, the elbows of his brown jacket threadbare, which meant there was probably no wife to sew on patches. Eyes like polished pebbles met hers with a piercing directness, which at once assessed her status, her clothes, perhaps what lay beneath. Oddly there was also something lulling in the gaze, a mesmeric quality.

She decided to return the directness at least. 'I'm afraid I'm not here for a consultation, Monsieur.'

The doctor's disappointment was palpable. Paying patients were not in great supply, it seemed. But his eyes remained unblinking. 'How can I help you then?'

Only now, as he put it down on the desk, did she take in the photographic apparatus he was carrying. So it had been a camera flash she had seen on the field.

'I'm here on behalf of a friend. But let me assuage my curiosity and ask you first, because it troubles me. Were you bent over a dead body atop a table in the neighbouring field not so very long ago?'

A shiftiness took him over. He found refuge in the papers on his desk and mumbled so that she could barely hear. 'Bodies of all kinds make up my practice.'

'You work with corpses?'

As if his nervous impatience had now got the better of him, he thrust his response at her. 'I work with the sick. If it disturbs you to consult a doctor who also performs autopsies on behalf of the judiciary and the police, then let me apologize in advance. But we are now in the twentieth century. And such scientific work is necessary. Even in the provinces.'

The portentous way in which he pronounced the word 'scientific' and underlined the new century reminded her of some of the earnest young students with whom she had attended lectures at the great Parisian hospitals. The body was still uncharted terrain, the abode of chemical mysteries, which called out for mapping and taming.

'Indeed, it is. Very necessary.' She smiled her respect.

His tension went with it, leaving only its ghost in the lines around his eyes.

'Who may I ask were you examining?'

'I'm not at liberty to say, Madame.' He glanced out the window, then lowered his lanky shape into the chair behind his desk. 'Perhaps you'll be kind enough not to spread word of my secondary activities too far and wide either . . . Some of the old people here can be a little superstitious, which I sense Madame approves of as little as I do.'

She nodded. 'Yet you perform your autopsies outdoors? Is that not irregular and a little too public?'

'You must have had the good fortune of spending much of your life in an advanced modern city, Madame. Here in the provinces, we are not in Paris.' He uttered the name of the capital with a mixture of awe and resentment. 'When it's colder outside than in, we work where we can and as quickly as we can. Bodies decompose, you know. There's also a question of light.' He was warming to his subject. 'Particularly in this dark time of the year. Candle and gaslight flicker too much for the delicate work.'

'I see. And you remove the organs?'

'When it seems to be called for. For laboratory examination. And I take photographs. I'm afraid in Montoire, there is a lack of professionals, not to mention facilities. Ascertaining the manner of death is still a new science. But we are making great strides.'

'And the manner of death of the man you were examining was suspicious in exactly what way?'

He was instantly on his guard again. 'May I ask why you are interested in these questions, Madame? You say you saw me in the field. Could you see the cadaver as well? Was the person known to you?'

'Please Doctor,' Marguerite cut him off. 'There's no need for misgivings. My interest is altogether general. I have a friend in the police force in Paris and we sometimes discuss such things. In fact, I've come to see you on quite another matter. On behalf of a friend of the family, as I said. A Mlle Branquart. Her sister, Yvette, is causing her some concern. She hasn't heard from her in several months. She was working at the Tellier House and it was from there I was directed to you.'

His wariness failed to dissipate. Quite the contrary. He deftly moved the police form off the table.

'Really? Now that surprises me. Madame Tellier has rarely put a high value on directing attractive women my way.' He bowed with a gallantry that seemed foreign to his earnest demeanour.

'Is that so?' Marguerite smiled. 'But then Madame Tellier was away. The person who mentioned you was a Madame Molineuf. The house-keeper, I imagine.'

He considered her again, his eyes astute. She could feel him wondering whether she was someone he needed to dissemble to.

'Put your mind at ease Dr. Labrosse. I have no intention of reporting our conversation to anyone in the Tellier House. You can be frank about Yvette with me.'

'Her sister, you say? I didn't know she had a sister. She never mentioned one. So her sister is worried about her health?'

'That too.'

He tapped out an impatient rhythm on the desk. The nails of his fingers were buffed and manicured. It surprised Marguerite.

'The girl wasn't well. A little high-strung compared to the usual maids I see. I wanted to conduct a thorough examination, but Madame Tellier prevented me. I recommended that she come and see me here. Recommended it to her rather quietly and to be utterly frank'—he smiled in a disarming manner—'secretly. Madame Tellier, gave me every reason to understand that she wasn't interested in paying for Mademoiselle's invented ailments.'

'What had brought you to the Tellier house in the first place?'

'Madame Tellier suffers from two unmarried daughters, amongst a number of other perennial complaints. She is a frequent patient. But the family is hardly amenable to scientific diagnoses. Not that I should speak ill of Monsieur Tellier, whom I have only met once. He is rarely in Troo. For Madame and her daughters, I usually prescribe a tonic and go on my way. But on one of my visits, her little maid, Yvette, as you say, fainted in my presence. I feared she was seriously anemic . . . But I'm speaking out of turn.'

'No, no. Not at all. Please go on. So Mlle Yvette came to see you here?'

He leapt up abruptly. 'She didn't. No. I gave her a prescription. The chemist will know whether she heeded it. I'm afraid that's all I can tell you, Madame. I have not seen her in some months either, come to think of it.'

'How did the girl seem to you generally, Monsieur?'

He shrugged. 'I sense the household she was working in was hardly the most wholesome of environments. Need I say more?'

'Was it Monsieur Tellier? Did they beat her?'

He looked around nervously. 'I know nothing about that.'

'Do you have any notion of where she might have gone? Did she have any friends to turn to?'

'She was from the region. She probably knew as many people as I do, if not more. I wish I could be of more help, Madame, but I'm afraid I must get on.' He pulled a gold watch from his waistcoat pocket and studied it with too much attention, simultaneously taking a sheet of paper and a quill from his desk drawer.

'Her sister is very distressed. If you hear anything, or something significant occurs to you, please do come to see me at La Rochambert.' Marguerite gathered her skirts.

'Yes, of course. Of course. La Rochambert.' He straightened his shoulders in military fashion at the mention of the address, and flicked specs of lint from his lapel.

She hesitated. 'Tell me, doctor, your police case? Was it the man found on the tracks. The suicide?'

Yes, the self-murder.' Gloom took the energy out of his features and made them almost ugly. 'Or so I was told by the police.'

Marguerite leapt at the casually offered information.

'You mean the poor man didn't fling himself in front of the train?'

'He was certainly under the train. Whether that's all that killed him, we have yet to learn . . .'

She stared at the Doctor. So little blood. She had wondered at that. And that vacant eye, too soon after the supposed death.

'You mean he died of a prior dying?'

'That's a quaint way of putting it. But yes, that's what I think. A prior dying. A double death, if you like.'

'Someone else brought him to the tracks?'

'So the bodily evidence would lead me to believe. So far in any case.'

'A murder then?'

He didn't answer.

'And do you know what killed him?'

'Not yet.' He shrugged, rubbed his eyes and suddenly looked tired. 'Not that the police, let alone the investigating magistrate, will necessarily believe me. But I shouldn't be saying all this. I talk too much. I must be very tired. You'll forgive me Madame. This is no conversation to be having with a woman. '

'This woman promises that it will go no further.' Marguerite smiled. 'If you tell me who the man is.'

He shrugged. 'That's just it. No one is certain. There was no identification on him. He's quite unknown to me, as he seemed to be to the two men who came to have a look at him. The people around here can be strangely secretive, you know. There's a chance of course that he's not from around here. No one seems to have reported an absence.'

'Well, if I can be of any help to you in the future, Doctor, please don't hesitate. Or if you need any support in your researches . . . I can sometimes facilitate things.'

He bowed. 'Thank-you, Madame. That is very kind.'

She had almost reached the door, when she turned back.' By the way, doctor, there is something else you might be able to help me with. Have you or any midwives you know come across a woman who might have lost a child recently?'

He didn't respond. She hadn't made herself clear.

'A baby has been found. In the river.'

He leapt up from his chair. He had misunderstood her.

'I'm not in the habit of throwing out babies, no matter what state they've arrived in, Madame. There are enough infanticides in these blighted provinces without my help. The Republic must do something about it, must somehow make men and women equally responsible for their offspring.He stopped himself, then rushed on, his eyes burning. And if you think . . . if you think Mlle Yvette was pregnant, I know nothing about it. Nothing. You, Madame, if I may say so, have an unhealthy preoccupation with death.'

_ 6 _

Outside the mist had grown denser. But Martine was not waiting in the carriage. The coachman informed Marguerite that the girl had grown impatient and gone for a stroll. She had gone in the direction of the market square.

Perhaps she had remembered a contact, Marguerite thought. It didn't really matter that they would be late home. As it was, she had taken far too long with the doctor.

Was he right about her? Had this last year of the century, heavy with loss, left her with an unhealthy preoccupation with death and the ordeals of the past?

She gathered her long fur more closely round her and sat back into the seat as Georges moved the horses slowly towards the square. Passersby had the wavering outlines of phantoms. The hawkers, muffled against the cold, seemed to be performing their business in some kind of shadow play, their arms waving in random gestures. The gas lamps in front of the shoe shop were already lit. The trees shivered. Drops of moisture clung to the bare branches despite the lack of rain.

Marguerite watched. Yes, it was true. She was being thrust into the company of the dead again, as if her very fascination propelled corpses into her path. Much as she refused this line of reasoning, it had its own logic. Death had long ago started to weave its fatal web round her, as though it was toying with her. She heard its call in the strains of certain melodies, in the judder of a piano chord or sweet sigh of a violin, and in the sudden panic of a nighttime awakening.

Here, now, in these old haunts, it seemed to her it must all date back to that childhood moment when her father had announced that her mother was dead. Had she seen her lying there on that bed her father had always called her mother's bed? She didn't know. Nothing about her mother was accessible to her, except that portrait, and very occasionally the soft pitch of a woman's voice.

The deaths she remembered had started with her animals. First the kitten she had nursed with a dropper who had grown into a sizeable enough creature before vanishing into the woods where, distraught, she had found him bloated with maggots, his fur matted and bloody. She had wanted somehow, against all odds, to revive him, and when that proved impossible, she had wanted more than anything to join him. She remembered lying on the leaf mould beside him, the earth damp and cloying and giving off some heavy smell which was simultaneously sweet and acrid.

After that, there had been her father's dog, who was also her own, a glowing, russet setter with a soft, unforgettable gaze. He had gone to sleep in front of the fire one night and never opened his eyes again. She had lain on top of him and sobbed. She had pounded and pummeled him in the hope of response. She had wondered what it was that made him dead rather than alive, since he looked exactly as he always looked except motionless.

Without quite realizing it, Marguerite had abandoned the carriage and begun to cross the bridge. Now she found herself staring into the waters and thinking about the foundling who had miraculously escaped drowning. Escaped death. Was that what made him so dear to Olivier? Or was it rather that he had been saved from the clutches of death by Olivier himself?

Marguerite shook herself, looked up and realized she was standing close to a riverside *blanchisserie*. Steam leaked from the cracks in the door and the frames of windows. Of course. Where did maids go, when they wanted to leave the world of service, if not to a laundry or a milliners, work which was often supplemented, in Paris at least, with sexual service. So many of the great *horizontales* had followed that trajectory. The woman in the blanchisserie might be able to help.

She slipped through the door and found herself in a fair-sized room. Sheets and clothes hung everywhere on wires to dry, giving the place the look of a washerwoman's garden on a hot afternoon. Pushing aside whites and embroidered tablecloths, she picked her way between petticoats and drawers and shirt fronts to arrive in the vicinity of a large table covered with calico at which six or so women were engaged in ironing everything from bodices to pockets. Their bonnets kept the perspiration from running down their faces. Their cheeks glowed pink. A sprite of a girl fed coke into the stove on which the irons heated.

'What can I do for you, Madame?' a portly older woman addressed her.

Marguerite met the woman's eyes and smiled confidentially. 'I wonder if I might have a word, Madame? In private, perhaps.'

She gestured the woman behind a large white sheet that hung to the side of the room, then asked her first about Yvette Branquart. There was no whiff of recognition in the woman's face, but she promised that she would ask all her girls, if Madame could return later in the week.

Marguerite nodded acquiescence, then tried to phrase her second question about the abandoned babe with enough delicacy so that it didn't solicit the kind of reaction she had had from Dr. Labrousse. It didn't prevent the woman's face from shutting down and her shoulders taking on a disapproving rigidity.

'There is nothing like that amongst my girls, Madame can be certain. They are good girls, all of them. I wouldn't allow for less. Not in my establishment.'

'But perhaps, Madame,' Marguerite asked solemnly, 'one of them might have heard something from a friend or . . .'

The woman's lips formed into a tight and even primmer line. 'I shall ask, Madame. But don't expect to learn anything here.'

Leaving the premises, Marguerite realized that her search for the foundling's parents might prove far more difficult than she had bargained. For even if anything was known, it would be hidden, certainly from someone of Marguerite's class.

One would think that the spiraling rate of illegitimacy, some said as much as fifty percent, or of children given up to orphanages, was provoked by disembodied creatures or the proverbial stork, who never stepped into a laundry or a hospital or indeed anywhere that Marguerite might choose to direct her questions.

She noticed the old Benedictine Priory just across the way. The door into the grounds was open, beckoning her through. She slipped round the single marked grave into the tiny ancient chapel with its trefoil of apses. It was empty, hushed. She let the silence play through her and breathed deeply.

The fresco depicting the virtues and the vices which had always intrigued her as a child was still there, the eyes of its gathered figures blind, unseeing. It gave them an otherworldly aspect: they could see into the invisible, she had thought. It was exactly what she needed to do now.

Not so long ago, she had read that the painted saints' blindness wasn't intended by their makers. The fresco artists of the Romanesque period had simply added eyes and beards to their images once the plaster was dry. Over the centuries time had eaten away these superficially applied features and deepened the mystery of the remaining figures.

On the low vaulted ceiling, angels surrounded a triumphant Christ. A Christ of the Apocalypse. The Christ who raised the dead. Her head arced backward in an awkward position, like the dead man's on the makeshift table in the field. He too had lost an eye, she remembered and shuddered. Shuddered not only for him, but because she had an inexplicable sense that she was being watched again. Yet it was impossible that anyone could hide in the tiny chapel. It had to be as deserted as when she had come in.

She hurried out from those thick stone walls which oozed the damp of centuries. She made her way back towards the river's edge, then stopped abruptly. There, half hidden by the trunk of an ancient chestnut, stood Martine. The bright blue of the beret on that golden head was unmistakable. Yet, the girl's posture was odd. She seemed to be pressed into the tree's trunk, her arms raised to ward off something frightening yet invisible. As she hastened towards her, Marguerite saw the reason for her fear.

Looming over Martine was the strange, giant youth they had seen at the Tellier's. He had edged close to her. He was running a finger down her cheek. It looked as if it might soon encircle her frail throat with only a little help from his thumb. The girl's mouth was open, but no sound emerged from it.

Marguerite screamed for her. The youth leapt back. He enacted an odd little dance, his big feet shuffling back and forward, his shoulders swinging and then he was off before Marguerite could come close enough to speak. Despite his bulk and the unwieldy gait, he disappeared quickly downriver along a shrub strewn path.

'Are you alright, Martine? Did he hurt you?'

The girl stood mute, as if she weren't altogether sure. Her words, when they came were delivered in a cracked whisper, only gaining strength when Marguerite wound an arm through hers and led her back to the street.

'He caught up to me before. I can't stand him. I can't. He scares me. P'tit Ours, they call him, but he's more like a big bear. A very big bear. He was trailing me. He walks so softly, I didn't hear. Despite his size. Then I thought he might want to tell me something about Yvette. That he had sought me out.'

'And did he?'

'I'm not sure. I don't know.'

'Just tell me what he said to you.'

They had crossed the bridge now and Marguerite could see the carriage waiting on the corner of the square. It had an inviting air. Georges had lit the lanterns and the flame danced in its glass casing.

'Take your time, Martine. It may be important.'

The girl didn't speak again until the carriage began its slow clatter along cobbles.

'The thing is Madame, I didn't understand him. Not really. Not altogether. He's not always very clear. He said something about smells and flowers. I think he was talking about Yvette. I don't know. He makes rhymes sometimes. "Pretty rose and flows," he said. Then something about a sack in the back. And a strong man and fire and oil and a winged monster. I just don't know.' She shook her head. 'Look, there he is again.'

The youth she had called P'tit Ours was standing in a narrow lane near a shop which bore a bold chemist's sign, Tournevau, Fils. He was being addressed by an officious little man who was a head shorter than him and was angrily waving an admonitory finger. The youth alternately cowered, his bushy eyebrows converging to a point on his broad forehead, then seemed about to hit the man.

'Shall I ask Georges to stop?'

'No, no.' Martine almost shouted. 'No, Madame. Not now.'

'Do you know who the man talking to him is?'

'I think he said something to me about an errand at the chemist's. He certainly said chemist.' She shivered, was silent for a moment. 'He also said . . .' she paused. 'I'm sure he said it. A platter with breasts on it. Breasts like blanc mange. Horrible.'

'A platter with breasts. How bizarre.'

Martine shot a glance at her, then determinedly looked out the window. The town had quickly given way to countryside, not at its loveliest here in the dirty light. But one field had produced a bright crop of garishly painted wagons of the kind fairground people used. In front of a red and white one, a woman squatted by a small fire. Beside her was a man with a large drooping moustache. He was wearing leotards beneath a heavy jacket. His bulk identified him as a possible strong man. Behind him, a juggler was practicing his art. His back to them, a man with a white turban sat on a barrel. A goat poked his head desultorily round its side. Two wolfish dogs barked and barked.

Marguerite was tempted to ask Georges to stop, then thought better of it. She wasn't with her artist friends now. The Paris ways which had become second nature to her would shock the locals. She couldn't first rush off to stare into a desolate field, then go and address mountebanks, without the whispers somehow getting back to Olivier. So she would have to return.

How she wished Chief Inspector Durand were here. Travellers always knew things. Nor, did they usually share the hypocritical morality of the townsfolk. Could it be one of their band who had left an unwanted baby to float downriver? Or one of their number who was now lying unidentified behind Dr. Labrousse's surgery? Come to think of it, the giant youth had mentioned a strong man. His words might be baffling, but they were evidently not devoid of sense.

Martine must have been thinking along the same lines. 'Maybe . . . I don't know. Maybe he thought I was Yvette.'

Marguerite sat up very straight. 'Thought you were Yvette?'

'Yes, yes. We're a lot like each other.'

Martine's head was still turned to the window. She seemed to be talking half to herself.

Marguerite looked at the stiff little back, the nervously bunched shoulders and wondered for a moment if she had perhaps taken on more than she had bargained in promising to help the girl. A vision of Olympe among the trembling madwomen in the wards of the Salpetriere hospital invaded her mind. There had been so many deaths in that madhouse. And before death, a living hell, a life with too many hurdles and pitfalls, exacerbated by the limited opportunities available to the poor creatures. On top of it all, they had to contend with the conflicting images of themselves men flung at them. Priests, journalists, even doctors insisted on their feminine virtue. But they were all too happy to seduce it away and turn them into women of that easy virtue which only served the opposite sex.

'Do you think Yvette might have decided to go off with travellers?' Marguerite asked just as Martine startled her with a half heard sentence.

'Yvette used to talk of breasts on platters.'

'Breasts on platters. Really.'

'Yes. Yes. She loved . . . she loves,' Yvette corrected herself, 'she loves stories of the saints. One of her favourites is Saint Agatha.'

'Tell me,' Marguerite murmured. Her education hadn't stretched to the lives of the saints. Her provincial childhood had been far too unorthodox. And what she had heard, later, from a stream of governesses, had repelled her in its blatant physical violence.

'Agatha was a beautiful and wealthy girl, Roman I think, who vowed her virginity to Christ.' A blush rose in Martine's face. 'But she was forced into . . . into bad ways, then tortured. Her emblem is a dish with blessed loaves on it. They stand in for her breasts which were . . .'

'Removed,' Marguerite finished for her when she hesitated. 'These saints stories hardly seem salutary in our modern times. One always hopes they've been subject to a great deal of exaggeration. Like fairy tales. Don't you think?'

Martine's features struggled with some difficult emotion. 'My sister never thought so. She believed in the lives. Our mother read them to us. From when we were very little. They were her models in courage.'

'I see. Is this what made Yvette so much braver than you?' Marguerite's image of the young woman, of both the sisters, had suddenly undergone a radical shift.

'Yes, in part.'

'And why do you think Yvette told P'tit Ours about the saints, or at least this particular saint?'

'I don't know. I don't know, Madame.' Tears gathered in the blue eyes. 'Perhaps she wanted to educate him. Before our aunt died, there was some talk that if we didn't get married straight away, we might consider becoming teachers. There are all these new schools for girls. Yvette was very keen on that. Then, when we were left with nothing . . . well, maybe for Yvette talking to P'tit Ours was a way of being something of a teacher.'

'Talking to him of breasts on platters,' Marguerite said with an edge in her voice.

Martine leapt to her sister's defence. 'She wouldn't have said it like that. That's P'tit Ours . . . Or at least,' she brought a handkerchief to her eyes. 'At least that's what I heard.'

Marguerite buried her hands more deeply in her muff. If this Yvette was silly enough to speak to an impressionable and unpredictable youth of private female parts, it was no wonder that Martine was so worried about her.

'Do you think Yvette provoked P'tit Ours to anything with these stories, Martine?' she made her question deliberately direct.

'I don't know . . . I don't think so. She's not like that. She's like . . . she's like Joan of Arc.'

'And yet P'tit Ours, mistaking you for her, was stroking your cheek?'

'He wasn't, Madame. He wasn't?'

'I must have seen incorrectly.'

'I think he wanted to. He was saying something I couldn't understand about a horse. Maybe it was his horse. Héloïse, he called her. He strokes her, I guess. He was showing me.'

'You as Yvette?'

She nodded. Tears filled her eyes again. 'I fear he doesn't see all that well. He goes by smells. I smell like Yvette. I still have a little of the Lavender water Aunt used to make for us. Oh Madame!' She gripped Marguerite's wrist with unexpected force. 'What have I done? What have I done?'

_ 7 _

The next day, milky sunlight propelled her out of the house early. She asked Jeanne to tell Olivier she was going riding. One of the stable boys saddled her favourite stallion, a spirited chestnut who went by the name of Mohawk, and she set off across fields and valleys, exhilarated by the wind on her face and the galloping speed of her horse.

The riding wasn't random. She had a destination. She was headed for an address in Château du Loir which Madame Solange had mentioned. She was in search of the maid called Louise who had left the château at harvest time for a family in the area.

Marguerite had made discreet inquiries amongst the staff at La Rochambert about the character of the two young women who had left, one soon after the other. It was clear enough from the slight nervousness or flushes on the faces of the males that either of the two could have engaged in relations with a man there or elsewhere; in particular perhaps, the man who had given notice soon after they had left. Though, of course, nothing was spoken. Only Madame Solange had been bold enough to presume aloud to a mistress she had known since childhood that one of these might have given birth to the foundling.

At the solid, double-turreted house in the riverside town, a great fuss was made of Marguerite's impromptu arrival. But the girl, Louise, it turned out, had left long ago, having stayed at her new posting for a mere two months, before going off with a sufficient reference in hand to an unknown destination. No one had any idea where she might now be. What was more, no one, certainly not the pretty, fluttery mistress of the house, seemed to have any inkling whether the girl had been pregnant or not. You might, Marguerite thought to herself on the way home and not for the first time, begin to surmise such conditions were altogether invisible in the valleys, except where four-legged creatures were concerned.

She returned to La Rochambert feeling well-exercised but more than a little despondent. She had hoped for something from this particular expedition. She was now sorry that she had not accompanied Martine. It had been arranged that the young woman would go to her hometown of Vendome in the old barouche that morning and spend the day talking to family friends who might be able in person to give her some better inkling of her sister's whereabouts. Marguerite sensed, too, that seeing familiar faces would cheer Martine, perhaps even relax her a little.

She stabled her horse and wondered whether it would make sense to return to Dr. Labrousse's this afternoon, despite the fact that she hadn't left him on altogether the best of terms, in order to elicit a list of midwives from him. The maids' trail having gone temporarily cold, it would be a midwife who would be best placed to know of any children born in the area. And she didn't want to involve their old family doctor, who would be sure to raise the matter with Olivier.

No sooner had she stepped into the house, however, than she was told Olivier wanted to see her immediately. The order conveyed urgency. Without changing her black riding habit or washing the perspiration from her face, she made her way to the library.

A cigarette in a silver holder in his left hand, monocle at his eye, Olivier was poised by the window of the long rectangular library. There was a man next to him, sitting at the heavy oak reading table. They were both examining a picture held up to catch the light.

'Ah Marguerite, there you are.' Olivier turned as she came in. He was all courtesy rather than impatience. It puzzled her.

The man beside him rose. He was wearing a fine black cassock which fell so smoothly from trim belted waist and broad shoulders that for a moment portraits of Renaissance cardinals, more profane than sacred, flashed through her mind. A fine gold cross swung across his chest. The skin on the closely shaven face had the healthy firmness of a child's. The solemn, grey gaze, the strong nose, the chin tilted in vanity, the smooth light hair, all seemed to hint at a man who might be more interested in power than sanctity.

'Père Benoit has taken over the parish in the wake of Père Philippe's death. I believe I wrote to you about it.'

The man bowed deeply.

She had liked the harmless old priest with his comfortable belly and sweet face. This man was of a different cut. He commanded the space around him in a way which made her wary.

'Old Father Philippe was much loved in these parts. I knew him from my childhood.'

'Indeed,' Olivier cut her off. 'Père Benoit has come to us directly from Rome.' He named the city with a touch of awe which took Marguerite by surprise.

'There have already been great improvements both to our chapel and to the church. New pews. A far better organ. Père Benoit has ideas for our little valley.'

'Really?'

'Yes, Madame.' The cleric cleared his throat and addressed her in a suasive, slightly pompous tone, one she sensed he cultivated for the minor but troublesome species amongst which the genus wife fell.

'Your esteemed husband and I have had several conversations. I imagine he has told you. In the wake of the sad death of Monsieur René Fretin, I am convinced that were Monsieur le Comte to stand as our deputy, we would see him at the Assemblée. And I am not alone in not being able to think of a better candidate for the Catholic Party.'

Marguerite veiled her astonishment.

Olivier had swollen under these words to regal proportions. His shoulders were now straight. His eyes shone.

A nervousness took her over. Of course, this was it. The explanation. The explanation for everything. Including the good deed of taking on the babe. Of calling her here. Of insisting on her presence. Of wanting a firm grip on her whereabouts.

Was it possible that Olivier had become so enamoured of country life that he now accepted all its values? The Olivier she thought she knew would not begin to consider a late career in politics, let alone joining the

Catholic Party. It was unthinkable that he would link himself with a reactionary faction which had put all its religious fervour in these long years of the Dreyfus affair into fomenting hatred, into defending a retrograde France of the imagination, one that had never really existed in the placid, yet heroic, feudal parochialism they evoked.

'Rome has given you an interest in politics, I see Monsieur,' She converted her uneasiness about Olivier into a focus on the young priest.

'It has indeed. The role of the church is central to the moral strength of France. We must prevent these urban Republicans from contaminating all of our lives with their excesses, not to mention their financial intrigues. They bleed the countryside, the core of our nation, of its spiritual wealth.'

The man had all the arrogance of youth compounded by the righteousness with which his vocation endowed him.

'Really?'

Olivier caught the combative edge in her tone and stepped in to distract her.

'Look what Monsieur le Curé has brought for my collection.'

Marguerite glanced at the small painting her husband held in his hand. She wasn't sure she knew anything of a collection of Olivier's, but if this was to be part of it, she would have to withhold her opinion. She could understand this lapse of taste no more than his sudden interest in the Catholic Party.

The picture showed a robed and bearded priest of some antique sort, his hands clasped in prayer. In front of him were two men, their limbs bared and intertwined whether in a struggle or capture wasn't clear. The man in front had his hands raised to the skies and a suffering expression on his face. The whole was executed in miserable fashion.

'It's Saint Benoit healing a man possessed by the devil.'

'I see.'

'Do you?' The priest's voice arrived with a coolness which verged on the rude. 'It's a copy I made of a fresco in a cloister in Bologna. A fresco by Louis Carrache, a master of the Bolognese school.' He enunciated each word ponderously, as if he were talking to an illiterate schoolgirl.

'Do you dabble then, Father?' Marguerite met the man's eyes with the full force of her own. 'Yes, I do see now. The great Bolognese School of the counter-reformation. I must admit, I have a taste for earlier, rather less excessive work than this. Work where the devil holds less sway.'

His cassock swinging, the man had the courtesy to perform a small bow. He mumbled something in Latin about taste.

'I omitted to mention to you, Father . . . my wife is rather well-versed in the arts. Is herself a tolerable artist.'

It was the first time since her arrival that Marguerite had heard Olivier's droll tone. Perhaps this new solemnity and correctness was merely a facade.

'I haven't seen the latest additions to your collection, Olivier. You must show me.'

He waved towards a waist-high set of drawers edged into a far corner of the room at the base of the book shelves. 'It's mostly in there. I have framed none of them yet. We'll look later. My dear,' he added, with a faint smile. 'I believe Monsieur le Curé has some news he wanted to tell us first.'

The cleric looked at Marguerite and licked dry lips with a fleshy tongue. 'I'm not sure if Madame . . .'

'Madame has heard most things at least once before, mon père. Don't be embarrassed by her presence. I am sure you shall yet grow very fond of each other.'

She felt the curé's gaze fall on her. Did those cool grey eyes betray just a hint of malevolence? She had a niggling sense that the man saw her as a competitor for Olivier's attention. Had it been excessively devoted until her arrival?

'I do want to change before lunch, Olivier, and perhaps look in on the babe.' She smiled sweetly.

'Of course, of course.'

The men exchanged a glance and nodded mutual approval.

Marguerite hesitated at the threshold. 'Incidentally, Monsieur le Curé, my husband told me you checked with the police to ascertain that there have been no kidnappings in the vicinity.'

'Yes, yes, of course.' The man beamed good will at her. 'Of course. And while we're on the subject, Madame, I am sure Monsieur le Comte has mentioned the urgency of a baptism to you. You will have to agree on a name. Monsieur I know is quite partial to Charles Gabriel. We want the child protected.'

She understood by how he touched his cross that he meant protected against an eternity in limbo. She couldn't stop herself confronting him.

'Nurse tells me he's a strong little soul. In due course, Monsieur. I have really only just arrived and I must make certain we are not robbing some poor woman of her offspring. Too often such women are so badly treated, so maligned, so lost, as to prefer to murder or abandon their children rather than be discovered. If that is the case here, and I can find her, I would rather do everything in my power to help the poor woman, than to take over her child.'

'Marguerite,' Olivier snapped.

But she had already closed the door behind her.

The long table beneath the dining room's painted ceiling, with its plump cupids and plumper clouds on a sky of clearest blue, gleamed with silver and an array of delicacies. The muted rose of the walls urged calm. But there was tension in the atmosphere. Not that it diminished the men's appetites. Olivier, Villemardi and especially Père Benoit ate with an open carnality. They also drank their way through half a dozen bottles of wine with a heartiness Marguerite would have liked to attribute to the country air, but secretly felt was the product of their surprising hostilities.

The proud new curate treated the sculptor with contempt. The two men vied for Olivier's approval like rival sons contending for a disdainful father's attention. Or unmarried sisters competing for the hand of a single suitor. Spellbound by the spectacle, Marguerite forgot to preside as the young men hurled only slightly veiled insults at each other.

'And how has the stone responded to your blows these last days, Monsieur Villemardi?'

'As well, no doubt, as the serving girls to your catechism, Father.'

Villemardi was so brazen, Marguerite found herself warming to his energetic refusal of the curé's ever more soulful sanctimony.

'If you and your kin didn't with one voice champion the large family and the virtues of many children and with another decry the loss of female virtue and the poor illegitimate bastards who result, these girls wouldn't get themselves into such a twist, and end up abandoning or murdering their offspring. Use your pulpit to blame the men who seduce and abandon, if you have to point your punitive finger at someone.'

'Shall I blame you then, Monsieur Villemardi? Shall I preach a sermon to convert you to chastity?'

'Yes, I do see that with the church's patriotic logic, chastity is what will increase the population of France, so that we catch up to our fine German neighbours, as you so loudly proclaim you wish. Yes, I do see.'

'You are incorrigible.'

'And you and the church have forgotten the meaning of forgiveness. I do hope, Olivier, that if you're going to run on a Catholic ticket, it'll be one that sides with the Republicans and says death to the old celibate orders, death to the rich and unholy congregations. Give their land, their brain-rotting schools to the poor. Take away their political power.'

Villemardi laughed at his own effrontery while Olivier chided and the curé reprimanded in the severest of terms, threatening the sculptor not only with hell, but with banishment from his Patron's house.

Only when the cheese was served, did Marguerite begin to suspect that the two young men's ire might be fuelled by more than the bill currently making its way through the Assemblée and general political disagreements.

Covertly she watched Olivier. She wondered if it was precisely for the spectacle of these two younger men's acrimony that he brought them together. He did little to abate their rising vitriol. Like a Roman at a gladiatorial combat, he observed, at once immune to and excited by the possibility that at any moment the contenders might draw blood.

With the last draining of glasses, Marguerite felt she could put off the question she wanted to ask the sculptor no longer. 'I gather, Monsieur Villemardi, you weren't able to recognize the dead man who had a card from your family firm in his pocket.'

The curé put his glass down with a clatter.

'Really, Marguerite. We are still at table.' Olivier reprimanded.

Villemardi paid no heed. 'Non, Madame. Though I was tempted to ask if I could do a death's head of him. It was quite a remarkable face.

Sculptural in its grossness. Particularly with that missing eye. I could imagine it as belonging to a Bacchic figure, to be positioned at some interesting angle in the woods.'

'That's enough, Paul.' Olivier pushed his chair back emphatically.

They followed in his train to take coffee in front of the fire. A feeble sun was already beginning to sink in the afternoon sky.

'I wonder if I might be invited to see the pieces you're working on before the light goes altogether, Monsieur Villemardi. It would give me great pleasure to do so.' Lunch had sparked Marguerite's interest in the sculptor.

The man performed a small military bow then flung his head back so that the hair flew.

'I would be honoured, Madame.'

Villemardi had converted two old outhouses at the far side of the chestnut grove into a conjoined workspace. His materials, marble and the white stone of the region, lay loosely covered under a tarpaulin, sheltered beneath a sloping half-roof on the outside of the structures. Inside, a small tile stove barely threw the worse of the chill from the long, dusty rooms. A series of work smocks hung from hooks on the door and Marguerite would have been happy to don one. It wasn't offered. Instead, Villemardi abruptly cloaked himself in sullenness, as if he were expecting to have to ward off blows from the neatly aligned series of hammers and chisels.

Marguerite said nothing at the display of temperament. She was used to artists and their complicated dance. They tended to welcome attention with a first step and reject it with a second, compounding desire for recognition with a sensitivity that shouted it was hardly necessary.

She was, however, surprised to see pinned to the walls a series of photographs, perhaps by the American Muybridge and evidently clipped from some journal. Motion studies, they depicted a woman in a long dress, leaping over a stool, each lift of skirt and arm and leg, embodied in a separate image. There was a running figure, too, calves tensed mid-air in fugue, then a horse trotting, and finally a sequence of clouds, larger, smaller, whisking across a flat sky. She wondered what part, if any, all this played in the man's work, but his expression forbade questions.

In the far room, white sheets covered a series of mysterious shapes. As Villemardi removed them, she saw figures, far lighter than the stone they emerged from, all but dance across the room. Two of them were of the same young woman taking on the fleeting pose of a classical nymph. Her cloak, intricate in its folds, defied gravity. It flew through the air. Everything here was light and motion as if to spite the materials which shaped it. The carved figures gave off the very breath of freedom.

She saw now why Villemardi was interested in the photographic studies.

'These are good.' Marguerite said in a soft voice. 'Very good.'

'It surprises you.'

'Not at all. Are they recent?'

'I've been working on them on and off for over a year. I hope to have them placed in the gardens this summer.'

'May I ask who served as your model?'

'One of the maids.'

'I should like to meet her. To compliment her on her transformation.'

'You'll have to travel to do that. She's no longer with the household.'

'Oh.'

'Yes. Madame Solange saw to that. But don't expect me to carry any tales.' He crossed his arms over his chest in a stubborn gesture.

'What was her name?'

'Louise.'

She stared at the man. 'I see.'

'Do you?' he asked, ever brash.

'I'd like to talk to this beautiful young woman. Do you know where I can find her?'

'Talk to Madame Solange. I have no idea.'

'Sad to lose such a talented model. What was her family name?'

'Do servants have family names?

The facetious grin played over his face as he pulled a drapery back emphatically from another figure.

Elbow poised on knee in a forward thrust, Marguerite recognized Olivier emerging from stone like some Medici.

'You've given him a very stately air.'

'Do you think I've been obsequious? Like our dear curé?' Villemardi met her eyes as if he expected an honest answer, not one from either a flattering patron or a dutiful wife.

'You see Olivier as a strong, somewhat arrogant man. It isn't untrue to him.'

Villemardi gave her his first open smile of the day. 'It's not finished yet.'

Marguerite nodded. 'May I touch?'

The stone was cold and not quite smooth.

Villemardi examined her without making any pretence of doing otherwise. 'You're not as I imagined.'

She met his gaze with her own direct one.

'I won't ask what you imagined. But tell me . . . you don't like our new curé very much?'

'What makes you say that?'

Her laugh rippled. 'Come Monsieur Villemardi, don't make me re-estimate your intelligence.'

'All right, but not for reasons you can imagine.'

'Oh. Let me try. Did he abandon a sister or a cousin of yours at the altar?'

Villemardi chuckled in a not altogether friendly fashion.

'No. Though he could have. And he would have made it seem as if it were an act of tribute to his God.'

The fierce undertow in Villemardi's voice amplified her sense that the two men had a history, that their spats bore the venom of an age-old grievance.

'You knew each other in a previous life?'

'Is it obvious?'

'I am hardly new to society, Monsieur.'

'We were at the same school. In Tours. He was a terrible bully to us poorer boys. Always mocking—our clothes, our clogs, our ways of speaking. Organizing cabals against us. Dare I say he wasn't known for his charity.'

'His own parents have wealth?'

Villemardi shrugged. 'I no longer know. I suspect there may have been some decline in their fortunes. Over the Panama affair. They fell for the golden bait like so many others. In any event, I think it was around that time that our local devil developed a vocation.'

'And he remembers you?'

'I had no reason to change my name. Isn't it interesting how it is only criminals and those with a vocation who change their names with such facility?'

There was more bitterness in his voice than Marguerite had bargained for. The childhood scars were still raw.

'In any case, Monsieur, I suspect where art is concerned, you have certainly surpassed your schoolmate.'

Villemardi gave her a small bow. 'But don't underestimate our dear curé in other areas, Madame. That would be a mistake. By the way, Bertin was the girl's name.' He paused. 'Many men, you know, like bees, are attracted to wayside flowers. But there are those of us who prefer rarer varieties. I would be honoured if you would consider posing for me, Madame.'

She wasn't altogether sure why, but she felt the compliment was double-edged.

_ 8 _

Martine folded nappies. The squares of cotton mounted, bright against her dark-grey, high-necked dress, which bore all the additional trimmings and displaced buttons of a hand-me-down. The girl's hands moved mechanically. Her eyes never left the babe.

The makeshift nursery had so swiftly acquired the necessary trappings that it was hard to think the child hadn't always been here in this blue and white room with a dormer window which looked over the small orchard. A crib had appeared from nowhere, a small tin tub, even a wooden rattle. A door to the side showed the nurse's room. The stout Celeste was making her bed.

'I hope you don't mind, Madame,' Martine turned as Marguerite came in and gave her what was almost a smile. 'But Celeste said she had so much on her hands that I offered to help.'

'That's fine, Martine. If it distracts you.'

Martine had returned from her journey to Vendome the previous evening with no news of her sister.

'It does, Madame. And . . . and I hate doing nothing and being so beholden to you.

'All the more reason then.'

'He's so sweet.'

They stared at the sleeping face of the infant, the shadow of thick lashes on milk-soft skin. The cheeks had filled out, even since Marguerite had been in the house. There was a kind of carnal plenitude about them. It was hard to think that such a brief span ago, the creature had been all but dead.

That was one good thing, at least, Marguerite mused. She ran a finger along that elastic expanse of cheek. The eyes flew open with a single swift movement. They focussed on her, deep and dark in their gaze. If she looked down, down into the pupils with the kind of attention the mite focussed on her, would she find the photographic imprint of his mother—the first face ever to leave a trace there. A face which wasn't the one she could see now.

As she brought her own closer, a smell of incense rose to her nostrils. On the flannel sheet to the child's side, she now noticed a small, but sturdy gold heart from which the scent seemed to emerge.

'What is that, Celeste?' she asked the wet nurse.

'It's his sacred heart, Madame. It keeps him safe.'

'I see. I see. From Monsieur?'

'I don't know, Madame.'

'How old do you reckon the mite is, Celeste? Do you think he was abandoned straight after he was born?'

'Difficult to say.'

She lifted the child with a single certain movement, propped him on the changing table and stripped him down.

Round naked limbs flailed the air in random playfulness.

'He's filled out well. But I'd say he's still under a month. Probably born just before Christmas.'

Marguerite nodded sagely and turned back to Martine. 'I was planning to pay a visit to Madame Tellier today. I imagine she's back from Tours. Would you rather stay here, Martine? Or shall we go together?'

The girl's cheeks grew pale. 'Oh Madame. If you don't mind. I so hate that place. If only . . .'

'You stay here and help Celeste out then. You could also undertake some secretarial tasks for me, if you felt like it.'

'Ah, Madame. Of course.'

Before Marguerite could say any more, Jeanne burst through the door. She was flustered.

'There's someone here for you, Madame, I didn't catch his name. But he looked nice enough so I invited him up to the library, the way we do in Paris. But I bumped into Monsieur le Comte and he wasn't pleased. I didn't know what to do.'

'So you came to find me. That's altogether fine, Jeanne.' Marguerite calmed her. 'He's still in the library I take it.'

All Marguerite saw when she came in was a narrow back suited in rough blue wool and a dark head bent over a volume.

'Monsieur?' she murmured. The man leapt back and snapped the book shut as if he'd been caught in an illicit act. 'You asked for me?'

He turned and bowed deeply, but she had already recognized him from his height.

'Madame, I was in the vicinity. I hope you don't mind my stopping by unannounced. You have a very fine library here. I envy you its contents.' Dr. Labrousse rattled on, his colour deepening.

'Indeed. My father was something of a scholar and added liberally to what he had inherited.' Her eyes twinkled. 'I believe the cellar still houses his collection of specimens. He liked to preserve parts in alcohol. For comparative study, you understand. My husband has long wanted to rid himself of them. Perhaps you might like to look at them. She stepped closer to him. 'What have you been reading so fervidly?'

'A volume of the Encyclopédie. An original.'

'Ah yes.'

'Yes, yes. But of course, that wasn't what I came for.' He looked at her beseechingly as if she might understand his errand without the need for words.

'I . . . I was sharp the other day. A little rude. I wanted to apologize. So many people here won't accept what I say. Because I'm from elsewhere. But perhaps you don't know. It makes me tetchy.'

'Montpelier, the diploma in your office said.'

'You noticed.' He chuckled, relaxed with the sound. 'Sometimes I also think I'm from another epoch, too, or indeed from our own but have landed in the dark, feudal past. Even stethoscopes, which our great Laennec invented as long ago as 1816, seems like magic to some of my patients. They refuse to believe that I can hear their chests and diagnose. You're probably not privy to the superstitions the locals hold. It all makes me a little thin-skinned . . . my temper . . . I'm sorry.'

Marguerite rescued him again from his floundering. 'Your apology is accepted, Doctor. Please.' She gestured him towards the leather armchair. 'Have the police made any progress with the identity of your cadaver?'

He examined his shoes as if they might reveal a secret. 'It's one of the reasons I came. The police have grown rather lazy over the matter. And I . . . well I suspect there really is foul play involved, not only of the self-murdering kind. I thought, since you mentioned a friend in the police, you might try to use your influence with the force here to ensure a more complete investigation.' He paused, looked down at his heavily-booted feet again. 'I went to enquire of the travellers.'

'Oh?'

'Yes.'

'And?'

'Well, they weren't altogether helpful. They don't trust outsiders.'

'Just like the good people of the region then. And perhaps with more reason?'

He nodded. 'They said none of their group had gone missing. Nor had anyone left them since they'd set off on their travels from Marseilles.'

'I see. From Marseilles.'

'The thing is I didn't believe their denials.'

'Why not?'

'I don't quite know.'

'You don't think these people are capable of the truth?'

'Perhaps. I'm not free of prejudice, it's true. But there was something else.'

'Oh?'

'They were made nervous by my enquiry in a way I can't pin down. Particularly one of the women. Her eyes . . . they had a particular kind of brightness. I don't know. There was something. When she looked at the picture.'

'The picture?'

'Yes, I showed them the photographs.'

'I would be interested in seeing them.'

'That won't be difficult.' He rose to rifle through the bag he had left at the far side of the room. 'I made two copies of the best of them. Things can go missing in our magistrates' offices.'

He brought the pictures to her and displayed them with all the enthusiasm of a man engaged in sharing a passionate hobby.

Marguerite gazed at the shadowy, pock-marked face of the dead man. There was a brutishness in the angles, yet it was strangely peaceful, despite the cuts and bruises. Both eyes were closed, which perhaps accounted for the odd serenity of the expression. Like the frescos of the saints in the church.

There had been photographs of poor, dear Olympe, too, but those had borne no relationship to the living woman.

The photograph dropped from her hand. She grasped the back of a chair.

'I'm sorry. How stupid of me. This is distressing for you. I don't know what I can be thinking of . . .'

'No, no please. A moment's clumsiness.' Marguerite took a deep breath. 'I'd like to look again. Have you learned anything more from your examination of the body?'

'Oh yes, Madame. To make the body speak. To make it reveal its secrets. That is what scientific medicine is all about. You see here . . .'

He pointed to a bloated, darker area around the left eye and forehead. 'This is a contusion. Bruising. The vessels ruptured after some kind of fall or attack and blood spread making a discoloration. Therefore, it must have happened before he died. Now here and here,' he pointed to lines on the cheek and forehead and around the eye which she knew was missing, 'these are distinct scrapes, and cuts, where the face landed on the rails. But there is no discoloration, no bruising around them. Therefore it is likely that the blood was no longer flowing. The man, as I suspected, was already dead.'

'And here?' Marguerite pointed to some marks on the neck, evenly positioned, as if small buttons or perhaps even a rope had left traces.

He stared, moved the photograph closer. 'I shall have to look at that under the magnifying glass. I hadn't noticed it before. ' He paused. 'This is not really a suitable subject for a lady. Your husband will . . .'

Marguerite cut him off. 'Do you have any idea how the poor man died, if it wasn't by doing away with himself on the railway tracks?'

'That's just it. I can't be sure.' He lowered his voice. 'I suspect there was poison in his system. The liver was irregular.'

'From drink, perhaps.'

'No, no. Not just that. His eye, too, strangely a single eye, the other having been ripped by a scavenging bird, I imagine. Or some particularly ruthless murderer. Well, the single pupil was contracted into a tiny point, which indicates opium use of some kind. I tried running some laboratory tests, but so far have found nothing conclusive. It has been cold, you see, and from one point of view the relative lack of decomposition is helpful. From another . . .'

'There you are, Marguerite.' Olivier strode in, stopping the doctor's flow. The look he cast over Labrousse was one of haughty disapproval, as it moved openly from the poor cut of his blue jacket, the frayed cuffs of his shirt and mismatched waistcoat, to the straggly lines of his beard and hair.

'I don't believe we've met properly, Monsieur.'

Dr. Labrousse hastened to put the photographs away, his gestures clumsy with nervousness.

'Have you not?' Marguerite soothed. 'I would have thought you were already acquainted with the medical examiner in the region, Olivier. But it's true, Dr. Labrousse has not been all that long in the area. I am sure you will interest each other.'

'I dare say.' Olivier was less polite than if he had caught them in an embrace.

'I don't quite know how the Doctor votes, but perhaps his influence . . .'

Olivier moderated his expression slightly, cleared his throat. 'He's very welcome, of course.'

'I didn't know Monsieur le Comte had announced his candidature?'

'In three days' time. I haven't mentioned it yet, Marguerite, but there's to be a little ceremony here. In the morning.'

'I shall try and be here, Monsieur.' The doctor was disarming. Marguerite wondered if he had heard what party Olivier was standing for.

Olivier nodded and turned back to Marguerite. I thought you'd want to know, my dear. There's some post for you. From Paris.'

Labrousse looked quickly at his pocket watch and picked up his case. 'I must go now in any case. Madame, Monsieur le Comte.' He bowed

'I trust I shall see you very soon, Doctor,' Marguerite called after him. 'We must continue our discussion. And I'll see what I can do.'

Dressed in the full splendour of his blue and gold-braided livery, Georges conveyed her to the Tellier house in good time. On their last visit with Martine, the time he had spent at the Inn had yielded only a little information. He had learned that the family was considered rich, owned a good deal of property in the area, spent a substantial amount of time in Tours, and wasn't much loved. Madame, in particular, thought herself too good for her neighbours. As for Yvette, no one seemed to remember her. She had evidently never gone to the Inn.

Marguerite decided that on this visit, it would be best if the carriage took her all the way to the house. Having reason to believe that Madame Tellier might be impressed by such niceties, she had Georges deliver her card ahead of her.

The woman came to greet her almost as soon as Marguerite was through the door. She had a singular face, long and irregular, mismatched of feature, with protruding yellow teeth and a pronounced nose beneath which the dark shadow of a moustache cupped her bow-shaped upper lip. The masculine features were in stark contrast to her hair which was arranged in the same girlish empire curls Marguerite had noticed through her carriage window. Her wine-red dress with its white stripe and lavish displays of lace at sleeves and bodice, had more flounces than her girth called for. But it was her eyes which trapped the attention. They darted. They leapt. They bulged with appreciation, envy and malice in rapid succession.

'Madame, this is indeed an honour. I am most gratified.'

Marguerite returned the compliment. 'It is kind of you to receive me at such short notice.'

She had a sense the woman needed to be treated with circumspection, like some poodle whose coif pretended to a civilisation that might at any moment drop away into yapping and biting. Or a wild horse, who had been left too long and only been partially broken. Looking at her, she also felt certain that the woman held the secret of Yvette's whereabouts.

Madame Tellier ushered her through a hall filled with portraits and an assortment of rifles and revolvers into an over-furnished drawing room. Her deluge of words evoking a crowded life in Tours, headquarters of Monsieur, her husband's importing firm, matched the excesses of the room. It was packed with bric-a-brac from the far corners of the world. There were tables inlaid with ivory. Others, sported vast bronze trays from leather thongs. There were elephant tusks hung on the walls, rugs with an assortment of rich patterns and peacock feathers protruding from urns. There were armchairs with clawed feet and a vast bergère, and some heavy, carved benches. There were glazed boxes replete with giant shells and others containing rocks in outlandish colours. On the mantel of the blazing fireplace, there were stuffed birds, and on the wall some grey, furry creature with an arc of whiskers.

'A veritable empire of a room,' Marguerite murmured.

Madame Tellier beamed with pride, 'My forebears were ships' captains and merchants who travelled the world. Far and wide. Far and wide.'

'How lucky for you to have inherited such a varied collection. And for your daughters. Will they join us?'

'You know my daughters?'

'I have heard about them. Charming girls, I'm told.'

Marguerite wondered if she was overdoing her brief. The woman's face had turned sceptical. She was not devoid of intelligence.

'They will be down in a moment, if you like.' She bared her prominent teeth in what was not altogether a smile, picked up a bell from a side table and shook it back and forth.

Madame Molineuf appeared so quickly that Marguerite was certain she had been listening at the door.

'Bring tea, Huguette, and ask the girls to come down.'

'Oui, Madame.' The woman gave Marguerite a conspiratorial grin she couldn't quite interpret.

'And what brings you to us in Troo?' Madame Tellier leaned back into her chair. They were sitting opposite each other at a small table in the half alcove formed by a window.

'A double errand, Madame.' Marguerite made up her mind on the instant. 'My husband is hosting a party in some weeks' time which I hope you and Monsieur will be free to attend. I wanted to alert you in person, before the invitation came, since we haven't had the occasion to meet before.'

'Thank you, Madame.' The woman bowed her head with due decorum.

'The second thing is I wanted to ask you about the sister of a young secretary of mine who was in service with you and who has disappeared. We're all worried about her. Her name is Yvette Branquart.'

'Yvette Branquart?' the woman's face stiffened into an equine mask. 'A dangerous girl. I had her leave months ago now. Violent, she was. And wholly unreliable. Why one day I caught her in her room with a riding crop in her hand. It was bloodied. Can you imagine? And the minx wouldn't tell me how it had got that way. There was blood on the floor, too.'

Marguerite sat up very straight. 'You have no idea where the blood came from.'

'No. I can only imagine she had vented her violence on some animal or . . .' Her gaze flew to the window.

Marguerite followed it. In the distance swinging from the overhanging branch of a tree was the lumbering youth she now recognized as P'tit Ours. He was lowering himself onto a high wall, his eyes fixed on a woman below who moved slowly towards him. Then he leapt into the neighbouring property. Marguerite held her breath. The woman standing there was regal in her proportions. Like the high priestess of some antique cult, she handed him a cup, watched him drink. She stroked his hair and the youth preened, his grin as big as his face. From the depths of his jacket, P'tit Ours brought out a jar and like some chivalric knight offering a precious tribute to his lady, handed it to her with a flourish.

Even from where she sat, it was clear to Marguerite the woman was dark, a mulatto, with an intricate coiffure of gleaming oiled hair. She thought of Baudelaire's mistress, Jeanne Duval. She thought of the stone-throwing children she had encountered thelast time she was in the village. They had probably never seen an African before.

'Is that the woman the children call the witch?' she heard herself ask Madame Tellier.

'I have no idea.' The woman was fuming. 'She has no business being here. None at all.' In a second, she was up from her chair and out of the room without a word of apology. Through the half-closed door, Marguerite could hear her screaming at Madame Molineuf about her degenerate son.

The stout servant seemed immune to her screams or the clatter of a window being recklessly heaved upwards. She appeared at the door bearing a tray and deposited it on the table in front of Marguerite, poured tea and grumbled a litany of plaints.

'Trouble. Only trouble ever since he came onto this earth. And now he wants a woman doesn't he? Somewhere to stick it in, like all of them. What am I to do? It's not as if he hasn't had plenty of people to learn from around here. Alright, so I'll beat him again, for all the good it'll do.' She paused to look out the window. 'He's gone now in any case. What's the use? No discipline. And the old master's as drunk as a ship's captain on a stormy night. Only the storm's gone on for days and days.'

'What you mumbling about, woman?'

The wreck of a giant Marguerite had glimpsed on her first visit appeared in the doorway and came in with a lunge. 'Is that my breakfast then?' he pointed a gnarled finger at the tray. 'Don't stretch to much these days, do we?' His face might be a mass of ruptured veins and jowls, his walk a slippered shuffle, his thick, velvet robe and knotted scarf spotted with the remains of she didn't know what substances, but the eyes he directed at Marguerite had a dark lustre about them which made her sit up in her chair as soon as they pinioned her.

'Or is she my breakfast?' A malicious laugh broke from the man, as he patted and pummelled the red setter who trailed him. He relished Marguerite's discomfort.

Madame Tellier came racing into the room after him. 'You're up, Papa,' she said in a small girl's piping voice. 'That's good. That's good.' The sound altered her face, her gestures. The large, middle-aged, woman was transformed into a skittish maid.

'Here, sit down here. You'll be comfortable here.' She plumped pillows and tended to him. 'Huguette will bring you a proper breakfast.'

She seemed to be in a trance, as if the man Marguerite had mistaken for her husband, were a mesmerist rather than her father.

'What's that one doing here?' He pointed his stick at Marguerite as he lowered his bulk into an armchair. Madame Tellier propped a foot-stool under his leg and placed a tray table in front of him.

'Pay no attention to her Papa. She's only come for me. She wanted to know about Yvette. You remember Yvette, don't you. A cheat, you called her.'

'A bribing, blackmailing strumpet is what I called her.' The old man leered at Marguerite. 'Friend of yours, is she? You here for money too? Everybody wants money from old Napoleon. Everybody. Even the puffed up priests. Bribing, cheating, blackmailing. What do you cost?'

Marguerite rose. 'Best if I go now, Madame, and leave you to your duties.'

The woman whipped round to face her. Marguerite stepped back, suddenly afraid. There was violence in the air.

'You know what that girl did? That Yvette you're looking for. She knocked him out. Knocked him cold. A helpless old man. Dangerous, like I told you. Good riddance to her. An animal.'

'Do you know where she might have gone? Where she might be now?'

The old man cackled, as if she had addressed him. 'If someone hasn't done her in, she's in a brothel I imagine. Playing a tasty little virgin.'

'Now, Papa,' Madame Tellier chided him in her little girl's voice, a coy look on her face. 'You know you don't care a fig for all that. You know you don't.'

'Thank you, then. Goodbye.'

Marguerite's mind reeled. She had to get out of the house quickly. The Telliers filled her with a kind of clammy shame, as if she had walked into a house of ill-repute thinking it was an ordinary family home and was now covered in some kind of invisible pig swill.

On the journey home, she tried to separate out atmosphere from information and make sense of what she had heard. Yvette Branquart had a bloodied riding crop. Yvette Branquart was dangerous. She was a strumpet and a cheat, a blackmailing, bribing strumpet.

She thought of Martine, who said she looked like her sister, a frail, rather innocent slip of a girl and the words on the lips of that repulsive man filled her with disbelief and rage. It must have been the other way around. Of course. The man had tried to force himself on Yvette, perhaps even tried to bribe her into performing sexual favours, and she had pushed him away, perhaps used a riding crop. What then?

Marguerite imagined a scene of violence. The giant of a man would certainly have emerged the winner. And Yvette? Could the girl be lying dead somewhere in a shallow grave, victim of that monster's rampant desires? Or of that huge simpleton's she had spied in the garden? Always wanting to stick it somewhere his mother had said, not mincing her words.

Marguerite shivered. She looked through the carriage window and above her in the distance saw a curtain move and a large head fill the space. The woman from the garden. The witch. Once more, Marguerite saw the woman beckon to her with a gracious, yet incomprehensible gesture. It occurred to her that she should ring her bell. But it was too late today. She would come back.

At the railway crossing, near the river, a queue of vehicles waited while the signal announced the coming of a train. The hoot and charge of the engine brought with it memories of her recent journey: the sudden stop, the shrieks, the dead man being carried away, his mottled face. Martine had fainted, confessed a misrecognition. With a twist of the mind's kaleidoscopic, the doctor's photographs appeared before Marguerite. She could now see the resemblance, too. There was something about the dead man, perhaps it was just his larger-than-life size, that brought to mind the old reprobate she had sat with in that overcrowded drawing room.

Martine had been frightened not only because of the recognition. She thought her sister—brave she had called her on another occasion— had hurt the man. Had Yvette written to her, telling her of brutalities Martine didn't dare repeat to Marguerite? Had she really in fact injured the old reprobate, as Madame Tellier claimed, and then run from the house? Run to the doctor, P'tit Ours had said. Perhaps she was injured herself. But Labrousse had stated he had never seen the girl in his consulting rooms.

How many of these informants could she trust, Marguerite wondered as the carriage took up its swaying, bumpy progress once more.

And what part of what they had said bore a relationship to the truth? Half lies could be as revealing as whole truths, but only if one had the key.

If Yvette had fled, where could she have gone? Why hadn't she gone to her sister in Paris? That could easily be explained by a lack of funds. Paris was a long way to walk. She could walk to her friends in Vendome, on the other hand, even if it might mean a day's trek. But the friends said they hadn't seen her. Why hadn't they? Why didn't she go to them?

Marguerite closed her eyes and imagined the Tellier house again. What if the girl felt as she did: soiled, ashamed somehow, too ashamed to tell anyone? Where did helpless, impoverished, perhaps ravished girls go when they felt ashamed? Maybe the old man—Napoléon, he had called himself—hadn't been lying. A brothel, he had said. It was all too easy for a young woman to disappear into a brothel. It was a destination one couldn't even tell a sister about. You had to be brave in a particular way to choose it over other courses. She should have thought of it sooner.

On a whim, Marguerite redirected Georges to Montoire. She would send a telegram to the Inspector.

About to announce his candidature, Olivier would have her locked up sooner than discover that she had been frequenting the very kind of sites he used to visit for other purposes.

PART TWO

DEAD WOMAN RUNNING

_ 9 _

While she waited for a reply from the Chief Inspector, Marguerite set out to do what she had intended ever since the babe's existence had been announced to her.

She rose early. A circle of wintry sun on the horizon bode well. She packed her saddle bag and started out without alerting anyone to her plans. The morning hoar frost crackled beneath the horse's galloping hooves. The wind flushed her cheeks and whipped her into alertness.

Olivier and Villemardi had been walking with their fishing poles on the day they had found the babe, so their route would have been different. They would have gone round the valley into the woods and down to the river. Instead, just where a small island rose from the reedy waters, as green and graceful as an abode for nymphs, Marguerite's path took her up onto a sinuous track and into the woods. She pulled up short and dismounted where the woods grew dense on either side of the track. Tethering the horse's reins to a bough, she opened her saddle bag, looked round and listened. There was no sound of hooves coming her way, no crackle of footsteps on twigs and dry leaves.

She vanished into the woods and shielded herself behind shrubbery. Here, she pulled off her riding jacket and skirt. She hadn't bothered with her top hat this morning. Beneath she was wearing men's trousers and a rough brown sweater. From the bag she took a thick, blue working-man's jacket, quickly donned it, then folded her skirt into the pouch. The jacket pocket yielded a large cap, into which she tucked all her hair. As she rubbed just a little earth onto her cheeks to smudge them into disguise, a girlish mischief played through her.

Antoine was now all but ready to do the sleuthing he could do so much more comfortably than his sometime-mistress. Marguerite tucked the pouch neatly into the saddle, took a pair of galoshes from its other side and leaned against a tree stump to pull them on.

A scarf wound round her neck and she was ready. She gave the horse a pat, then headed off into the woods and back down to the river's edge. For the first time since her arrival, she felt utterly at home on this bank, amidst these trees and shrubs and spiky thickets. Her feet grasped the ground firmly. She could run and bend, even swing from branches. She felt like a girl again. Or rather, a boy.

But it wasn't for all this, she reminded herself, that she had donned the guise of Antoine. The youth might be an adept of Paris streets, but he had never before dared to come to La Rochambert. There had never been the need until now.

Whatever he might have said when she first arrived, Olivier didn't really want her to trace the babe's origins. Nor did Père Benoit. The priest had joined them for dinner last night together with some bigot of a politician from Tours. She was prepared to strangle him well before the evening was over because of his high-minded stupidity. If he really thought France needed less industry and more farmers after the horrors of the last agricultural depression, all she could recommend was that he give up his post and live a peasant's life for a few years.

Olivier had once more swollen to the heroic proportions of a grand and charitable seigneur in the waif's beaming, anonymous stare, let alone that of his new-found flatterers. But he would be less than happy to find himself giving succour to the bastard offspring of named and disreputable individuals. Indeed, he would be altogether miserable to find anyone turning up in the course of time and demanding hush money. What would happen to the child then, a child who might be old enough to understand matters?

It surprised her that Olivier hadn't considered any of these eventualities. The countryside had put his jungle instincts to sleep. Hers were still awake.

Today Marguerite was determined to find out at exactly what points a basket might be left at the river's edge and be propelled safely by the current to the spot where Olivier and Villemardi had told her they had found the babe.

She had wondered whether someone might have borrowed a boat from the island and rowed a little way upstream to a safe spot. But seen from her present position in the woods on the opposite bank, the pretty little island, with its mill, had too open an aspect. Winter had denuded the willows. In summer, they wept heavily into the river, shrouding the area beneath and providing perfect hiding spots for boats. Now eyes could fall upon you from any point.

She tramped on, her boots crunching through the sharpness of the frost to squelch the leaves beneath, sticking a little in patches of mud where the ground was open and warmer.

Why was it that she imagined a woman carrying the baby in the wicker basket, rather than a man? In fact it would be far easier for a man to trudge through woods like these unnoticed, prodding at points in the bank with a stick, just as she was doing now.

She considered this and paused to look around her. The woods, when she stopped walking, were preternaturally still. No wind whistled through bare branches. There wasn't even the chirrup of a bird. Everything had stopped to watch her passage.

She stepped on a twig and heard a loud snap. It broke the hush. It also alerted her to the fact that this spot wore all the marks of Olivier's description. She prodded at the bank, a little steep here, but not too steep to step down carefully. Beneath the swirl of the grassy waters, wedged amidst pebble and mud, she made out a log. It climbed towards the shallows where it lay just below the water's surface. That log could easily have been what stopped the basket's progress down river.

Now, instead of imagining an unpredictable current, she considered an alternative possibility. She imagined a woman walking, a desperate woman, looking for a spot where her child wouldn't be harmed. She imagined her carefully stepping down this slippery bank and thanking the stars for her good fortune. If she wedged the basket well enough right here, it might just be found before the river carried it further. Might even be found by one of the passing skiffs or small barges.

She would have lifted the baby out before leaving it, hugged and kissed it, certainly also given it suck, and then allowed the waters to rock the cradle, gently enough. Perhaps she had even hidden behind the trees and waited with the infant. Waited to make certain that it was found. That would mean she might even know who had picked the child in his basket out of the river.

Marguerite watched the waters and reflected. All this—except the feeding—could have been done just as easily, in fact more easily, by a man. Where would this man or woman have come from?

It was too late to find footprints, even if any had been left on the cold ground. But on a whim and because of the lay of shrubbery and trees and leaf mould, she decided to walk away from the river for a distance. The sliver of a path might emerge somewhere telling.

She pretended she had a sizeable basket on her arm, kept shifting its position slightly to make up for height. She looked out for markings on bark or snapped shrubs. She had done this as a child when she played with the local children. Her father had given her the *Leatherstocking Tales* to read and they had pretended they were in the terrifying wilds of America, rather than here on the borders of the Loir where no Natty Bumpo and Chingachcook trawled the forests. It had come as something of a disappointment, when she had learned only a few years ago, that the creator of these great stories of the wilds of the new world had written many of them not so very far from her Paris house.

Marguerite stopped. There, hanging on a low and prickly thicket branch, was a piece of ripped cloth. She eased it carefully from the thorns. It was a worsted black fabric of good enough quality. A woman then. A black skirt caught on a low lying thorn. Not the poorest of women either. But she mustn't jump to conclusions. People came through here for purposes other than leaving infants in the river.

She folded the cloth into her trouser pocket. Did this part of the woods still belong to the family estate? She no longer knew, if she ever had. She trudged on uphill and came to a field. There were no houses in view, so she retraced her steps until she came to the area where she had found the piece of cloth and now turned to her left. This wasn't terrain she recognized.

Her thoughts moved to Martine. She had only told the girl a very little about her visit with the Tellier's. There was no point worrying her needlessly. But she had asked whether Yvette had ever written anything specific about the old man.

'Only that she didn't like him. Not one little bit,' Martine had murmured. 'But she was probably trying to be brave. Braver than me. I told you how he scared me. A terrifying old drunkard. Once, in his own house when I had to go on an errand, he just sat there in a black stupour staring into space as if he were already dead. Didn't even see me.'

Marguerite had asked delicately whether he had made advances to her and Martine had blushed and said once, but she had run like the wind and though he had cursed her, he couldn't follow after, because his legs weren't that good.

Marguerite walked on, inspecting ground and shrubs. More than anything she would have liked to talk the whole matter over with Raphael. How she missed their roaming, speculative conversations. But there was nothing for it. Raphael was thousands of miles away and immersed in his own preoccupations. She was no longer even certain what they were.

As for Olivier, though she put the best possible face on it, he had begun to frighten her far more than he ever had before. He had grown monomaniacal about his plans and determined that she be included in them.

She shivered, unsure whether the cold had come from her thoughts or a drop in temperature in this shadowy area of the woods. The trees were taller here, dark sycamores whose bare branches swayed like grasping arms in the wind. She hastened her pace. And then, from behind one of the thick trunks, Olivier appeared.

At first she thought she had conjured him up with her thoughts. But no, he was there, his strides certain, his walking stick prodding the earth with unhesitating assurance. He stopped in front of her. His eyes played over her in cool assessment. She felt a flush rising in her face, remembered she was Antoine, and thought it must grow even brighter. Would he recognize her?

It was worse. She could feel from the nature of his gaze, the sudden thrust of his chin, the casual hand placed on his hip, that this was the old Olivier, the one she had only ever seen in action once before. Were the woods a favourite haunt of his? A meeting place? Did he think Antoine might be fair game, a passing youth who wouldn't mind a little adventure?

'Where are you heading, lad? What are you up to? Mischief, I imagine.'

Marguerite didn't trust her voice. She lowered it, grumbled in a rustic manner, fabricated. 'To Montoire. I'm late.'

She could feel Olivier considering. She circled round him. 'G'day, Sir,'

The stick was suddenly in front of her, tripping her up, preventing her passage. 'Not so fast. Don't we raise our caps anymore? No respect?'

She barely righted herself, used a tree for balance. 'Sorry Sir.' She moved round again, hurried on, murmuring, almost in tears. 'Don't want to be late, Sir.'

'Next time you come this way, give yourself more time.' Olivier shouted after her. A laugh came from him. Loud. Gruff. Not altogether friendly. It echoed in her ears. She hurried.

He hadn't recognized her—not unless he was capable of an elaborate joke. And he wouldn't pursue the boy Antoine. No, not that. She started to run. Ran until she was breathless. When she couldn't run anymore, she stopped to look behind her. No, no. He hadn't bothered.

Relief coursed through her, robbing her of energy in its passage. She breathed deeply. Collected herself. Walked on. She didn't want to think. No, it was best not to think.

A small clearing appeared. She stepped into its tall grass, its brighter light. Crows swooped and cawed their menace overhead. There was no sun to give her a sense of her direction. Was she lost? Her head was swirling. She should turn back to the river. No, no, There was a pile of heaped logs at the far end of the clearing. Which meant she must be near a house. A house where she could ask questions tomorrow. A house where someone might have seen something, a woman with a basket, a servant running . . .

She headed towards the logs and on uphill. There was a distinct path now, closely bordered by bramble, trailing green vine and hawthorn, narrow and oddly steep. With no notice, it abutted on a wall—an ivy-covered wall, so that she hadn't taken it in at first, had assumed an extension of the woods. The wall was of substantial height. It indicated a place of some importance on the other side.

Marguerite racked her memory. She couldn't think of what the property might be, whom it might belong to. Nor could she see a door in the wall, which was odd, given the path. The twigs and vegetation on the left looked as if they had once been trampled. She headed in that direction. Some twenty metres on, she noticed what seemed to be a portcullis, its heavy bars hiding a moss-covered door.

She pushed and prodded against both to no avail. Nor was there any purchase to be had on the wall. Even Antoine couldn't scale this height. She looked round to see if there was another path from the door leading down towards the river. But, except for the direction from which she had come, everything was covered in thick undergrowth. She retraced her steps to the clearing. Only then did a downward possibility present itself.

It was steep again here and sombre. Strange how she always remembered these valleys as warm and pleasant, with perfume in the air. The memories were warmed by childhood, warmed by summer and birdsong. Now everything was cold and still. Oddly still. She felt it as the stillness of threat. She hurried on, her heart racing, perspiration seizing at her armpits. Would Olivier in his predatory guise be waiting round the next tree? The undergrowth was tricky here, thick with twining vine. It clutched at her heavy, unfeeling boots so that she had to keep her eyes to the ground.

As a child, she remembered, she had liked that. She had watched the earth with all its buried and hidden life for hours, had stood spellbound by the regroupings of an anthill as she prodded it with a stick, or waited with baited breath at dusk for the arrival of a mole's snout at the mouth of his mound. Natural marvels, their mystery had filled the childhood space of wonder. A space which for Martine and her sister had been taken up by saints.

She reflected on this for a moment, then sighed with relief when a silver glimmer in the distance announced what must be the river. She ran towards it, her heart light again, her eyes focussed on her destination. She was almost tempted to hail a passing boat, if one should come. Anything to take her away from here and to people.

Her boot caught in a tangle of shrubbery. She fell, fell downhill, face forward, her cap flying, her gloved hands stretched in front of her only in time to prevent her head hitting the ground with a heavy thud.

She lay there without moving until her breath had come back. She seemed to be intact. Nothing broken. Only when she stood, did she see that she had torn her trouser leg. Her knee burned. And her cap had landed at some distance. She must fetch it. Must. It was the most important part of her disguise. She trod back to where it had fallen.

It was then that she saw. Saw it with a lurch and heave of her stomach which chased away all thoughts of Olivier or uncovered hair or anything at all. Saw the obstacle she had tripped on. It was a leg, a leg stretched across the path. The bottom half of a woman's leg: the calf prettily turned, the stockings, cotton or wool ruched around the ankle in a bunch.

She took a deep breath. Thoughts of the vanished Yvette pounded through her mind as loud as the pulse in her ears. Her own legs were in irons. She was too weak to move them the few paces into the shrubbery.

At last, with an enormous effort of the will, she crouched down for a closer look, bent back prickly branches.

There was more than just a leg. There were two. They were half hidden by a red dress which was worn by a woman whose face was turned downwards into the cold, cold ground. The woman's hair was long and dark and curly. Not Yvette then. With a shudder, she turned the woman over. She was too heavy. She was dead. There was no doubt of that. The maggots were already at her face. A thin trail of dried blood ripped like a scar from the side of her mouth.

Marguerite put a hand up to her own. She didn't know whether she was going to cry or retch.

That was when she heard it. It made her leap up. A great noise of twigs and branches, a lunge like an animal coming towards her, a blow and a growl which knocked her to the ground, and then the sound of running. The thud of feet on massed earth and crinkling leaves. And then nothing except an unnatural quiet.

She didn't know how long she waited before she got up. Got up slowly, in confusion. Very slowly, because now panic had shrouded her ability to move. It confused her senses, made the near far. She could hear a low rushing sound. Where was it? Where?

She waited for the vertigo to pass, remembered the slab of chocolate she had put in Antoine's pocket and slowly, very slowly reached for it. She let it melt on her tongue, then so slowly she thought she might never get there, she began to walk towards the river. She walked and walked and walked. She had hoped for the miracle of a boat. A fisherman. Neither were to be seen. Some instinct reminded her to leave a marker. She twisted Antoine's scarf round a bough. When she looked back at it, it was floating innocently in the wind, like some wordless banner inciting the woods to protest.

_ 10 _

Without knowing quite how she had got there, Marguerite found herself lying on a high narrow bed under a diagram of a leg. There was a room screen in front of her. She called out. An aging, sweet-faced woman, a crumpled bonnet perched on her wispy hair, appeared. She was holding a cup.

'Don't say anything, Madame. Just drink this. Drink this first. I'm Madame Germaine.'

Marguerite felt the heat of brandy in her throat.

'All of it.'

'How did I get here?'

From behind the screen, Dr. Labrousse appeared. He bowed briefly. 'I found you, Madame la Comtesse. Found you slumped over on your horse as I was heading towards Poncé late this morning. I brought you back here. You needed some stitches in your arm. You'd lost a good deal of blood.'

He looked at her with a mixture of compassion and curiosity.

She stared down at her bandaged arm which lay like an inert object on the sheet that covered her. It all came back to her.

'How does your head feel? I don't know whether you've had a fall or . . .'

'Never mind about that, doctor. There are more important matters we have to deal with. And quickly. There's a dead woman in the woods. A woman in a red dress. Someone would rather I hadn't found her. I don't know who. You must get the police there. And in a hurry.'

An image flashed through her mind, fugitive, like a rushing animal, a boar in the undergrowth. Its snout became the face of . . . who was it?

Olivier. Could it have been Olivier? The face swam into that of Dr. Labrousse.

'You've had some kind of accident Madame de Landois. Your imagination may be working . . .'

'I'm not prone to imaginings, Doctor. You need to alert the police. I've left a scarf tied to a tree by the riverbank to indicate the place or near enough. A boat might be quickest. It's down river from here.'

The doctor stared at her, reached for her pulse. 'I was about to send for Monsieur le Comte.'

Her throat grew drier. 'No, no. Better not. He's busy.' She controlled her voice. 'Best not to trouble him. Just have someone let him know I'll be back later.'

Before the doctor could protest, she added. 'I'll hire a carriage.'

'In fact, I would rather you rested a little longer. Some hot soup would be beneficial. I'll send to the Inn. It wouldn't be wise to get up just yet.'

She smiled at him, her face stiff.

'You must believe me, doctor. The police will have to go quickly if they're to find her. I'll rest better if you alert them straight away.'

When she woke again, it was to see the sweet-faced old woman balancing a tray. On it there were two covered tureens and great hunks of country bread. The sight of them brought hunger and with it alertness.

'We'll have you right as rain in no time, my dear. It's these horses. They get skittish at this time of year. I reckon he must have thrown you onto some rocks. But you climbed right back on. Brave of you. And lucky that the doctor was heading that way.'

'You're quite right, Madame Germaine. That must have been it.' There was no point explaining that her fall had taken place earlier. Marguerite allowed the woman to help move her aching body into a chair. The soup was thick and hot. The bread moist and yeasty. She was hungry. And the dizziness was gone.

Madame Germaine's friendly, wrinkled face twinkled at her. 'Good isn't it?'

Marguerite peered at the face. 'I know you, don't I?'

'You do indeed my dear. I was hoping it might come back to you. Years ago now. I worked in your father's house. You must have been about ten. Your father liked me to instruct him on the medical properties of the forest plants, and the herbs. You used to tag along and listen.' She laughed. 'You wore trousers then, too.'

'So it was you . . .' Marguerite was filled with relief. She was wondering who had undressed her, found Antoine's trousers beneath her hastily donned skirt.

'Yes, and I gave you just a little wash. The doctor had already done his business on your arm. You have more scrapes and bruises on you than you did as a child. Though I imagine they won't do you any more harm now than they did then.'

Marguerite saw the woman give her a distinct wink.

'It's good to see you again, Madame Germaine. Very good.'

While she ate, the woman regaled her with stories of the old days, little tidbits about her father. Marguerite felt strength coursing back with the food and the kind, humorous voice. When she had finished the last morsel on the tray, she insisted on taking a stroll at least round the room.

'The doctor, I take it, makes his home here.'

'Yes, my dear. He'll be in to see you as soon as he's back. Don't you worry.'

'Tell me, Madame Germaine.' Marguerite lowered her voice. 'Can one see from a dead woman's body whether she's recently had a baby?'

'You mean the woman you think you saw in the woods?' Madame Germaine had all her wits about her.

'I *did* see. And her killer—or someone—was still in the vicinity. He knocked me to the ground. I'm convinced of that.' A trembling took hold of her.

'There, there, my dear. I'm going to brew you one of my special *tisanes*. It will see you right. Calm you, too.'

'But can you tell? About the baby I mean.'

'Oh yes. Easily enough.'

Her words filled Marguerite with relief. Whoever the dead woman was, if she had recently been delivered of a baby, Marguerite's misadventure wouldn't have been altogether in vain.

There remained the question of who the woman in red might be. But that would be determined soon enough. Madame Germaine herself, who delivered so many of the babies of the region, might know.

She hoped with all her being that Olivier himself had no hand in the fact that she was dead. That he hadn't, through some mistaken wish to make the child he now called Gabriel wholly his, helped the babe's blood mother to her end. It would account for his lack of worry about the child's parentage.

But these were wild speculations, fantasies worthy only of her exhaustion.

The next time she woke up, it was to find Martine and her little maid, Jeanne, hovering over her in the cramped space behind the screen where the body part diagrams floated on the wall.

'Oh Madame,' Martine was tearful. 'I'm so glad you're awake. I mean, I'm so sorry about your accident. Monsieur sent us. He sent us to fetch you.'

'Yes, Madame,' Jeanne smoothed the hair from Marguerite's brow. 'He wants you straight home. He won't stand for a 'non'. No Madame, he won't. I shall do your hair, while you have something to drink. That Madame Germaine said you had to. Drink, that is. Then Georges is waiting to help.'

Marguerite smiled at both of them. 'I'm glad you've come.' She glanced at the clock on the mantel. Not yet four. 'Very glad. Now, Jeanne, before you do my hair, I want you to tell Georges to rush over to the post office and see if a telegram has come for me. No, no. No protests. Straight away. It will be from Chief Inspector Emile Durand.'

She flinched as she waved the girl away. Her arm was very sore.

'Oh, Madame.' The colour had drained from Martine's face making it paler than the starched cotton of her shirt. Marguerite thought the girl might faint and she ordered her somewhat brutally into a chair.

'Drink something, Martine. Here. And tell me what's wrong.'

'It's your arm, Madame. The rawness. And the welts.' The girl trembled.

Marguerite looked down. Madame Germaine had put an unguent over the stitches to speed the healing and had left the arm to air unbandaged.

'It is ugly isn't it? We'll cover it up, soon enough. Did you get lots of cuts as a child? I was terrible, always falling about.' She made light of the wound.

'Ah no, Madame. It's not that. It reminds me. Reminds of Yvette.' Abruptly she clamped a hand over her mouth.

'What does it remind you of?' Marguerite asked softly.

'No, no. It's nothing.'

'Tell me, Martine. It may be important. To help us find her. Anything you can tell me is important. Is she marked in some way?'

Martine tore the woolen hat off her head as if it sat there with the weight of an iron case. Her hair was pulled back tightly from her face today and caught in a wispy bun. Long fingers played with it, trying to tuck stray curls. It came to Marguerite that Olivier might have said something to the girl about her slightly disheveled appearance. 'It really is important, Martine.'

'She . . . Yvette. She had a lot of cuts. Blood, too. It made me . . .' The fingers coiled into a tight fist on her lap and grew white. 'Welts. She did it to herself. To punish herself, she said. Because she was wicked. Because it made her feel better afterwards. After she had been punished. And it did make her feel better, Madame. Her eyes would grow all clear. Do you feel better, Madame?'

Marguerite stared at her. The conversation she had had with Madame Tellier—whom she had judged more or less lying, perhaps even mad—took on a different configuration. Was it Yvette who was the greater hysteric? Was the girl inflicting harm on herself in a systematic way?

'Do you think Yvette could . . .' She chose her words carefully. 'Could punish herself so badly that . . . that she couldn't move?'

Martine shook her head uncertainly. 'I don't know, Madame. I don't think so. I don't. She never did before.'

'What about someone else? Could she hurt someone else? While she was punishing them, of course?'

'She never hurt me. Never.'

'But she frightened you?'

'Ladies.' For lack of a door to knock on, Dr. Labrousse spoke his presence, 'May I come in?'

'Of course,' Marguerite called out. 'Tell me the news, doctor. About the woman.'

She glanced at the doctor and saw that he was staring at Martine. 'But of course, you haven't yet met. This is Martine Branquart, Dr. Labrousse. Yvette's sister.'

'Yes, I see. I see.' He bowed slightly.

'My husband has sent the carriage for me. He insists I return.'

The doctor was still staring. 'You're very like your sister,' he murmured.

The colour rose in uncomfortable flecks on Martine's cheeks. 'Yes,' she turned away.

'Very pretty, Mademoiselle.'

Martine flashed him a shy smile.

He looked at his feet. Like a boy, Marguerite thought, timid despite all his experience. But she needed him alert.

'Martine, why don't you go and see if Jeanne is back yet.' She didn't speak until the girl had left the *cabinet*. 'Please doctor, tell me what you found.'

He placed his hand to her forehead and then putting a lens to his eye, lifted her arm to examine it better. 'Remarkably like her sister,' he murmured again, still troubled. 'I do hope the poor young woman is alright.'

Marguerite was growing impatient. 'The woman in the woods, doctor. The woman in red.'

'Oh yes, Madame. She was just up the path from where you left the scarf flying. The constable confirmed it to me on my return here. I owe you an apology once more it seems.'

'And who is she?'

'That I can't help you with, Madame. I had rounds at the hospital to make and I haven't yet seen her. Tomorrow I will examine her.'

'I see.' Marguerite wished that Olivier hadn't sent for her, but now there was no way she could stay here and wait for the doctor's autopsy. 'That will make two bodies for you in under ten days, doctor.'

'Yes, that does rather exceed our usual rate.' He met her eyes. 'I sense what you are thinking, Madame. But you must rest. I am sending Madame Germaine home with you. To look after you. She is wholly reliable.'

'Thank you, doctor. Thank you for coming along at the right moment too. Who knows, you might have had three bodies to contend with.'

'That is definitely not a matter to joke about, Madame.' He stood sternly to his full height and took on the aura of a stern patriarch.

'I am very grateful to you doctor. Perhaps, I was destined to become your patient after all. By the way, I hope that very soon we shall have a senior member of the police *judiciare* with us. That should be of some help in following through what are now your two cases.'

_ 11 _

The bedroom she used when she came to La Rochambert had once been her mother's. Olivier had transformed it from the empire burgundies and golds it had worn in her childhood to coolest celandine and silver. It held a large whitish bed in provincial style draped on three sides by yards of finest muslin, almost like a girl's bed. There was a small matching boudoir next to the room, complete with chaise longue and a fine rococo writing desk. The little boudoir occupied one of the château's rounded towers.

It was here she reclined, freshly washed and powdered in her heavy silk robe, its deep forest green encrusted with gold thread which caught the fire's light. On the table in front of her sat a carafe of brandy and a book Olivier had evidently left for her. She opened it to find it was a volume by Maurice Barrès: *The Garden of Berenice*. Had Olivier intended it as provocation, an education in the wifeliness she so patently failed to display? Clearly he must know that the inventor of the cult of the self, with his love of priests and prayer and native soil, his stance against Dreyfus, was hardly amongst her favourites.

She couldn't concentrate on Barrès' encrusted prose. There was little she could concentrate on. Even her own thoughts were unclear. Her body ached far more than she had thought possible earlier. Pain had set in once it knew it was safe to do so. But was she safe, she wondered? Someone had seen her in the woods beside the dead woman. Someone who might be Olivier. Someone who might or might not have recognized her in the guise of Antoine.

Marguerite gazed at the leaping fire in the hearth. Was it weakness that now made her so uncomfortable and so suspicious? There had been a barely restrained scowl on Olivier's face as he watched her slowly take the stairs with the help of Madame Germaine and Martine.

She had sent both of them away now to visit Gabriel and in order to have some time to think on her own. Not that Madame Germaine had been any help on the Gabriel front. She could think of no woman she knew of in the immediate area who had disappeared during or after a visible pregnancy to reappear without the child.

In other spheres, though, the woman was a mine of information, even asserting with a smile that gossip was part of her profession. She had babbled on happily about the Telliers when Marguerite had asked, telling her what she already in part knew, but giving it all a vividness it had previously lacked.

The Telliers were Troo's most despised and simultaneously revered family, hated and admired in equal measure for their wealth, profligacy and baronial temperament, even though there were no titles to permit it.

Over the years, the family had accumulated sizeable properties both in the area and in Tours, where the men spent much of their time when business concerns didn't also take them further afield. Monsieur Tellier was older than Madame, probably as old as her intemperate father, Napoleon Grandcourt Marchand, who had been notorious in the area in his debauched youth, years ago now. He was a scoundrel of the first order; a lumbering giant of a man with pitch black hair and eyes and a an even darker disposition. The brother was no better. And there had been some funny business with the sister as well, a broken engagement or some such. Anyhow she had left, and the brothers had started to travel. The region breathed a sigh of something like relief and went to feed its appetite for gossip elsewhere. Madame Germaine had had little contact with them of late. She was only irregularly called to Troo, which had its own midwife.

A loud, unmistakable knock on the door announced Olivier's presence. He didn't wait for her to bid him in. Nor did he sit. He stood over her, his features heavy, dour.

'You should know, Marguerite, that I am less than pleased at your misadventures. Of course, of course,' he held up a hand as if she had been about to interrupt him, 'I'm sorry that you've taken a fall. But what you think you were doing traipsing round the countryside on your own, making a spectacle of yourself, ending up prostrate at the house of that less than savoury Dr. Labrousse . . . Really, Marguerite. This kind of behaviour is better suited to a kitchen maid then a countess.'

Perhaps he didn't know, then. It was Labrousse who worried him.

'A countess soon to be the wife of a deputy, you mean.'

'That too.' He was immune to her irony. For a moment, it even came to her that he might be jealous.

'Have you been told about the woman?'

She watched his face carefully.

'What woman?'

'The dead woman. The one whose body I found not far from the point where I believe you discovered Gabriel.'

'Really?' Some emotion she didn't recognize distorted his features. He brought them quickly under control and folded his limbs into the chair opposite her chaise longue. He adjusted the crease of his houndstooth trousers, the knot of his perfectly casual tie.

'Yes, really.'

'How annoying for you. For her, too, I have no doubt. Who is she? Who was she?'

Now, he was watching her, his eyes nervous despite the ease of his posture.

'I don't know. Doubtless someone will.'

'And you, of course, think she is Gabriel's mother.'

'Have I said that?'

'No, but the implication was there. She delivered herself of her illegitimate child, had just enough strength to carry him to the waters as she dreamed of Pharaoh's daughters, and promptly went off to die, leaving a trail of blood behind her, I imagine.'

'You imagination has grown colourful, Olivier.

'Not yours?'

'Not really. Though I think there might just be a link between the two events.'

'Why? Infants are often left, most often to die. Bodies rarely.'

'You're rather callous today.'

He didn't answer.

She lightened her tone. 'Have you met Madame Germaine before? She's a nurse. And a midwife.'

He didn't rise to the bait.

'Did I tell you I knew her when I was little?'

He gave her his cold stare. 'You seem to have known everyone here when you were little. It will no doubt be a boon to my candidacy. Which reminds me, Père Benoit has offered to come up to you. To give you solace.'

'He's not where I would most prefer to seek solace.'

'Isn't he? Should I find that offensive?'

She shrugged. 'You've changed, Olivier.'

'For the better, I hope.' He leapt up unexpectedly. He came close and laid a hand on her shoulder.

She flinched.

'Confession would do you no harm, Marguerite.'

The notion startled her. What were Olivier and the priest up to?

'But it's been years, Olivier. More than I like to count.'

'In the eyes of God, it's a mere trifle.'

She wanted to say childishly that Olivier was being sententious, that he had no way of knowing. But she kept silent. It came to her with the chill of an ill wind that Olivier wanted access through the cleric to what Marguerite might be hiding. Had he in fact recognized her after all in Antoine and conveyed this to Père Benoit? Worse, could he have pushed her himself and wanted now to know whether she had recognized *him*?

Why couldn't she rid herself of the sense that the men were in some kind of cabal together which did not have her best interests at heart?

'I will consider it,' she murmured. 'I'm too weary, now. But tell me truthfully, Olivier, if the babe and the dead woman are found to be linked by some unusual chain of events, would you still feel the same way about Gabriel?'

'I am certain they won't be. So why don't you just set your mind at ease and rest, my dear.'

She wasn't immune to the threat in his voice.

'I want nothing more than to rest.'

'Good. Because I want you in fine fettle for the day after tomorrow. Up and about. At least around the house. I have a surprise for you. My candidacy is being announced in a rather wonderful way. There will be people here. It would be appropriate if you were at your best.' He rested his eyes on her, his smile tight.

'You can be beautiful, Marguerite, but a little less thinking and a little more rest, will help the process.'

'I have a friend coming from Paris, that day, Olivier. I trust he'll be welcome to whatever you're planning.'

'All your friends are welcome, Marguerite. As long as they're also my friends.' With a stiff bow, he was away.

She looked at the door he closed behind him with a mixture of relief and trepidation.

She had a sense that she needed a sturdy ally.

A dream gripped her with terror in the darkest hours of the night. She couldn't fall asleep again and she turned it round and round in her mind.

It started calmly enough. She was dressed as Antoine. He was riding through the woods, passing by some of the very spots where she had walked not all that long ago. He was somehow managing to ride without getting his cap caught in low-lying branches and without his horse protesting at scrub. She could see him clearly from the outside.

It was when he walked into the water that everything grew frightening. Mud clung at his boots. The current swirled. It enveloped him and then he was swimming against it, thrashing, catching at branches. A log came into view—a log, like the one she had seen at the spot where she suspected Gabriel's basket had been left. He caught at that too and it stopped his progress. He heaved himself up towards the bank, clutched and pulled and then something that he tugged at gave a little and he clutched again. It was a woman's leg. Her body clad in a red dress followed. He flung himself back into the waters and away. Further upstream, he managed somehow to clamber up the bank. He returned to the woman. He could see her now. He turned her over.

The woman in the red dress wore Marguerite's features.

It was the sight of her own dead, inert face being pulled up by the Antoine she also was which had woken her in terror. She was wet through, her nightgown a rag of perspiration. She was unable to move, transfixed by the sight of her double with her Medusa's head of blond, snaking curls caked in river mud.

From somewhere she heard Olivier's cold laugh.

_ 12 _

There were more people on the hill than she could ever remember seeing. There were children in a motley assortment of uniforms, teachers from state as well as religious schools, and bearded headmasters. There were farmers in scarves and caps and clogs, and servants in a variety of livery. There were notables, walking sticks in hand, bellies and top hats in place, kicking the ground as if it might produce some warmth despite winter. There were officers in full regalia from the local garrison in Blois. There was even the mayor of Montoire, his tricolor sash tight over his frockcoat. It was like a fête except that all eyes were pointed in a single direction.

At the top of the little hill, just where the trees began, floated a vast air balloon with bright blue and red trimmings. A large cane basket hung from it, tethered to the ground, and dripping great sacs and ropes. An attached banner advertised its allegiance to the Catholic Party.

To the side of the basket stood Monsieur Mirtout, the ancient, portly head of the Catholic Party in the area, who had been ancient even when Marguerite was a child. She could only partly hear the words of his speech. Despite his funnel of a loud speaker, despite the evident weight of pomp and circumstance his oratory held, the brisk morning wind dispersed it as lightly as crisp leaves. She either heard or imagined something about the greatness of *la patrie,* the dangers to church schools and the family the radicals represented, and the pride of naming Monsieur le Comte de Landois as their candidate.

Père Benoit and the local bishop nodded their affirmation with a monotonous rhythm of the head. They were mimicked in swift succession by Olivier's retinue of loyal aristocrats, only two of them with their wives, hefty women in funereal black, with hats as broad as parasols. There were a few lawyers as well, and an unctuously charming banker who had just opened a branch for the people of Blois, since—as he had told her almost with his first words over a preliminary breakfast—there was a great deal of spare money around, what with salaries rising so quickly, even for the workers.

Olivier, himself, cloaked in a vast fur which made him look like a Russian bear preparing for a circus dance, kept his comments minimal. A few words of thanks and of rousing cheer, certainly no mention of the two deaths in the near region and an abandoned child, and he was off into the balloon's basket next to his captain.

A small, uniformed brass band burst into a chorus of the Marseillaise. Everyone sang and as the balloon began to rise, Olivier waved, waved to all of them. The crowd waved back and cheered. The children jumped up and down with the thrill of it all. The basket bobbed and shuddered and then the wind whipped the balloon sideways and up over the trees.

Even from her distance, Marguerite could see that Olivier had his great box of a camera in front of him. He was taking photographs. Photographing everyone. Perhaps that was why he had chosen this escapade as a way of announcing his candidacy. No need to stay behind now and actually talk to the people. He could fly up into the sky and enjoy his latest passion, leaving the rest to her. She was to smile and shake hands and urge everyone to partake of the brioche and pastries, the drinks and fruit and chocolate that were now piled high on linen-covered trestle tables in front of the château.

With the balloon now a mere speck in the atmosphere, the curé approached her. 'The Count's bravery is exemplary, Madame, don't you think? He's like one of our old French heroes. And his charity is exemplary, too. I'm thinking of little Gabriel. You must admire him for it.'

'Indeed. And you, Monsieur, must be grateful to him for taking the banner of the Catholic Party up into the heavens. Where I'm certain it belongs.'

He bowed slightly, a little uncertain of the intent of her words.

Marguerite merely smiled. Leaving him behind, she wove her way through the crowd, urging all and sundry towards the tables and playing the role of châtelaine as near to perfection as the stiffness of her limbs permitted.

She noticed the lumbering youth from the Tellier's coming up the hill in her direction. A vision of an animal force rushing out at her from the forest tangle of brush leapt into her mind. She watched P'tit Ours carefully, his clumsy, yet sure-footed gait. He was being followed by a gaggle of youngsters from the village school. She wondered if some of them might be the ones who had thrown stones at the supposed witch immured in that walled house. They were baiting him, tugging at him.

'What d'you think of that, P'tit Ours? Pretty spectacular, eh, eh?'

'Ever seen one of them before? A balloon big enough to carry two men? Might even be big enough to carry you.'

The ungainly youth pushed them aside, but they kept at him, like wasps at a piece of meat.

'Wanna go up? We could ask Monsieur le Conte. P'tit Ours flies.'

'They say pigs can fly.'

P'tit Ours shook his heavy head. 'No, no.' He took off his old cap and passed a hand across his tow-head.

'They say it's colder than underwater after a frost up there.'

'Colder than a witch's teat. How's your witch, P'tit Ours?'

'That's why the count was dressed like a big bear. Cause it's so cold. A Grand'ours.'

The children tittered and giggled. P'tit Ours lashed out at one of them with a kick. They ran, then re-grouped around him.

'Did you see what the balloon was called?'

'It had its name written on the side. In big letters. Above Catholic Party.'

'Go way. Go. You know P'tit Ours don't read.'

'Pegasus. That's what it was called. The flying horse. The teacher told us. See. Maitre Pascal is over there.'

'Pegasus,' P'tit Ours repeated. 'Horses don't fly.'

'Yup. Pegasus. He was the horse that carried Zeus' thunderbolt.'

P'tit Ours cuffed the boy hard over the head.

Marguerite intervened before things escalated. 'Go and get yourselves something to drink, boys. Hurry up, or it'll all be gone.' She pointed towards the tables in front of the château. 'And you, P'tit Ours. I'd like a word with you.' She approached him a little warily, yet she felt sorry for the hulk of a lad, the teasing he had to put up with.

P'tit Ours great, wide eyes bulged at her. She was reminded of what Martine had surmised. Perhaps the youth didn't see all that well. But his next words confounded her.

'You find Dr. Labrousse?' he asked, his mouth a cavern around his uneven teeth.

'Yes, thank you P'tit Ours. Thank you. I wanted to ask you something else. The woman who lives next door to you, who is she?'

A stream of language poured from him, so fast she couldn't make out the individual words. What she thought she heard was, 'Amandine witch. Good witch. Good to P'tit Ours. But everyone bad. To her. Master bad to her. Poor Amandine. You help Amandine. Yvette help Amandine.'

'Yvette?' Marguerite leapt back from the spray that came with his words. 'You know where Yvette is, P'tit Ours? Tell me, please.'

The youth pointed and started to race up towards the house with his odd, lolloping gait.

The sun had taken on a new lustre and in its hard, clear light, the château shone so white that all the figures in front of it appeared as dark silhouettes. It seemed the group P'tit Ours was running towards was comprised of Martine, plump, little Armand who was never far from Celeste, the wet-nurse, and her charge. There were some others, too, cooing into the baby carriage, but she couldn't quite distinguish who they were. Villemardi hovered at their sides, and Marguerite wondered if the sculptor was unsure where he belonged—whether amidst the servants or with the guests. Or was it that he fancied Martine as a subject? She wondered if she should warn the girl. But first, she needed to talk to Ville-mardi.

P'tit Ours had now reached Martine. He tapped her on the shoulder. So the strange youth really did still mistake her for Yvette. The girl leapt back and away from him, her fright visible. Villemardi interposed herself, hardly a bulwark against the young giant.

Before Marguerite could catch up to them or see how the scene would play itself out, she was hailed by Père Benoit again who positioned himself squarely in front of her, this time with two other clerics who wanted to meet Madame la Comtesse. She couldn't brush them away and she carried on a desultory conversation until the curé suddenly trapped her entire attention.

'I'm glad to see you're feeling so very much better after your nasty fall, Madame. It was in the woods, wasn't it? The woods where the body was found.'

'I fear so.' Marguerite nodded. She had been certain that Olivier had already told the man everything, so there was no need for his question.

'Not a good lot, those people.'

'What do you mean, mon père?'

'Have you not heard? They've identified the body.'

'I heard that,' one of the other older clerics intervened. 'Terrible influence these people. I've warned my flock. Some of them are from Spain, you know. We've had too many of their lot over here of late. Even if they are Catholics.'

The three sets of cassocks traced shadows like scythes on the ground.

'Who is she?' Marguerite kept her voice cool. She felt she needed to hide her rabid interest.

Black robes swayed in unison. What was it that struck her as ominous? Something she had forgotten.

'It seems she came from the travellers' encampment just outside of Montoire. You know, the fairground people.'

Père Benoit said it almost as if fairground and people were a contradiction in terms.

'How do you know?'

'The police. One of the vagabonds, the one from the East, the one with a turban, he went to see Monsieur Mirtout in Montoire.'

'Monsieur Mirtout? Of your party?'

'Yes.'

They had reached the tables on the terrace in front of the house and before she could hear anymore, she had to wait for the priests to fill their plates with fruit and pastries.

'You were saying, about Monsieur Mirtout?' Marguerite prodded the curé.

'Yes, it seems the vagabond thought Monsieur Mirtout was a wise man of some kind, because of his advanced age, and these people believe they must register their complaints with sages or nobles. Of course, Monsieur Mirtout promptly took him to the police. All this was some days ago. Anyhow, this man, Rama . . . I don't remember. He's from India. This man wanted to report that a woman had disappeared from the encampment. Danuta the Dancer. His snake had disappeared as well. The snake was called Harinasa or some such. He insisted both had been kidnapped, stolen. Odd little man. The police didn't believe him. Not wholly reliable, I fear.'

'The police or the man who made the complaint?'

'The man, of course. The woman even less so.'

'You know them personally?'

'My duties take me far afield, Madame. I have been to the site where these people are currently stationed.'

'Père Benoit has built up a wide following in the region, Madame,' the other young priest murmured.

'So I see.'

She wished she could see further, wished Labrousse or Madame Germaine were here to tell her what the body revealed about the poor woman's death and a child she might have given birth to before it. The woman in red. Danuta the Dancer.

There would be no more dancing for Danuta.

Marguerite had a sudden, overwhelming desire to cry.

She sat in the long, mirrored orangerie which was her music room and played, her body at one with the chords and trills her hands brought forth from the gleaming old piano. Chopin. A nocturne for poor Danuta the Dancer.

The crowd had dispersed and Marguerite had retired to her instrument. Only Martine was in the room with her, sitting a little to one side of the piano, visibly moved by the music.

The music soothed. It spoke for her. It allowed her mind to make the connections that too much thought often refused. It also gave her patience. She needed it, she thought, as she let her eyes rove through the row of

French windows onto the grounds from which the sun had now vanished to leave everything an uninflected, uniform grey.

There was no sign of the Chief Inspector. His train must have been delayed.

The rise and fall of the music took her attention again and she poured her sadness over the death of the woman whose body she had found into its strains. Had Olivier had anything to do with her death? The thought floated up into the room's painted ceiling where a mythical Pan wooed nymphs with his pipe and lost itself amongst fleeting clouds.

There was another death to mourn, she remembered, although she felt more distant from it. The man on the tracks, still unnamed.

She saw his face again, as she had seen it in those grainy photographs Labrousse had shown her, all bruised and lumpy, pores enlarged. Suddenly, something glimpsed and unfocussed swam into her vision. Another picture, this time in oils, mustard colours and sienna with glints of pink in the skin above a blue, braided uniform. In Madame Tellier's house. The two images slotted in, one over the other. Yes.

Her fingers tripped producing the clatter of a false chord. She lifted her hands from the piano.

'Martine! Martine.' Her tone made the girl leap nervously from her chair. 'Martine. Do you remember you said to me you thought the dead man on the tracks was someone . . . someone you knew? Big and ugly. You were thinking of Madame Tellier's father, you said.'

The girl hung her head, 'Yes, Madame.'

'Well, do you think you might in fact have recognized him, really recognized him, because he was the incarnation of a painting you had seen on the stairs in Madame Tellier's house? Some kind of relative, no doubt.'

Marguerite gave her a look of consternation. 'I don't know, Madame. I don't know.' She closed her eyes as if she were trying to recreate an internal sense of the house that so distressed her. 'Maybe,' she murmured. 'Yes, hanging next to a portrait of the old master.' She shuddered. Her eyes started open and grew wide. 'Do you think it was him, Madame? Do you think it was that man?'

'It could well be, Martine. Since both of us noticed the resemblance . . . without at first realizing it. We shall have to tell the police.'

Behind her, Marguerite heard a throat being cleared.

'Docteur Labrousse is here, Madame. Will you see him?'

'Yes, of course, Jeanne. Show him right in.'

Labrousse was wearing a well-brushed frock coat and what looked like a new tie carefully propped over a hi-necked collar. It was clear he had been expecting a confrontation with Olivier, who might loudly resist the services of a less than impeccably turned out doctor.

'How are you feeling, Madame?'

'Quite well, as you can see,' Marguerite brought out a chord with her injured arm and smiled at him. She started to unbutton the myriad tiny buttons on the sleeve of the burnished soft woolen dress she had worn precisely because of this feature. Jeanne rushed to her aid.

'I trust you've brought me news, as well as new dressings, doctor. I'm hungry for news. It will do me far more good than any unguents.'

He glanced at the two young women, greeted Martine with a little smile which softened his long face and said nothing until Marguerite had waved the girls from the room.

'Were you able to examine the woman, doctor? I heard this morning she was identified as Danuta the Dancer, one of the fairground performers.'

Labrousse's face grew longer with visible discomfort. He was paying attention only to her arm.

'Well, were you doctor?'

'Only cursorily, I'm afraid.'

How did the woman die?'

'From what I could see, a blow killed her. To the head. There was another at the nape of the neck. Violent. Of course, the second could have provoked a fall which caused the first.'

'A blow form a bare hand?'

'I could detect no sign of a weapon, but as I say the examination was cursory. She might have fallen after a struggle. Either way, the police are simply not interested. The woman's not important enough to waste their time on. It's just like the man on the tracks. Their line is simply that she was up to no good in the woods, fell, injured herself and died of cold. If someone knocked her about, that's par for the course. She was reported missing, it seems, some days back.'

Labrousse wasn't meeting her eyes. Now that he was finished with her arm, other objects in the room had taken on an inordinate interest: the polished candelabra atop the grand, the gilded frames of the many mirrors, most certainly his own boots. Once more she was aware of the southern aspect of him, the olive tinge to his skin.

'What is it, doctor? There's something you're not saying to me. Did you get a chance to see if the woman had recently been delivered of a child? Madame Germaine told me it was a simple matter to check for.'

'Been delivered of a child? Why . . . oh I see . . . you think the foundling . . . But Madame, that's simply not possible.'

'Why not?' Marguerite hid her disappointment in curtness.

'Well . . .' he met her eyes at last with his polished ones. 'Danuta the Dancer . . . I saw her. Saw her perform. Not so long before Christmas. On her horses. She twirled and turned and leapt and stood upside down. Difficult enough without the protuberance of a pregnancy. And there certainly wasn't one visible through what was a rather scant costume. So if I'm to trust my eyes, as you say . . .'

He turned a face on her which was all innocence. 'But there is something you might like to know.' His features grew heavy again.

'Go on.'

'She was the woman I told you about. The one I was certain had recognized the dead man in the photographs. She was there when I went to the camp site.'

'I see,' Marguerite started to pace. 'So there is a link between the two deaths. We simply don't know what it is.'

'My fear is that I may in some way I don't understand have contributed to the poor woman's demise.'

She stared at him. 'Doctor, both Martine and I thought of something, just a short time ago. We both think we recognize your dead man. We think he is the same man as one depicted in a painting in Madame Tellier's house. I want you to go and check. It could be very important.'

'Madame Tellier's?'

'Yes.'

'If the police, and particularly the investigative magistrate, care not a jot about these cases, have ceased to pursue them, there is little I can do.'

'I can assure you, doctor. They will pursue them. Don't let their momentary lack of interest hold you back. For the sake of your own conscience, too.' She paused. 'By the way. I notice you are nervous of my husband. Would it help if I knew why?'

Labrousse straightened his tie as if Olivier had walked into the room.

'He shan't be back until tomorrow.'

'I . . . I don't know. He . . . he may have heard some of the rumours about me. They're rife, you know. And I haven't told you. Perhaps he has. They say I let my brother die. And it's true, Madame. That's why I left Montpelier.'

Tears welled in the man's dark eyes. The well-scrubbed hands clenched into tight fists. 'I take complete responsibility. But it was an exercise of misjudgment not of lack of medical knowledge. Or so I tell myself.'

'Tell me,' Marguerite said softly.

'I didn't get to him in time, you see. I didn't think it was serious. He was always complaining, calling for me. A stomach ache it was this time, apparently. So I didn't rush over.'

'You were busy with other patients.'

'Yes, yes. You understand. I tended to what I assumed were more urgent needs. I had no idea.' He sat down in a chair and buried his large head in his hands. 'By the time, the servant found me again, it was too late. Acute appendicitis. There. Now I've said it. Before you hear it behind my back. If you haven't already.'

'And Montoire presented itself?'

He nodded. 'Now I'm assiduous in tending to even my most plaintive of patients.'

'Even Yvette and Madame Tellier . . .'

She didn't understand the look he cast her, but she went on.

'I'm glad you've told me, doctor. I shall quash any rumours I hear. I'm certain you have paid enough of a price.' She waited a moment. 'As for these other matters, I would be truly grateful to you if you paid a visit to the woman and had a good look at her picture collection. The police would certainly trust an identification based on your scientific assessment and backed by Martine and myself.'

'Martine saw the resemblance too?' His face brightened.

Marguerite sighed. 'Who knows . . . an identification might even take us a step closer to her sister!'

After he left, Marguerite returned to her piano. She found herself playing a fugue, lost herself in the counterpoint of voices, the identities which turned away into differences, the flight of her fingers like her racing legs masquerading as Antoine. All the while her mind hurtled through the woods and back to the Tellier house, the old man, Yvette, so like her sister, the portrait. She barely heard Martine come into the room.

When the crash came, she leapt as from a trance. The heavy satin train of her dress caught on the piano stool, trapping her, so that for a moment all she saw were shards of glass rushing towards her. A window pane had been smashed. Pieces lay scattered over the gleaming beech floor. Through the French doors, in the murky half-light that marked the coming of dusk, she now saw a growling, bare-headed P'tit Ours. The buttons of his ragged trousers were open to display a half-erect member. She moved backwards, slowly, imperceptibly, as if in a dream in which her legs were paralyzed.

Martine was screaming. She had fled to the far side of the room. Before Marguerite could unlock her legs, behind the bulk of P'tit Ours, she discerned a second shape. That second, smaller form was holding the giant youth's arms pinned back in a sharp grip. It was the effort of struggling to break free that must have resulted in the broken window.

Now Georges and one of the groundsmen ran up to take hold of P'tit Ours's arms. Behind the burly youth, she recognized the barrel-chest, well-brushed coat and bowler hat of Emile Durand. It was a relief and pleasure to see the stout, dapper little man with the heavy brows and big broom of a moustache.

'Perhaps you should have him do his trousers up, Chief Inspector. My young companion here is still at a shockable age.'

'I'm sorry, Madame. This was not the entrance I had planned.'

Emile Durand extricated himself from the group and stood directly in front of P'tit Ours. He smoothed his coat, stood to attention with military precision, bowed, and doffed his bowler hat.

'I do apologize Madame, but as we drove up I saw this large figure by the window. It took me a moment to realize that he was staring in at you. You were outlined in the light, reflected in the mirrors. You and the girl,' he bowed now toward Martine. 'When I realized what this lout of a peeping Tom was up to, I raced here.'

A loud wail came from P'tit Ours. 'Let go. Let go. Let P'tit Ours go.' He lunged and tried to shrug the men off, but despite his bulk they kept a firm grip. Tears were pouring down his face. His mouth was a cavernous hole with unruly stumps of teeth. 'Let go!'

'You were bad, Ptit Ours. Very bad.' Marguerite said, surprised at her own gentleness. The overgrown boy terrified her more than ever, yet still he evoked her pity.

'Maman say P'tit Ours bad. But not bad. P'tit Ours not bad. Not lazy good for nothing. No dragon. No tattoos. P'tit Ours listen to sounds. Sad sounds. Like river. Running. Sad running. Sad. Big sad.'

The tears still poured from his eyes and as they all tried to make out what he meant, he lunged again, this time backwards, and with a wild shriek broke the grip of the men. And then P'tit Ours was running. Running like some kind of untamed creature. Hopping, shuffling, running for all he was worth, down the hill and into the copse and away.

'Let him go, Inspector. I know where to find him if we need to,' Marguerite said, hoping she wasn't doing the wrong thing.

_ 13 _

Little had gone as she might have wished since she had come to La Rochambert, but Marguerite judged herself lucky in the timing of the Chief
Inspector's arrival. Not only because it coincided with P'tit Ours's disturbing and potentially dangerous intrusion, but also because it coincided
with Olivier's absence. Her husband would spend the night in Tours. The
Chief Inspector and she were free to talk and talk until the small hours if
necessary. Certainly until her strength or his gave out. She was so relieved
to see his face with all its worn humanity that for the first time since she
had arrived at La Rochambert, she relaxed utterly.

Her first task was to introduce the Inspector properly to Martine.
She had the young woman tell him in her halting way about Yvette's disappearance and the lack of headway they had made in locating her.

Moved by the girl's narrative, her worry, and her elfin charm, aware
of the shock P'tit Our's eruption into their midst had caused, the Inspector
treated her with such gentle protectiveness, such paternal warmth that she
might have been his own child. Marguerite knew that he had two of his
own, a daughter of thirteen, not all that much younger than Martine, and
a smaller boy. She knew that he doted on them, though occasionally the
remarks he let drop gave her intimations that his relations with a plaintive wife were less than ideal. None the less, he was a firm believer in the
family, and was prone to rant periodically against escalating divorce rates
and loose morality. It came to her that despite his ardent Republicanism,
on that score at least, the Inspector would not find himself all that distant from Olivier's new position.

Martine basked in Durand's warmth and talked with more freedom
than Marguerite had ever quite witnessed in her before. Perhaps the

Inspector allowed her to forget that she was the recipient of favours, something Marguerite, because of her position, had been unable to do. Gratitude, in Marguerite's experience, was rarely an emotion that came without a darker side.

Yes, Durand distinctly had the common touch. She had discovered recently that he was one of seven children from a poor farming family on the further reaches of the Ile de France. He had worked himself up by dint of his own efforts and with the selfless help of a village schoolteacher who had seen potential in him. The experience had made him into a firm and shrewd meritocrat. With thrift and education and effort, anyone could make a go of it, he believed. His past made him hard on criminals. They were intent on cheating or destroying the society which had been kind to him. It made him hard on slackers and on a self-indulgent aristocracy. It also made him excessively kind to Martine and for some reason to Marguerite, whom he had exempted from the crimes of her birth.

When Marguerite focussed in on the Inspector's interview once more she heard Martine telling him something Marguerite hadn't yet heard. She was confessing to him she thought Yvette would not have been as frightened of P'tit Ours as she was, not even today.

'And why is that, Mademoiselle?'

'Yvette is strong. She likes helping people. All kinds of people. She can talk to anyone. It's probably why P'tit Ours keeps coming here.'

'So when he came to the window, you think it was for you. You as Yvette?' Marguerite asked in great excitement, since it confirmed her suspicions about where they might find the girl. With her greater experience of the world, she read Martine's comments as an indication of Yvette's more indulgent, if at times self-punishing ways with men. Her hopes that Yvette might be traced to a brothel, as so many vanished young women before her had been, kept her greater fears for the young woman at bay.

Martine was blushing scarlet. Had she followed the full trajectory of Marguerite's thoughts?

'I don't know, Madame, I really don't'

'But that's been very helpful, Mademoiselle. You skip off now and rest after all the excitement, while Madame and I talk things over.' The Inspector smiled his warm, disarming smile, as if he were simply an ordinary chap who enjoyed a little chit chat, not the cool, punctilious observer Marguerite knew him to be.

Having shooed the girl away, it turned out he wanted to conduct a thorough Inspection of the Château before they did anything else. He had a notion that P'tit Ours might come back. He was also concerned that it had needed his arrival to alert the household of the giant youth's presence at their windows.

'Madame should not discount the possibility that other foul acts will occur. They rarely come singly. And sometimes it takes a rank outsider to see even the most obvious things. People in the area will undoubtedly know that you've been taking an interest in the cadaver. They may not like it. This oaf may be a spy in the interests of someone else and simply taking his perverted pleasure on the way. And if he's had it once, he'll come back. We can't be too careful.'

Marguerite waited for her moment to tell him about Danuta the Dancer and how she had been assaulted in the woods. Meanwhile, the Inspector tried doors and windows, noted the position of stairwells and servants' quarters and greeted an array of chambermaids and footmen with an affable smile that permitted him to watch the degree of nervousness his title evoked.

When they finally sat down to dinner in happy seclusion, it was to a feast she trusted Durand, who was something of a gourmet, would welcome after his exertions. She had alerted Madame Solange who had prodded cook to excel. The ate a Crème Germiny followed by a buttery fillet of sole, a boeuf en croute prepared to perfection and garnished with green beans and parsleyed potatoes, a plateau of cheese, fruit and petits fours, all accompanied by an array of wines from Olivier's cellar and a fragrant after-dinner Courvoisier to sweeten the Inspector's pipe tobacco.

With all the detail she could muster, because she knew the Inspector relished detail to bite on as much as a good piece of beef, Marguerite told him everything she had learned about Yvette, her employers and her sister. Then she launched into a rather grisly rendition, given the food in front of them, of the cadaver on the tracks and what the doctor's autopsy had laid bare. She told him, too, about her current hunch concerning the corpse's identity. Then skirting over Olivier's presence in the woods, and her terror at the charging beast of a man, she unfurled the account of the woman in red she had found dead, how she had been knocked down and who the woman had turned out to be.

Durand asked pointed questions and savoured his food, mulled and considered. During the last part of her narrative, his eyes spoke his disapproval. He chastized her for her daring.

'You really must take care, Madame. I implore you. Two deaths unaccounted for always makes me worry about a possible third. Murder grows easier, I've learned. For the murderer, at least.'

Marguerite nodded. 'Yet you see, Inspector, the police here are ready to dismiss both possible murders, because the victims are simply not citizens they recognize as needing their time and attention. They see them as tramps and vagabonds. Expendable. That's one of the reasons, I so wanted you to use your influence.'

'Tomorrow I shall pay a visit to the *Commissariat* and have a word, if it's possible with the magistrates as well.'

And there is another matter, Inspector.'

She told him about the foundling and how she had failed thus far in her attempts to uncover Gabriel's origins.

The Inspector didn't fail to note that this matter lay particularly close to her heart.

'So you see why I needed your help, Inspector. Help on several fronts.'

The Inspector swirled the golden brandy round in his glass, sniffed with pleasure and nodded sagely. 'And I need yours, Madame.' He filled his pipe and Marguerite could see in the deep breath he took, that he needed to unburden himself of his own worries. She encouraged him.

It seemed a Parisian scandal was brewing over a high-ranking politician from the Radical Party who had purportedly been selling state honours to the highest bidder and using the money to subsidize rather unsavoury activities, some of them with the children he met in the Palais Royale or around the boat lake in the Luxembourg Gardens.

Durand's unhappy task was to ferret out the truth with the minimum publicity; and having done so to demonstrate to the politician in question—whose name he only mentioned once and then in a whisper—that instant resignation, followed by quick emigration was the best possible solution for all concerned, unless he fancied years behind bars. What he wanted from Marguerite was advice on tactics, as well as on who might be connected to whom and know what, so that pressure could be applied in appropriate ways. And first of all, he had to ascertain that the politician hadn't been set up by an envious rival, superior at the moment, but perhaps not for long.

Marguerite sharpened her wits on the intrigue. By the end of the evening, after they had debated the pros and cons of various approaches and gone into the secret lives of a number of influential parties, she had altogether forgotten that she was not in Paris and ready for an excursion to the Chat Noir where a panoply of her friends were certain to be gathered for an evening of scurrilous chansons and pungent wit.

Yet it was La Rochambert which concerned her most nearly now.

When she went to bed and inadvertently leaned on her injured arm, she thought of Danuta the Dancer stretched out on the dark, cold ground. The wind at the shutters and the chilling hoot of a prophetic owl intensified her sense of impending disaster.

'The snow's coming,' Madame Solange murmured at breakfast. She was hovering over them, as bleak as some Greek oracle.

On the horizon, the clouds were dark and heavy. The pale yellow of the room's walls felt like an intrusion.

'We'll have to take the carriage then,' Marguerite said half to herself. She had hoped she and the Inspector could ride cross country or unnoticed in the old barouche, but snow would make that difficult.

'I'll alert Georges.' Madame Solange took in everything.

Marguerite sensed she was uneasy about Durand's presence; couldn't work out whether he was a genuine guest or somehow a member of staff sent for to discover the babe's parentage. She knew Durand would soon seduce Madame Solange into good will, particularly if his compliments and murmurs of 'delicious,' persisted. The Inspector looked particularly bright this morning. The château evidently provided a holiday from the travails of Paris life.

Villemardi burst into the breakfast room, just as Marguerite was about to ask the Inspector about his children.

'Ah Madame,' he looked curiously at Durand and in afterthought straightened his tie and bowed to them both. 'I've just heard that you'll be driving into Montoire. If I might come along, I'd be grateful. I need to deliver a few sample drawings to the mayor's office. I'm told he's looking for something to grace the square in front of the Mairie with.'

'How altogether citizenly of him,' Marguerite had an image of the Mayor's rotund presence draped in the tricolor. 'But perhaps we could drop the work for you. The Inspector and I may be gone some time.'

The last thing she wanted was to have Villemardi trailing them from Montoire to the brothels of Blois and reporting on everything to Olivier.

The sculptor's face radiated disappointment.

'Excuse me, Madame, if Monsieur . . . is it . . .'

'Villemardi,' the sculptor filled in for Durand.

'If Monsieur Villemardi wishes to accompany us with his packages, all he need do is let his horse follow on behind the carriage.'

'Of course. A happy solution, Inspector.' Marguerite smiled at Villemardi. The sculptor might wish to assuage his curiosity about the Inspector, but Durand, she realized had an equal wish to find out what the sculptor might know and she hadn't yet managed to discover.

They were almost out the door, when Martine was upon them.

'Madame, Madame.' The girl was breathless, her hair bursting from its pins. 'Look what blew in through the broken pane in the conservatory. I thought you might want to see it.'

She smoothed a bit of rumpled paper with long, trembling fingers. 'It may be nothing, but . . .'

Marguerite examined the paper. There was writing on it, a childlike scrawl in large, ungainly printed letters. Full of misspellings. At first, she thought of schoolboy pranks, some game the young ones had indulged in on the day of the balloon flight.

'Help me. Pleese. I am prisner. Aginst mi will. Pleese.'

'What do you think, Madame?'

'I'm not sure.' She passed the paper to Durand, who was looking at Martine impassively.

He read the note quickly. 'What does this message make you think of, Mademoiselle?'

Martine's eyes grew wide.

'Do you recognize the writing, my dear?' Marguerite asked.

The girl shook her head. 'No, it's just, I thought maybe it came with P'tit Ours. Maybe he wrote it. It made me think of Yvette. Yvette locked up somewhere. I don't know. I had a vision of an island. Yvette can't swim.'

'Devil's Island, perhaps.' The Inspector said gently. 'It's been much in the papers.'

Marguerite doubted the Inspector's connection. She had yet to see Martine reading the papers. But there might be other prisoners in P'tit Ours' vicinity. That link of Martine's felt altogether appropriate. It would be worth investigating, particularly since she felt another visit to Madame Tellier's would soon be necessary.

Snow had started to fall. Thick, wet, drunken flakes of it blown by an ogre of a wind. The ploughed fields on the horizon turned white in a twist of the road. The dark steeple in the distance disappeared and refused to appear again. The sky was white. The air was white, too, where the flakes met to leap and dance. The rare coaches and wagons moved with a regal slowness, fading away then utterly swallowed into milky whiteness. Only the river remained dark with a kind of swirling anger.

No one but she noticed. Durand, wearing an expression of profound attentiveness, was busy drawing Villemardi out concerning the day on which little Gabriel had been found.

'I trust artists' perceptions, Monsieur. I have been led to trust them,' Durand was saying. Like some telegraph operator, he tapped out his thoughts on his knee with his unlit pipe. 'Artists are experts at observation, like detectives. Describe it to me, Monsieur. Describe Monsieur le Comte's expression.'

'Horror,' Villemardi burst out, his face pale with his passion. 'Utter horror. Both of us. We had been off for an innocent morning's fishing. And we were convinced the child was dead.'

'Did you have any immediate thoughts, wild leaps of the imagination, about whom it might belong to?'

'Non, Monsieur. Certainly not. Though I think Monsieur le Comte might have imagined it was the offspring of one of the former maids. I wasn't sure. The swaddling was good quality cloth. No holes. And the babe had been washed, at least once. Which meant that he hadn't just popped into life behind a thicket nearby.' He lowered his eyes. He refused Marguerite's interrogative glance and with a look, the Inspector forbade her to speak. In any case, Villemardi was now rushing on. 'There was no question of keeping it, once we found it was alive. None at all. Until the curé stepped in, that is.'

'Père Benoit,' Marguerite elaborated for the Inspector's benefit.

'Père Benoit, once André Marchand.'

'Marchand?' Marguerite echoed.

He nodded, still without looking at her.

'Go on.' The Inspector said.

'Well, it was all his doing, really. Noblesse de la robe,' Villemardi scoffed, venting his dislike of the curé as Marguerite had heard him do at every possible opportunity. 'He convinced Monsieur le Comte that the child was a sign of grace or some such . . . that a true seigneur of the old school would always take a foundling in. And there we are.'

The Inspector nodded sagely and glanced towards Marguerite for a moment. She had suddenly sat up very straight, as if someone had been tugging at her fur-trimmed hat.

'It was nothing Inspector. I just hadn't heard the expression 'noblesse de la robe' for a long time. It set me thinking.' What she had been thinking was indeed about gowns, black cloth. That's what she had found in the woods before that second more terrible finding. A woman in red and a piece of black cloth.

'By the way, Madame. I remember you asked me about this and I shall soon have the opportunity to find out. I need to make a trip to Blois and I shall see if I can locate Louise Bertin's family there. Perhaps they've heard something from the girl.'

'That would be extremely useful, Monsieur.' But Marguerite wasn't thinking about Louise Bertin. She was wondering whether, even though

Marchand was a common enough name, there might be any link between the curé and the monstrous old Napoléon Marchand, Madame Tellier's father.

When she focussed in on the Inspector's veiled interrogation, it was to hear Villemardi describing his experience of seeing the cadaver found on the tracks.

'But you had never to your knowledge seen the man before?' Durand double-checked. 'Not even though your family firm's card was found in his pocket.'

'Non, Inspector. As I explained to the police here, my father—who runs the firm—leaves our cards everywhere that he can to drum up business, particularly with undertakers and notaries.'

'So we can assume that before he died, our unknown man made a visit to a local undertaker or notary. Château du Loir, isn't it?'

'Yes, but the cards probably travel as far as Blois.'

'I shall check this out with the local police,' Durand nodded sagely.

The travellers' encampment, as they approached, offered an odd spectacle. Clothes lines had been pulled up, fires quashed. The barrels which doubled as chairs or braziers were gone, together with the random assortment of cases and baskets and utensils which had previously marked the area. There was nothing left on the site except a line of colourful coaches, more garish than ever against the pallor of snow. They were moving slowly towards the road.

'Oh no, Inspector. The travellers must be going. We must catch them before they do.'

'I think they'll be attending a funeral before they vanish.'

Only now did Marguerite see the wagon coming towards them. It was draped in black, its driver in tails and top hat. One after another, the bright coaches fell into line.

There was a strange dignity to the procession: the hearse, sombre, onyx black against the snow; the carriages, their curlicues and animal pictures alight in brightest azure, red and gold; the drivers, their expressions solemn, their posture pulled stiff and upright by some inner injunction.

Trailing behind on a rope tied to the last wagon came two beautiful horses, as white as the snow. Their pink nostrils quivered, their well-tended manes flowed in the wind. The children lined up by the side of the road and waved, calling out by name to their favourite performers.

Fifteen slow minutes through the town to its nether end, with a stop to drop Villemardi off near the Mairie, brought them to a small, walled cemetery. The gravediggers stood by the open pit. They clapped their hands together for warmth and stamped their feet. The grave was filling with snow, a lace coverlet dropped into the depths. A frail, old priest or brother with a kind, wrinkled face and a potato of a nose greeted people as they gathered. It felt, at first, as if the Inspector and she were the only ones present who didn't belong. Their clothes were too good, their boots polished, their gloves and muffs intact. They elicited stares, both curious and hostile.

A clarinet began to wail its music to the open skies. It acted as a signal. Local children crowded in from all sides to this pied piper's magical call.

This piper wore a scarlet tunic and silver-threaded jodhpurs. A jeweled turban rested on his gleaming head. His silky moustache curled dramatically. His eyes shone, brighter than the jewel.

Around him, like a retinue for some regal maharajah, stood a strong man with a shaved head and vast biceps; an old crone whose bosom heaved as she cried copious tears; various acrobats and jugglers and dark-eyed women clutching ragged children by the hand.

There was a hurdy gurdy man with a tiny monkey on his shoulder and a saltimbanque in jester's motley with a ruffled collar. His face, beneath the close-fitting pointed hat, had a heart-rending aquiline beauty, neither male, nor female, but somehow both. His hooded eyes stared into the pit with a sadness which tore at Marguerite. She wanted to go and put a reassuring hand on his shoulder, tend to his wounds, but there was no comfort for that melancholy, not even the priest's words, as Danuta the Dancer was slowly lowered into her last resting place.

Marguerite waited for the ceremony to be over, for the clarinetist to blow his final clear note. When he began to leave his spot by the graveside, she walked over to him. The Inspector was right beside her. Behind him, standing next to the strong man, she glimpsed P'tit Ours. Madame Tellier's housekeeper's giant of a son was everywhere.

Tears were streaming down his face and the strong man had a comforting arm around him. She didn't have time to ponder connections. Eyes were on her, narrowed, chary.

'Monsieur,' she addressed the Indian. 'My condolences to you all.'

He turned towards her. Initial suspicion was converted into a bow.

'I wonder, Monsieur. Do you speak English? If so, it might be best.' Marguerite made a small gesture at the crowd, smiled reassurance.

The man stared for a moment. His teeth gleamed.

'If Madame so would prefer,' he replied in perfect English.

'I . . . I was the person who found your friend.'

'You found the lady Danuta?'

Marguerite nodded, walked slowly with the two men towards the edge of the crowd. She didn't dare introduce Durand yet. These people would be suspicious enough of her without the added burden of a policeman. She hoped Durand's smattering of English would come in useful.

'Yes. In the woods. It was not a happy finding.'

'No. No. Most sad. Most terrible. Most unpropitious. Myself, I had warned her. Had warned her about that gentleman. She insisted. Insisted.'

'A gentleman? So she wasn't stolen away against her will.'

'Will. What is this will? She could dance. She could twirl on the horses. But this Danuta could not think. She had a madness of an idea. A new life. To begin a new life. I ask you, how many times can a person begin anew? She left. She came back. She left again. Cats, they have nine lives. Danuta, she thought she had ninety-nine. One with every no-good man she met. Now she has a completely and utterly new one.'

With an air of utter despair, he looked back at the pit, half filled with earth now.

'Meanwhile her dancing horses pine and weep. And my serpent, my precious cobra is gone. Gone forever. Irreplaceable.'

'Your serpent?'

'Yes. My Nasa. My friend. My livelihood.' He made a graceful spiraling motion in the air. It took Marguerite a moment to realize he was miming the upward coiling of a snake. She hadn't realized. He was the travellers' snake charmer.

'Your Danuta took him with her?'

He shrugged. 'I don't know. I don't know. I think she had some idea of doing magic with her lover. But I don't know. I will never know.'

'And your serpent, Sir, is he venomous?'

'But of course, of course. He must be returned to me immediately. Immediately. Or there will be more trouble. I told the old gentleman. This Monsieur Mirtout. I told him. I warned him. But the people here are so stubborn.'

He shook his head, let the smile flash across his face again. 'Not the honourable Madame. No, no.'

'Rama, Rama.'

The man turned.

'We're off. Get over here.' The strong man was calling.

The Indian bowed in Marguerite's direction.

'Where are you all heading, Monsieur? I hope you are not leaving the region?'

'Hope is not enough Madame. We have been ordered. Ordered in terms which were hardly pleasant. We have overstayed our welcome. So we must set off. '

'Ordered?' The Inspector echoed, then asked in French, 'Ordered by whom?'

'By the police. By the mayor.'

'But how will you discover what happened to Danuta? Or your snake?'

He shrugged. 'We may not. That is the way of authority. It is not interested in our wishes. Goodbye Madame. Thank you for your interest.'

Marguerite chased after him, her heavy coat and dress lifted awkwardly, her feet crunching the gathering snow. 'Tell me, Sir. Please. Was this Danuta with child? Was this one of the reasons she kept going and coming back, going and coming back?'

'With child?' The man looked at her as if she had lost her senses. 'How would poor Rama know? What is clearer is that she was with snake.'

Marguerite exchanged glances with Durand and reverted to French, 'Perhaps, Sir, given the inclement weather, I could arrange for you to spend another few nights in the area. I shall go straight away to the Town Hall. Worse comes to worse, I can offer you one of my meadows for the night.'

Marguerite had an image of Olivier's face if she came home with a band of travellers. She wanted to shudder and laugh simultaneously. 'Perhaps even a few nights. Though it would mean going in the other direction.'

'Auguste.' He called the strong man over. 'A proposal has been put to us.' He repeated her words.

The wrestler looked her up and down, his expression surly. He grunted something to the effect that if they didn't leave here in the next half hour they would be snowed in, in any event.

'That settles it, Messieurs. You go back to the camp site, and leave the rest to me.'

The chief Inspector stopped her on the steps of the carriage. 'If you permit me to say, Madame, this latest generous offer of yours, if I understood you correctly, seems to me something of an extravagance. I wonder if Monsieur le Comte will look upon it kindly.'

Marguerite smiled. She had forgotten something else. Chief Inspector Durand might be as staunch a republican as Olivier was a royalist, but between them they would happily build a wall round France to protect her from foreigners and vagabonds.

'I shall deal with Olivier.' Marguerite put far more certainty in her voice than she felt. 'When and if the need arises.'

The need didn't arise. While Inspector Durand went off to talk things over with the local police, Marguerite managed a five minute visit to the Mayor, who was as obsequious as someone waiting for the imminent return of one of the mighty Louis. She convinced him that it was inhuman, unChristian and certainly unpatriotic to send the travellers away in weather like this, after the sadness of losing one of their members. It would all reflect very badly on the town. Undoubtedly they would be deprived of fairs and mountebanks, much loved of the people, in the future. The travellers had their own grapevine and it functioned effectively, of that he could be certain.

The mayor nodded gravely, thanked her for her renewed interest in the commune and called for a messenger.

By noon, when she left the Mairie, the skies had cleared and a pale sun glimmered like a lemon lozenge on the starched linen of the snow-decked town.

The Inspector had still not returned to the carriage, so she told Georges she would pay a quick visit to Dr. Labrousse. When she arrived in his consulting room, he ushered her through in front of an old woman and a gnarled man who were waiting.

'As your physician, I must tell that you should not be out in this weather.' Labrousse shook his narrow head.

'I simply wanted to know, doctor, whether by any chance you had an opportunity to pay a visit to Madame Tellier.'

'I called in on my way back from La Rochambert, yesterday.'

'And . . .'

'None of them were in. Let me have a look at your arm, while you're here, Madame.'

'So you didn't go in?'

'I did. Madame Molineuf escorted me.'

He paused.

'And . . .' Marguerite was impatient, but she noticed that the doctor looked tired. The skin around his eyes was drawn, his cheeks had grown paler against the bristle of beard.

'Yes . . . yes . . . I did think there was a resemblance between the portrait on the stairs and the cadaver.'

'A mere resemblance?'

Labrousse heaved his shoulders with a sigh. 'I must be cautious, Madame. We never saw the man alive. Gesture changes everything. Colouring. Nor are portraits necessarily accurate. On top of it all, time passes. Change takes place. Decay sets in.'

'So Madame Molineuf told you something which made you doubt the resemblance your eyes perceived. As did mine.'

'Perhaps.' He gave her a soft smile. 'To build up our diagnoses, we doctors listen to what people tell us, as well as examining their bodies.'

'No doubt. What did she tell you? How did you put it to her?'

'I asked her who that fine portrait was of, next to the one of the young Napoleon Marchand.'

'So the other portrait is of the father.'

He nodded. 'She told me it was a painting of Monsieur's brother. He had left France a very long time ago, had sailed to the Caribbean. To Martinique, Madame always said.'

'Did you mention the body on the tracks to her? Convey a message to Madame to come and see him?'

'That's hardly my business as her physician.'

'The police then. You'll tell them.'

He nodded slowly. 'Madame Molineuf was adamant though. When I said I thought I had seen that man, she was certain I must be mistaken. Why if he had been in the country, he would certainly have come to visit his family. His brother, his niece, his grandnieces whom he had never seen. Which makes sense, doesn't it?'

'Families rarely make sense,' Marguerite murmured. 'Whatever ideologues might like to tell us.'

He stared at her.

'Well, according to Madame Molineuf, whom I'm inclined to believe rather more than Madame Tellier, herself, never mind the old man who drinks so much he couldn't see straight if he tried, no one has seen hide nor hair of Napoleon's brother for years and years.'

'Except you and me,' Marguerite said with a touch of scepticism. 'Not to mention his murderers. I'd like Inspector Durand, who has arrived from Paris, to see the body, if that's still possible.'

'I've managed to keep him back until today. Unlike Danuta. Luckily it's been very cold. 'The gravediggers don't like being pressed to burial in the cold.'

'I shall send the Inspector over. Meanwhile, doctor, it occurs to me. I never visited the chemist you said had handled Yvette Branquart's prescription. She may have gone back to him without any of us knowing, so he might even have some knowledge of her whereabouts.'

Dr. Labrousse gave her what wasn't his friendliest look, but he pointed her in the right direction and said he would wait for the Inspector's visit. She didn't test him on her hunch about brothels. Labrousse, despite his scientific frame of mind, preferred a sentimental idea of women and would be little help in that direction.

Monsieur Tournevau's pharmacy on the market square sparkled with mahogany and glass. Jars and phials displayed liquids of aquamarine, indigo, ruby red and dandelion yellow. Powders were neatly arranged. Patent medicines, mineral waters and blood purifiers, were lined up like so many soldiers, their banners announcing their regiments in copper plate or bold print. Scales stood on the gleaming counter. A door to the side displayed the word 'laboratory' in proud gold letters.

The man behind the counter was measuring out a powder from a large jar. He had a sheaf of straw-coloured hair and watery eyes. As she approached, he spilled some powder on the counter. He cleaned it away with an awkward hand.

'Monsieur Tournevau?' Marguerite asked.

The man nodded.

She introduced herself, then rushed on. 'I'm interested to learn when Yvette Branquart last had you fill a prescription given her by Dr. Labrousse.'

'Yvette,' the man repeated with a mooning expression that made her think he was a little slow.

'Yes, Yvette Branquart.'

The door on the side opened and an older man appeared. He was wearing a white coat. Spectacles sat at the edge of his nose. Hair bushed from the sides of his balding pate giving him the air of a brown owl.

'What is it, Jacques?' He was truculent until he took in Marguerite's presence. He offered a little bow. 'Is my son helping you adequately, Madame?'

She smiled, repeated her query.

'Let me check in the ledger. You are . . . ?'

'Madame de Landois. Her sister is working as my secretary and is worried about Yvette.'

'Of course. Of course.' He brought out a thick leather volume with embossed letters on its right. He flicked the pages with great authority.

'Yes, here we are.' He adjusted the spectacles on his nose. 'Yvette Branquart. All paid and up to date. Ah yes, even the two repeats of her prescription. Let's see, October 15th was the last.'

'October 15th?' Marguerite edged closer to the counter to stare at the ledger. That was well after Martine had last heard from her sister.

'Yes, that's right. Let me think. That's right. That's right. The girl did not come herself. Who was it now?' He tapped his fingers on the counter.

'It was Frère Michel,' his son called out. 'You remember. You shouted at me because I went after him, even though Madame Forestier was here. Too late. He'd vanished.' The young man was wild-eyed, almost in tears.

'Frère Michel, that's right,' the father repeated equably.

'And where can I find this man?' Marguerite asked.

The chemist raised his hands and shrugged. 'That Madame, I'm sorry to say, is not always simple to determine. He comes through Mont-oire now and again. He stays with various orders. He moves about.'

'I see.'

'Madame is disappointed. But never fear. He'll be back. Next time he comes in my son will question him. He is more than eager to locate the young woman. He lost his heart to her. I fear he also lost his head. It has done nothing for his efficiency. Nothing at all. Well, Jacques. Are those salts measured out yet?'

The son was blushing to the roots of his hair. Marguerite began to feel sorry for him.

'Please, if you see him, let us know. Let us know straight away. Send a message to La Rochambert. Or better still, alert him. Tell him we wish to speak to him.'

They had almost reached the door, when she turned back. 'What does he look like, this Frère Michel.'

The chemist shrugged. 'What they all look like, Madame. Until the Republic puts an end to these religious orders. Brown soutane, Scapular. Except he has more wrinkles. Not that he's a bad man, this one. Quite amenable, if a trifle over-superstitious. Kind to the poor. Good walker, too. Walks everywhere. If the church gave sainthoods for walking rather than silly young women's visions, Frère Michel would be a saint. Frère Michel of the highways and by-ways.'

Marguerite stared at the chemist who was evidently not of her husband's party. She wished she had come to him earlier. She had a terrible feeling that she had seen Frère Michel just a few hours ago. Seen him without knowing and missed the first significant lead they had come across in all these days.

_ 14 _

The snow had already begun to melt. Great sucking noises accompanied her boots' passage. She could feel the wet accumulating on the hem of her dress and petticoat and rising in uneven stains.

In the market square, with its fine array of buildings, the last of the vendors were packing away their wares. Marguerite hurried towards the river where she wanted to inquire quickly once more at the *blanchisserie* to see if any information had come to light. But the manager recognized her as soon as she came into the warmth of the steam-filled room. She ushered her out of her girls' line of vision behind a vast white sheet, shook her head and said none of her girls, as she had known, could help Madame. She was sorry.

Marguerite rushed back towards the carriage which was parked to the side of the market square. Stepping round a crate of potatoes, she all but collided with the Inspector. 'Ah Madame, I was just coming to find you. The local police have been most amenable to my persuasion. They will keep the cases open for a little while, but . . .'

Marguerite interrupted him. 'Well done, Inspector. In that case, you must go straight to Dr. Labrousse's surgery and ask him to show you the body. I'm hurrying back to find the travellers. There may be someone with them who can help us to locate Yvette and save us a great deal of time with our enquiries.'

'Not without me, Madame. I meant to say to you . . . I don't know if you noticed, but that degenerate, that P'tit Ours as you call him, was amongst them. He may be dangerous to you. Watching him, I was quite convinced that he could easily be the man who knocked you down in the woods when you found Danuta. And he certainly must have known her if he was at the funeral. He may have recognized you and wishes you harm. Which was one of the reasons he came to La Rochambert yesterday. I suspect he is not altogether in charge of his actions or his strength.'

She didn't contradict Durand, didn't say that it was unlikely that P'tit Ours had seen through her disguise as Antoine, even if her cap had fallen off, given that his sight wasn't all that good.

'But he can't do me any harm in broad daylight.'

'No, I insist, we must go together or not at all.' He lowered his voice. 'The police have also kindly supplied me with a list of names of all the girls in the one local brothel. Yvette Branquart doesn't figure amongst them, though of course these women can be adept at changing their identity. I shall make enquiries while you wait. As for Blois, it's as you thought. They have no lists here, so the journey is unavoidable.'

Marguerite stared at him. She hadn't considered that the Inspector would be unwilling for her to go into the establishments with him. She needed to go with him. She had an ulterior motive. She wanted to ask the women if any of their fellows had left because of pregnancy. It was unlikely, since most of the prostitutes used pessaries, but accidents happened. She thought she might be able to elicit information from them, certainly read their faces better than Durand would, for all his surface affability.

'Given the hour, Inspector, the weather and the length of the journey, I suggest we delay the trip to Blois until tomorrow. And I do need to be with you.'

He examined her, his astuteness all in his light eyes which were just on a level with hers. He coughed, his bushy brows rising, then in a soft voice as if he were breaching a line of privacy, murmured. 'I understand Madame, that you might want to enquire after the foundling at the same time, but I think I can be instrumental there as well. However, if you insist. And if Monsieur le Comte will not take it amiss, should he find out.'

'I insist, Inspector. You see, I think there is little likelihood that we will find Yvette in Montoire. I doubt that the girl could be so close without anyone at all recognizing her, particularly the chemists' son, who I now realize was in love with her. However, the mother of our little

Gabriel, may well not be very far. Ah look. There is Monsieur Villemardi. If he accompanies me to the fairground, you can see Dr. Labrousse first of all, and have a bite to eat at the Inn, Inspector.'

She waylaid his protests, 'No, no, I'm not at all hungry, really,' she insisted, thinking that Olivier might disapprove more of her being seen with the Inspector at the Inn, than of her going discreetly to an establishment no one they knew visited. 'Then we shall go together to our local temple of vice. I must hurry Inspector, if I'm to find my man.'

The horses moved slowly in the melting snow. The fields at the edge of the small town loomed as uncertain as a white-crested sea through the mist on her window. Only Villemardi's voice was clear. She half-listened as he talked excitedly about possible new work, flinging his long hair back every few moments as he did so, his face a swirl of expressions. But only when she heard him pronounce Martine's name, did she focus in and away from her own thoughts.

'I wonder if Madame would mind if she posed for me. I know Mlle Branquart is on edge, because of her sister, but it might relax her. And she would make a wonderful dancer. On one of my rare trips to the capital, I saw an exceptional figure by Manet. I can see mademoiselle in a similar pose. I could do something good.'

'You must put it to her, Monsieur Villemardi. She will have my permission. But tell me, there's something else I've been intending to ask you. You said Père Benoit's name at birth was Marchand. Is he by any chance related to the Marchands of Troo?'

'As far as I know, Madame, all the Marchands in the area of Tours are related, though I have never specifically had occasion to enquire of our good curé. I shall ask him for you, if you like. It will give me pleasure.'

The travellers were back at their encampment, their wagons and caravans stationed in a semi-circle. Some desultory fires burned, meager protection against the bitter cold. At a little distance, two children were rolling out the base of a snowman.

Marguerite looked round for Mr. Rama, since it was with him she had set up some kind of relationship. She was directed to his caravan, a sumptuously coloured affair, with a great cobra coiling round it. He appeared at his door almost before Villemardi had knocked.

'Ah my lady. Welcome. Welcome.'

'I have what I hope is good news for you, Mr. Rama. You have permission to stay here for the time being. The mayor understands your predicament and how sad it would be to have to leave so soon after the funeral of one of your colleagues.'

Mr. Rama hopped out to join them on the ground, as if he didn't think it appropriate to be standing so far above them.

'That is indeed, good news. We must tell Auguste and the others.'

'Before we do that, do you know, Mr. Rama, whether the brother who officiated at the funeral service was Frère Michel?'

'I believe so, Madame.'

'Is he still with you?'

'That I do not know. We shall see. We shall ask Auguste, who is his particular friend here.'

Auguste occupied the third wagon along. With its brash depiction of a strongman in a leopard skin leotard lifting a weight, it could hardly belong to anyone else. When Mr. Rama knocked and called out Auguste's name, the door opened on a spectacle which made Marguerite take a backward step in sudden fear.

Bald-headed and bare-chested, the strongman's arms and head gleamed with oil. Emblazoned on his torso was a dragon breathing fire. As he bent toward her, the beast leapt forward. It took her a deep breath and a long moment to realize that she was looking at an elaborate tattoo which moved with the man's muscles. Standing to his side was P'tit Ours, a bottle in his hand. He was staring at them, waving the bottle. He looked as if he might run straight out and over them.

The strongman growled, his features fierce with untrained as well as trained pugnacity.

Marguerite could only stare at his chest. Something Martine had reported that P'tit Ours had said on that first meeting in the grounds of Saint-Gilles came back to her. A winged creature. Fire.

So despite the difficulty they had in understanding him, the strange youth spoke sense.

'Madame has kindly come to tell us that the mayor has agreed to let us stay.'

'Bully for him,' Auguste slurred. His eyes didn't quite focus.

'You must thank, Madame.'

Auguste mumbled something and slammed the door.

Mr. Rama's face grew long with dejection. 'I am sorry, Madame. Auguste is very upset about Danuta. I thank you for him, Madame.'

'That's alright, Mr. Rama. And Frère Michel?'

Rama looked round dispiritedly. 'I believe he's already left, Madame. Ah, but look.' He pointed in the direction of the road. Walking away from the site, they saw a thin figure cloaked in brown.

'Run after him for me, Monsieur Villemardi. I need to speak to him.'

Villemardi raced away, while Marguerite said goodbye to Mr. Rama and told him to communicate with her if they met with any problems or if he had any news which might help them locate the person responsible for Danuta's murder.

The man's brow creased beneath the jewelled turban. 'So you think it was murder, Madame? Not an accident.'

'I believe so, Monsieur.'

She could feel his eyes still on her as she walked towards Villemardi and the Friar. Children were following her now, one of them holding out his hand in a begging gesture. Mr. Rama slapped him away and held them back.

The pair were waiting for her by the side of the road, and Marguerite urged them towards the carriage where they could sit in greater comfort. But the friar held back. He had a thin, hollowed-out face, as old as the caves of the region. But a calm sweetness hung over him. His soft voice commanded attention. Marguerite took an instant liking to him.

'Non, Madame. Thank you. I prefer to walk. But Madame wished a word with me?'

'Mon Frère,' she lowered her voice because the curious children had followed them, a small procession, hanging about as if waiting for a performance. 'I was told, by Monsieur Tournevau, the chemist, that you had picked up a prescription some time back for a young woman I am trying to trace.'

The friar looked at her. His eyes were watery. Only now did she notice that they were asymmetrical, one a deep sea blue, the other as pale as a cascading stream. She had a feeling of slight vertigo as she looked into them.

The man said nothing and after a moment, she understood that he wouldn't divulge anything unless she explained further.

'She is the sister of a young friend, my current secretary, Mlle Branquart. This sister is frantic with worry. She fears she may be dead. She has heard nothing from her for many months.'

'Too many months,' Villemardi echoed with a note of threat.

The friar looked only at her. He studied her, then gazed through the shadows cast by the straight line of bare trees and up at the darkening sky. Marguerite wondered whether he was entering into some form of communion or asking heavenly permission to address her.

At last he said, 'Please tell her sister, that as far as I know Mademoiselle is safe. There is no need to worry. But she cannot receive visitors. Not at the present time.'

'Why ever not?' Marguerite was more abrupt than she had intended. To have found this man and then not to find anything out was more than her patience could bear.

He gave her his slow, watery stare, as if he were plumbing some depths of soul and integrity she wasn't certain she possessed.

'Her sister cannot bear it,' Marguerite said. 'They were very close. Orphans. They have only each other.'

'Silence is imposed on me from above, Madame. There is nothing I can do for it. Her sister will have to wait. But let her wait in peace and pray.'

He nodded once, offered a gesture which she thought might be a benediction and started to trot down the road, his shoes, too large for his feet, squelching as he went.

Marguerite stared after him. The man seemed oblivious either to slush or cold. She wondered whether the silence imposed on him from above was the silence of the confessional or something quite different.

Montoire's single brothel occupied a small nondescript stone house in the less salubrious part of the town, beyond the Priory, right at the end of one of the old winding streets on the ruined fortress side of the river.

Town had almost become country here. There was a small stable to one side. The sole distinguishing feature of the place was a series of curving wrought iron railings at gate and windows. They gave the premises the air of an abandoned Spanish hacienda which had migrated to the wrong part of the world. It wanted only women in veiled coifs peeking out through half-opened shutters to complete the picture.

Emile Durand gave Marguerite a look somewhere between exasperation and admiration at her tenacity as he helped her out of the carriage and ushered her up the short path to the front stairs. He pulled the bell cord quickly.

A sturdy young man with a gash of a mouth displaying large, crooked teeth opened the door to them. He couldn't have been more than twenty and he was improbably attired in a frock coat that was too large for him and striped trousers. The locale had aspirations to a certain kind of gentility. But when the Inspector announced who he was, it was clear that these didn't extend to unknown members of the police force.

The door was closed in their faces only to reopen a moment later on a well-rounded woman in a low-cut satin gown and a bodice which propelled her bosom forward. The strong scent of her perfume and powder forced itself on the cold air. The shape of her mouth, despite the slash of lipstick, announced her relationship before she spoke it.

'My son said you wanted to see me, Monsieur.' The 'Madame' came as an afterthought. She barely looked at Marguerite.

'May we come in?' The Inspector gestured vaguely indicating that their conversation was not one for open air. He gave the woman a brief smile and she stepped back to usher them to a darkened hall, then on second thought into a small salon, hung everywhere with red drapery. The floor was a faded carpet of floral inspiration which boasted a few Turkish bolsters. In the dimness of scattered candlelight, they had only a passing glance at three women who sat in an alcove playing cards. Marguerite noticed that they were scantily clad, one in a dancer's tulle skirt and a flimsy bodice, the other in a shift ruched up to her knees. One was a redhead, one dark, the smallest blonde. All three seemed too old to be Yvette. Before she could ascertain any more, the curtain on the alcove was released by their Madame, and they disappeared behind red velvet that had imbibed years of tobacco smoke.

'I haven't much time,' the Madame said. 'We're busy in the cold weather.' She stared at them suspiciously.

'This won't take long. We're looking for a young woman by the name of Yvette Branquart, blonde, blue-eyed, slight . . . she might of course be using a different name.'

'No one here like that. All my girls are legal. Clean. They go for regular examination. What's she done?'

'She's come into some money, Madame,' Marguerite intervened. 'She would be grateful to you for locating her.'

From beneath mascara-thickened lashes, the woman's small brown eyes suddenly took on a gleam of greed. Marguerite felt their examination, now, as they moved over her, taking in her worth, noting the fur on her coat, the sweep and the cut of it, the discrete but well-made matching hat, the soft gloves.

'She could have come to you at any time since the summer. Perhaps she didn't stay long.'

Calculation played over the woman's face. She didn't look at the Inspector any more. 'There was a girl who worked here briefly, but she went . . . when was it, September. Not that name, of course. But it's possible . . . I'll just check with the girls. Is there a reward?'

'Yes, Madame.' Marguerite nodded. She felt a sudden rush of hope for Martine.

The woman was about to disappear behind the curtain when the Inspector pulled it back for her with a graciousness which masked his real intent. The three prostitutes seemed not at all troubled at their presence and as soon as the Madame put the question to them, they started to chat away, making an inventory of the women who occasionally came to swell their numbers in busier seasons.

'Remember, when I was sick over the summer, there was that cousin of Marielle's who came in?'

'Dark as coal. No way she was a blonde. And thirty, at least.'

'No, no, not that one. The one old Monsieur Plon took a shine to. Tubercular she was. On her last.'

'Oh ya. What was her name?'

'Louise.'

Marguerite drew in her breath and held it.

'Louise Vanès.'

So it wasn't the maid that had left La Rochambert.

'Don't know where she went. Probably dead by now. So cold.' The redhead drew a shawl over her shoulders.

'I wonder,' Marguerite intervened, remembering something else. 'have you had any African women here or from the Caribbean colonies.'

'Certainly not.' The Madame was adamant.

'Don't know why you say it like that.' One of the women giggled. 'There's one or two of our regulars who'd like a little variety. Keep them from going all the way to Blois. Fargeau told me he went there just for that. The spice of life, he said.'

'And tell me, ladies, have any amongst you or who have come through had the misfortune of conceiving.' The Inspector put it bluntly before Marguerite had a chance.

A hush fell over the room. Two of the women crossed themselves quickly. The other shuddered and seemed about to tip off her stool.

'What kind of question is that, Monsieur? Really. I told you this is a clean establishment.'

'Accidents happen,' Marguerite murmured. She had a sense that the blonde might recently have had an abortion. Was it possible in a town as small as Montoire, she wondered.

'Upsetting my girls, like that. If anyone was pregnant it was that Louise girl. Pale as sin. And with a mouth on her to take on the President.'

So it might just be La Rochambert's Louise after all. They would have to find the girl. If she had come to Montoire after her post in Château, it was likely that she would stay in the vicinity.

The Madame's eyes darted towards the door where Marguerite saw her son had come in. He had another woman in tow. A girl. She looked barely old enough to be out of school. She stared at them in terror.

The Madame made a quick calculation. 'If you leave me your card, I shall let you know if this Yvette you're looking for comes to someone's mind.'

'The thing to do, Madame, is to contact Constable Rosier at the Prefecture. He'll know where to get hold of us.'

'But Madame said . . .'

The muted clang of the bell interrupted them.

The Inspector gave Marguerite a quick look and turned to the brothel owner.

'Madame, it would be best if your client is shown to a different room while we take our leave. If you can help us to Yvette Branquart, have no fear about your reward.'

Having left his young charge in a corner chair, Madame's son was already at the door.

'Take him upstairs a moment, Hebert.'

Marguerite lowered the fishnet veil she had worn specifically for this eventuality and turned up the collar of her coat. Walls in small towns had eyes. Once more she rued the gold crest on the carriage door, which advertised its owners to all and sundry.

_ 15 _

Despite Durand's insistence that they had done enough for one day, Marguerite wanted to use the rest of the light. Olivier would inevitably make it difficult for her to go out tomorrow. The day of his grand party approached and she would be needed.

'It's only a small detour, Inspector. And since you've just seen the cadaver, it will be fresh in your mind. To take in the painting straight away can only be a plus in terms of identification.'

Reluctantly, since he had a habit of being gallant and was thinking of her state of inevitable feminine fatigue, Durand agreed.

Marguerite had an ulterior motive for going to Troo. She didn't speak it, since she sensed the Inspector wouldn't approve her chasing after child's play. But like some terrier worrying a bone, a part of her had been gnawing away at the strange, scrappy note with its cry for help that had blown into the orangerie. Martine had shuddered over it, saying it made her think of Yvette, not of some children's game. But what if the note were both? What if it had been brought by a child, or even P'tit Ours, as he stood there peering in at them from the window, but was a genuine plea for help from some poor, incarcerated being?

With his insistence on facts, only facts, Durand would consider all this fanciful. And after they had shared their impressions of the brothel and what Frère Michel might have meant by his comments, they fell into a companionable silence for the remainder of the journey and concentrated on their own thoughts.

Marguerite's certainty that the dead man had some link to the Tellier household made her more worried than ever about Martine's sister. Could the girl be being kept hostage somewhere?

Servants were so often privy to secret knowledge it would have been better not to have overheard. Had Yvette gleaned or discovered something that incriminated her masters? Was she as a result a prisoner held in one of their properties? Is that what the friar had meant when he said that the girl was alive, but couldn't be reached now? Could Frère Michel's vow of silence really be a promise he had made to the Telliers in exchange for their keeping the girl alive, rather than dumping her, too, on some lonely stretch of track?

Questions. All she had were questions. Marguerite wrapped her coat more firmly round her and rubbed the mist from her window. Above its wall, the Tellier house rose solid and square in the near distance. Again she had an intense sense of Martine's delicate look-alike sister being pummeled and buffeted by her coarse masters. A fine-boned bird amidst predators who were holding her in a cage.

There was another possible prisoner in the vicinity. Marguerite thought of the handsome, dark woman she had seen in the adjacent garden, the woman the children called the witch. P'tit Ours had leapt down to her all smiles and offerings. But Madame Tellier had bristled and flared, surprised by her presence. Whether it was because she had something against her race or because she recognized her or both was unclear.

On a whim, Marguerite pushed the little flap on the window separating them from Georges and asked him to take them round to the Tellier's from the other direction. They would stop, if only for a moment. Amandine, P'tit Ours had called her. Amandine, who had made what could well have been a supplicant's gesture towards Marguerite.

The visible windows of the house were shuttered. The premises looked desolate. No lights flickered. Could the witch have moved or been moved away? The high, heavy wall now sported a snow-covered ledge where a robin perched, its breast blood red against the white.

She asked Georges to ring the bell at the gate. Quickly she explained to Durand, who nodded affably. Again she had the impression the Chief Inspector was finding his country escapade something of a relief after the pressures of Paris where ministers breathed down his stiffly-collared neck with too much regularity. Perhaps the tragic circumstances that had thrown the dapper little man into her salon and then kept him in the world of the

Faubourg and the Assemblée because of his ruthless honesty, had removed him from work he ultimately preferred.

She was besieged for a moment by waves of sadness. Sometimes, it was hard to remember that Olympe was really gone, Olympe and her sister, and Mlle Norton and her brother, Rafael—though happily he was only on another continent.

From somewhere she heard the howl of a dog. It seemed to be coming closer and fiercer, but the thick wooden doors in front of which Georges stood didn't budge. And there was still no glimmer of light from the windows. If the so-called witch Amandine was being kept prisoner here, she was no longer even able to come to the windows.

There had been a change, too, at the Tellier house. It was not Madame Molineuf who opened the door to them, but a dour, stolid man, with a square face and a flattened nose that had been visibly broken in several places. He was improbably decked out in a uniform of a dove grey far subtler than his voice.

'Madame and Monsieur are away,' he grunted at the Inspector's query.

'And Monsieur Marchand? Is he available?' Marguerite intervened.

'Monsieur has gone home.'

'And where is that exactly?'

A hefty young, beribboned woman with a craven look in her eye peered out from the depths of the hall.

'Ah, Mlle Tellier.' Marguerite guessed. 'How kind of you to come down. I'd been hoping to meet you for some time.'

The ungainly girl stepped forward with a mixture of curiosity and fear.

'Yes, yes, I'm the Comtesse de Landois. I wanted to see a member of your family. Perhaps your grandfather, since your parents are away. May we come in?'

She pushed past the footman, Durand just behind her. The girl was standing not too far from the pictures Marguerite wanted Durand to inspect, but no sooner had she stepped inside than she noticed that they had been moved. Two dusty rectangles lined the wall in their place. Madame Molineuf must have talked to her mistress straight after seeing Dr. Labrousse.

Marguerite hid her disappointment. 'Where might I find your grand-father, Mademoiselle? I have never visited him at home.'

'His house is just past the orchard, on the next hill. But I don't know if you'll find him there,' the girl said in the small, plaintive voice of some-one whom life regularly disappointed. 'You can't miss it, though. There's a new porch been built. With columns. Maman designed it for him. As a birthday present.'

'What a nice idea,' Durand murmured. 'Madame la Comtesse told me you also possessed some fine family portraits.'

The girl flushed and picked nervously at a curl which was twisted in exactly the same fashion as her mother's. But her white blouse was mod-est, indeed severe. It was ruched over her capacious bosom and high at the neck like some cleric's collar. The girl looked behind her to where the portraits had hung.

'Maman decided to have them cleaned. All of them. She said they had grown dark with the years. Too dark.'

'How sad that I shall miss them then! Perhaps another time. Do you know who painted them? Or perhaps there were various artists?'

'I think they were done while grandpère lived on the islands. But you can ask him when you see him.'

'And I hope we shall see you. At la Rochambert. On the 28th. For the party. You shall meet Yvette Branquart's sister there. She's my secretary.'

Flecked brown eyes grew round in consternation.

'You don't perhaps know where Yvette herself might be found, Made-moiselle?' The Inspector asked.

'Maman says she should be two metres under,' the girl blurted out. 'She was a terrible maid. Disobedient, disrespectful. Disreputable!'

The voice that emerged was an uncanny echo of Madame Tellier's. Marguerite found herself veering round to look for the absent ventriloquist, even though she knew the words had come from the girl in front of her.

'It must be difficult getting good staff around here,' the Inspector offered like a pacifying sweet.

'Very difficult, monsieur,' the girl said still in her mother's voice. She glanced in fear towards the footman who was standing by the door. 'But sometimes we're lucky.'

'Is Madame Molineuf away with your mother, then?' Marguerite asked.

'Non Madame, she's not well. She's resting. She had something of an accident. On the stairs.' All this was still spoken in the parroting voice which made Marguerite's spine crawl.

The Inspector lit his pipe as soon as they were out the door and puffed at it excitedly.

'The fact that the pictures were moved is an indication that someone in the family definitely knows something. I'll wager it's the old reprobate you described to me.'

'I hope it's that easy, Inspector,' Marguerite murmured, remembering old Napoleon Marchand's mad, crafty eyes. 'I wish we had a better case tying the dead man to him than just the resemblance in a painting we no longer have to hand. I imagine Madame is shrewd enough to have the whole thing repainted rather than simply cleaned. Then, too, Madame Molineuf swore to the doctor that the man had never been to the house.'

'There are other houses.'

A fat round moon rose sat lazily above what they determined must be the home of Napoleon Grandcourt Marchand. It was at the base an old stone farmers' house, typical of the region. A rounded bread chimney arched out at one of its sides. But the house had grown wings and accretions and floors, as well as a large U of a drive edged by beech trees, their dry reddened leaves still clinging to branches. Smoke drifted out of a chimney, indicating a presence. Marguerite found herself shivering in anticipation of a meeting with the old drunken devil.

'You wait here, Madame. I'll go and present myself, sniff around and insist that Marchand come in to Montoire tomorrow to identify the body. I'll just say that someone in the area recognized the man as a relative of his.'

'But I'd also like a better sense from him of Yvette, Inspector. He might be holding the girl somewhere. I swear he's capable of it. Say she overheard something she shouldn't have. Something incriminating. Perhaps involving the scheme which would result in the cadaver now lying in the cold outside Dr. Labrousse's consulting room.'

The Inspector's features took on a sharper focus. The air of benign self-satisfaction, which served falsely to assuage the fears of those he interrogated, was replaced by a fox's cunning. 'That's very good, Madame. Very good. It gives us motive. Motive for Yvette's Branquart's silence as well as her disappearance. Yes, she overheard something.'

Marguerite smiled at him. 'Our servants always know far more about us than we know ourselves, Inspector. It can be a dangerous life.'

He nodded at her. 'Let's hope in Yvette's case, it hasn't proved fatally so.'

He trotted up the flank of semi-circular stairs and made his way to the columned porch Madame Tellier's daughter had alerted them to. They gave the house an air of classical grandiosity. Madame Tellier evidently wanted her father's stature in the world improved. Marguerite couldn't imagine him caring. He was not, in her brief experience of him, a man who gave a *sous* for social niceties. Quite the contrary. He seemed to take a pleasure in confounding all expectations.

The door had yielded to the Inspector's insistent knocking. In the lamplight, a thin, twisted figure of a man appeared. He raised his bent head to stare at Durand.

With a start, Marguerite recognized him. It was the ancient, emaciated manservant who had opened the gate to yell at the stone-throwing children when she had first tried to find the Tellier house with Martine. Hercule. That was his name. Hercule who had ordered her rudely away. If he was here now, then the witch Amandine was probably here too. And both of them had something to do with Napoleon Marchand, even though his daughter had claimed she knew nothing of Amandine.

Marguerite found herself examining all the upper story windows of the house, but there was no light or movement visible.

She opened the door of the carriage and was about to alight, when she heard the ancient servant growl, 'I told you. Police or no police, there's no one at home. No one. Now skedaddle. Scoot.' He slammed the door in the Inspector's face.

Marguerite watched Durand all but trip on an ornate box that stood to the side of the door. She gazed at its peculiar shape, like a coffin but too small. It was a finely carved wood with exotic whorls and shapes.

'Not very polite in the countryside, are we?' Durand muttered as he took up his place beside her.

'What did he say?'

'Whatever he said, he was lying.' He closed the carriage door with a clatter, before Georges could get to it. 'There was certainly somebody else in there. Unless that desiccated old man has taken up smoking fine cigars, not to mention something more potent.'

'And that desiccated old man, I'll wager, Inspector, is also guarding a woman called Amandine, a woman who for some reason they want none of us to see or have access to.'

With a sudden wave of despair, Marguerite sat back in her seat and looked out at the bulbous outcropping of the house against the hill. 'Let's hope we get to her and to Yvette in time. If it's not already too late.'

PART THREE

SUBTERRANEAN

_ 16 _

Carriages gleamed in the moonlight and lined the drive as far as the eye could see. The guests had started to arrive from mid-afternoon and had come from far and wide: Blois and Vendome and Château and La Chatre and even a small contingent from Tours. With a deep bow, Olivier greeted the arrivals as they entered the hall. Heels clicked over marble and shining parquet, grew muted on Aubusson rugs. Furs were carried away by a flurry of maids, fluted glasses proffered.

Men's chests sprouted decorations pinned on the dark grain of fine suits and uniforms. Women dazzled with an array of jewels on perfumed skin and hair or waxed secret behind a modesty of lace. Slim-fitting skirts rustled with ample trains of printed meteor silks, pliable satins, glistening taffetas and frothy aeoliennes. Bare shoulders glistened above the forward thrust of this season's bosoms or the plateaux of a provincial yesteryear. Voices rose and fell and tinkled into laughter.

If the mirrors and chandeliers sparkled rather more than the wit, Marguerite was happy enough to see her childhood home brimming in this unaccustomed way. Old family friends had honoured them with a visit: the Marquis de Conflans, whose monocle kept falling from his eye as it had always done when he took her hand between his two gnarled ones; the Countess de Cambremer whose red sequined turban grew out of her highly rouged cheekbones and who still loved to inject English phrases into her speech, so that Marguerite was greeted as 'darling,' her dress proclaimed, 'divine,' the champagne, 'excellent,' the canapés 'just super'.

General Narbon of the great hooked nose had come, accompanied by his wife who had so shrunk with the years that she appeared to be a diminutive child, until she raised a haggard powdered face at you. There was also Monsieur Mirtout, a number of priests, two resplendent bishops, at least two mayors, not to mention landowners, lawyers, several judges, captains of local industry, a handful of merchants, doctors, an assortment of wives of varying degrees of beauty and capability, and even the editor of *Le Journal de Blois*—in short, as Olivier had emphasized to her, a broad and democratic selection of the neighbouring community, all of whose votes he would need in the next election and would win with his good wife's help.

Madame Tellier had accepted the invitation. Marguerite was pleased. She wanted to observe the woman, who looked rather grand tonight in a myrtle-green satin dress and an encrustation of rings which would have done an old Spanish dowager empress proud. Madame had brought her daughters. There was Laure, who turned out to be a great pudding of a girl with feet the size of paddles and an expression of disdain which did nothing for her beauty. There was also the younger Hortense, whom Marguerite and the Inspector had already met. Madame was intent on showing the girls off to any available men and Marguerite promised herself she would line some up.

Docteur Labrousse was there, too, his black beard freshly trimmed. He had come with the local investigative magistrate she had insisted they invite. Both had survived Olivier's inevitably frosty reception, though he had forced the semblance of a campaigner's smile on his face. She in turn had been particularly kind to both.

From her welcoming position near the doors of the large drawing room, Marguerite now looked out for Durand. Many of the men had gathered to play billiards before dinner, but the Inspector was here, dutifully engaging Docteur Labrousse and Madame Tellier.

'I'm told you have relations in the Caribbean islands, Madame.' Durand was saying. 'I confess I have long wanted to go there.'

'Really, Inspector? For myself I have never had the least interest in that direction. It is the men in my family who are the voyagers.'

'As is only appropriate Madame. We travel so we can come back and regale our wives with tales. Like Odysseus.'

Madame Tellier looked at him with a blank expression. 'Spices. That's what my grandfather came back with. From Martinique. And then chocolate. My father when he was young apprenticed with the Grocers Guild.'

'You never told me,' the plump Laure reprimanded.

'The Guild controlled a highly lucrative colonial traffic, Mademoiselle.'

'So you know about them, Monsieur?'

'In Paris, they know everything,' Docteur Labrousse said, a note of longing in his voice.

The Inspector's chest took on even more barrel-like proportions. 'I should very much like to hear your husband's and your father's stories, Madame.'

'I would welcome you to our house, Monsieur. But unfortunately they are both in Tours.'

'Perhaps, then, when I make my visit to the city. I may do so while I am in the region.'

Marguerite didn't hear Madame Tellier's reply in the wake of a new group of arrivals. She smiled to herself as much as to her guests. With that economy of movement and gesture which never ceased to surprise her, Durand would quietly make the rounds of the party finding out what people knew about the suspicious deaths and pregnancies without issue in the region.

It was as they were going in to dinner that she glimpsed Martine rushing from the room. There were tears in the girl's eyes, a nervous quiver in the wrist which held up her dress as she made for the stairs. The dress was a soft velour of palest celandine, one of her own which had been adjusted for the girl for the evening. With her aureole of pale hair, she looked like a flower rising from a swaying stalk.

Marguerite excused herself and followed after her. She did so with an unhurried tread and a face which gave away none of her concerns. What could have happened to upset the girl? Had she seen P'tit Ours peering through a window? Had someone insulted her? Not Olivier, she hoped. Martine had been filled with youthful delight at the prospect of the party. She had also been excited by the notion that amidst all the gathered guests, she might find someone who had information about her sister. And now, this rushing away in the midst of things . . . It made no sense.

Martine had been so much calmer these last days, so much more measured in her responses. Marguerite could swear she had even filled out a little. Best of all, she was beginning to learn to trust her. It was Marguerite's own weakened and slightly tremulous state after her fall in the woods that had brought them closer.

Marguerite caught up with the girl in the corridor. The tears were streaming down her face. It was clear she could no longer see where she was heading.

'What is it Martine? What's happened?'

The girl wrung the hankie in her hands, sobbed convulsively, shook her head.

Marguerite murmured, calmed, asked again. She couldn't stay away too long or Olivier would notice.

'Please Martine. Tell me. And I'll see what I can do.'

'There's nothing to be done, Madame. Nothing. It's the priest. He told me I was damned. Damned for all eternity. Ungrateful.' She sobbed again.

'How dare he! Which priest? Père Benoit?'

'No, no. The small one. With the squinty eyes.'

That surprised her. 'Do you know him?'

She shook her head, tried to catch her breath. 'He said I was a wretch. After all he had done. The treachery. I was damned. Doomed. I would burn in hell.'

The tears were pouring down her face again.

'But Martine, if the man doesn't know you. Then he must simply be wrong. Wrong.'

'He probably thinks I'm my sister. So she's the one. It's so dreadful. She . . .'

Marguerite took her to her room, had her sit down. 'Now listen Martine, I can't stay here with you. You rest. Wash your face. And stop thinking about him. I'm going to have a word with the silly man. Perhaps this is a boon. A key to where your sister is.'

The girl stared at her with widening eyes.

'Now go on.'

As she moved back into the hubbub of the party, she reflected that they could do with a new lead. Durand had spent a day in Blois getting lists of registered prostitutes, visiting a few brothels, but it had led nowhere, certainly not to Yvette or to a woman mourning her lost babe. Nor had he been able to locate the vanished maid Villemardi had named as Louise Bertin.

Olivier had kept her so busy that she hadn't been able to go with the Inspector. It was clear from his constraint and his barely veiled insults that someone had informed him of her activities in Montoire. She hadn't even been able to accompany Durand on a visit to Napoleon Marchand, though that too had not led very far, since the man still hadn't been there, or hadn't permitted entry. A visit from the Montoire constabulary, had led no further. After this evening, the two of them would have to make a concerted effort, if Paris duties were not to rob her of the Inspector before they had made any headway.

Marguerite noticed Olivier looking down his aristocratic nose at Durand. He had the air of a sultan exchanging words with a negligible emissary from some unknown province where the smell of dung was omnipresent. She wondered whether she should go and protect the Inspector from her husband's arrogance. She approached, saw Durand shuffling his feet, then in the humblest of voices complimenting her husband on his great charity in adopting a stray child. A second later, the Inspector was extricating the exact details of the story from Olivier. She smiled to herself and left the men to it. The dinner table needed her attention more.

It was a grand affair. In the mirrored expanse of the great hall, the tables stretched in two ranks. A retinue of servants had been brought in to pour the wines and serve the truffled pâtés and bisque and game, the carrot purées and the diced potatoes, the tarts and fruit elaborately heaped on giant silver platters. Meanwhile, on the frescoed ceiling, nymphs and cupids danced their revels amidst racing clouds.

Durand, Marguerite noted, was positioned behind a gold-leafed column, watching and listening with all the alertness of a terrier on the hunt.

Olivier had placed her at the end of a table between the Marquis de Conflans and the General. She kept the conversation light. She had been warned.

There were to be no confrontations with the good people of the region. Her views were entirely a private matter. When she had asked Olivier what subjects he thought appropriate for the wife of a candidate, who as yet had no children of her own and thus could have no views about education, religious or secular, he had scowled and told her that she could talk about art, about changes to the château.

'And gossip?' she had intervened.

'As long as it's in good taste.'

Marguerite kept her gossip in good taste, just as she had changed her dress at the last moment at Olivier's request, to one which exposed rather less bosom and shoulder. Jeanne had rushed her into his chosen wine-red, long-sleeved gown of shimmering brocaded silk and a sparkling ruby necklace. The rich colour brought a glow to the tired pallor of her face, while the jewels accentuated the lights in her hair, looped and twisted and topped by a single feather by her skilful maid.

'Appropriately regal,' Olivier had offered with a tight little smile. 'Your bohemian aspect is best saved for Paris.'

Now, she shivered the scene away. She asked the Marquis and the General about the people round the table whom she didn't know. She learned from the Marquis, who had come to conversation in times less puritan than the ones Olivier was now trying to impose, that the Bishop had once been known for his great flair with the ladies, that it was even rumoured that a certain Mother Superior, once upon a time the broken-hearted Mlle de la Vaudreuil, had had a soft spot for him.

Her eyes moved along the table and she noticed that Père Benoit was preening himself before that very Bishop. And there was Paul Villemardi glowering in good artistic style at a dowager, before he hid a yawn in his hand. Laure Tellier had somehow contrived to sit next to him instead of her sister. Inspector Durand, meanwhile, was listening intently to the investigating magistrate she had placed beside him, a small spectacled man with rat-like features that quivered as he spoke.

Olivier was holding forth at his end of the table. His tones reached her, though the words were lost. There were nods of satisfaction from listeners, which could only mean he was mouthing appropriate matter. A wicked thought flashed across her mind as she noticed the editor of the *Blois Journal* making mental notes, but she imagined the paper didn't resort to scandal-mongering in the manner of the Parisian press. Not that she approved of the latter.

There were probably only a handful of politicians in all France who could stand up to having their private lives examined. What rankled was public proclamations altogether antithetical to what they lived. She had little doubt that she would have felt differently about Olivier's candidacy, had he espoused a set of political ideas more closely aligned to his own experience.

The curé's eyes were on her. Had the insidious man read her mind? She smiled at him in vague acknowledgement. Her attention roved again round the tables. With the invisible care of a practiced hostess, she noted with no ostensible sign the boredom or vivacity on a face, a flirtatious smile, a secret shudder, the lay of a plate or the lack of a salt shaker, the requisite movements of servants.

The General was addressing her and she gave him her eyes. Not once had he mentioned the Dreyfus Case and she was grateful to him for that. But now he wanted to know whether she was as troubled as he was by the continuing encampment of the gypsies on the outskirts of Montoire. Since they had arrived, there had been more crimes in the area than he could ever remember.

'Did you know the dancer who died, then, mon Général? Did you ever see her perform?'

The old man touched one of his medals with a bony hand. 'From a distance. I wouldn't be surprised if someone murdered her just for showing all that nudity.'

'But surely flesh comes to us from God,' Marguerite murmured.

'What was that, my dear?' the Marquis' thin lips were shaped into a brazen grin.

The General hadn't taken in her aside. 'Why just the other day, I caught two of my maids at the camp making eyes at that snake charmer. A Jew from the look of him, hiding inside a turban.'

Marguerite choked on her wine.

'Your maids came to no harm, I trust. His snake has vanished I'm told.'

'I wouldn't be surprised if we found it with its fangs buried inside the mayor's throat. That's the thanks we'll get for letting them stay for so long.'

Marguerite made a plea for charity, which must have been too vocal since the old priest who had so upset Martine now looked in her direction. She was relieved when Olivier stood, marking an end to this part of the evening. He took her arm to lead her to the drawing room where coffee and chocolates, brandy and liqueurs were waiting. He was smiling, at his most gracious and for a moment Marguerite was lulled into thinking that she had stepped into an altogether ordinary marriage with a man like any other. It was only the way in which he forcibly propelled her towards the ancient priest that reminded her otherwise.

The man had colourless eyes beneath spectacles which kept sliding down a diminutive nose.

'I wanted to greet you properly, Madame. I knew your parents. Truly an exceptional pair. I married them.' He gave her a thin-lipped smile

'Ah mon Père, what a pleasure to meet you, to welcome you here. Again, I imagine.'

'Yes. But after a great many years. You see, the war took me away and when I came back it was to another parish and I had no occasion to visit.'

'Well, you are most welcome now, Father. Most welcome.'

'Your mother was a pious woman, Madame. Were you ever told that she had once been drawn to the religious life? As a girl . . .'

'No, mon Père, I didn't know.'

'No, and your father had quite other ideas, of course.'

'Yes.' She took in his words, wondered how she might now bring up the subject of Martine, when Père Benoit was suddenly prominent at their side. 'You must come and visit the château chapel, mon père. And our church in the village. It has been recently restored.'

'Indeed, thank you, thank you. I'm feeling a little tired now.'

Olivier ushered the man towards a chair, leaving Marguerite with the younger priest.

'Père François is a saintly man, Madame. One of the most devout in the region. But you, too, must make a visit to the chapel, Madame. I had been hoping you would already have done so.

'So my husband has informed me.' Marguerite kept her voice gracious.

But the curé seemed to intuit her dislike. He gave her a hard-edged look which contained a barely-veiled contempt. 'I have done a great deal for your husband, Madame. Has he told you that as well? Can you not see it? His little eccentricities are quite gone. Family life restored. I would have thought it could only be to your benefit.'

Marguerite's shock could not have registered on her face, for he stepped closer. She had the impression the pompous young man fully intended to reveal the extent of her husband's eccentricities here and now given half the chance.

'Oh, I am certain it is, Monsieur, quite certain everything you do is to my benefit. You'll excuse me.'

She turned away, a flush in her cheek. Her benefit, indeed. Had Olivier perhaps told him that the foundling was a boon to their marriage? Yes, she could almost hear him saying it. But how objectionable that this stranger should think he had any right whatsoever to knowledge of their intimate life. All at once, the perfidy of confession struck her. Just exactly how much did the young priest know about her husband?'

She thought of Martine and her dismay at the old priest's words. It wasn't dissimilar in a way. Men, dressed as God's minions, infringing private boundaries by right. The prurience of the righteous.

The smile on her face stiff, Marguerite looked round for Martine. The girl was nowhere to be seen. Nor was Durand now. She wanted him near. Amidst this frenzy of strangers, the Inspector emerged as her most trusted friend. Odd how home could feel like the most alien place of all.

She exchanged pleasantries with the guests at hand and gradually wound her way towards the music room. The quintet which was to provide the evening's entertainment was tuning its instruments. She waited for the music to begin, then fled upstairs in need of a brief respite. On a whim, she stopped in the babe's room and startled a dozing Celeste. The mite, too, was asleep, his face basking in a fullness which could only mean peaceful dreams. As she looked at him, he raised a tiny hand and made a random, floating gesture. Almost a wave. Or a benediction. The benediction of an innocent.

Still feeling peculiar, Marguerite slipped into the library. Her father's ranked books would calm her, bring her back to herself. But there was already someone in the room, someone who had lit a lamp and was half reclining in a chair and staring up at a folio-sized sheet of paper.

'I'm sorry. Sorry.' Paul Villemardi leapt to his feet and bowed deeply as he recognized her. 'I didn't mean . . . I was only . . . I . . . Too many people bore me.' He gave her his abrupt laugh. 'Perhaps you feel the same?'

'What are you looking at?'

'This? From Olivier's collection. Have you not seen it?' He passed an ink drawing towards her. It was crowded with people gathered around a tomb in what was either a classical cemetery or a church. Only slowly did she realize that the people's expressions and postures were out of the ordinary. They looked not unlike the hysterics she had seen when attending Charcot's lectures at the Salpetrière. But the people here were pressing against the tomb of a saint, it seemed. The infirm waved crutches in the air, the exalted thrust their arms and eyes towards heaven, others lay on the ground in positions of supplication or ecstasy. A priest-like figure was tending to a convulsive woman. A baby was being stretched towards the tomb. Here and there, boy vendors, offered the crowd portraits of saints.

'It's eighteenth century,' Paul Villemardi offered.

'An extraordinary scene.'

'Like Lourdes today. The crowds for Bernadette grow larger with each passing year. Our lady of Lourdes heals. Just go to Bernadette's grotto and all will be well. I thought I might have a look myself. For inspiration you understand.'

She nodded, unsure whether he was being serious or irreverent, or perhaps both simultaneously.

He took the picture from her and laid it carefully back in a large open drawer.

'Do you have other favourites?' Marguerite asked, not wanting him to know that she had never seen the pictures in the collection.

He pulled open an upper drawer and took out an etching, another holy scene with a struggling woman, her head thrust back so that it looked as if it might snap off.

'Olivier is interested in exorcism.'

'Yes.' Marguerite said, keeping her voice even. She didn't give anything away, but she was shocked by this turn in Oivier's interests. She hadn't suspected, when he had shown her Père Benoit's present to him, that there was this host of images here, one more excessive than the next. Flagrant beatings, convulsions, devils to be driven away. Madness.

When she returned to the music room in time for the last plaintive moans of the violins, it was with a sense of profound exhaustion. Olivier had always presented a troubling mystery. Now she felt more than ever his prey, as if vampire-like, he would sap her remaining spirit, in order himself to remain whole.

He was leaning against the wall listening to the musicians, his eyes slightly narrowed, his arms crossed over his chest. A prepossessing man. She saw him with the gaze of Paul Villemardi, who had made him into a Medici—cold, regal, authoritative. He had that look about him now. Power.

It took a moment for her to realize that all of it was being directed at the young pianist, whose body swayed in vigorous accompaniment to the chords he was beating out. When the young man stood to take his bow, his fine mop of hair swinging towards the ground to reveal a delicate neck, a predatory expression sharpened Olivier's features. She wondered whether anyone else could see it. It was as if her husband had been transformed into a force whose unique direction was the curve of the young musician's torso, the play of his limbs as he moved away from the piano.

Olivier followed the musician, aware of nothing, no one, not even her absence and return, which, had he noted it, would have irritated. The entire world had been curled into that young man. She watched transfixed, watched him reach the far door of the room in the wake of the quintet, watched his expression which now had something maidenly about it, watched him disappear behind the door.

A moment later, when she had already moved into action and was introducing Durand to the old Comtesse de Cambremer and asking Docteur Labrousse whether he had enjoyed the Brahms, she was astonished to see Père Benoit opening the far door and following in Olivier's tracks. The priest's face wore a scowl.

She didn't see either of them for the rest of the evening, not even after the last guests had left or been safely tucked up in their rooms; not even after she had had a final word with Madame Solange and the staff and thanked them for their hard work.

Only much later when little Jeanne was helping her off with her gown and brushing out her hair, was there a knock at her door. It opened before she could speak to reveal Olivier. His features were drawn, his eyes bleary, but he was holding himself very erect.

'You'll leave us,' he gestured to Jeanne, who raced from the room in fear. He closed the door behind her and turned the key in the lock.

Marguerite stayed at her dressing table. She picked up the brush Jeanne had put down. In the mirror, she saw Olivier moving towards her. He stopped just behind her and ran a fingernail along her shoulder where the nightgown left it bare.

'You're a beautiful woman, Marguerite. Despite the passage of years.'

'There's no need for this, Olivier. No need for pretense now.'

'Pretense. I don't know what you mean. A man coming to visit his wife after a successful soirée strikes me as something altogether ordinary.'

'Yes, ordinary. Far too banal for us, Olivier.'

She rose and reached for her dressing gown. He stopped her hand.

'Let me look at you.' He raked his fingers along her back from her shoulders to her thigh—as if she were an instrument whose sound he hated, but he had none the less learned to tune.

She moved away from him. A prickle of dread had started up in her spine. He couldn't. Not now. Not after all these years. It was unthinkable.

'Yes, Madame de Landois. Marguerite de Landois, A great beauty they tell me. Coveted by all the young bucks in Paris. They think me a lucky man.'

'Go to bed Olivier. You've had too much to drink.'

'Not at all. How much is too much?' His laugh was a scoff. 'You know why I've come Marguerite. I've come to thank you. Thank you for joining me in such a splendid evening. Thank you in the way husbands thank their wives.'

He was suddenly too close to her, pushing her down on the bed. He took off his jacket, turned down the light, all with those swift mechanical gestures which did nothing to mask his dislike—of her, of himself, of the couple they formed.

'Go away, Olivier. I want none of this. I need no thanks.'

'No thanks at all Marguerite? None at all?' He took hold of her hair and with a painful twist pulled her head down on the duvet. She pummeled his shoulders.

'You know, Marguerite, I often feel you are my most intimate enemy.'

His voice had grown hoarse, edged with cruelty. Her resistance had excited him. His hand was on his crotch and he drew hers after it. She pulled back and saw him working his penis into stiffness. She averted her eyes, tried to goad him into reason.

'What's prodded you into this, Olivier? This charade? This unnecessary make-believe.'

'You have, my dear wife, only you.' He was ruching her nightgown up over her thighs. She shivered, tried to pull away, but he was too heavy for her. His arms held her down while he rubbed himself against her. There was an edge of disgust in his eyes. A mockery. Directed at them both.

She lay very still, felt him grow small again. But he was determined, his implacable will guiding his body best it could. He closed his eyes now and she could feel him willing himself to believe that the thighs he pressed himself against were that boy's, that the cavity he blindly groped for was another's. She tightened herself against him.

'I shall scream. Olivier. I shall scream for your priest.'

As she mentioned the curé, he shuddered.

The shadowy lines of his face produced a revelation. She saw the black-clad form of Père Benoit chasing through the salon, running after Olivier and the musician.

'No, Olivier, No.'

Her voice stuttered out of her, torn on the knife of her thoughts. 'He's the one who's sent you here? To me? Is that it? Penance. A proper marriage as penance for past sins. You let him have this power over you? You let him . . .'

'Shut up.' He slapped her hard across the face.

'You let him,' she whimpered.

He slapped her again. The slaps drove him on. His face was heavy with perspiration and cruelty. He forced her legs apart, his breathing raucous.

Tears streamed down her cheeks as she tried to push him aside.

'This is madness, Olivier, madness. How could you allow him?'

He twisted his fingers round her throat. 'Shut up, Marguerite. You're no better than a whore. You even frequent their brothels.'

The violence drove his excitement.

But as if the word 'whore' had given her a strength she didn't know she possessed, she now arched a knee and jabbed it into his groin. He recoiled. Swiftly, she slid out from beneath him and made a lunge towards her little boudoir. She slammed the door hard, turned the key which happily sat in the lock, and pulled a chair against the knob for good measure.

She was breathing hard. She felt sullied. Dirty with a dirt water wouldn't wash away.

From next door, she heard Olivier muttering as if in some trance. 'Man and wife . . . I now proclaim us man and wife.'

When the bedroom door closed after an eternity, she still waited a few moments longer, then rushed forward to lock that, too. She determined her door would now stay locked forever.

_ 17 _

Martine was gone. Jeanne, her maid announced it in a frightened little voice when Marguerite finally permitted her to come in half way through the morning.

She had wanted to see no one. Had wanted time to reassemble herself. Had really wanted to run through the grounds, shake everything off, flail her arms and scream and fling herself down on the cold earth. Had been thinking that now more than ever she must extricate herself from Olivier, from this prison of marriage, from this vulture in black who called himself a priest and was a tyrant, from this sense of duty which always and ever coiled itself round her. And from this whole business of adopting the babe. Somewhere during the long night she had also promised herself that she would concentrate all her energies on locating Gabriel's mother.

She had certainly wanted to hear nothing like this.

'Yes Madame. She wasn't in her room this morning.'

The tears she hadn't yet properly shed stung at Marguerite's eyes. Visions of disaster. Martine gone. Poor, frail Martine. She had failed her too. Like Olympe.

'Are you certain?'

'No one has seen her, Madame. No one can find her. Not even in the coach house or the stables. Inspector Durand went himself to look.'

'I see. And Monsieur le Comte?'

'I don't believe he's up yet. Nor have the other guests come down. Though coffee has been brought to them.'

Marguerite hastened through her morning toilette. Her eyes were bruised, her face shadowed. There were reddenings on her cheek, where

Olivier had slapped her. Jeanne said nothing and repaired the damage best she could. Marguerite fixed her thoughts on Martine. Had she paid too little heed to the girl's troubled state last night? Or was it even worse? Had someone in their midst, perhaps the very person who had acted against Yvette, now targetted her sister?

Dire images of near ones who had taken their own lives also flooded her mind. Women. Always women. They seemed so little attached to life when despair took hold of them. Like she felt today. Had Martine, too, become infected by despair—a guilty despair at ever again finding the sister whose fate she had sealed by changing places with her?

Marguerite hadn't been able to help. The very task she had set herself in leaving Paris was the one she had failed at.

Ever darker thoughts fed on her own sombre mood and invigorated shadows from the past. They brought Martine into the tragic circle of Olympe and her sister. A torpor fell over her, like a paralysis. She had to force each gesture. With an effort, she also forced an act of mental gymnastics. She imagined Martine escaping, not in danger, but simply running away from a situation which made her miserable, running away because for all her promises Marguerite had brought her no closer to her sister and had failed to give her enough time last night. Was this possible? A pure escape from everything that tied her down. An act composed in equal parts of adolescent peevishness and rebellion.

As she went downstairs, Marguerite admitted to herself that this was forcing a sunny gloss on things. The points of her conversation with Martine the previous evening came back to her. The girl's fear, her tears, her despair, were like a premonition of her own.

The house wore no trace of her mood. Everything was alive with morning bustle. Servants came and went. Furniture moved. Rooms took on their usual aspect. A buffet of rolls and brioche and conserves, of cold meats and mustards and fruit had been laid for the guests in the breakfast room. But it was downstairs in the kitchen that she found Inspector Durand. He was sitting at a corner of the long wooden table with one of the footmen who had been brought in especially for last night's gathering.

Freshly-shaven and pink-cheeked, the Inspector was making some notes in his little pad. The writing was miniscule and Marguerite wondered once more whether the note taking was done more for effect than for any mnemonic purposes.

'Good morning, Inspector.'

Durand bowed and appraised her.

'I trust you have slept well,' she said, not quite meeting his eyes.

'The country air does wonders . . . though I have had a lot to think about. As you have had, I see.'

'And now this news of Martine . . .'

'Yes. We have just learned from Jacques, here, who was at the door, that the young woman was indeed seen leaving the house. Well wrapped, she was too. And alone.'

'Yes, Madame,' Jacques intervened, his fear that he would be blamed evident in his tumbling speech. 'I thought nothing of it. Nothing. The young lady said she wanted a little air. A walk. She was well wrapped up for it. So I saw no harm. None at all. The girls are always wanting a breather. A look at the stars. They like that sort of thing.'

'Did she have a look of distress about her?'

'No, Madame. At least I don't think so.'

'But you never saw her come back in?'

'No I didn't. I didn't. But that's not to say, she didn't.'

'Did anyone follow her?'

'People were starting to leave by then. It got very busy. There were carriages to bring forward. Ladies to help. Old gentleman. One of them all but needed to be carried. I . . .'

'It's alright, Jacques. Did you see what direction, she walked in?'

'I told the Inspector, Ma'am. I told him. Straight down the drive she went. I didn't pay much attention though, once she had crossed the threshold.'

Celeste, the wet-nurse, had come into the kitchen. She was carrying the babe and crooning to him softly.

Of course, Marguerite slapped herself mentally. Celeste was closer to Martine than anyone here, apart from herself. They had spent most time together. She called the woman over and questioned her.

'Oh yes, Madame, Martine came in to see us last night. The first time in her beautiful gown. How lovely she looked. And the second time before she went out for a breath of air, to say goodnight to us. She was a little upset, I thought.'

'Had she changed?' the Inspector asked.

'Well she wasn't in no ball gown when I saw her,' Jacques intervened. 'A hat. And gloves. And a warm blue jacket, I think, and some dark skirt.'

'So she changed deliberately . . .' Marguerite said.

'I'm sure she'll be back, Madame,' Celeste erupted. 'She wouldn't leave us without saying a proper goodbye.'

'Yes, This is a good house.'

'Thank you, Jacques. Tell me Celeste, did Martine confess any likings for any particular man to you? An old sweetheart, perhaps.'

'Ah no, Madame. Nothing like that. She said Gabriel was her sweetheart.' The woman giggled.

Marguerite met Durand's eyes at last. 'Inspector, perhaps one of the footmen can save us some time by running a message to the Préfecture in Montoire about all this . . . and indeed in Vendome, where Martine's friends must also be contacted. On balance, even if Martine went out for a walk, I don't think she left us of her own free will.'

The Inspector nodded, and Marguerite called for pen and paper. While they waited, he tapped his fingers on the table with the same rhythm that his pipe would take later in the day.

'My own feeling, like yours, is that Martine might have gone for a walk of her own free will, but would already have come back unless she was prevented from doing so.'

'I wonder whether the person who might have been responsible for Yvette's vanishing might not be responsible for Martine's as well. But that would probably mean that the culprit is somebody from the past, somebody who has nothing to do with the Telliers, someone from Vendome. Though Martine went there on her own when we first arrived in the area and came back unscathed.'

Durand shook his head. 'Non, Madame . . . I'm afraid my own suspicions fall on that giant of a youth whom I found hanging about the windows and spying when I first arrived. He manages to appear out of nowhere and is everywhere. He's also silent, despite his bulk. And he wanted that girl. I know it.'

Marguerite shivered, remembering the first time she had seen P'tit Ours with Martine, the way he had tried to caress her cheek, the way he had appeared, his trousers unbuttoned, at the orangerie window.

'Yes, P'tit Ours must be our first priority.'

The wind was up. Clouds raced across the sky leaving their shadowy imprint on the chalky ground. The world felt unstable as they bumped across the pitted roads.

Unusually, the main gate of the Tellier house was locked. Their repeated ringing brought the manservant they had seen just a few days before. 'Madame is indisposed,' he said in a surly voice. 'She wants no visitors.'

'It's Madame Molineuf we've come to see. Madame Tellier would not wish us to be turned away, I can assure you.'

The man registered the latent threat in her voice, shrugged and unlocked the heavy gate. They followed him up the slope to the door of the house. He left them standing in the dark lobby and bellowed a 'Madame Molineuf . . .' towards the back of the house.

From upstairs, there was the crash of something heavy, a rush of cursing from a male voice. Marguerite met Durand's eyes. He was as curious as she of that sound. Madame Tellier had told them quite distinctly that the men in her family were both in Tours.

Looking as if she had just been pulled from bed, despite the lateness of the hour, Madame Molineuf appeared at the stairs—a stolid, aproned, angry presence. Her recognition of Marguerite did little to dent her hostility.

'What do you want this time?' the housekeeper addressed her, but she was staring at Durand. 'You've brought the police, have you? None too soon, with all the cursing in this house. Morality police, that's what they need.'

Close to, the woman's cheeks looked mildewed, eaten away by some inner trouble.

'This is Chief Inspector Durand.'

The little man bowed while the woman fixed him with bloodshot eyes.

'What's happened then? Out with it.'

'In fact, chère Madame,' Durand was impeccable in his politeness. 'We've come to interview your son. Will you fetch him for us?'

'My son! What's that good-for-nothing done now?' She was grumbling. Speaking to herself as much as to them. 'A double pain he is, now. Thinks he's a man. Out all hours. He never came in last night. Stayed away. Maybe at the other place. How should I know?'

There was another crash from upstairs, like that made by a wild animal let loose in a room full of furniture. Madame Molineuf seemed oblivious to it.

'Always in trouble. Always. Don't get me wrong, He's not a bad lad. Just a bit . . . well, on the simple side. I warned him. I did.'

'We need to see him urgently, Madame.'

'Urgently, eh? Well, he's not here. No, that's not him upstairs. I don't let him up there. He's probably out and about in the fields. Or the orchard. I told him. Told him not to bother coming home unless he could bring some wood back with him. No food unless he does what he's told. No more. Keep him out from under my feet.' She looked up at the ceiling as if there were more she'd like to sweep outside.

'Can you direct us to him?'

She shrugged as if the effort were too much for her. 'You can't miss the orchard if that's where the good-for-nothing is. Between our house and the next one. He'll be out there somewhere. Dreaming instead of working, no doubt. Wandering.' An air of despair came over her. 'I warned him. I did. It's not to do with girls, is it Inspector? I'll beat him black and blue. I told him. I warned him. Stay away from the women. It's the old master who leads him astray. He doesn't understand. I'll have to beat it into him.'

Settled in the coach once more, Durand shook his head and cracked his knuckles. Belligerence warred with sadness in his features.

'That women drinks. And drinks. I thought it was a vice of the urban proletariat But no. Did you take a look at her skin? No surprise the boy is simple. Degenerate.'

He sat back in the seat and stroked his moustache reflectively, then embarked on another chapter in his intermittent disquisition on the rot of the underclass.

She had heard much of it before and knew better than to interrupt. Degeneration was one of his bugbears. According to the Inspector, and he was hardly alone even amongst the ranks of the progressives, the world, at least the French bit of it, was rapidly moving to an end because of the demon drink, his sister opium and a generalized lasciviousness, The drinkers and the drug takers produced the babies while others refrained. And what they produced were degenerates, feeble, sometimes emasculated offspring, inheritors of vile criminal blood, a terrible underclass who would bring France down.

Since the Inspector knew a great many more criminals than she did and since degeneration was a fashionable field of speculation, Marguerite rarely bothered to oppose him—even if she thought that alongside the Inspector's 'bad blood,' poverty and misfortune had to be equal players in any description of what he called the criminal class. Only when he chose to add female freedom to his overall portrait of the ills of the time, did she jump in to argue. Just because men controlled the state and production, there was no need for them to feel they had sole authority over reproduction, too.

Today she stayed mute. She didn't want her feelings about Olivier to infect her reason.

'Not that Madame Tellier spares herself the tipple either. I had to stop her snoring during the concert last night. Then she had to be heaved into her carriage. Can you imagine the impact of living in a house like that on a pure young girl?' The Inspector's face was bleak.

'You mean on Martine's sister? Did you have a chance to speak to Martine last night, Inspector? '

'No, not during the party.' He was gazing out the window. 'But earlier in the day.'

'Did she say anything that might help us?'

He tapped his fingers impatiently on the window. His gaze was fixed on the fields, searching out anything that moved.

'Her sister had evidently described the horrors of her posting with graphic precision. I asked her whether I might read her letters to see if I could find any clues in them. She said she hadn't brought them with her.'

'Shame.'

The Inspector wriggled. 'I didn't altogether believe her.'

'Why?'

'There's something that girl is hiding from us. And now it may have come back to take her away . . . Ah, the orchard.'

'Let's carry on until we spot him, if we can. It's chill out there.'

'Madame will wait while I talk to him. The lout isn't to be trusted with women.'

'That may be, Inspector. But the boy will recognize me as a possible friend . . . He's not stupid. Remember I've had conversations of a sort with him before. That may make finding out about Martine easier. That's what we want first of all. And you, you will be my protector.' Marguerite smiled, knowing the Inspector could never refuse an act of gallantry.

'If Madame insists,' he murmured. He clenched his fists in preparation.

Round a bend, they saw something moving behind one of the rows of pear trees. A bulky figure was tossing a bough into the air and catching it as easily as if it were a twiglet. There was both strength and awkwardness in his gestures, as if the youth's hands were paddles which didn't know about gripping until too late, but did so in any event. The bough caught, he broke it effortlessly in two and now threw the parts up into the air, only to catch and break them again. It was a kind of game.

When he heard them he forgot to catch the pieces. Instead, he picked a basket up from the ground and started to trot in the opposite direction.

Marguerite called out, 'P'tit Ours!' and waved. 'Wait, we need to talk to you. Wait.'

She kept her voice light, all the time looking round her, superstitiously fearing that as part of his game P'tit Ours might have tied Martine to a tree trunk.

The youth slowed, glanced at them, then picked up speed.

Marguerite shouted again. Meanwhile the Inspector wove his way round and came up on P'tit Ours from the other side.

'Police, Molineuf. Stop. Or look forward to a life behind bars.'

The threatening tone had its effect. P'tit Ours stopped, shuffled from foot to foot, swung his basket round like a mace.

They were at the very tip of the orchard. The ground was hard from the cold, littered with twigs where the old, gnarled trees had cracked.

From the end of the row they could see across the fields to what from this distance she could only guess was Napoleon Marchand's house. On the other side was a high wall which edged into a dark hillock of almost the same height. Beyond it, where a low cloud hung, there were the houses of Troo which she would have supposed nearer. The fields played tricks with perspective.

As Marguerite drew closer to the two men she saw that P'tit Ours had put his basket down and was holding a piece of wood remarkably like a cudgel. He dwarfed the Inspector.

'Put that down, Molineuf. No funny business.'

'We just want to talk to you, P'tit Ours,' Marguerite tried a different tack, her voice soft as she held the boy's eyes. They were round and large and protruded slightly. 'We wanted to know whether you talked to Martine yesterday. Or saw her?'

He looked at her blankly, and she repeated, 'Martine.'

The youth's sudden movement made her leap backwards. The Inspector stepped in front of her. 'That's enough. Talk now or I'm taking you in.'

The youth started to edge backwards, as if he were planning either to launch himself at them or make a getaway. Only now did it come to Marguerite that the boy might not be clear on Martine's name. The girl herself had said she thought he mistook her for her sister.

'Did you see Yvette yesterday?' Marguerite tried again. 'Do you know where she is?'

'Yvette. Yvette.' The boy rubbed his squash of a nose, smiled, did a little clumsy dance on his paddle feet. 'Your house. Your house,' he repeated.

'Yes, she was at my house,' Marguerite smiled. 'But she went away. Did you see her?'

An excited coil of words rolled off the boy's thick tongue, too fast for sense. They got trapped in his jagged teeth and splayed lips so that they had to be spat.

'The doctor's did you say?' The Inspector had understood better.

'Doctor, doctor,' P'tit Ours repeated and then looked sad. With the sadness the words grew slow. 'Yvette gone. Witch gone. Danuta gone. All gone. Into the ground.'

'Into the ground?' The Inspector repeated.

Marguerite shuddered. Another young woman she had let down.

The youth repeated it again, like a song. 'Into the ground.' He hopped from foot to foot. Picked up a bough again and threw it into the air. This time he let it fall on the ground, forcing them to step away. The Inspector growled a threat.

Marguerite couldn't tell whether P'tit Ours' gesture had been one of anger or a kind of desperation. A kind of compassion wouldn't allow her to believe that the boy was all bad. He had been mistreated, shaped by his drunken masters.

'The witch, you say?'

'Gone gone. All gone.'

'She went away. Like Yvette. Went where?'

'Gone. All gone. P'tit Ours cry. Like Auguste. Auguste cry. Dancer dead. In the ground. The ground.'

'Yes.' Marguerite looked at the ground. The basket with the twigs rested near them. It had the same weave as the basket Gabriel had come in.

The Inspector put an arm on the youth's shoulder. 'You'll come with us now, Eustache Molineuf.' It was the first time Margeurite had heard the youth's proper name and she wondered at the extent of Durand's investigations.

With a sudden heave and a duck, P'tit Ours shook the Inspector off, picked up the basket and raced away with his odd hop, weaving through the trees. Durand went straight after him. But despite the youth's clumsiness, the Inspector was no match for speed coupled with knowledge of the fields. P'tit Ours dodged and parried, finally to leap over a low point in the wall in one bound, leaving the Inspector to clamber and tail after him.

'There's no sense to this, Molineuf,' Durand shouted. But now, he was shouting into the void. The giant youth had vanished.

After a protracted moment, he shrugged and turned back towards Marguerite.

Suddenly there was a crack from behind him and a stick came whizzing through the air and over the wall. The Inspector stepped aside just in time.

'There's no question of it. The oaf is dangerous.' He was breathing hard when he reached Marguerite. 'He'll have to be locked up. We'll beat Martine's whereabouts out of him.'

'He must have shimmied up a tree.'

Together they examined the distance from where the stick had come minutely. Nothing stirred. Not a branch or leaf. A hush filled the cold air. Even the birds had gone quiet. On a meadow in the valley opposite, some cows grazed in bovine tranquility.

The earth had swallowed P'tit Ours.

'He's cleverer than we thought.'

'Strength, more than often, stands in for cleverness, Madame. Believe me. Not too many of the murderers we round up have degrees from our leading schools.'

Marguerite's hand flew to her mouth. 'It's just come to me, Inspector. I've worked it out. I know. I know where he's gone. Come on. I shall have to go home and get some clothes.'

'You think he'll still be around when we return.'

'Oh yes, Inspector. He's in the ground.'

_ 18 _

She no longer cared what Olivier thought if he saw her. She changed into an old pair of trousers borrowed from a servant and held tight with a leather belt, donned her riding jacket and boots, and tried not to think about anything except what was in front of them. They would need a lamp. That was essential. Her father had always taken a lamp. And warm gloves. She recommended to Durand, who was game, that they leave the carriage at home and ride cross country to the spot. It would save time.

The Inspector stared at her with an expression which was hardly one of approval, though there was a twinkle in his eye.

'Madame will make me forget that Georges Sand was never my favourite model of womanhood.'

'We haven't time for all of that, Inspector. Where we're going hardly produces the right atmosphere for my best dresses.'

An hour of hard riding later, the orchard appeared before them on its slope, its trees ranked, but bare like an army devoid of uniforms. Scanning the vista, Marguerite suggested they tether the horses near the wall. They would be least visible from there, should anyone approach.

The sun's position was in their favour. Their shadows were obliterated by the ample one cast by the wall, so long as they kept close to it. They reached the hillock she had seen from a distance that morning. She examined its outer hump and noted, with relief, the existence of a partly obscured opening. She had been right. She hadn't dreamt or imagined it. There was a cave.

Durand moved aside the fronds of copper beech which had been used to mask the opening. It was narrow, but ample enough for the Inspector to ease himself through. She heard a muted thud as his feet touched earth. Not too high a leap then. She saw the flickering of the lantern he was holding and lowered herself through the hole after him.

She didn't quite know what she had expected. Perhaps a corpse half covered with rubble. Or Martine tied up, terrified, next to her the mulatto woman. Instead in the wavering light, she made out a roundish cave about seven metres in diameter and tall enough for Durand to stand in comfortably. Near the entrance, on the ground lay some half-burned twigs arranged in the shape of a fire. And by the wall there was a small heap of potatoes and turnips. This was definitely P'tit Ours' hide-away.

'Look Madame,' Durand pointed to an opening in the wall. Then to another. The cave gave way to tunnels, one slightly to the left of their entry place, another almost straight ahead.

'I suggest we start with the one at the back.' She had lowered her voice to a whisper. Sound funneled and echoed through the tunnels with eerie amplification.

She should have considered all this before. Her father had told her years ago about the tunnels that crisscrossed the region, tunnels which led to dungeons, tunnels between châteaux and from châteaux to river along which endangered nobles had been spirited away as long ago as the days of Richard the Lion Heart, and throughout the various battles of succession and religion. In revolutionary times, escaping nobles had been joined by clerics in the tunnels which led between cloisters and safe houses and chalky caves. Spies, too had used them as recently as the Franco-Prussian War. And now?

The tunnel space was low, the earth around them as cold and moist as a tomb. A smell of damp and rot, like putrefying eggs, rose from the walls. Her hat scraped the ceiling. Durand took his off and, where the tunnel grew narrower, she did too. She was glad of the lamp, though the shadows it cast on the grimy walls could all too easily grow into childhood nightmares, magic-lantern magicians with pointed chins and accusing noses hurtling towards her, ogres wearing the face of P'tit Ours and behind it that of the man they called the Old Master, Napoleon Marchand.

They trudged until her feet were frozen inside her boots. She could see that Durand was stiff with the effort of bending. It was impossible accurately to predict their direction. At one point she had the impression they were moving precipitously down hill. Here the tunnel joined another. They carried straight on, though she had lost her sense of direction. Their path now rose little by little, so that her legs had to work harder.

'Do you know where we might be heading? And for how long?' Durand whispered. 'I don't want the lamp to fail us.'

'Let's give it another few minutes, and we'll try another direction.' No sooner had she spoken, than the tunnel came to a dead end. Stopped abruptly without the opening out of a cave. There was nothing in front of them. Just an earthen wall.

Durand crouched for a moment against it so that he could straighten his neck. He looked up at her.

She shrugged, avoiding his question. As she did so, she noticed a faint shift of light above his shoulder.

She ran her hand along the wall. Her fingers felt the change before she saw it. Earth had become wood. Between them was a tiny crack which had produced a sliver of light.

Durand leapt up. He placed his hand where hers was, edged forward. 'Yes, Yes, Madame.' She heard the click of a latch. One push and they were through a door into what could only be, judging from the dusty array of rope, bottles and old barrels, a cellar room. Above them a trap door stood partly open. Here was the source of the light.

With a quick glance at her, Durand lowered the ladder tucked into the side of the door. She put a hushing finger to her lips. She half expected to hear a scream from an imprisoned Martine. Half expected the bulk of P'tit Ours to loom before them, cudgel in hand.

They climbed up, hurrying over the creak of boards. They emerged beside a sack of flour leaning against a wall. Next to it, stood another of rice. Jars lined the walls. Marguerite tiptoed towards the door. It opened. They were in a kitchen. Silence echoed around them.

The room was less than clean, the window dark with accumulated grit. Through it, she could see into an expanse of garden and beyond that the gentle rise and fall of fields. She stood very still for a moment, gazing, then changed position. The change brought everything into focus.

Durand was at the door and gesturing her behind him. He put down his lamp and peered out slowly with the air of a man who expected to hear a bullet whizzing past him at any moment. When it didn't come, he tiptoed out.

They were in a box-like hall now, to its side a dusty half-furnished drawing room of no particular style, but not poor. A bourgeois house. Marguerite hastened to the windows again, shuttered here, so she had to steal a peek through slats. The sight of the high wall made her certain. They were in the house the children had called the witch's house. Which meant there was probably no one here. No one alive, in any case. The body she had half feared they would find in the cave might well be somewhere within these rooms.

She sniffed the air, wondering if there was decomposition mingled with the pervasive dust, and signalled to Durand that she wanted to have a look upstairs, while he explored down here. He shook his head and pressed ahead of her. The stairs creaked. There were no pictures to examine along their length, only oily wallpaper of an uncertain colour.

A few endless seconds later, they were in a shuttered bedroom. The bed was tousled, unmade, a nightgown tossed across it. A glass of murky water stood on the night table, an array of abandoned jewellry. Whoever had been here had left in a hurry.

In an alcove stood a cabin trunk of sea-going size. She hastened to it, read its tag, Amandine Septembre. There was an address, too. Martinique. She almost shouted to Durand, then, remembering, clamped a hand over her mouth. A.S. The initials on the handkerchief found in the pocket of the dead man, along with the card for Villemardi Fils, stonemasons. Had the dead man planned a death for Amandine Septembre, only himself to suffer one first?

She didn't have a pencil and pad to jot the address down, and she hailed the Inspector. His eyes grew wide as he took it in. He gave her a little smile, then reached for his pad.

The windows sported two layers of curtain, one heavy, one transparent. It was probably behind these very ones that she had seen the woman pace and listen to the taunts of the children. Amandine Septembre. She knew her full name now.

She pulled open a wardrobe and was astonished by the collection of gowns and shoes. She was a big woman, and not poor, no, judging by the fabrics. So why had she ended up in this sorry state, kept prisoner here, perhaps, certainly forced to leave her lodgings in a hurry, taking little with her. Fleeing. Where was she now?

Marguerite ran a finger across the dressing table and saw the trace in the accumulation of dust. No one had cleaned here for a good week or more.

She noticed a piece of paper on the table. Something she couldn't make out in the murky half-light was written on it. She folded it quickly into her pocket and followed Durand into the next room. Another bedroom. Men's clothes in this wardrobe. She wished they could get the measure of them. No time. Someone could come in at any moment. P'tit Ours. Where was he? The Inspector was scanning the desk. She felt as much as saw the small notebook on the bedside table. She put it in her pocket and looked round for a second trunk. None here. Time to go. Quickly. Their luck mightn't hold. She was already breathing too hard.

Durand tried the front door. It wouldn't give. It had been locked from the outside. To lock someone in or to keep people out? There were no keys in sight. He waved her towards the back of the house into the store room. Here a large key was looped prominently round a nail. He fitted it into the lock of the back door.

They were on a small verandah from which steps led down to what must once have been a kitchen garden. Down the hill and then above them, she could see the Tellier House.

'Better this, than the tunnel again.'

'We may not be able to scale the wall,' Marguerite murmured. But she followed him. She had no desire to find herself once more in the tunnel. Though she was already wondering where the other paths led and whether she had condemned Martine to another miserable night in captivity.

They kept close to the wall she had seen P'tit Ours scale from the tree on its other side. She hoped no one in the Tellier House could see them from the window. If they did, it was unlikely they would be recognized. That was the good thing. The bad thing was that there was no way

Marguerite could climb onto that wall and jump down the other side. And if she scrambled onto Durand's shoulders, he would then be trapped here. No trees, like the one P'tit Ours had used were in evidence on this side of the high wall.

On the horizon, the sun had already disappeared. Dusk would soon give way to dark. When the mound at last emerged from the shadows like some great sleeping beast digesting its prey, it seemed to have grown so large as to be unscaleable.

'You wait here, Madame,' Durand whispered. I'll wriggle up, get the horse's reins and launch them down to you to tug you up by.'

She didn't protest. She was suddenly weary. Weary with too much fear for those they might still find in 'the ground' P'tit Ours had evoked.

Durand started to worm his way up. Soon he was a mere presence in the gloom of the late afternoon. She could tell by his breathing when he had reached the hump and was over. In the distance, she heard the restless whinny of horses, and took a deep breath. Only a few more minutes now.

A cry burst on the air like cannon fire. A terrible cry followed by a thump and the sound of feet pounding across ground, running, running heavily.

Then everything was far too still.

'Inspector,' She ventured a call after a few minutes. She had a terrible presentiment. That heavy tread. Those feet hammering the earth. It could only be P'tit Ours. Was it the same strange animal tread she had heard in the woods the day she had found Danuta the dancer? Her legs turned to stone. And now the Inspector . . .

The ogre of a youth must have found the horses and been lying in wait. He understood more than they all gave him credit for. That's what had fooled her. She hadn't liked to think that his strangeness inevitably made him a criminal. So she had been led astray by her own unwillingness to accept what Durand and all the others took for granted. A degenerate. Capable of murder. A murderer. Durand had threatened prison. Durand was not a friend.

'Inspector,' she called again, more loudly now. Tears rose to her eyes. Durand had been assaulted. Worse. He could be lying dead on the other side of the wall. Or dying. Her fault. She started to scramble up the steep hillock, using her feet to wedge herself where she could, inching along, slipping backwards where the ground had grown wet with the gathering cold. Persisting, despite the tears. At last, her head was over the top. She heaved herself up and slid down the other side, bumping her way to the bottom.

She walked slowly, her ears alert to any tread. P'tit Ours could still be in the vicinity. Waiting. Waiting for her. She scanned the area for the sign of an attack, for the Inspector's body, if it had been left here.

A horse snorted. She was almost back at their departure point. So P'tit Ours had left the horses behind.

When she reached the tethered animals, they responded nervously, whinnying and rearing. Only then did she notice the ungainly bundle draped over one of the saddles.

'Inspector,' she cried out, then muffled her shout.

He was strapped to the horse with the very reins he had been going to use to help her climb.

She touched his cheek, reached for his pulse. He was still warm, breathing. She took a deep breath herself.

When his voice came, she was so relieved, she started to sob.

'Madame. If you could untie me, please.'

She pulled at the knots with clumsy fingers.

'That dolt was waiting for me. He took me by surprise.'

The Inspector rubbed the back of his head. He looked shamed and angry by turn . 'I suppose he thought the horse would run off with me.'

'Thank our lucky stars, he didn't. He was probably waiting for my mare, who was still tethered.'

'And you, Madame, are you alright?'

Marguerite nodded. 'Well, at least we know what we're up against now, Inspector.'

'We've got our culprit. I'll wager a proper exploration of the tunnels will lead us to Martine, as well.'

'And to Amandine Septembre. The only problem is I don't altogether see what ties P'tit Ours to the dancer. Nor what his motive might be for killing the man on the tracks as well. And what of Yvette? Has he had her buried underground all these months?'

The Inspector shrugged and shook his head reflectively. 'The thing is, Madame, with these brutes, it's easy enough. He might have killed out of simple jealousy, just like that, a moment's rage. Let's hope he's sweet enough on your Martine for that not to happen—certainly not while he's got her locked up.'

Marguerite winced. 'Or maybe, Inspector, he doesn't need a motive. He's working for someone. And that's the very someone we didn't find in on our last visit.' She pointed past the trees, into the distance where Napoleon Marchand's house lay.

'That's possible, too.' The Inspector was rubbing the back of his neck with his hand. 'Yes. We'll pay a visit to Marchand as soon as I've contacted the police in Montoire.'

'You remember, P'tit Ours' mother talked about the old master, the old master corrupting him. The old master whose portrait has disappeared from their hall, alongside that of the relative he will certainly now identify for us.'

'The relative he had killed,' the Inspector finished for her. 'Or killed himself. I need to go to Montoire, Madame. I need to send some telegrams to Martinique urgently.'

'But Inspector, surely you need to rest first, to have your head seen to?'

He shook it, to prove it was still in operation. As if the gesture had reminded him of something, he dug abruptly into his pocket. Relief flooded his features. He brought out his little notebook. It now contained an address in Martinique. That would certainly speed their searches.

She had only been back in the Châateau for some three minutes when Jeanne rushed towards her. Her look of astonishment reminded Marguerite that she was not in a fit state for general inspection.

'Monsieur has been asking for you, Madame. He's in his study.'

The way the girl looked down at her feet and fingered the edges of her white apron indicated that Monsieur was hardly at his sweetest. Marguerite, had she allowed herself the anxiety of anticipation, would have expected no less.

'Thank you, Jeanne. Please tell Monsieur I shall be with him in an hour. Then come and help me change.

Marguerite was as good as her word. There was little point in putting the inevitable moment off. And her mind, now, was filled with so much else that confronting her husband about last night's ordeal seemed almost trivial in comparison. Martine was gone, her disappearance a matter of life and death, given the dangers this afternoon had revealed.

In fact, as she made her way towards Olivier's study, she decided to pretend that nothing much was amiss in her relations with him. There would be time enough for all that. She didn't want to be laid even lower by the sharpness of his tongue and the malice he could unleash. And Olivier could hardly be planning to make his nighttime visits a regular occurrence.

He and the curé had made their point. In the light of day, it was clear she was something of an unhappy bystander whose body was needed but whose presence was superfluous to the act of penance being undergone.

She forced away the waves of shame which coursed through her, compelled herself to knock.

At Olivier's 'come in,' she opened the door, her little speech about Martine's absence and the need to find her already on her lips.

'Ah, Marguerite, good,' Olivier smiled at her with innocent pleasure.

It surprised her as much as Paul Villemardi's presence at her husband's side. The relief she felt indicated to her the depth of her prior fear.

She greeted them both. They were standing on the same side of Olivier's large mahogany desk, looking at something. Light streamed through the window above, illuminating them with a biblical cast, as if they had stepped out of some minor Dutch master's scene of Saint Jerome addressing a follower.

'I hope Jeanne explained.'

'Yes, yes. About Martine. I imagine she met someone to her liking last night and decided on a little escapade.'

Marguerite stepped back with something like shock at this casualness. 'I doubt that somehow,' she said in a low voice.

'That's because you always think the worst first. She's young after all. I saw her talking with Monsieur Bonpierre's son.'

'Did you? And you really think she went off with him, went off with-out telling any of us. It would be rather irresponsible of her.'

'My dear, you understand young women these days far better than I do. Perhaps she couldn't find you. Didn't want to tell a servant for fear of gossip. What do I know? She might already have had a flirtation with the boy. You told me she was from the region.'

Marguerite didn't reply.

'But it's not because of her, I asked you to come here. I thought you'd like to see these. My footman has just picked them up from Legrand's stu-dio in La Chatre.'

Marguerite bent towards the desk and saw a sheaf of photographs laid out in what was evidently an order. At first she couldn't make out what she was seeing. Then it came to her that all these were aerial shots, marvels of the new technology, taken during Olivier's balloon trip. As her eyes grew accustomed to a perspective which shrunk everything yet simultaneously introduced a panoramic vista, she grew excited.

'I've never seen the country like this. Never. La Rochambert is so flat, like an ancient earth work. And the lines of the trees, so strange, just a blur of shadow. And everything's so . . . so close together.'

'They're beautiful,' Paul Villemardi murmured. 'The photograph will displace us all.'

'But you use three dimensions, Paul. Not the same thing. Not in any way.'

'None the less.'

'Is that why you chose to work in sculpture rather than paint? Because of photography?' Marguerite asked.

The sculptor shrugged. 'Not altogether, but perhaps. Next time,' he addressed Olivier again, 'I'd like to come up with you.'

'So would I,' Marguerite heard herself say, then clamped her lips shut. How could she have said that? Let herself be carried away by the excitement of the images? Olivier would think she acquiesced to his brutal behaviour.

'I'll arrange it.' She could feel his eyes on her back.

'The camera's at a tilt, isn't it?' She changed the subject. 'It makes me feel quite dizzy. And this field here, just to the north of the house, is at a strange angle.'

'It takes a while to learn how to decipher these images. I think I'll mount them. Put them up in the hall as a sequence. You see, here, here is the large wood and the river, just a swirl of ribbon, really. And the vineyard. Like a bit of corduroy.'

Marguerite stared. She was beginning to find her bearings amidst these oddly abstract shadows which gave only the contours of shape. Like looking at a puzzle or a set of abstract forms. The curl of the river, the look round a smudge of an island, the wood she had walked in during her misadventure . . . Her eyes raced. No, she couldn't distinguish a clearing. But the wall, she was certain the wall she had seen was there and beyond it, at a good remove, a house which created a flattened U from the sky.

'Where's that?' she asked innocently.

'That's a house, quite a big one. I'm not sure exactly where. What I should really do is get Monsieur Lemaitre to identify all this. Since he's always up there, he'll know. Then we can give the photographs captions.'

'Excellent idea,' Paul Villemardi said without much enthusiasm. 'I think I'll get back to work.'

'Before you go, Monsieur Villemardi,' Marguerite stopped him. 'Did you by any chance speak to Martine last night? Overhear anything?'

'Your Durand has already asked me. None too politely, either, I should point out. He couldn't have been less polite if he was accusing me of tying the girl up in my studio and covering her in plaster.'

'I apologize for him. The police have their ways.'

The man bowed. A little smile played over his lips. 'The only thing of interest I managed to notice last night was that our dear Père Benoit was in a terrible temper. What did you say to him Olivier to get him so worked up? I would have thought God didn't allow it in his intermediaries.'

'I didn't notice,' Olivier was curt. He tapped his fingers on his desk, willing Villemardi to leave. Marguerite was about to follow after, when he called her back.

'There was something I wanted to mention to you, Marguerite.' The face he turned on her was a mask of pleasantness. But the crack in his voice belied both the importance of what he was saying and his anxiety about her answer. 'The notary is drawing up the adoption papers for Gabriel. Charles Gabriel de Landois is the name we approved, remember? He'll be coming round with them next week. And then there will be the baptism. I'm assuming that will be convenient for you.'

'If it isn't, I'll give you good warning, Olivier.'

She could see his instant recoil. The façade of courtesy cracked.

As she pulled the door shut behind her, she heard his slightly menacing, 'I trust that won't be necessary.'

_ 19 _

The morning brought a message from the Inspector, who had spent the night at the Inn in Montoire. He had been too tired to return after the misadventures of the day, and he awaited a response to his telegram. A visit two constables had paid to Napoleon Marchand's house just outside Troo had yielded nothing. The man wasn't there. Nor was P'tit Ours in either house. Durand was insisting that a watch be put on old Marchand's house and had also communicated with the Préfecture in Tours to ask them to pay a visit to the man's address in that city. He would write to her again later, if anything turned up. She was to spend the day resting. That was an order from the Paris police. If he, himself, was anything to judge by, she was probably more tired than she knew.

Marguerite stepped into her bath. The steaming water was scented with rose and lime blossom. Madame Germaine had supplied the mixture days back, along with the poultice for her wound. She had also told her to breath deeply of the steam, to let the brew seep into her body until the water grew tepid. She had promised it would relieve her aches.

Marguerite hoped it would work on her new ones as well. The scramble up the hillock had resulted in more bruises and scrapes.

She had secretly hoped that the day would have produced a message from Martine, but nothing had come. She cursed the fact that the area hadn't yet been wired for telephone. It slowed everything about their investigations. Perhaps it would also slow the speed of impending disaster. It might give them the time of a reprieve in which to snatch friends from the scythe of death, so busy of late in these valleys.

Something niggled at the back of her mind as she completed her toilette, something about Martine she sensed she had forgotten. She went over the girl's behaviour the night of the party step by step, included the flirtation she hadn't seen with this Bonpierre lad that Olivier had cattily referred to. It came to her, while Jeanne helped her with the corset she would have liked to refuse, that even if their principal suspect were P'tit Ours, someone needed to go and interview the people Martine had talked to that night. In particular, the old priest who had so upset her had to be seen. Père François might have said more to Martine than she had let on. She would have to ask Olivier where the man could be found.

Olivier. She stole a quick look at her body and shivered. She still did not want to confront all that. Yet thoughts of rape had punctuated her night with a terror greater than that of the tunnels. She had imagined Leda and Europa. She had been visited by a cascade of antique nymphs taken against their will by divine beasts, terrifying creatures who drove them mad or in turn transformed them into trees or pools. Transformed them so that they were no longer thinking, feeling humans or nymphs, but parts of unspeaking, only semi-sentient nature. Vegetable or animal matter.

Marguerite refused their muteness and suffering for herself. She tried to tell herself that whatever had happened with Olivier was not really happening to her. Any other woman would have done as well.

But wasn't that the very nub of the horror? The shame. This trampling of individuality. The sense of being no one in particular, yet somehow chosen by fate. Olivier was the incarnation of her brutal fate, cruel and smiling by turn.

She wondered how he could live with himself and this new series of lies which pretended that he had somehow changed, when the look in his eyes the night he had followed after the musician proved altogether differently. She didn't know whether she loathed him more for his attempted rape or for lying to himself and pulling on the cloak of supposed virtue the curé had supplied.

She hadn't always loathed Olivier. At the beginning, she had been half in love with him. No, that too was a lie. She had been wholly in love with him, as her seventeen-year-old self then understood the matter—a matter influenced by her father and her great-aunt's wishes, but also by Olivier's charm, his knowledge of the world, his sharp intelligence. To him, then, she had probably seemed not all that far away from a boy—a boy who had learned to wear dresses.

Not enough of a boy, however, for he lost interest in her soon enough except in the most superficial of ways. He continued to pay attention to her appearance. He loved her to look beautiful. He loved to dress her, to be there when the couturier paraded his models, to suggest a fabric here, a snip and pleat there, a row of buttons, a smattering of lace or braid. He loved to choose the evening's jewels for her, her hats, her gloves, even her tea gowns with their peacock colours. When her façade particularly pleased him, his eyes shone—as if he had given to the world a masterwork of his own creation.

If she hadn't misunderstood his sexual abandonment of her, hadn't imagined a mistress and in her youthful ardour followed him into the brothel's depths, who knew but that they might still be one of those fashionable couples of a certain age who pursued life amicably enough, both together and separately, in the Saint-Germain-des-Prés. Couples who pretended that their sexual inclinations were neither more outré nor more limited than everyone else's.

But she had been too naïve, too eager for truth, too scandalized and uncomprehending when she had ferreted it out in that tawdry bordello where the boys and the men met. She didn't regret her detective work. Not at all.

Nor did she regret the separation she had enforced with the threat of blackmail. The independent life suited her. Before this visit, she would have thought Olivier would have acknowledged that it suited him too.

Now everything had changed for the worse. Olivier was obviously struggling to redefine the accommodation they had reached. He wanted to redefine it in the name of some mad political aspiration born out of vanity and boredom. Or perhaps a delusion, a punitive religious delusion. The child was part of it all.

She paused, stumbled in her thoughts. She saw her eyes reflected in the mirror—large, clear, golden, flecked with darker tints, searching. They were telling her she was blind. Stupid. Why hadn't she seen it before? Olivier was communicating something with his brutal act. He was telling her that, even now, he was capable of bedding a woman. He was telling her, however covertly, however subterranean his manner, that the babe was his.

Yes. Of course. Wasn't that what Madame Solange had intimated when she had talked about the brazenness of the servant girls? And Villemardi . . . He had suggested much the same thing about the girl Louise—and he knew her well, after all. She had been his model. Marguerite had misinterpreted him. She had assumed the standard story of the artist and his model. She'd assumed he was deflecting attention from his own interest in the girl by generalizing it. What was it he had said? All bees were attracted to wayside flowers.

In her mind, she had gone through all the men in the house—except Olivier. In her knowledge, Olivier's tastes tended towards the exotic— towards the hothouse rather than the wayside.

She remembered that conversation now in its fullness. Was it Villemardi or one of the servants who had also intimated that Louise was the kind of young woman who, if she found herself with child, would have little hesitation in confronting the father squarely.

This was precisely what the girl had probably done. In one way or another she had brought the babe to Olivier, and Olivier knew it.

Villemardi had told the Inspector he was going to Blois and would try once more to track this Louise down. At least, unlike the Inspector, he knew who he was looking for. Marguerite must prod him.

She didn't realize she was standing there, at the window, her nails biting into her palms, her eyes unfocussed, until a horse came into view. It emerged from the poplars in a flare of red and white like a dream mare bearing a ghostly Napoleonic soldier.

As the pair drew closer Marguerite recognized one of Danuta's horses. The man riding him was more difficult to identify, but when she did so she raced for the stairs.

She didn't wait for the servants to gawp at him and give him a difficult time of it.

'Mr. Rama,' she said, as soon as the door was open. 'How good to see you.' She addressed him in English.

The snake charmer bowed with military precision and thrust an envelope towards her. 'I have been asked by Chief Inspector Durand of the *Judiciare* to deliver this to you, Madame.'

'Indeed. Come in Mr. Rama. Please. You will take tea with me.'

'I would be honoured. Madame is very kind.'

'The small drawing room, Jeanne. Bring tea and some light refreshment for Monsieur.'

The girl was staring as if eyes and ears, both, had given birth to hallucinations. Marguerite prodded her. 'That done, we do not wish to be disturbed.'

'A most beautiful palace you inhabit, Madame.' Mr. Rama was taking everything in with his bright eyes. He sat down carefully on one of the upholstered armchairs by the fire. He kept himself quite stiff. Perhaps he feared he might be asked to leave at any moment.

Marguerite tore open the Inspector's letter. He had made preliminary contact with Martinique. So far it tied in with their speculations. He would tell her more tonight. But he wouldn't return to the Chateau until then. Meanwhile, he hoped she would take time to talk more fully to his messenger. He suspected he might know things he didn't speak, or perhaps didn't even know he knew.

Marguerite allowed herself an inward smile. The content of the letter, which was no real content at all after her earlier message, was precisely why she so enjoyed the Inspector's collaboration. It was the messenger who was important. Grand, universalist theories might occasionally divide them, but when it came to assessing people, they were most often in accord.

'How are you and your friends faring, Mr. Rama?'

'Not so very badly Ma'am. Nor so very well. There is much upset about Danuta. And for me, on top, about my livelihood. Soon we must move on.'

Marguerite nodded in sympathy, exchanged small talk until the tray had been brought, the tea served. Then she grew more serious.

'You told me when we first met, Mr. Rama, that your snake had been taken, perhaps by Danuta. Did the snake have any particular home that he lived in?'

'But of course, my lady. A very fine home. Especially carved for him by my cousins in Bengal. The best rose wood, beautifully punctuated with breathing holes for my poor Nasa.'

'Yes, Monsieur, I can imagine.'

'If you see such a box, you will tell me.'

Marguerite had already seen it, but it was best not to reveal this yet to Mr. Rama, though from the look in his eyes she suspected he had already guessed but was too polite to press her.

'Tell me, when we last spoke amidst the sadness of the funeral, you painted a picture for me of Danuta's love for a man. Did you ever see this man?'

'No Madame. Danuta did not bring him to us. It would have driven Auguste to distraction. Already he was made furious by the name she chose to give him, as if he were such a very special man.'

'Oh?'

'Yes. "Mon empereur," she called him.'

'Her emperor. You're certain?'

'Oh yes, Madame.'

'What did Auguste do when she taunted him?'

'Oh no, Madame. No, no, you mistake our Danuta. She was not like that. Not at all. She did not tease poor Auguste. He is capable of fury without much provocation. In fact, Danuta calmed him. She said the man was so old he had nothing to worry for. His demands on her would not be so very great. And he was rich enough for all three of them. In fact she knew how to get money from him for the whole group of us.'

'She said that?'

'That is what Auguste now tells when he sings her generosity, her praises. She had, it seems, already given him some of these riches. He spends most liberally now, our Auguste. Most liberally. Buys us all brandy. But have you ever seen a big man crying, Ma'am? A very big man? It is sad, you believe me?'

'Very sad, Mr. Rama. Very sad. Please will you have a little more tea, and some cold meats. I am sure you must be hungry after your ride.'

'I am wondering if I could become the rider of Danuta's horses. Did you see me? I am not so bad, eh? And bare back, too. But I do not know that I can twirl.' He looked into the distance with a profound sadness.

'You will learn, I feel certain of it. Tell me, Monsieur, when Dr. Labrousse, the tall man with the big beard came to you to show you the photographs of the person found dead on the tracks, did you recognize him?'

'I might have seen him in the crowd. But I couldn't be certain. A proper identification is important. It is no point saying I think . . . or I might . . . or anything at all. I know this. To my pain. In this country, they think all Indians looks exactly alike. Too stupid. So I do not wish to commit the same stupidity.'

'Very wise of you. Very wise. But Danuta, she recognized this man?'

He gave her a wily look. 'Danuta was very brave with her nine lives. I told you this.' He stood, as if he had said enough.

'One more thing, Mr. Rama. I am concerned about that young man they call, P'tit Ours. Was he a particular friend of Danuta's?'

'He is more a friend of Auguste's. Our strong man sees in him a kindred spirit. Danuta . . .' he shrugged. 'Ah, Madame. With women, women like her, I mean, one never knows.'

Marguerite smiled. 'Please come back and see me, before you leave the region, Mr. Rama. And perhaps even bring your friend Auguste. We can try to cheer him a little.'

'You are kind, Ma'am. I am not certain he wants kindness.'

The atmosphere at the lunch table was frosty for more reasons than she could determine. There were the three men, whom she had begun to consider as the household core, and herself.

Olivier had seen Mr. Rama riding away. He had managed a few jibes about the company she kept and how he was less than pleased to have such riff-raff in the house. But she had let his comments pass.

In fact, she wanted everyone in an easy mood. For once, she too, was eager to see the arrogant young curé who had so transformed her husband.

'Do tell me more about the saintly Père François,' she addressed him as soon as the marinated pike was on the table and the first glass of wine poured.

'You liked him, Madame?' The curé's eyes narrowed into little slits of calculation.

'Yes, I did. He talked to me of my parents, you remember.'

'Happy those who are made happy by talk of their parents,' Paul Villemardi muttered, loudly enough for everyone to hear.

'You are not happy talking about your parents?' Marguerite couldn't resist the sculptor's taunts.

'Not particularly, Madame. They do not interest me. Though perhaps they interest me rather more than our dear curé's parents interest him.'

'And what is that supposed to mean?' the curé snapped

'To mean? To mean? Why nothing at all, or simply that God the father displaces all others, I guess. You have altogether abandoned your origins. You never even visit your old mother, who is, I'm told, in sorry straits these days.

'Who told you that? Who?'

'Monsieur le curé has so many duties, I do not wonder he has no time to ride to Tours every day,' Marguerite intervened.

Olivier was staring at her, blinking slightly, as if unsure whether this change of heart towards his preferred priest carried a sarcasm he couldn't detect.

'Indeed, Madame.'

'And I'm sure Monsieur is solicitous of his family closer to home. The Marchands isn't it, mon Père? Do you visit the old man when he comes to Troo? I'm told he had quite a reputation in his youth. Even now. He's apparently rather difficult when he's had too much to drink, though. He, too, I imagine is in need of attention.'

The curé's face had grown contorted with emotions she couldn't altogether decipher, though panic was uppermost in them. He seemed to be straining against some weight. A weight of expletive perhaps, given the angry red which had risen in his smooth cheeks. His eyes shot bolts through her.

'Perhaps you saw his daughter here the other night. She's a Tellier now, as you know. She came with her own two daughters, Laure and Hortense.'

A strangled sound came from the curé's throat, which was neither a yes nor a no.

'Am I wrong, Monsieur? You are not a Marchand, then. Who could have misinformed me? I thought it was the Bishop himself who had said something.'

A cackle come from Paul Villemardi. She ignored it. Olivier looked alarmed. She had forgotten how much lineage meant to him. Evidently the curé had never mentioned anything as unspiritual as direct parentage. He would be less than pleased to find his favourite churchman related to Madame Tellier whose vulgarity he had already twice mentioned to her.

'A very distant relation, Madame,' Père Benoit had found his voice. 'Altogether negligible really. But charity is always necessary. You asked me about Père François?

'Yes, yes.' The man was nothing if not shrewd.

'This will interest you, I feel sure. Père François has long had a concern for the education of women. The appropriate, Catholic education, I should stress. He has overseen many conventual schools, acted as confessor to the girls and to the sisters.'

'Charming,' Paul Villemardi muttered.

Marguerite was suddenly struck by the sculptor's resemblance to the satyr in the oil behind him. She was surprised Olivier hadn't yet seen fit to replace the Dionysian scene.

'In fact the good father talked to me only recently of his hopes for a new establishment in our little town of Montoire, which is growing as you know. He asked me if I cared to be involved, and I assured him that I would be more than happy, indeed, to take a lead. The Bishop of Blois, for whom Père François works, supports the project.'

The curé was now in full control of himself again, brimming with unrestrained egotism, convincing himself of the urgency and importance of this demanding work. His lips moved to produce phases, which swayed him, above all.

'This may well be something Madame herself would like to have a hand in, close as I imagine the education of women is to her heart.' He looked from Olivier, who nodded, to Marguerite who smiled in encouragement.

'The government is intent on secularizing education. We must fight back, particularly since there is now also a threat to the closed orders. Their lands will be taken from them if we are not careful. Yes, we must fight back. And one way to do so is to ensure that the catechism remains at the heart of education, a girl's education. We need to train the future teachers, whether they become professionals or stay in the family.'

'Indeed,' Marguerite voiced her enthusiasm. 'I would do much to help with the education of women. With education will come the vote.'

The priest's face fell. He turned his attention to his plate which still had a few slivers of magret on it. Olivier meanwhile had started to rap his fingers impatiently on the table. If there hadn't still been desert to come, she thought he might already have stood.

'Oh yes, mon Père,' she continued innocently. 'You must engage the church in the struggle for women's right to vote. After all, with so many women firm believers, it might indeed, in the end, further your political ambitions. I am sure that Pope Leo, with all his feelings for social justice, his support of the Republic before his French brothers turned against him, would see the reason in this.'

Olivier was gazing at her in confusion, once again unsure of her intent. Père Benoit was clearly looking for a retort, but hadn't yet been able to find one.

'Yes, and I am most interested in making sure that all the women we have in our service now have achieved a high enough level of education. I am certain we would see less of that horror we have been so subject to of late if this were the case. I mean the abandoning or killing of infants. Which reminds me, Monsieur Villemardi, have you had any success in tracking Louise, our one time maid, for me . . .'

The curé choked on his wine. He and Olivier exchanged baleful glances. She intercepted one and had a glimmering sense once more of being at the centre of a plot she couldn't quite unravel.

Paul Villemardi flung his hair back in his dramatic manner.

'I have been remiss, Madame. I haven't located the young woman myself. But I happened upon Madame Germaine, you know, the midwife, and she told me that she had been approached by a young woman called Louise Limbour, which I believe to be Louise's mother's name by a second marriage. The woman, who from Madame Germaine's description, might well be our Louise, wanted to know how she could go about becoming a midwife. I imagine the girl has decided to take on her stepfather's name'

'Why have you not told me this sooner, Monsieur Villemardi?'

'I only learned yesterday. I chanced to be visiting those uninteresting parents of mine, in order to help my father out with a difficult commission, and Madame Germaine happened in on my mother. Since the two good women are champions in the sport of gossip, I took my opportunity. This particular Louise, if she is indeed ours, is definitely living in the area of Blois. Madame Germaine will provide us with the details.'

'Excellent, Monsieur. The sooner, the better. You didn't by any chance hear from your champion gossips anything about my poor, missing, Martine.'

'Non, Madame.' He seemed to be about to say something more when the sound of Olivier scraping his chair back from the table put an end to the conversation.

'I think I won't join you for coffee, gentlemen,' Marguerite announced with her most fetching smile. 'I want to go and see how little Gabriel is faring.'

She had also just remembered that she had never emptied out her jacket pockets. In all the turbulence of the attack on Durand, she had forgotten about the items from Amandine Septembre's room that she had placed there.

_ 20 _

Marguerite tethered her horse at the far end of the wall which gave onto the orchard and looked around her. Everything was quiet. The valleys were at lunch. A pale sun lay at the height of its winter trajectory.

She pulled on the cap she had decided to wear to protect her hair from the grit of the tunnels, adjusted the belt on her borrowed trousers and walked downhill to the low point of the wall near the hillock.

She was surer of her destination today. Last night in the geographical section of her father's library she had found an old book that detailed some of the tunnels of the region. It was a revelation. As long as her luck held and she didn't bump into P'tit Ours in the cave, she now knew which of the underground paths would lead her to Napoleon Marchand's house.

If the police couldn't gain access to interview the old man who was still away, she hoped she could at least get into his house. She would certainly be able to lay her hands on documents to match the story told in the notebook she had found in the house Amandine Septembre had been held in. She was more certain now than ever that the woman had indeed been held.

The notebook was in fact a diminutive accounts ledger, or a summary of one. She had had to read it several times before its sense came clear. Who it belonged to was plain enough though. That was written in decisive letters on the front page. Xavier Port-Royal Marchand: what exact relation this person had to Napoleon Marchand wasn't clear from the notebook, though he was probably the brother who had been mentioned to her. What was incontestable was that they were or had been in business together. A trading enterprise based in the colony of Martinique in the town of Fort de France.

Trade was good. There were lists of supplies of rum and spices which set sail for Marseilles, ships hired, costs incurred. The problem, it seemed, was that the products had never been paid for and the sums owing grew larger year after year. There were also details of other joint enterprises—a distillery that had gone bankrupt because profits had been drawn in France and never re-invested; a dyeing establishment that had gone to pay for a property in France for which the deeds had never been sent. There was more than ample reason here for Xavier Port-Royal Marchand to journey home and confront his relative, Napoleon Grandcourt Marchand. In fact, the points were summed up at the back of the notebook under a thrice-underscored heading entitled: OWED.

There was also ample motive for Napoleon to do away with his probable brother, if demands or threats grew too vocal. The sums involved in the business were substantial.

It was clear to Marguerite that if Yvette, in her role as maid, had been privy to any of this, there was reason for her to vanish. As there was for the woman called Amandine Septembre who must have sailed to France as Xavier Marchand's companion. As for Danuta the Dancer, given what Mr. Rama had told her yesterday, she had dealings with a man she called the Emperor. Her emperor was no doubt Napoleon. Napoleon Marchand. Danuta, too, must have overheard something of the two Marchands' dealings.

Marguerite remembered that the first time she had met the horrendous Napoleon with his daughter, he had talked of blackmail—a 'blackmailing strumpet' is what he had called Yvette. Was it possible that this girl who had no compunctions about drawing blood, who was bolder than her sister, who was, it seemed, frightened of neither P'tit Ours nor her master, really had tried to blackmail the man? As Danuta could well have, too. Money for sexual favours would be even larger if an element of bribery entered the picture. And Mr. Rama had said there was plenty of money.

But what about Martine? Marguerite could only think that Napoleon's henchman, P'tit Ours, really did think the girl was Yvette and had stolen her away to bring her back to Napoleon Marchand.

Would she find her in Marchand's house? It was primarily because of this that she had set out without waiting for the Inspector. If the girl was there, perhaps hidden in some dank cellar like the storeroom they had found in Amandine's house, and Marchand was away, the likelihood was that she was safe. There was no time to lose. P'tit Ours wouldn't act without his master's orders. He had seemed to like the girl.

One more thing worried her, but not with the same urgency: P'tit Ours' refrain that Yvette had gone to the doctor, to Dr. Labrousse. Had they beat her up. Did she need medication? Was there something Labrousse was keeping from her out of fear? He had made an impromptu confession to her about his brother. In her experience the easy confession often signalled a deeper, more secret, guilt.

First things first, however. She lowered herself into the cave, sniffed a pervasive dampness, a smell of rot and mould, and peered round. Something scurried across her boots and she leapt back. Rats. She wasn't used to creatures any more. She lit her lantern with care and had a better look. A potato or two had been gnawed at since her last visit with the Inspector. But the ashes at the base of the small fire were cold.

She hurried through the alternate opening this time. Her path lay uphill. Unless she was imagining it, there were fresh footprints here. The prints clogs made, their uneven undersides imprinted on the moist earth. P'tit Ours, she imagined and shuddered. Though it could be any one else. She stopped to listen. Quiet. But her lantern flickered. There was a draft of air coming from the direction of her destination. She hurried on, fearful now that her light might give out.

What felt like a long time later, she reached an arched, thick-slatted door. It stood just a fraction open. She almost shouted with relief, then tripped on something, righting herself only at the last moment. It took a second for her to realize that she had stumbled on a twig, This was what ensured the door didn't creak shut. Could this, too, be a sign of P'tit Ours?

Taking a deep, calming breath she let herself in, slowly, slowly, so that the groan of the door was minimal. She made sure the twig was back in its exact place.

A quick sweep of her lantern indicated she was in a narrow wine cellar. Barrels and bottles lined the walls. There was rum, too. She paused at a label. Martinique. Its presence reassured her that she was in Napoleon Marchand's house. As softly as she could she made her way up creaking cellar stairs. The door at the end opened easily. She found herself in a kitchen. The light startled her. It came from a high window out of which she couldn't see. The slope of the hill must mean the kitchen wasn't on a level.

There were pots on the stove, still warm, a pervasive scent of spice. Cinnamon and nutmeg, something stronger, too. Did that old vulture of a servant, Hercule, cook for himself? The Inspector had told her no one had answered to the police and she had assumed he, too, would be away. Or were there others here, as she had suspected? Others who had been warned not to open any doors?

Her pulse quickened. With a sudden worry, she placed her lamp carefully on the second cellar step to ensure a quick retreat should she need it, then tiptoed across the room towards a stairwell.

Voices came at her from somewhere. Loud, then soft. She followed the sound, up the stairs and into a square, sombre hall, none too clean and hung with rifles and walking sticks, and coat hooks sporting an assortment of cloaks and caps. In front of her was the main door of the house. Four other doors gave off the hall, two behind her, two in front. The one at the back, left, near the stairs which led to the first floor, was ajar. It was from here the voices came, as well as the main source of daylight.

One voice was distinctly a man's. The second was uncertain. It was soft and slurred, She couldn't make out the words.

Holding her breath, Marguerite crept towards the door. She flattened herself against the wall and peered in. She saw a ramshackle drawing room with an assortment of worn armchairs and footstools and peeling wallpaper. On the table closest to her stood a bowl with an assortment of pipes, long handled pipes. Opium pipes. Opium. Of course. The dead man's single pupil had been contracted in the way of opium smokers. But there was no one in here. The voices came from further away through a set of double doors thickly curtained in old bronze velvet to keep out the cold.

She tiptoed over and stopped by the curtains. She could see clearly enough through the crack where they hadn't been fully pulled together.

A fire crackled and blazed. It was a smaller room, much of its space taken up by a lumpy claw-footed sofa on which large gold flowers grew as resplendent as the Emperor for whom the fashion had been named.

The couple sitting on the sofa startled her. She only stopped her rush of breath in time.

The crumbling old giant who was Napoleon Marchand, with his straggling unkempt hair and massive features was resting his large head on the copious, chocolate brown cleavage of Amandine Septembre. He was patting the woman, stroking her bare statuesque shoulders above the thick drapery of her violet gown. His eyes, which looked straight towards Marguerite, lolled. His lips were loose, his expression lascivious. He was mumbling something she couldn't make out. Endearments probably.

So the woman was his mistress, Marguerite thought with uncustomary distaste. He kept her here for his pleasure. She had misunderstood.

Amandine was sitting very straight, somewhat stiff. A deep, yet soft voice suddenly came out of her just as Marguerite was about to creep away across the room again. It took a moment for Marguerite to attune her ears.

'Why can't I go out, papa?' The mellow voice caught on a sob. 'Amandine is going crazy. Crazy with being locked up. Hercule doesn't let me out.'

'Soon, my fragrant beauty. Soon. Soon Papa will find the right place for you.'

'What kind of right place?'

'Far from here.'

'But Uncle Xavier. Where is Uncle Xavier? He said he wouldn't be gone long. But it's been weeks, Papa. Weeks. We have to wait for him to return.'

'You smell so nice, ma petite Amandine. Put your hand where Papa likes it. Then Papa will be kind. Papa will be in a good humour. Come Amandine.'

A shock ran through Marguerite. It made her knees weak. So the woman really was being held captive. Not any woman either. Amandine was the old reprobate's daughter. Daughter by a woman he had either bedded or bigamously married in Martinique. And now he was demanding his daughter's sexual favours.

She wanted to rage. To scream at the injustice of it. But intervening right now would do no one any good. She had neither the necessary force nor police authority to stop the man. On the other hand, witnessing what the monster was going to tell Amandine about the whereabouts of Uncle Xavier would certainly land him in jail for the rest of his days.

Amandine had wriggled away towards the end of the sofa and now Napoleon was coaxing and cajoling.

'A little more rum for you, my island flower? Yes, yes. Then you'll be kind to your old Papa.' He picked up the bottle, but nothing flowed from it.

With an effort, he heaved himself up and shouted. 'Empty. Empty! Where is that no good oaf? P'tit Ours,' he bellowed, bellowed so loudly that Marguerite sprang back. From upstairs came the sound of uneven footsteps.

'P'tit Ours.' That terrible shout again.

Marguerite hid in the crack behind the door, pulling it as close as possible to her face as she dared. If she held her breath, P'tit Ours wouldn't see her. He didn't see well. The windows were shuttered. The only light came through the cracks and from the fire.

She said all these things to herself one after another to keep herself calm. Calm so that her breath came slowly.

She heard the heavy sound of P'tit Ours footfall as he rushed into the room. Meanwhile, through the doors, Amandine was asking, 'When will Uncle be back, Papa?'

'That again. Forget about him. Say goodbye to him. He went off with a fairground strumpet. A dancer. Fled. That's what I found out in town. I can bet you won't see him any more, that one. Not soon. No. Not soon.'

There was a sob from Amandine and then a torrent of words from P'tit Ours which sounded like emphatic negation.

'No, no. Wrong. Wrong, witch. Uncle bumped down stairs. Push, then bump. Bump bump. Then to tracks. Uncle a sack on tracks.'

'Shut up, P'tit Ours!' The old man screamed. 'Hold your tongue. What did I tell you. Out of here. Out.'

She could imagine the spittle leaping from that gargantuan mouth.

There was the sound of a slap. Heavy, hard. She felt its impact, felt that it must be P'tit Ours who had been cuffed. Poor, strange lad. Then came footsteps. The curtain was being pulled to. But P'tit Ours didn't flee. Didn't leave her side of the double room. He stopped there. Stopped right to the side of the curtains, peering. She was trapped.

Amandine had started to cry, big full sobs. Then P'tit Ours began to cry, too, like a child in sympathy with a friend. A friend he had stood up for.

Marguerite turned her head towards the crack in the door. If she closed one eye, she could see.

'What will I do? What will I do?' Amandine moaned, rocked herself back and forth on the sofa. 'I thought I heard something. Yes, Papa. Yes. That night in the big house with all those whores. The night you shot your pistol at me. Shrieking. I heard shrieking. I dreamt of the peacocks. But they weren't peacocks.'

'Shut up.'

I have to get out. Have to. I'm going crazy. Like prison. I have done no wrong, Papa. No wrong, you hear me?'

The old man leapt up and shouted, cursed. His big belly wobbled with the effort. He reared his leonine head, his eye's bulged. His sagging jowls waggled. He slapped Amandine. One slap then another. His trousers were half way down his legs. He was baring his parts to her.

Marguerite remembered another slap and trembled for the woman. She wasn't thinking clearly anymore. What could she do? She pushed the door forward slightly and peered round the side to see where P'tit Ours was standing. He, too, had his member in his hand, now as if in imitation of his corrupt old master.

'Ungrateful bitch.' The man yelled. 'Where am I supposed to take you? Where? For a walk in the village? In town? In all your finery? On my arm? Bonjour Madame la Marquise. Have you seen your colour? Mud. Mud brown. Like your mother. The white bitch will kill you before she lets you out. Kill you if she hears who you really are and finds you here. Bad enough, she hates Xavier. His companion, I called you.'

The old man snorted.

Amandine had stood up. She was almost as tall as the ancient hulk and she looked stronger.

'Sister? Kill her own sister?' she shouted back.

'Not the first time. So shut up.'

P'tit Ours was so excited, he didn't see Marguerite. He was jumping up and down, staring into the room.

'Why should I shut up? Why? I'll go to the Police. Amandine Septembre is a citizen of France.'

'You know nothing, my girl. Nothing. They'll string you up before they believe you. String you up for the murder of Xavier. She'll see to it.'

She heard the scrape of the sofa's claws being pushed back as if someone had fallen on it, the groan of springs.

'I'm taking care of you. Protecting you. Aren't I? Now show me how you say thank you to your long lost papa.'

'Belly in her face,' P'tit Ours shouted, his hand still on his member. 'Belly in her face.'

Suddenly there was tumultuous crash from the room, furniture falling, the thump and thud of bodies. P'tit Ours pulled the curtains open and ran in.

His old master lay on the floor. A toppled table half covered him. The youth stared down in disbelief, as if he couldn't believe the proof of his eyes. Then, he shouted. Shouted and shouted, whether in fear or euphoria wasn't clear, since with each shout he landed a hefty kick on his master's inert body.

A table lamp fell.

Amandine Septembre grabbed it and stamped on the flame that had leapt onto the carpet. She took P'tit Ours's hand.

Marguerite found the shelter between the door and the wall again, just as the two came towards her. Though she wasn't altogether sure why, she felt it better not to show herself yet. She didn't know how the volatile P'tit Ours would react to her presence. Nor what the twosome might be planning. She also needed to make a foray upstairs for Martine, perhaps even for Yvette. Who knew what kind of brothel the old monster kept for himself.

'Amandine Witch killed the old master. Amandine Witch killed the old master!' P'tit Ours was chanting as they passed near her. His clogs tapped out the rhythm of a dance.

'Hush, P'tit Ours. Hush. Amandine has to go away.' The regal woman gave the youth a slow smile.

'Police man wants to lock P'tit Ours up. Lock up. Like Amandine.'

'We won't let them, P'tit Ours. We'll run away. Run away together.'

'Away?'

'Yes. You'll take care of Amandine. Is your horse here, P'tit Ours?'

'No horse. Come from ground.'

There was a sudden jarring noise. The bell.

Amandine and P'tit Ours raced from the room, hand in hand. She could hear them clattering down the stairs towards the kitchen, then another door opening.

She didn't stop them. She didn't want to. The police would do that soon enough. She made for the front door to let them in. A noise from behind her stopped her. She turned to see Napoleon Marchand's arm move and take a grip on the sofa. Then give it up to reach for the bottle.

So the old tyrant wasn't dead. Despite her better judgment, she was just a little sorry.

But there was all the more reason, now, to hurry the police in. Amandine hadn't killed the old man. P'tit Ours's kick was only a misdemeanour. He felt to her like some unruly, overgrown child who had been misled into wrong doing. Now Napoleon Grandcourt Marchand would live to have his day in court where he would stand accused of two deaths.

She hoped with all her might that there were no others, that a trip upstairs would find the house empty of cadavers.

She pulled back the lock on the heavy front door and was about to turn the key when the voice behind it stopped her motion.

'Cousin. Cousin? Are you there? It's Père Benoit. You told me to come this week. Hercule? Is that you? Open up. Marchand's left an envelope for me. Open up.'

Did she want the curé here? More to the point, what did he want? And why hadn't the police who were meant to be watching the place stopped him?

Without pausing to consider any further, Marguerite ran upstairs. This might be her only chance to check for Martine and Yvette before old Gargantua rose from his stupour.

215

_ 21 _

She could find no one in the house. No one in the dining room with its fine mahogany table, where the wall sported a stuffed boar's head of deplorable ugliness. No one in the rooms upstairs where the gilded paper buckled on the walls and fell away in long shards. Nor was there any sign of Martine or Yvette in the tiny servants' rooms in the eaves.

There was nothing in Napoleon Grandcourt Marchand's house except an abiding smell of damp and dereliction. And drawers stuffed with an accumulation of papers. She started to rifle through these, hoping to spot instant corroboration of what she had found in Xavier Marchand's notebook. Instead she found a drawer full of property deeds. She noted their presence with the thought that they might just name a house where the Branquart sisters were being kept, since they so palpably weren't here. But searching now would take more time than she felt she had. This detailed work would have to be left for another day.

Half way down the stairs, she stopped abruptly. The front door was open. How could someone have come in, or indeed gone out without her hearing? Who had a key to the lock? She crouched low on the landing. Could Marchand himself have got up, Lazarus-like, from his swoon, and escaped before the police arrived? She pricked up her ears.

There was a sound coming from the room where she had last seen the man. A mewling sound, like a child's whimper.

She moved softly towards it. The sight which greeted her, made her rush once more for the safety of the curtains. It wasn't so much that she feared being seen now, but a kind of modesty overcame her, a visceral embarrassment.

Madame Tellier was there. She must have come in as silently as a ghost. She had propped her father up in an armchair or perhaps he had managed to get into it himself and he was reclining, his eyes open but glazed. She was crouched at his feet, her head on his lap, her hair, her most beautiful feature, a tumble of loosened locks meshed around his fingers. The daughterly posture wouldn't have troubled Marguerite, except that it wasn't altogether daughterly, not in any ordinary way. The woman was talking in a little girl's voice, rich with lisps and endearments, stroking her father's hands, stroking his face, stroking where Marguerite didn't want to look.

'Ah papa, mon petit papa, what has happened to you? What has happened to you? All because you wouldn't let your little Estelle in earlier. Or yesterday. You barred the door. Naughty Papa. But now you've opened it and you'll be kind to your little Estelle, your Estelle who loves you, who loves only you. Yes, mon petit papa.' Her voice grew more urgent. She was rocking herself against the man, who sat there, impassive, staring into the flames, grunting at her caresses.

Suddenly, the woman sprang to her feet. Her eyes smouldered, huge in that long odd face. Marguerite stepped back, shuddering.

Estelle Tellier had picked a brightly patterned embroidered bag from the floor. A howl came from her. Her nostrils flared. 'So you have had her here. You've kept her here. All along. All along. Where is she? I'll tear her eyes out.' Her breath rasped. 'It is her, isn't it? Not just his companion. Where? Where is she? Where are you hiding her?'

The woman was panting. Her expression tortured, demented. She pulled at her hair. 'How could you? How could you, Papa? After everything I've done for you. Everything. I'll kill her. That'll be the end of it. The end of both of them. One, two. The end.'

The face was terrible in its contortion. A dark energy came from the woman that made Marguerite think that like a steam engine she would mow anything down in her path.

'You love her, don't you. You love her. That black bastard of yours. Where is she. I'll kill her. You love her more.' The woman was sobbing now. 'It killed Maman.'

A vase flew across the room and landed near Madame Tellier with a crash.

'Stop your whining, woman. Get a hold on yourself. Or I'll put Amandine in for her share of the will after all. She's a kind soul, like her mother. My very own "island Josephine". Not like that greedy, nagging bitch who was yours. A schemer incarnate.' A mad laugh erupted from him, loud, curdling. 'Your blackness is all on the inside.'

'This is her bag. I recognize it.' Madame Tellier's voice was sharper than a knife through her sobs.

'You mean the sweet little Creole tart went off without it?' Napoleon taunted her. 'I'll have to find her. Where could she have gone? Maybe she's learned to fly now. All those magic tricks they have.'

The man was brutal, savage. Marguerite judged he would commit a murder as easily and with as little conscience as a child might crush a beetle. Anyone could be his beetle.

'I've had enough. I've had enough of you.'

'Quiet. If you want to scream like a fishwife, go and do it at that good for nothing husband I bought for you. And behave yourself, or I won't buy any for your daughters.'

The howl that came from Madame Tellier was followed by another object hurled across the room.

'How dare you insult me like that?'

Marguerite raced softly for the front door. It still stood half open and in a moment she was outside, outside where the sun was swathed in pink mists on the horizon. She felt utterly exhausted. A herd of raging animals had trampled over her and left her flattened on the ground.

She breathed deeply, hoping the crisp air would wipe out what she had seen. Wipe out the perversions of love she had witnessed in these last hours. They made her want to shut herself up in a cloister or ride eternally over some unpeopled desert, free of families.

Yet there was something pitiful in the woman's jealousy, in this childhood enactment of a love that should never have been. She loved the monster, despite everything. Despite the wrongness, despite the humiliation.

Perversions of love. They were everywhere.

Marguerite shivered. She started to run, run wildly through the copse, down the hill and away.

She had almost reached the orchard where she hoped her horse was still tethered when she saw a wagon winding up the road towards her. She was surprised to recognize Dr. Labrousse and next to him Chief Inspector Durand, bundled up as if for an expedition to the Arctic. Following on behind them was a constable on horseback.

Worried that they wouldn't recognize her, Marguerite waved them down.

'Ah Madame, I've been anxious about you. You mustn't undertake these escapades alone. Your messenger didn't find me until late. I was buried in the post office, waiting for that telegram. It came finally. It gives us everything we need . . . and then as I was setting out, I met Dr. Labrousse.'

The Doctor interrupted him. 'Yes. Madame sent her man for me. It seems her father has had a fall.'

'I'll tell you everything I've discovered while we drive, Messieurs. Perhaps the constable can fetch my horse for me and bring it to the Marchand house.'

The Inspector helped her up into the wagon. She squeezed gratefully into the seat next to him and quickly began to tell the men what she had witnessed. She left out the prurient detail, only emphasizing the depths of Marchand's cruel amorality and the grip he had on P'tit Ours, as well as his daughter. She could gauge Durand's response from his clenched fists.

'A degenerate monster,' he muttered.

The doctor was more difficult to judge. She had a passing sense that he already knew something of the family's corruption.

Marguerite told them she was certain they would find P'tit Ours and Amandine Septembre at the other end of the tunnel in the house bordering the Tellier property. Their more urgent business, however, was with that depraved old murderer, Napoleon Marchand, the mastermind of the valleys' ills.

'We have everything we need to take him in,' Durand grunted. 'And if I have anything to do with it, he won't ride across these hills again, Madame. The Martinique lot have confirmed that Xavier Port-Royal Marchand, partner to Napoleon in the firm of Marchand et Marchand sailed to

France on the cargo ship of the same name, which belongs to the French part of the firm. He sailed with one Amandine Septembre who is a Creole and his housekeeper, though rumour widely has it in Fort de France, that she's either his niece or daughter, her mother, Josephine, having been employed in the same house for many years before Amandine's birth.'

'And they came here to extract funds owed to them by the old man. So he decided to get rid of his brother and keep Amandine as his mistress.'

Her stomach heaved. Only after a pause could she go on to mutter, 'I'll show you the notebook listing figures when we get home, Inspector.'

The forced grandeur of the run-down house now looked doubly unwelcoming. The door was closed and as Dr. Labrousse pulled the bell, Marguerite heard a slithering sound from the side of the porch. She took a step backwards. Somewhere a magpie set up a terrible screech. She had forgotten about Mr. Rama's box. His snake was evidently still in it, somnolent in the cold, but still active.

As the door opened to them, a red-faced Madame Tellier appeared. With her came a whiff of what suddenly struck Marguerite as the house's abiding odour, an undertow of excrement and sewage. Father and daughter, in their moral corruption, were like an emanation of the house's physical decay.

'Doctor. At last. It's my father. He's delirious. He's suffered a fall, I believe. Or someone has knocked him over. Perhaps with a poker. I think I know who it might be.'

She stopped as she noticed the Inspector and with something of a double-take, Marguerite, who had removed her cap, so that at least her hair might make her recognizable to the woman.

The Inspector didn't give her time to query their presence. 'Madame, we were with the doctor when your message came. We thought he might need help. Your father is a large man. There are also some questions I must put to him.'

'This is not a time for questions, Inspector,' the woman said crossly.

Marguerite could hardly bring herself to meet her eyes after all she had witnessed. She focussed instead on her dress, a brown-red, the colour of dried blood.

Napoleon Marchand, a vast, filthy, wool dressing gown draped over his shoulders, was half reclining in an armchair, his legs stretched in front of him and propped on a footstool. Behind him was a rich peacock tapestry which looked decidedly Persian. She hadn't spotted that before. Nor had she noticed the hanging which had been violently torn from the wall and lay half spread across the floor. Could that have happened since she had left?

'This is your doctor, is it?' the voice the old man propelled at his daughter was like a fist. He was staring at Marguerite from canny eyes, licking his full lips slowly with an animal tongue. His teeth emerged as large tobacco stained stumps. 'More fit for the bedchamber than the hospital ward, by my reckoning. I've seen her before haven't I? The Comtesse of something or other. These countesses are always playing at being boys. I have nothing against boys. What bit of me does she want to see?' His hand was already on his trousers.

Dr. Labrousse and Durand stepped in front of her more swiftly than a military escort.

'You've had a fall, Monsieur Marchand. Or so your daughter tells me.'

'Don't believe a word she says. I've been assaulted.'

'Assaulted by whom?'

'And who are you?'

'Chief Inspector Durand of the Paris Police.'

His eyes narrowed and for a moment Marguerite had a clear sense of the malign intelligence that lived within the man's drunken excesses.

'You've come for her, have you?'

'For whom?'

The man's mad laugh wheezed. 'For my torturer, who else?' he turned his vast head towards Marguerite. 'When I was young, women were saints. Soft, beautiful. Now! Now you're all potential poisoners! Hurlers of vitriol! Each and every one of you. Oh yes, Madame de . . . Old Napoleon reads the newspapers. Burning out the eyes of the lords of creation.

That's what you're best at. One-time sweethearts, wives, ungrateful daughters, all attacking their masters. Isn't that so Chief Inspector? Isn't that what the vixens do best now! Snakes, they are . . .

'Quiet, papa,' Madame Tellier growled. Not the little girl, anymore, but like the incarnation of everything he evoked.

'I noticed you have an interest in snakes, Monsieur Marchand,' Marguerite said innocently.

'Let me feel your pulse, Monsieur.' Dr. Labrousse had approached Napoleon.

'Snakes!' The man shook him off as if he were one. 'Hate the creatures. Devils. Satan's offspring. Every one of them.'

'But surely there's one in the box on your porch.'

'Not mine,' he growled. 'Belongs to the fairground folk.'

'Can we have a tisane for him, Madame. He needs liquid. Lots of it. Water as well, first of all. And then something warm. He's burning.'

Madame Tellier threw a suspicious look round the room, then at an authoritative gesture from the doctor, hurried down to the kitchen, her untied hair swinging behind her like a shroud.

'Fairground folk? 'Marguerite brought his attention back to her. 'You mean, poor Danuta the Dancer!'

'Poor!' Napoleon's guffaw filled the room. 'Poor. After everything she's blackmailed me for. All of them blackmailers these days. The women, The men. The men in skirts.' He roared at his own joke.

'Come on Marchand,' the Inspector intervened with none of his customary civility. I've had enough of this. You know you had her killed.'

The man sprang out of his chair and lunged towards the Inspector, who stepped deftly backwards, so that Marchand would have fallen, had Labrousse not seized him and with a heave, shoved him back into his chair.

'Killed. What are you talking about?'

'Murdered.' Durand elaborated. He looked towards the door of the room, where his constable now stood.

Old Napoleon's face had grown blotched with purple He lashed the stick at his side against the table, a riding crop to spur a horse on. 'Oh no. You can't pin that on Napoleon Marchand. Cheeky strumpet may deserve to be dead. Nothing better than a whore. But that's nothing to do with me. Nothing. Now get out of here. All of you. Leave me alone.'

His eyes bore down on Marguerite as he tapped his stick on the floor, each tap a threat. 'Your idea, is it. Madame de . . . ? Well. You're wrong. So get your ass out of here. Out of my house. If you think old Napoleon has respect for your kind, you're wrong. Remember . . .' He narrowed his eyes, watched her leap of fear, then guffawed again. 'Death is a democrat. Takes your brothers and your masters.' He raised his stick in the air, held it like a scythe.

For a moment, Marguerite felt the man's hypnotic power. He had been handsome in his youth, Madame Germaine had told her. A Heathcliffe of the tender river valleys. He had made the young women swoon and had his pick of them. It was those dark, glowering eyes. She couldn't shake them off now. She felt she had met a latter-day Caligula, or an incarnation of the grim reaper and her end was at hand. She couldn't move.

In one swift movement, the Inspector broke the spell. The stick was propelled from the man's hand and he and the Constable were ranked at old Napoleon's side.

'Here's the tisane, doctor. And a pitcher of water.' Madame Tellier had come into the room. Her full skirts brushed past the Inspector, forcing him away from her father. She looked down at Durand from her impressive height, as if he were some unwanted worm who had stupidly dared to crawl into her orchard.

'Have you not noticed, Inspector, that my father is ill. Delirious with fever?'

'Your father is under arrest, Madame. We are taking him in for questioning.'

Marguerite was keenly aware of the woman's resemblance to her father which the difference in age and sex so often masked. The same long face, the same protruding features, that sallow drinker's skin with its ruptured veins, the sheer size of hands and feet and face.

'You must be mad, Inspector. What can a sick old man do?'

'This particular sick old man is responsible for the death of one, Xavier Port-Royal Marchand, who sailed here to lay claim to the debts his partner and brother, your father, had thus far refused to repay. The sum is sizeable. The motive in place.'

'Stupid fool fell down the stairs, didn't he?'

Marguerite and the Inspector glanced at each other.

'Not before he'd managed to take in a great deal of poison, not to mention opium. I notice you have a plentiful supply of pipes here. I imagine those and a little push had something to do with it all. Otherwise, why dump his body on the tracks?'

'This is madness Inspector. You have proof of nothing. This is pure conjecture.'

'Don't you worry, Madame. We have sufficient proof.'

Old Napoleon had leaned back in his chair and was staring off into space. For a moment, Marguerite thought the man might faint again.

'Who would have thought, eh? Who would have thought.' Tears gathered in his eyes and started to pour down his face. 'Everyone taking advantage of old Napoleon. Everyone. Danuta, the beautiful dancer, that arrogant shit of a curé, even Yvette. And I thought she was a Saint. Nothing more than a blackmailer. All of them. Money, money. Napoleon's treasure. Because I'm old. Spent. Even that dumb Xavier. After everything I did for him. All those years. Everything . . .'

'Napoleon Grandcourt Marchand, I'm arresting you for the murder of your brother, Xavier Port Royal Marchand.' The Chief Inspector stepped forward again.

'Murder? Murder? There was no murder. The stupid oaf fell down the stairs. That's what stupid drunken oafs do. And if someone brushed past him and helped him on his way, that's certainly not murder. Not murder I tell you. If you want murder you'll have to go elsewhere.' He shook his large head, then glowered at his daughter. 'After all those favours.'

'Drink this, Monsieur. You're dehydrated.' Labrousse forced liquid down the man's throat. After a moment, Napoleon took the glass in his own hand and drank thirstily. The sound of his swallowing filled the room.

'You did things for your daughter, Amandine, too. Did you? Favours. Like keeping her locked up.' The Inspector wasn't sparing his punches.

Madame Tellier walked up to him and seemed to be about to grab him by the scruff of the neck and eject him. She placed herself between her father and Durand. Shadows from the flames augmented the ferocity in her face.

'My father has only *one* daughter, Inspector. I don't know who's been carrying tales to you. By all the laws of France I am that daughter.'

'Some fifty percent of births, Madame, fall outside of the law. Being outside the law doesn't make your father's progeny any the less flesh and blood.'

'Plenty of flesh,' the old mammoth growled.

A look of such venom passed over Madame Tellier's features, that Marguerite found herself taking refuge behind the sofa.

'He's delirious, Inspector. I told you. You must go now. You can come back in the morning when his temperature has abated. He can't be moved, can he doctor? She challenged Labrousse.

'Aren't you afraid to be left here alone with this violent murderer, Madame?' The Inspector was on a new tack, his voice low, confidential. 'I know your father spends much of his time away from here. Perhaps you're not aware just how dangerous he is. Quite depraved and deranged, Madame. I wouldn't wish myself alone next to him.'

'Dangerous, Violent!' Marchand's ears seemed to be as acute as a young man's . 'Is that what the she-devil has been saying about me? Ugly bitch. Keep your eye on her and you'll see who's violent. Should have sent her to her Aunt right from the start. That would have cleaned her up. She could have prayed for my sins. Prayed for my sins.'

The thought brought forth laughter like a clap of thunder. It provoked wheezing. He started to cough, spat a gob at a bronze spittoon and missed.

'He's raving, doctor. Give him something.' Madame Tellier muttered.

Labrousse was already stirring a powder into the tisane, which he now handed to his patient. Napoleon Marchand took it from him. While he sniffed it, he tilted his head towards Marguerite in the manner of large, shaggy dog. Again she had a sense of a malign intelligence lurking beneath the strutting surface of the man's behaviour. The oafish clown, the deranged tyrant were real enough, but they were also poses. 'Pay no attention to her, Comtesse. She's mad.'

'Drink up now, Monsieur. It will help calm you.' The doctor gave the Inspector a meaningful look. 'You'll feel much better. Much better in the morning.'

'Do you know where we can find Yvette, Monsieur. Yvette and her sister? They're both missing.' Marguerite pricked up her courage to ask.

'Yes, speak up Marchand. If you tell us where you've put them, I'll put in a word with the investigating magistrate.'

Dark eyes rolled over the Inspector. 'Ask the bitch, why don't you? Ask her. Old Napoleon knows nothing. Old Napoleon just wants to rest.' He drank noisily.

A look passed between Labrousse and Madame Tellier. Marguerite intercepted it. She didn't know what it meant.

'I think he'll sleep now,' the doctor said. 'He'll sleep until morning, Inspector. Why not leave the constable here to watch over him and you can have him brought in the morning. A little less alcohol in his system will make him far more amenable to questioning. And to identifying the body. He'd be a bit heavy to move, if he weren't willing.'

'That's right, Inspector. Madame Tellier was suddenly all complaisance. 'I'll come in with him if you like. I only knew Xavier from his portrait, but I'm sure if the body is his, I might recognize it too. I had no idea he was in the country. Papa never said anything. He always keeps things close to his chest.'

'Does he now?' The inspector cracked his knuckles as if he wanted to hit somebody. 'All right, Madame. As a favour to you. But I want him in Montoire before lunch. I shall come personally to fetch him.'

Marguerite felt a great wave of tiredness swirl over her. She swayed a little, clutched the back of a chair.

'Madame needs to be taken home, Inspector.'

'Why don't you do that, Labrousse? I'll stay on here to explore a little, and keep Madame Tellier and the constable company. I'm sure Madame will do the honours of the property for me, won't you Madame Tellier.'

'Of course, Inspector. The company will be most welcome.'

'Remember, Madame. No alcohol. Even if he begs.'

'Maybe just a little drink for the Inspector and myself.'

Watching the gracious smile play over her face, Marguerite began to wonder if she had imagined all the rest.

_ 22 _

Freshly white-washed, the ancient church stood square and fortress-like beneath its black sloping roof and rounded cone of a steeple. Its stolid aspect, its heavy bells, its very lack of beauty served to remind that it had been there for longer than anyone could remember—longer than most of the small hamlet that surrounded its bulk, longer than the trees which stood bare and wintry at its side. It would undoubtedly abide whatever the whimsies of its sometimes errant, more often faithful congregation.

Or perhaps this was simply the meaning Marguerite chose to attribute to the church today. She had effectively been coerced into attendance by Olivier. In a voice that brooked no dissent, he had announced at breakfast that it really was more than time the wife of the Catholic candidate came to mass with her husband.

She was happy enough to join him. She had an ulterior motive. She wondered, too, whether the drive in the carriage, which provided no easy escape, might offer the right moment in which to confront him directly about Gabriel.

But she wasn't thinking very clearly about all that. She was still too deeply shaken by yesterday's experience of the Marchand house. She had not wanted to accompany Inspector Durand back there this morning. Her dreams had been filled with the slow repetition of scenes, memorized despite herself. Amandine, P'tit Ours, Madame Tellier and the monster, their words and actions played themselves over and over in her mind, as did imagined scenes of Xavier Marchand, bumping down a staircase. In one version he was dead, his body unfeeling, but for some reason, already one-eyed. In another, he was screaming, his hand clinging to Danuta the Dancer, whom he pulled behind him.

For all their repetition, neither of the scenes altogether gelled. Nor did what she had witnessed in the house. There was something, she wasn't grasping. Then, too, despite Napoleon Marchand's depths of depravity, she had felt that his surprise at learning Danuta was dead was genuine.

She grappled with what he had said about Yvette as well and with the look that had passed between the doctor and Madame Tellier. She wished Martine were here to talk it over with and she only hoped the girl would turn up as soon as the police had apprehended P'tit Ours and Amandine Septembre in the house next door to the Tellier's. She couldn't imagine the youth doing the girl harm within the Creole woman's commanding presence.

The restless night had brandished another possibility. It had brought with it the notion that Martine, like Marguerite's one-time protégée, Olympe, might have been troubled enough to abscond in a walking trance, a fugue state in which she was no longer aware of her surroundings or indeed who she was. She hoped this was her own ghosts and worry speaking, the after-effect of wanting to run from the corrupt monster's presence.

Preliminary police searches, instigated by Durand in the Montoire and Vendome area, had so far brought no sighting of Martine. Nor had she been seen by old family friends. Marguerite had now written to the Priest, Père François, who had so troubled Martine at the party, though she had little faith that she would elicit much from him in this way. She would go and see him as soon as she could.

Bonneted peasant women and a few old men in caps walked through the church doors. The more affluent members of the congregation were already in their pews, as was a gaggle of children from the local primary school. Marguerite allowed Olivier to lead her in. He stood very tall and straight, the astrakhan collar of his coat high and splendid over the glistening white of his shirt and his dark cravat.

The scent of incense pricked at her nostrils. The invisible organ played above and around them, its rich chords forming their own architecture as solid as the church walls. The wood shone, the pads on the kneeling stools were new, the altar was dressed with a rich cloth and the old frescos above it had grown brighter, whether with paint or cleaning she couldn't tell from her distance. She nodded at the fellow members of the congregation as Olivier and she took their places.

Outside the tiny family chapel in La Rochambert, this church was the closest one to the house and one of three in the rural parish over which Père Benoit presided. There he was now. Pristine, lace-encrusted white covered his black habit. He took his place in front of the altar and stretched out his arms. His Latin voice was sonorous. His eyes gleamed. His plump face was composed in a mask of good will. She suddenly saw him, not as himself, a wily priest intent on boosting his place in the hierarchy, but as someone who incarnated a role that had passed through time and which was larger than himself, larger than his pettiness.

She stole a glance at Olivier. Was this how he saw the curé? She hadn't understood. She had utterly missed a ritual significance which transformed the priest into someone other. He was a medium between a terrestrial and a heavenly sphere.

She watched her husband surreptitiously through the length of the mass. With the scripture reading from Paul's epistle to the Romans, a change came over him.

'God also gave them up to uncleanness through the lusts of their own hearts, to dishonour their own bodies between themselves . . .' the curé intoned.

Olivier gripped the seat in front of him with such force that his knuckles turned white. His lips curled into a snarl. He was staring at Père Benoit with an intensity of hatred, like a man staring at an enemy, or worse, a friend by whom he has been utterly betrayed. Had she missed some cues? Had there been a startling row between the men? It made no sense. It was Olivier, after all, who had insisted they come here this morning.

The sermon, forcefully argued, invoked them to a purity of body and spirit. Marguerite was fascinated by the way in which everyday politics entered its core so naturally as to make the secular part and parcel of the spiritual sphere. The Republic, too, must be pure and expunge its alien elements, the curé argued, giving his congregation a political brief that seemed to come from God. Why, in their very midst they had seen what havoc debauchery could bring: a lewd gypsy dancer had invited murder, had been struck down; a man, too, a stranger in their midst.

So that was the way the Church yielded its influence, Marguerite thought: the line came down from the centre and made itself felt in the smallest congregations in the land, in the most mundane and local of community responses. She had never felt the everyday workings of churchly power quite so nearly.

She stole a glance at Olivier. The strain in his face was intense. It was as if he felt each and every one of the curé's words were directed only at him. She thought he might leave. He didn't. A kind of rigour, or perhaps it was fear, kept him in his place until the curé raised the host aloft.

Père Benoit did it with striking operatic gestures that underlined the importance of his task. His legs were astride, his head flung back, his shoulders straining as his arms rose to bear their sacred weight. He was holding high the body and blood of Christ, not an ordinary receptacle.

Again, it was as if she were observing the rites of an unknown tribe for the first time. She felt both distant and impressed, irreverent and admiring. Whatever the curé's personal failings, he had a marked talent for the theatre of his profession. She could see him officiating in a grand Gothic cathedral, his robes resplendent, his sacred vessels encrusted with jewels, his voice resonant with his sacral mission.

Olivier didn't take communion. That surprised her. Was it that after the curé's sermon he didn't feel pure enough today for the Eucharist? She certainly wasn't. She hadn't been to confession since her wedding. Nor was she about to bare her soul to Père Benoit, whatever her transient sense that his office made him greater than his mere person.

Yet she needed to speak to the priest alone. She followed Olivier out and waited her moment. The cold, clear air seemed to snap her husband from some painful reverie. He paused on the porch and was quickly at the centre of a small gaggle of parishioners she didn't recognize. She stepped back into the church. As the last of the congregation trailed down the aisle, she saw Père Benoit disappear through a door on the side. She followed quickly, her shoes now setting up an echo in the empty space.

She knocked on the door and without waiting for a reply allowed herself in.

Père Benoit was standing behind a large desk and looking out through a mullioned window.

'I wanted to speak to you, Father.'

'Oh?'

He turned towards her, his face stern with youthful self-importance.

'Yes. I found your service . . . well . . . impressive.'

A small smile settled on his lips. He nodded once, accepting her acknowledgment as his due, yet evidently pleased.

'Yes. Something kept troubling me, however.'

'Oh?'

'Yes. Yes. You see I visited your . . . is it grand-uncle, yesterday, or your cousin. Napoleon Marchand. And he said something . . .' She looked down at her gloved hands, played with the soft leather of fingertips.

'What?' The question was a bark.

'I'm not sure the word is appropriate in these premises.' Marguerite stared at the desk. The pen and inkwell stand were in gold, the leather rimmed blotter unmarked.

'What word?'

She shot a glance at him, touched the brim of her hat and looked down again.

'Blackmail,' she murmured almost beneath her breath.

'Blackmail,' the curé repeated. 'Blackmail,' his voice rose, forcing her to look up. His smooth cheeks were tinged with red.

She nodded once.

'If that scoundrel names it blackmail for me to take just a little from his ill-gotten gains in order to pay back the Church for the amount it has given to sheltering his bastard and that whore of a mother, than so be it.'

'Your uncle was involved with a whore?' Marguerite murmured in a shocked tone.

'Servant girls, whores . . . is there really a difference, Madame? You of all people must know that.'

'Still, mon père, blackmail in a man of the church so close to my husband, and his campaign . . .' Marguerite shook her head with regal weariness. 'It won't do. It will certainly not do Olivier any good.'

'So that's it, is it . . .' He clamped his hand down on hers, imprisoning it on the desk. 'If you think, Madame, that your husband has any chance at all without me behind him, you are hardly as intelligent as I have always estimated.'

His eyes gripped hers as fixedly as his hand still pinned down her fingers. 'There are things I know about your husband, Madame, things, which, believe me, would not sit well in the public eye.'

He had come very close. She could feel his hot breath on her cheek

'Matters extracted in the privacy of the confessional, I imagine. I had always been told it was a secret place.'

'Not only in the confessional.' His voice grew low with hissing menace. 'If Madame places so little value on my role in exorcising her husband's demons, if she rushes to convey to him what she has learned from an ogre of depravity, than I shall be forced to do that which I would loathe. I should be forced to expose him.'

'I see.' Marguerite released her hand from the one that still clenched hers. 'Blackmail again. I suspect, Monsieur, that in shaking off what you call his demons, my poor Olivier has saddled himself with ones that are no less tractable. I may in all honesty have to say this to him. And remember, Monsieur, his demons break no laws of our Republic. I fear that yours may.'

She nodded once brusquely and turned on her heel before he could again lay a hand on her.

Olivier was waiting in the carriage. He didn't ask her where she had been. He barely greeted her. He was consumed in his own thoughts.

'Do you want to tell me what's troubling you?' she asked softly, once the bump and roll of the road had started.

He shook his head with abrupt emphasis.

'Has that priest begun to blackmail you?' The question had involuntarily come to her lips. She hadn't intended it now. She turned to look out the window.

His eyes were on the back of her head. She could feel them. Hot. She didn't want to meet them.

Spring would bring all its lost beauty back to the gentle roll of the countryside. She hoped she could experience it again without seeing

Napoleon Marchand rise in front of her. So much had been lost in this last year.

'How did you know?' Olivier's question rose above the voices inside her and startled her out of her reverie.

She turned back to him.

His face was ravaged. 'He made me come to you. It was him. I wouldn't . . .' His clenched knuckles grew white.

She nodded. She didn't want to hear this. Not now. He looked like a frightened, distressed boy in need of a mother. She knew he was about to cry.

'Let's leave it, Olivier. Never again.'

'No, you have to understand. He scared the young musician. Forced him away. I had become pure, he said. Cleansed of evil. Free of sin. I had to prove it. Prove it that very night.' He paused, his eyes filling. 'I thought he was doing it for . . . for God, for me . . . Now he humiliates me, even in public. And he insists on Paul going. He hates Paul. He has threatened . . .'

'Did he talk you into keeping Gabriel, too?'

Olivier stared at her, his face taut, as if he hadn't considered this. His handkerchief was to his face. A sob cracked his stony features.

There was one more question she wanted to put to him, but it would wait. Wait until he had pulled himself together. She sensed it would be better for her not to witness too much of his discomfiture. Olivier was not a man who wanted compassion. He hated to display weakness.

She concentrated on the window once more.

They had not quite reached the house, when Olivier called to the coachman to halt.

'Forgive me, Marguerite. I need to walk. To think.'

She nodded. He was already out of the coach when she called after him. 'I was planning to have a word with his superiors in any event, Olivier. Now I certainly will. I don't think he'll trouble you much longer.'

No sooner had the carriage pulled up at La Rochambert, then Madame Solange herself came to the door and alerted her.

'The Chief Inspector wants you, Madame. At the Marchand house.'

'Why? Did he say.'

'The messenger said something's happened. To the Tellier woman. He needs your help.'

'I see.'

Marguerite didn't really see. But she knew she had to go immediately. Yet something unfinished played through her mind, something that had displaced the thrum of her rage against Olivier.

Armand, Madame Solange's son, was running across the terrace. He had a ball in his arms and coming up behind him was the wet nurse pushing Marguerite's old pram. The pudgy boy and the babe had become inseparable.

'Do you think your son could run an errand for me, Solange?'

'Of course, Madame.'

She called out and the boy puffed towards them.

'How are you, Armand?'

'Fine, Ma'am.' The child was shy with her.

'Will you do something for me?'

He nodded.

'I dropped Monsieur by the river. I think he'll do his usual walk. Towards where you found baby Gabriel. I'd like you to run and keep him company.'

The boy nodded.

'And Armand. Don't say I sent you. Just keep him company.'

'Yes, Madame.'

He rushed off on his stocky legs. Marguerite watched him for a moment. The river was high because of the snow and then the driving rain. In her imagination, she saw the reeds swirling in the waters, the new depth beneath them hungry, eager to encircle a body.

Solange was staring at her, her brow furrowed. 'I'm sure he'll be fine, Madame. And Armand will keep watch. They get on surprisingly well.'

_ 23 _

The police wagon stood in front of the Marchand house, a public warning that the forces of the law had taken over. Durand opened the door to her himself. The dank gloom of the hall behind gave him an added spruceness, as if the little man with the well-trimmed moustache and business-like suit had travelled through time as well as space to arrive at this dour spot in the ancient valleys.

He didn't mince his words. 'Marchand is dead.'

'What?' Marguerite stepped backwards, only noticing now that the box with the snake in it had vanished.

Durand joined her on the porch for a moment and lowered his voice.

'Apoplexy probably. According to Madame, when she came to find him in the morning, he didn't respond to her calls or questions or ministrations. He must have died in the night. Not altogether surprising perhaps, given his exertions of the last days. And the amount of alcohol that man pours down himself. I found both carafes of whisky empty and a number of half-consumed bottles of rum lying about.'

Marguerite stared at him. She hadn't expected this. Not this. Nor could she tell from Durand's unreadable public face, how much of his account was to be taken at surface value.

'Really, Inspector? You mean he drank himself to death! But Labrousse said specifically, he wasn't to drink. Is Labrousse here? What does he say? And your constable?'

'He heard and saw nothing. He was asleep. Asleep as only these country folk seem to manage. The sleep of the righteous,' the Inspector drawled. 'He neither heard nor saw anything. As for Labrousse, he's just arrived. I wanted you here, Madame la Comtesse, because I thought you might be able to help with Madame Tellier. She's inconsolable.' He lowered his voice. 'She's also in the way. She won't keep her nose out.'

'I see. Is she with her father?'

He nodded. 'Get her out of there.'

The smell assaulted her even before she had reached the room, a low pungent reek of excrement combined with something sweet and sickly she couldn't place. The body seemed to take up most of the free space on the floor of the room and all its air.

Napoleon Marchand lay, huge, strangely slack-jawed and waxen-skinned, at the base of the sagging Restoration sofa. It hadn't restored him and he must have rolled off it in some death agony. Or tried to reach for the whisky carafe, which stood empty by its side, and toppled off in a final spasm. His legs were splayed, one arm stretched outward in an extravagant appeal which had gone unheard.

Dr. Labrousse was on his knees to the side of the corpse, tapping and prodding, lifting one arm after another, looking at hands and nails, lifting eyelids to show constricted pupils.

Meanwhile Madame Tellier sobbed, her bosom heaving, her hair straggling free from its pins, her eyes wild. One hand trailed loosely across surfaces, tables, a display case, partly drawn curtains, as if the act of fingering were a necessary accompaniment to her grief. Dust flew in her wake. If the room had contained any foreign fingerprints, they were now certainly gone.

Marguerite put a handkerchief to her nose and moved towards the woman. She had identified that other smell now. It was vomit. It covered the old man's clothes. Perhaps he had gagged and choked on it.

Before she could reach Madame Tellier, Dr. Labrousse had her by the shoulders.

'Now look at me, Madame Tellier. Concentrate. How many times did he wake up after we left you? You didn't give him more of the medication than I prescribed, did you? I warned you.'

Madame Tellier stared at him from red-rimmed eyes. Her sobs turned into violent hiccoughs. She shook her head, launched herself into an armchair which almost fell with the violence of her weight. Beside her

237

the fire raged, recently stoked into fury. A white ash, bearing all the aspects of burned paper, lay heaped on the floor beyond its bounds.

'But you let him get to the drink. I specifically ordered that there was to be no drink.'

The sobbing grew louder. 'Have you ever tried to stop my father if he was intent on something. Have you, doctor?' She shouted between sobs.

Marguerite and Durand exchanged a glance.

She walked towards the woman and put an arm around her. 'Come with me, Madame Tellier. You need to relax. Deep breaths now. And a cup of tea. Madame Molineuf . . .' She saw the woman lurking in the doorway and called to her. 'Prepare a tray of tea, or whatever you can find for Madame. I'll take her upstairs. Away from this. It's too terrible for her. She can't be sitting here with the corpse of her father.'

'Quite right. Quite right.' The Chief Inspector took Mme Tellier's arm and together with Marguerite eased her out of the chair. 'Let the Countess look after you, Madame.' He gestured towards the young uniformed constable. Marguerite thought the man might burst into tears.

'I don't know how I slept through it. I don't know how . . .' His refrain, directed at the Chief Inspector who gave him the full benefit of one of his Parisian shrugs, also earned a venomous look from Madame Tellier.

'I tried to rouse you,' she shrieked. 'I tried. You're a miserable lump of a boy. You'll hear about this next time I bump into your mother.'

'Please, Madame.'

Marguerite noticed that the young man's eyes, which had now filled with tears were very blue, the pupils too small. It gave her pause. Like the dead man's. She would have to check with Dr. Labrousse. He must have given old Marchand morphine. Had some of it found its way into the constable? Perhaps via Madame Tellier? It would account for his heavy sleep.

Madame Tellier was still sobbing. Durand spoke soothing words all the way up the stairs. He found an open door which led to a bedroom and with visible relief turned the woman over to Marguerite.

'Now Madame, I recommend you loosen your corset a little and lie down.'

Marguerite plumped less than clean pillows. 'Your tea will be here in a moment.'

The room was large and shrouded in blood-red wallpaper embossed in a fleur-de-lys pattern. It was cold and dank. The high bed, with its heavy, dark wooden headboard, stood prominently on one side. On the other a chest, holding a vase of dusty dried flowers and an escritoire, its rolltop shut. On the bedside table, stood a bottle of rum, and another of Marchand's opium pipes. It was a wonder the man had lived for as long as he had.

'I can't believe it, Madame. I can't believe it.'

Madame Tellier must have heard her thoughts. She was propped against the bed's headboard, a wrinkled hanky to her face. 'He was a fine man, Madame. A towering figure. I'm only sorry that you had to see him when he wasn't at his best. That fall he suffered . . . it affected his temper as well as his manners.' The woman's face with its vast reddened eyes was a tragic mask.

'Yes. Yes. Don't worry yourself about that, Madame. I know you loved your father.' And she had, in her way, Marguerite thought. Love was a dangerous passion.

'But now, you must close your eyes and relax. I've learned in these circumstances it's a good thing to breathe deeply.'

The woman did as she was told. 'It's kind of you to look after me. Really it is, Madame.'

Marguerite hushed her, made soothing noises. All the while, she examined the room. The light fell in slashes from the corners of the drawn curtains. It cut the bed, the oval table and zigzagged along the escritoire. A piece of paper protruded from the base of its rolltop. That hadn't been visible yesterday. At least she didn't think so.

She glanced at Madame Tellier's bulky form. Her breath came evenly now. She moved towards the desk and gently lifted the lid. Beneath, a pile of documents and letters lay in disarray. They had been heaped higgledy-piggledy by someone in a hurry. One slipped to the floor.

'Just what do you think you're doing?' Madame Tellier's hiss startled her.

'One . . . one of these papers was protruding. I was trying to put it back.' Marguerite smiled reassurance.

'Make sure you do. Just make sure you do.' The woman threatened. There were no longer any tears in her eyes. The hysteria or its semblance had metamorphosed into cold control. 'That's Napoleon Marchand's desk.'

Her emphasis made it clear that Marchand had now joined his name-sake in importance, having always surpassed him in stature. But there was something else in Madame Tellier's voice which gave Marguerite pause. It was as if she were hearing old Napoleon Marchand himself, as if his daughter had now become the old man. Incarnated him in a new form. The realization created a pit in Marguerite's stomach. She smoothed her pale grey dress unhurriedly.

'You heard me.'

Madame Tellier's furious eyes dictated, so that the eruption of noise from downstairs came almost as a relief. The clatter was louder than gunfire. Fear flashed across Madame Tellier's face, robbing it of its cold authority. A convulsive shiver took her over.

'No, no. It can't be. Can't be him.'

Marguerite preceded her down the stairs, her skirts swinging with the speed of her movement.

On the ground floor, they all but collided with Dr. Labrousse and the Constable who were heaving the dead man through the hall. Madame Tellier leapt on them, grabbed hold first of the doctor's arm, then her father's hand.

'Not yet.' A sob broke from her. 'No, it's too soon.'

'We must, Madame.' Labrousse shrugged her off. 'We need to . . . to ascertain the cause of death.'

'What do you mean?' She repeated the words twice, her wild eyes aiming daggers at the doctor. 'No, no. I don't give you permission. Never. He's not to be cut up.'

The front door was already open, the police wagon parked directly in front of it.

'He stays here. With me. The family will want to see him. The priest must come. No.' She clung to her father's body. In her struggle with the doctor, the corpse of Napoleon Marchand tipped towards the floor.

The Inspector appeared just in time to tilt the balance. Another loud noise erupted from somewhere beneath them.

'What is that?' Marguerite asked.

'That's just what I was rushing to find out. Now leave the good doctor, Madame.' He took the woman's arm and maneuvered her skillfully away. 'Your father's body will be returned to you. Perhaps even later today. Soon enough, certainly. By Monsieur, the undertaker. You must prepare your father's best clothes. From what I understand of his position here, many will want to come and pay their respects.'

Madame Tellier nodded. 'A great many. My father was well connected. Before he started his travelling, he was in demand everywhere. Everywhere.'

The doctor and the constable had managed to use the interruption to ferry old Marchand towards the door. The Inspector was already making his way downstairs urging Madame Tellier before him. Marguerite followed after.

As they opened the door to the kitchen, they were met by Madame Molineuf and a scene of devastation. The shelves had been hit by what might have been cannon fire. Crockery lay shattered amidst an assortment of pots and toppled spice containers, their contents spilling reds and blacks on the tiled floor. A large carpet bag, partly obscured by a burlap sac, exuded hams and condiments. An iron casserole had landed upside down on the table.

'I tried to stop him, Madame. I tried. But it's no use now. He's too big.'

'Who?'

'My son, Inspector. I know you wanted to see him. He pushed me away and rushed out.'

'How could you let him go, you stupid woman? He might have been the one who gave my father the killing quantity of alcohol. You hear that Inspector? Get the lout. I always knew he was no good. He's killed my darling father.' Madame Tellier tore at her hair, her eyes wild.

'What're you talking about?' Madame Molineuf strode towards her, hand on bulky hip. Her voice came with low menace. 'Just watch what you say, you hear . . . Remember all the things I've seen around here. And don't get too big for your boots. P'tit Ours loves his old master. If he's run off, it's because he's got some woman with him. I know he has. All that food he took.'

'A woman?' Madame Tellier echoed.

The Inspector was already running up the wooden steps that brought him to a storeroom. Marguerite lifted her skirts and followed after him. Behind her, she could hear Madame Tellier's heavy tread.

The external door was open. It led into a dank field where stray bits of iron and old carriage wheels littered the ground. In the distance, jumping over a stile, they made out P'tit Ours. He had a bright sack in one hand, which looked stuffed to the brim and some kind of iron box in the other. Marguerite recognized the bag. It was the one that had thrown Madame Tellier into a rage. It belonged to her half sister. P'tit Ours had surely been in the house for some time and with his soft tread managed to help himself to whatever Amandine had asked him for. Marguerite had no doubt that the strange youth was now following a new set of orders. She hoped they were less violent.

'Stop him, Inspector. He's stolen things. Stolen things from my father.' Madame Tellier's voice was a shriek.

'In due course, Madame. We won't catch him now. And we have other more important matters matters to see to.

_ 24 _

The room the Inspector led Marguerite to was tucked away in a far corner towards the top of old Marchand's house. It was an odd place, a cross
between a child's room and servant's quarters. A China doll cloaked in
an elaborate Empire gown trimmed with gold sat in pomp in a small rocking chair in the corner. The rest of the dusty space had nothing to show
but a narrow bed topped by a bare horsehair mattress and a wooden chest
on knobby legs. The window was high and dirty and had a wall of old
heavy curtains to both its sides.

They had left Madame Tellier, who had at last drunk the calming
powder the doctor had provided, to her housekeeper's erratic ministrations.

'Do your instincts tell you she helped her father through that final
frontier, Madame?' The Inspector shut the door behind them and
addressed her in a low voice.

'Probably. If only so as to prevent him making his other daughter
public. And she burnt some telling documents.'

'It's true. I searched and couldn't find a will anywhere.'

'Though he might have deposited it with a notary. In Tours, I imagine. For all his excesses, old Napoleon Marchand seemed to be a shrewd
businessman.' A sigh escaped her. 'Families, Inspector! The things that
go on behind closed doors.'

'They are the backbone of the nation.'

'Yours is undoubtedly, Inspector.' She smiled at him, then changed
the subject. Durand idolized his children and only spoke of his wife in
terms of the greatest respect. 'Why have you brought me up here?'

With a dramatic flourish he pulled back the dank curtains on the left of the window. 'Because of this.'

The curtain gave way not to more windows, but to an alcove which contained what she could only think of as a shrine. There was a pretty little statue of the Virgin Mary, all blue and white and gold, her head inclined in prayer. The walls around her were in a deeper, almost midnight blue, through which gold stars peeped. At the Virgin's feet lay an assortment of shells and candles, some of them the old, stubby tallow kind that servants used, but the others tall and slender wax. Amidst the shells there were two locket-like hearts which gave Marguerite pause. One of them was remarkably like the incense-filled sacred heart that always lay by little Gabriel's side.

She fingered it.

'Relics and amulets,' the Inspector said. 'Not quite what one would imagine that old pit of corruption that was Napoleon Marchand bending his knees to.'

'No.' She paused, then grew excited. 'You remember how he said he thought Yvette was a saint. Could this have been her room? Her secret shrine.'

'That's why I wanted you to see it. But odd that she should have a room here as well as at the Tellier's.'

'A saint who also blackmailed him,' Marguerite mused.

They went softly downstairs. In the front hall, with its massed guns and walking sticks, they bumped into Madame Molineuf. The woman was grumbling again, her back to the door which she seemed just to have shut.

'Vultures. All of them. Fighting over the remains of the old master already. Barely cold, he is.'

'Who was that, Madame Molineuf?' Durand asked amiably.

'The curé, that's who it was. Missed the last rites, I told him. Special masses, he offered. But really came for his envelope, didn't he? I told him there was nothing. Nothing at all for him.' A triumphant beam illuminated her face.

'The curé,' Marguerite queried. 'You don't mean Père Benoit?'

'Who else might I mean? Always here this last month. Christmas greetings. New Year's greetings. Family greetings. Epiphany greetings. Any old greetings.'

'Our greetings to you, Madame' The Inspector tipped his hat. 'Take good care of your Mistress. Tell her we'll see her later.'

Close to Montoire, where the Inspector had rushed them in order to see the Investigating magistrate, they saw a lone figure in a red jacket limping towards them. There was no turban on his head, though as they watched, he paused, put down the large box he was holding together with a bag, took from it the missing headgear and adjusted the jewelled turban. He looked altogether forlorn. As they drew nearer, they could see that the Indian's face was bloated, one eye black and blue.

'Mr. Rama,' Marguerite called to him in English.

The man bowed. The horses whinnied and reared.

'It's that blasted snake of his,' Durand mumbled. 'Tell him to put it down or we'll have run-aways. The animal stinks. The police mares were not very happy, I can tell you, when we brought it back for him yesterday.'

Rama didn't have to be told. He had already put his serpent down carefully by the side of the road.

'What's happened, Monsieur Rama? Have you been in an accident?' Marguerite asked in French for the Inspector's benefit.

Durand helped the man into the coach. His face, usually so fine and smooth, showed cuts and contusions.

'I fear so. A kind of accident.' He sat back in the seat opposite them, his posture stiff.

They waited for him to say more.

At last, with a shrug, he offered. 'Auguste got very drunk. He mistook me for an enemy. Or maybe even a wall, to practice his kicks and punches on.'

'How terrible.'

'The man is a danger. We should lock him up.' Durand exploded. 'This can't be allowed. I'm surprised you didn't set your beast on him.'

Mr. Rama looked from one to the other of them. 'I told you. yesterday, Inspector, though I don't like to make this confession and it is only for your and Madame's ears. My poor Nasa long ago had his poison centres removed. He is a cobra with only the appearance of venom. He can leave his mark, but he cannot kill.'

'As he did on the neck of Hercule Marchand,' Marguerite murmured. 'But your friends don't know that?'

'It is best in this work of mine not to reveal all one's secrets.'

'Doesn't seem to have worked for the best today . . .' Durand smiled, not without a trace of wickedness.

'Ah that . . .' the Indian looked down at his lap, his expression weary.

'Where are you heading, Mr. Rama?' Marguerite asked

'To be honest with you, Madame. I do not know. I am simply heading. I cannot stay with my onetime family any longer. They are not my friends. Auguste, I fear, may kill me.'

'Kill?' Durand asked

The Indian waved his arm weakly. 'It is a manner of saying. But it is true, he has become a belligerent leader since Danuta's death. It is the grief, perhaps. And the drink. He has too much money to spend on drink. Rama has suffered for it.'

'And where does all this money come from? Business can't be very good at the moment.' Durand grumbled.

'Did Madame not mention it to you? I think it is money that Danuta got from her gentleman. Auguste repeats over and over, while he douses himself with the liquor he has bought with her money, while he weeps and beats his chest and beats Rama, "if only there had been no emperor, if only . . ."'

Marguerite and Durand looked at each other.

'Can you remember exactly what you did and said that led to this beating, Monsieur Rama?'

'I wanted to practice my riding on Danuta's horses. To improve my act. It was when I was mounting. He heaved me off. He said I wasn't to go.' Rama shook his head slowly. 'The alcohol has destroyed his seeing perhaps. He mistook me for Danuta. He threw my turban to the ground and said I didn't need feathers on my head for what I was about to do.'

'I think we need to see your Auguste,' the Inspector murmured.

'Not with me. Not with me, Inspector. I have enough marks on my body. I am not a brave man.'

The Inspector patted him on the shoulder.

'But you are a brave man, Monsieur Rama,' Marguerite intervened. 'You have travelled half way around the world with your serpent. That takes far more courage, I imagine, than the kind that can be found in a bottle.'

Monsieur Rama considered her.

'And to give up your work, your friends, because a strongman has decided to use his strength in the wrong way, is not a solution. Come with us, Monsieur Rama. We need you.'

'If Madame really believes so.'

'I do. But since my horses do not seem to feel kindly towards your Nasa, we will meet you at the site.'

The travellers' camp looked desolate in the late afternoon gloom. Many seemed to have abandoned it. Smoke rose from a single metal barrel situated in the midst of the semi-circle the carriages made. Two ragged boys played round it in a half-hearted manner, aiming pebbles which pinged against the tin. A man Marguerite didn't recognize emerged from behind a wagon and stared at them from suspicious eyes.

Durand tipped his hat. 'We're looking for Auguste,' he said.

The man pointed with a surly expression towards a carriage painted red and white.

Monsieur Rama had now caught up with them and the stranger shook his head at him as if he were a lunatic.

'I thought you were leaving.'

'I've come back.'

'You enjoy beatings, do you?'

'I do not. But Rama will not run.'

'No, he'll limp.'

The man shrugged and disappeared behind the wagon.

The Inspector was about to knock at Auguste's door, when Rama pointed into the distance. The strong man appeared in the shadow of the castle wall. He wasn't alone. He was accompanied by a man in a brown habit.

Marguerite stopped in her tracks. 'How fortunate. I wanted to talk to the brother again. I've been thinking about him.'

Durand looked at her as if she had lost her wits.

'It's Frère Michel.' Marguerite started to walk towards the friar and Auguste. The ground was cold and muddy in the drizzling rain, but she carried on regardless. Durand was right behind her.

'Don't do anything silly now, Madame. The man is dangerous.'

Auguste didn't turn away as they approached. Marguerite wasn't even sure he saw them. His head was bent, his shoulders slack. He stumbled across the uneven ground. At one point he fell to his knees and tugged at Frère Michel's habit. The brother helped him up.

'Let's wait,' Durand said.

When the men had come closer, he called out. 'Auguste, a word, please.'

'Excuse us, Monsieur, Madame.' It was the cleric who responded, bowing slightly in Marguerite's direction as well. 'My friend here has an urgent errand.'

'Our matter is urgent, too. Auguste has assaulted a fellow artiste, has chased him away from the only home he knows. Monsieur Rama is poorly, is distraught, and I suspect penniless, while Auguste squanders his dead fiancée's ill-gotten gains on drink and . . .'

A savage howl from Auguste interrupted the Inspector's speech. 'Rama! Rama!' the man shouted. He was still drunk. Barely upright, he lunged towards the Indian. The Inspector interposed himself.

Auguste flung his arms around him, whether in order to attack or simply to hold on wasn't clear.

'Rama,' he called again. 'God is my witness.'

He was hugging the Inspector, his head lolling over the smaller man's shoulder.

'I'm here Auguste, what is it?' Monsieur Rama moved behind the Inspector so that Auguste could focus on him.

'Rama, my friend. I'm sorry. So very sorry.'

Auguste had started to sob. Best he could, the Inspector eased the bigger man onto his own feet. He brushed off his shoulders discreetly, then catching the cleric's eyes on him, he stopped.

'Yes,' Frère Michel repeated. 'Monsieur Auguste has an urgent errand to attend to.'

'I'm going to the police, Rama,' the strong man shouted so that in the middle distance the two children stopped their play and followed them with their eyes. 'The police.'

'We have a policeman right here,' Rama murmured.

The Inspector shook his head rapidly. 'Best to go to Montoire.'

'I have been bad, Rama. So bad. Bad to Danuta. When she came out of that house. I waited for her. I waited. I was so angry. It is a sin to be so angry, Rama. Frère Michel has explained it to me. It is a sin because it makes you lose yourself in rage, do terrible things, stay angry forever. Angry at yourself. At the world. At God's creation. Yes, Rama. At you, too. But when I told the brother, he took the rage from me. Held it. Held it away.'

Rama shook his head sagely. 'The brother is kind.'

'I hit her Rama. So hard. Too hard. She fell. I took all her money and ran away.' Auguste started to sob again. 'When I came back, she wouldn't move. I wanted to bring her, to bury her. But this boy came. And I ran. Ran from a boy.'

'Antoine,' Marguerite breathed. She must have said it louder than she assumed, because the man looked at her.

So it was Auguste and not P'tit Ours or Olivier, as she had suspected by turn. Auguste, the strong man, battering her down in the woods, this side of the little clearing, as she tried to take in the dead figure of the dancer.

Auguste was still staring at her. She shook herself. 'Where did you follow Danuta to, Monsieur Auguste. Which house?'

'The Emperor's house,' Auguste said with a touch of pride. 'She went to the Emperor's house. Beaumont.'

'I see.'

'Come Auguste. We must be on our way.' The cleric's voice was gentle, but firm. 'Night is closing in.'

Marguerite gestured to Rama and Durand. 'Shall we walk with them,' she murmured. 'I would like a few words with Frère Michel.'

The men took up her cue and positioned themselves on either side of Auguste, who had started to weep again.

'Mon Frère,' she held the cleric back a little. She was struck again by his asymmetric eyes, one dark, one light, looking it seemed to her at different parts of human capability. She lowered her voice. 'Mon Frère, I wanted you to be amongst the first to know. I thought it might free you to speak about poor Yvette, Yvette Branquart. Napoleon Grandcourt Marchand is dead.'

Frère Michel crossed himself and murmured something in Latin beneath his breath. Then he fingered the heavy rope around his soutane and examined her face. 'I don't understand why you have brought me this news, Madame.'

'I thought . . . I thought your silence was due to him. That you were holding back her whereabouts out of fear of him; or perhaps out of some confidences garnered in the confessional?'

The man looked up at the unbroken sheet of grey sky, then gave her a smile of startling sweetness. 'Non, Madame. Non. Please tell her sister that she will hear from her when she is ready. May God be with you, Madame.' He went quietly towards his charge.

She caught up with Durand. They walked in silence for a moment. Then Marguerite burst out, 'I need to see Dr. Labrousse, Inspector. There is something I need to press him on. He knows something about Yvette. I don't know what it is. But I feel it. And Frère Michel, despite his gentleness, has provided no enlightenment. None at all.'

The Inspector didn't seem to be following her train of thought. His mind was elsewhere. 'So that old scoundrel of a Napoleon wasn't lying about Danuta.'

'It would seem not. Though if Auguste were less drunk, I would find his confession more palatable. Still it makes sense. Jealousy. Another perversion of love,' she added almost under her breath, but wouldn't explain when the Inspector looked a question at her.

'And Auguste has given us a lead. About a third of the Marchand properties. We shall need to check it out, Inspector.'

'First things first, Madame. If old Napoleon chose for some mysterious reason to tell the truth, then we must consider believing him about other matters, too.'

'If we're talking about first things, Inspector, then the safety of my two charges is paramount. When will the police go to the house I think of as the Witch's House?'

'That's precisely what I am going to organize now, Madame. Perhaps we might meet at the Doctor's?'

_ 25 _

The rain prevented the doctor from working on the cadaver in the open field. She found him under a kind of lean-to at the back of his consulting rooms, the man she had first seen him with at his side. They were both clad in surgical green. A gas lamp was propped to one side of them casting a murky yellow glow over everything,

Both men's eyes flew at her in a greeting which bore not a little irritation. Labrousse hastily drew a sheet over the naked corpse from whose pale, jaundiced flesh she had in any event instantly averted her gaze.

'I'm sorry, Madame. But you've chosen a bad moment.'

'I recognize that doctor. I just need five minutes of your time. Five minutes for the living. I think you'll understand. I wouldn't ask if it wasn't urgent. And it's a private matter.' She glanced at his assistant and with a quick nod went round to the front of the house and waited.

She waited for longer than she would have liked. It forced her to think impatient thoughts about Labrousse. She scanned the human parts diagrammed on his wall and wondered for a moment whether he cared more for the parts than for the whole, living person.

What kind of man was he really, this doctor with his gleaming skin, his shrewd, unblinking eyes. What kind of man was he above and beyond his professed modernity, his love of science?

'I'm sorry to keep you, Madame.'

Marguerite jumped. Had she been maligning him out of sheer exhaustion?

'Some things can't be done too quickly. And I shall have to test the samples in my little laboratory this evening if we're to find anything revealing at the earliest possible date.'

She nodded.

He took a deep breath and surveyed her. 'You wanted to ask me something in private? I trust you're not ill. Your arm hasn't taken a turn for the worse . . .'

She shook her head, shrugged. 'I noticed, when we were with Madame Tellier yesterday, that some secret information passed between you. A glance of understanding. It came when the old man mentioned Yvette, who as you know I have a particular interest in.'

'I, too, Madame. Has her sister returned?' he asked with a touch of fervour. 'I have been worrying about her.'

'No. I trust that has nothing to do with you.'

He was out of his chair like a bolt of lightning. The movement was so aggressive that Marguerite scraped her own chair backwards and found herself tiptilting precariously. She had pricked a raw nerve in the doctor.

'What has the woman told you to make you think like that? She's pure venom.'

'What could she have told me that would make you say that about a patient?'

His hands rose to his face and hid it from her. When he emerged again, his brow was furrowed with worry He gave her a dark look. 'Alright. You're a woman of the world. I'll tell you. But it isn't pretty. And it reflects well on no one.'

'I'm not interested in passing moral judgments, doctor. I just want to find the girl. I'm afraid for her. As I am now for Martine.'

He nodded, rubbed his brow with those long immaculate fingers.

'I'm not sure this will help you find her, but since you're intent on the truth . . .' He paused. 'A great German philosopher, if one's allowed to quote Germans around here—they were very good at laboratory medicine you know—said, "Give me beauty. Truth is ugly. We perish of truth."'

'I will try to stay alive, doctor. Please continue.'

Marguerite sighed. She was tired of the time these men took. In the name of gallantry. In order to preserve her from the experience any person with eyes could see.

He shrugged. 'After refusing the girl the care she needed, Madame Tellier sent her to me. She wanted me to induce . . .'

He stopped and surveyed Marguerite carefully. She had to urge him on again.

'She was certain the girl was pregnant. That she had been carrying on with every Jules in the region, the chemist's son included. She wanted me to induce a miscarriage.'

He said it evenly, but his eyes were on the floor.

'I told her I couldn't do that. She offered to pay me handsomely. She left money for me in an envelope on my desk. I tried to return it to her. She refused it. She said to keep it to buy myself some new instruments, the latest. She said she liked the girl, didn't want her life to go astray. I later realized that she suspected the child was old Napoleon's, her father's. So she'd do almost anything to get rid of it, and of Yvette.'

'The girl was his favourite?'

'If you mean in receipt of his questionable favours, then certainly Madame Tellier assumed so. His actions put her in a fury. I learned this from Yvette, not from her. Madame Tellier came to me, I imagine only because I was new to the region and would suspect nothing. In any case, I told her to send Yvette to me and I would examine her. She didn't come, and I thought the whole thing had passed. It happens you know. Girl's think they're pregnant. Then suddenly realize they're not.'

'Was she? She did finally come to you, didn't she? That's what Madame Molineuf's son said. It was the first thing I learned about Yvette.'

He nodded. 'She appeared late one evening. I was eating. Alone in the kitchen. Reading at the same time. It was summer, so there was still a little light in the sky.'

'And?'

He was staring out the window, as if he could see the girl. He didn't answer.

'You were fond of her,' Marguerite urged him on.

'Yes, she was a brave girl.'

'And?'

'Well, she told me she thought she was with child. It was a sin. But it would be a far worse sin to try and get rid of it, which is what Madame Tellier had been urging her to do. So she had run away. Yvette was a pious girl. She had spent the last two days in the caves. Praying, she told me. That

Molineuf lad kept an eye out for her. She liked him. But she couldn't stay there. And she wanted my advice. I was the only person she could turn to. She wanted to know if there was a place where she could go and be safe.'

'You kept all this from me?' Marguerite looked at him in despair. 'All this time, you knew. All this time while her sister was in misery.'

He shrugged. 'Yvette was my patient. What patients confide in their doctor is as confidential as what they tell their priests. It's the nearest thing we men of science have to a sacred trust.'

She stared at him.

'Even if it ends up by harming your patient?'

'Who are you to say what might be harm for Yvette? The choice was hers to make. She wanted secrecy. She made me swear.'

'But you're telling me now.'

'That Tellier woman will land me in jail, if she carries on. So you might as well have my version. And whether the poor girl was pregnant or not, it's now long over. She didn't want me to examine her.'

'So where is she?'

'I don't know that either.'

'You know. You won't tell me.'

'I gave her a bed for the night. I gave her money. All the money Madame Tellier had left for me. I told her there were some Poor Clares working on the far side of town. They had come from Blois to help with the sick. They would know better than I where she might go. I hadn't yet met up with Madame Germaine or I would have consulted her. But Yvette was very happy with what I had suggested. "Poor Clares," she kept repeating, as if the name itself was some kind of prayer. I took her to them. She said if she needed any more help, she would come back to me in the evening. She never did. She told me she knew I was doing her a special favour and if Madame or her father found out, they would be very angry. She was frightened of them. A lot of the people in the region are. With better reason than I had initially thought, it seems. I asked her to write to me to tell me how she was getting on.'

'Did she?'

'Yes, once.'

'Where from?'

'There was no return address. No stamp either. A crumpled note arrived at my door. It hadn't been delivered by the postman.'

'So she came back?'

'I don't think so. I don't think it was her. I would like to think if it had been, she would have knocked.'

The man was half in love, Marguerite thought. 'What did the letter say?'

'It thanked me. Said she was as well as could be expected. And that maybe one day we would meet again. In this life or the next.'

'That's terrible.'

'I agree. But only terrible for you and me. Yvette, I think, rather longed for the next life. I don't know what her sister's like in that respect.'

'So you think Yvette is dead? You keep talking about her in the past tense.'

He shrugged and got up to pace. 'I really don't know, Madame. I'd like to know. Had I thought my story would help you, I would perhaps have told you sooner. But I don't know where she went after I took her to the Clares. She couldn't have stayed with them for long.'

'And have you told me everything now?'

He smiled, a little sadly. 'Everything of moment. I hope you believe that I never colluded with Madame Tellier. If anything I was happy to get the girl out of her way. As far out of her way as possible.'

'Now, doctor. Tell me honestly. Has her sister, Martine, come to you in the last few days?'

'No Madame, how can you think it . . . I wish she had.'

He said it with an air of such longing, that Marguerite suddenly felt she might weep.

These last days were beginning to take their toll. She was tired, tearful, felt she had failed in too many respects. A man in love brought back all the vulnerability she worked so hard to distance.

'You'll excuse me. I must get back to the remains of Monsieur Marchand.'

She nodded and met his eyes. She had the impression the doctor, like her, had been running away from intimate matters by immersing himself in more distant problems.

You could, she thought, be overwhelmed by both.

A coughing took hold of her on the way home. Yes, she was bone tired, had probably caught a chill in the rain or in the tunnels or in Napoleon Marchand's house or indeed in the church only this morning. In the church with Olivier, who was more distressed than she had ever seen him. She shivered and tucked the blanket round her skirt. It had been too long a day.

Part of her was relieved that the Inspector had stayed behind in Montoire to learn the results of Dr. Labrousse's laboratory work and to stay close to the investigating magistrate. She needed some time alone. Time to think. She hadn't been thinking clearly enough. There was so much she had missed: about Yvette, probably about Martine, even about Olivier. She had been blind to a whole spectrum of motive and inclination and intent.

Faith. Belief. Ritual. Their comforts. Their attendant hierarchies of authority and of punishment, of guilt and of sin. They had so little play in her own life that she had been blind to the way they shaped or distorted the daily lives and passions of others. She had been blind not to religion's sway as a political or social force—these last years which had riven the nation had made that all too clear. But blind to the sway religion had over the individual conscience, over desires too, over aspirations and fears. Her sleep of reason had bred only one kind of monster—and it wasn't the one in play.

She should have seen it before. Yvette was a pious girl, inspired more by Bernadette and Joan of Arc than by the likes of Georges Sand. She was hardly alone if you were to judge by the ranks and ranks of women who filled the churches. It was one of the reasons the Republicans were against giving women the vote. They feared women in the sway of priests would vote largely for the religious right.

Marguerite looked out at the grey, winding river, with its graceful willows and poplars, its reeds, all bending in the direction the wind chose. She forced her thoughts back to the particular.

Everything she had been told about Yvette should have pointed her in the right direction. The girl was strong, unafraid, Martine had said, with just a little note of fear in her own voice. Virtuous. Little frightened her, not even blood: in fact she drew it herself, punished her body for its sins. There was that little shrine to the Virgin Mary in the old sinner's house. Frère Michel's cryptic words about silence were not cryptic at all, when looked at in the right light. Poverty. Chastity. Obedience. And sometimes silence. Silence could simply be one of the vows.

Where did girls go to disappear? Girls without money, girls with no one to turn to? It was the question she had posed herself about Yvette all along and she had come up with a Parisian answer, the answer of anonymous crowds and shop-filled streets and rows upon rows of houses. Houses of ill-repute, she had told herself. But brothels didn't take in pregnant girls.

The kinds of houses that did were holy houses. At the opposite end of the spectrum of vice stood virtue. There were two kinds of home away from home. The brothel and the convent. She hadn't considered the convent. Yet she knew that even as the state grew increasingly secular and Republican, orders, scores of them women's orders, had sprung up across the country. In many instances they offered women not only piety and the ascetic religious life, but a way of doing useful work in the world, a way of freeing themselves from the imposed and constricting choices of marriage or spinsterhood. For a troubled adolescent with no one to turn to what greater relief than to have order put into a disordered universe by a power greater than oneself.

She would find Yvette in a convent. She was now convinced of it. All she had to do was begin the search. As for Martine, it was becoming clearer to her where she might be. If that frightening bear of a creature, that P'tit Ours and his malign old master, hadn't stood in the way, she might have seen it sooner.

At La Rochambert, she was relieved to hear that Olivier had returned with Armand and his father, Henri, the gamekeeper. He had said he would do without dinner, just a bowl of soup in his rooms. He was feeling under the weather and wanted not to be disturbed.

Marguerite asked for the same.

But when she finally curled up in bed, she couldn't sleep. The sheets felt alien. The events of the last days whipped at her mind like angry wasps at a closed window. She was too tired to calm them and they buzzed round her, spiraling, intersecting for hours, creating waking dreams, so that when she heard a sound, felt rather than saw a shifting pattern of light, she jolted up in fear.

A thin stream played across the floor of her room, moved, gave birth to shadows. It was too late for light. But someone was walking along the hall. Who? Going where?

Softly, she stole into her dressing gown. The house was cold. She would have to have shoes. No, they would make too much noise. Was it her ruminations about the power of the clergy that provoked the thought that Père Benoit might be making a little free with their hospitality. All the doors of the house were rarely locked. He could easily come in. To find what?

Blackmail. The word resounded in her mind with all the clarity of a bell ringing out evensong. Hadn't he already threatened as much earlier that day? And one of his sources of extra cash had now given out. If the curé was to be accused—and he had certainly seen her carriage at old Napoleon Marchand's—then he would point a finger at Olivier in turn.

But what could there be amongst Olivier's papers that attested to his secret life? Surely nothing. This wasn't the stuff of documents.

Letters? Might there be letters? In the library. Had the light come from the direction of the library?

She was already in the hall, stealing after the flicker of the lamp. It cast a weak, yellow light, on the stairs now, no, not down, but up. That surprised her. She waited until it was only a gleam in the distance then crept up the stairs.

A shadow—robed, tall, broken at the legs. It loomed up the side of the wall. Then it was gone before she could decipher it. Through a door. The babe's room. She was certain of it. What could the priest want in little Gabriel's room? Was it possible that Olivier kept secret matter in there?

She took a deep breath and followed. She waited a few moments before turning the knob. But there was no point creeping. Or hiding. It was her house after all.

The figure sat in lamplight, his profile to her. He was staring into the cradle. He was so intent on what he saw that he seemed not to have heard the movement of the door. He held up the little glimmering heart-shaped amulet that lay in the crib and brought it to his lips. Marguerite stopped in her progress.

Olivier. It was Olivier in his long dressing gown which had played over the walls like the curé's habit. He was watching the baby with a concentration which blocked out all else. For a moment, she thought he might be sleepwalking. Or about to do the child some harm.

Then he turned to her, slowly took in her presence. His face wore the marks of the misery she had seen the first signs of that morning. The full-blown realization came towards her, like one of those engines travelling through the night of a moving picture screen. She had glimpsed the headlight before, cutting across the distance, growing brighter and brighter, Now as it threatened to knock her over, she was forced to grapple with the unmistakable beast.

'He's your son, isn't he Olivier? You know he's your son? You just haven't told me. It might have been easier to tell me.'

A strangled sound emerged from his throat. He repeated it more firmly.

'Yes.'

She held back, then uncharacteristically walked towards him and placed her hand on his shoulder.

'That's fine, Olivier,' she said. 'I just needed to know. To know the truth.'

His breath was ragged. He nodded once, a definitive once.

'And his mother is Louise who was once a maid here? Is that right?'

The nod again. This time he met her eyes. 'It was Père Benoit's idea. To make me go to her . . . I needed to be made whole. He said it would make me whole.'

'Whole. I see. I see.' She saw it with a terrifying clarity. The priest directing Olivier to Louise. To make him a man. A different kind of man. And then inducing him to come to Marguerite, herself. To prove it once more. To prove it, since his desires so palpably that night of the party had lain in another direction.

'I'm glad you've told me,' she said.

He stared at her. 'Are you?'

'Told me yourself.' She moved a step closer to the cradle. 'But I must go and see her, this Louise. Talk to her. You understand that, Olivier?'

He nodded miserably.

'If she's happy about it, we'll move ahead with the adoption. Perhaps you might just delay the notary for a few days.'

He looked back into the cradle. 'He's beautiful, isn't he?'

'Yes.'

'Marguerite . . .'

'Yes.'

'Thank you.'

PART FOUR

SACRED ENDS

_ 26 _

She woke late, but with a lightness in her heart which was difficult to attribute.

Could she really feel so much easier because Olivier had confessed to a paternity she had already half-suspected? Could she really prefer a truth ordinarily so difficult for a wife to swallow to the shadow play of concealment? She was, Marguerite reflected, just a little odd. Or maybe it was simply that she didn't consider Olivier's transgression a betrayal. Except in law, the larger part of their bond had long been broken.

Of the two of them, the curé, however, was decidedly the odder. Perhaps even the more transgressive. She could just about bring herself to see how he might find it within his understanding that Olivier be charged with performing his marital duty. She could not see how inducing him to bed a serving girl would transform his so-called sexual sins. Nor could she call to mind any scriptural instance in which sodomy was purified by adultery.

But all that finally had little to do with little Gabriel's future. She would go and see the girl Louise at the nearest opportunity. Today, however, she had a more urgent task.

No sooner had she rung for Jeanne, than the young woman was through the door.

'Ah Madame, I've been putting the Inspector off. I told him you needed your rest. You weren't well yesterday.'

'What is it, Jeanne?'

'He wants to see you. Before he leaves for Paris. He's been summoned.'

'Help me dress, Jeanne. I'll take my coffee with him.'

Durand was pacing the small drawing room impatiently. There were circles under his eyes. He had shaved without his usual care, and the stubble darkened his chin, giving his dapper air a dangerous edge. The Inn in Montoire, as he had told her before, had little to recommend it except a loose-tongued mistress and gossip exchanged round the blazing fire.

'I leave on the next train, Madame,' he said by way of greeting. 'There was a telegram waiting for me from the Commissioner when I got back here.' He adjusted his tie in unhappy anticipation. 'His patience has run out.'

'I'm so sorry, Inspector . . . I had hoped . . . But no, I understand. You shall be much missed here, however.'

A maid brought in a tray of coffee and brioche. The morning's post sat in a neat pile next to the silver pots.

'I wanted you to know, Madame, that our incursion early this morning into the property you call the witch's house, though in fact it belonged to Napoleon Marchand, was a complete failure. A failure in the sense that neither P'tit Ours nor this Amandine Septembre were there. Nor anyone else.'

'I see.'

Marguerite played with the lace of her collar and looked down at the black and white patterning of checks on her skirt. Half of her was relieved. She didn't want the Inspector to notice. She hadn't relished the possibility of Amandine Septembre behind bars on a charge Madame Tellier would inevitably have concocted. And the woman had only, after all, pushed Napoleon over in justifiable self-defence. She had a hunch the old man himself would never have pressed charges. He was not one to go to the police for justice. Though that, she reminded herself, was hardly a good.

'I was almost certain, that if they'd taken the tunnel route, that's where they'd be.'

The Inspector shrugged. 'I'm sure they'll be found in due course. I'm only sorry I won't be with you when they're apprehended. Or indeed until you find the Branquart sisters. I'm leaving behind too many loose ends. And Martine worries me. Such a tremulous young thing. Easy prey for any man.'

Marguerite sipped her coffee and told him of her hunch, only to see him smile and nod in that endearing way of his, as if the idea had been his all along, and she had now had the good sense to come round to it.

'As for the rest,' Durand added, happier now that the bad news didn't seem so bad to her, 'the examining magistrate and the constable are calling on Madame Tellier at this moment. There is reason enough to believe from Dr. Labrousse's report that she . . . or someone . . . had a hand in her father's death. The old man certainly had too large a dose of morphine administered to him. Suspicion, of course, falls on Madame Tellier,' Durand gave her a mischievous smile, 'particularly since our brave little constable was sent into dreamland as well. On top of that, the drunken old blighter choked on his own vomit. The local magistrate wants to press the case against her.'

'And will he succeed, Inspector?'

He shrugged. 'She may try and slip out of it by claiming that her father took the additional powders and the quantities of alcohol himself. But the magistrate says he'll persist with his interrogation, will not allow himself to be swayed.' The Inspector's blue eyes were at their most shrewd.

'You're not certain he'll resist her?'

He didn't answer directly. 'You said when you first went to see the old man he was already poorly. I suspect she may have been at her evil work for some time, though it's hard to come by proof. I have convinced the magistrate that a thorough search of both her own and her father's house is necessary. It should yield evidence of his defrauding of his brother. His estate, I imagine, will go to her.'

'He threatened not, if she annoyed him. It may just have been a ritual provocation, often repeated but never acted upon. He certainly wouldn't have had ready opportunity that night. Though I could be wrong. It may be the provocation that decided her to perform the ultimate act. That plus finding direct evidence of her half-sister's presence in the house would have tipped her over—from love into hate, I mean.'

'If only there was something to implicate Madame Tellier in the fraud against the Martinique branch of the firm, we'd be on surer footing with charging her. You know how these provincial juries are reluctant to trust medical evidence. Too new-fangled for them.'

'I shall pester the magistrate to make sure both houses are thoroughly searched, Inspector. Something may well emerge. But in any case, the commune must be grateful to you. Two murders solved.'

'Yes. Auguste confessed everything about Danuta, several times over. Funny.' The Inspector paused.

'What's funny?'

'How people seem so often to want to confess . . .

'He had the trigger of Frère Michel. Religion and its forms are everywhere, Inspector. Even when people don't believe.'

Durand nodded and pulled out his watch from his waistcoat pocket. He clicked open its lid with a decided snap. 'Reluctantly I shall have to leave you, Madame. I hope Paris will see you very soon.'

'Hold on one moment, Inspector.' Marguerite had just noticed, amongst the pile of letters, one which bore the crest she had been waiting for. 'There may be something here for the case of your Deputy.' She tore open the envelope, read quickly, then passed the letter to the Inspector. 'I think your Commissioner will be very happy, Inspector. You have been working for him, even while you've been away.'

Durand's smile grew wider than the window behind him. 'Ah Madame. What an intrigue. Our Deputy is selling honours to pay off a blackmailer! Past sins feeding present ones.' He shook his head sadly, but it did nothing to lessen his smile. 'It's as I've said to you before, Madame. We shall have to make you an honorary member of the force. I'm only sorry I haven't been able to help you with the waif. The child must be a great worry.'

'Ah that, Inspector . . .' She downed her coffee in a gulp and shook her head. A bitter-sweet expression settled on her lips. 'I'm happy to say our waif is now only half a waif. His father, who is known to me, has now come forward. In private, of course.'

Freteval, where the doddering priest who had known Marguerite's long-dead mother presided, was a flat, grey town, not really much more than a sprawling village with a smattering of old stone streets. It was served, however, by a smart, well-painted, little station, part of the Republic's attempt to bring the countryside into the present. It was also overlooked by a hill where the ruin of a hulking fortress marked the passage of the Lionheart.

The church, too, was a plain, grey affair, stripped of its ornament by the Revolution, though large enough on the inside to hold a capacious congregation. It also had beautiful stained glass windows through which the light glowed in a rainbow of colour over motes of dust. Two old women in identical rough serge dresses were sweeping out the area in front of the linen-clad altar with straw brooms. Marguerite watched them whipping up dust for a moment. The priest's handmaidens she found herself thinking. All the humility was with the women who served the church. She walked over to them. Jeanne, whom she had decided needed an outing, was right behind her.

'Do you know where I could find Père François, Mesdames?'

The two women looked up at her, then at each other. The one on the left murmured toothlessly. 'I know where. But I wouldn't if I were you. Find him, I mean'

'Why not?'

The women looked at each other again and now the other one spoke, tugging at her kerchief. 'He's out of sorts, Ma'am. Better not to speak to him when he's out of sorts.'

'What has made him out of sorts?'

The women shrugged simultaneously. 'Maybe it was the girl who tried to run away again.'

'She only wanted me to post a letter. It's the third time she's tried.'

'A girl?'

'Yes, Yvette he calls her.'

Marguerite stood very still. A long sigh escaped her. A part of her had still been afraid. Afraid that the girl might be dead—as dead as Danuta the Dancer in that wet wood.

'And did you post the letter?'

'No, ma'am. He took it away. Took it straight out of my hand. Poor little thing isn't looking too well with all that fasting, either. I told him. But he doesn't listen. Not anymore. And he doesn't see either. Sees less than my Pierre when he went off to meet his maker. He lost his specs ages ago. Broke them deliberately if you ask me.'

'And he called me Agathe the other day, when he knows perfectly well that I'm Marie. I've been doing for him long enough,' the other woman grumbled. 'And for the one who died before him. Time they sent us a younger man.'

'I fear I shall have to see him before that happens. Where do I go, Mesdames?'

They glanced at each other again, shrugged and pointed to a door on the side. 'If you don't find him, go up the stairs and across the hall to the house.'

Marguerite found Père François in his office. It was littered with paper and bits of left-over food. To the side of his desk, there stood a pew and above it a great wooden carving of a tortured Christ. More worryingly, in what looked like an umbrella stand, she spied an assortment or rods, thongs, whips and crops which made her think of a medieval flagellant's armoury, or one of those terrifying dungeons she had heard of in the centre of Paris where macabre practices were indulged in for sexual purposes. Pain for humbling the body, eradicating the shame and sin of pleasure, and pain for producing that very pleasure: the mysteries her fellow beings provided never ceased to astonish her.

Père François, who failed to recognize her even when she had stated her name several times, was no less of a puzzle. He receded behind his desk and pointed an accusing finger at her. 'Temptress,' he muttered, beneath his breath, and when she tried to remind him that she was her pious mother's daughter, and that he had seen her not so long ago at the Château, he flapped back and forth across the small space like some deranged bird.

His hold on lucidity was even more tenuous, though a momentary light flickered in his watery eyes when she said, enunciating with great clarity, that she was looking for Yvette Branquart.

'Cheating strumpet,' he squawked. 'She fled. Left us. She's sinful. Damned.'

'Are you certain, mon Père? I was told by your church associates that you were holding her here. Holding her sister, in fact, whom you have mistaken for her.'

The hollow face struck her as a death's mask, its empty stare inhuman. She looked down at the desk and there lying on top of a prayer book amidst the litter, saw an envelope in Martine's handwriting addressed to

Celeste Delmas at La Rochambert. It was the letter the cleaners had mentioned. She whipped it off the table and slipped it inside her cape.

'Well, mon Père?'

The man didn't answer. He was looking at her with a stricken expression, as if she were the incarnation of the whore of Babylon.

The old man was clearly demented. His superiors must have been shielding his lacks for some time. A flame of anger leapt in her.

'I shall just go and fetch her and take her home, mon Père. This is no place for a frail, young woman. For one thing, it's exceedingly cold.'

As she closed the door behind her, she saw the accusatory finger pointed at her once more, accompanied this time with a mumbled Latin incantation.

She shuddered. The man might be deranged, but the force of that finger, held aloft in the gesture of some medieval inquisitor, still touched her. She moved away quickly as if his invisible minions might fly after her.

She had no clear idea where she was heading. The letter might point a direction. Or the women in the church. She only hoped Martine wasn't being held in some freezing dungeon in accordance with the man's hoary fantasies. Half way down the sombre corridor, light poured in from a high window. She paused and tore open the envelope.

My dear Celeste,

I write to you because I am too frightened to write to Madame. She will be so angry with me. Properly so. But things just happened. And I wanted you all to know that I was all right. Well, almost all right.

I shouldn't have gone off with Père François without saying anything, but it just turned out that way. It wasn't intended. I was out walking and he stopped me again and started to berate me, tell me that I must do penance. I had taken in what Madame had said— that he mistook me for my sister—and I thought that if I went along with him, as he seemed to wish, even to insist, it would eventually lead me to her.

It all took place so quickly, I didn't have time to tell anyone. One minute I was walking. The next I was in his carriage, asking him to forgive me, I had been stupid. In due course, they might take me back, he said. I didn't dare ask who, yet. I just listened.

I'm still listening. I stay in this little room, which is like a cell, in his house. He comes to see me twice a day to test me on my catechism which he says is terrible and that I'm a bad, stupid girl, and gives me a great many Hail Mary's to repeat. I go to Church three times a day, too. I am not to speak to anyone but him, not even to the woman who brings me a tray with the minimum, when I'm not forced to fast.

You will think this very bad, but at confession, I say any old thing that comes into my mind. Yvette was always better at all this than I am. Nor have I learned yet where she is—or where I was.

Yesterday, no, the day before, I overheard him talking to Monsieur le Curé. Madame, it seems, is bad too. That's what the curé said. A bad influence on Monsieur. But marriage is a sacrament, said Père François. There is nothing for it.

I didn't listen for long, lest they catch me at it. I don't think Madame is bad. I think she is very good. Please ask her to forgive me and make it right with her.

Now I'm trying to find a way to go for a walk and post this. I hope I manage. I hope to see you soon. I really hope so.

Your friend, Martine

The letter brought a chill with it which was colder than the frigid quarters. She hurried towards the church, almost colliding with Jeanne, as she went.

'I've found her, Madame. I've found her. Upstairs. All the way upstairs. In the attic. I'm sorry if I was snooping . . . but I just thought, if there was a maid, like me, we could chat, and instead I heard this crying. Martine. I called to her. But she's locked in, Madame, I don't know how we'll get her out. Truly I don't.'

Jeanne, too, was in tears by the time she had finished her report.

Marguerite soothed her and went to find the women who were cleaning the church. She hoped they were still there. She realized that her hands were trembling. Not fear, no, she told herself. She could overpower that old man if she had to. But out of rage. A burning rage about the abuses the hierarchy shielded. She remembered now that her father, way back when, had already complained of the power of the clergy in the countryside. The corruptions of power.

Women were a negligible breed for so many of these cassocked men who took their cue from St Paul. They were mere vessels to be filled. Filled with whatever ideas they chose. Or more bodily matter, if ideas weren't in the offing. Even Olivier, under their influence, had only had a momentary compunction about using her in the lowest manner. And the maid, Louise, too—a vessel with a twin use, but still without mind or soul.

By the time Marguerite found the two cleaners, hanging up their aprons in a nether room, they would have had to possess the strength of Hercules to refuse her the key to the room in which Martine was kept.

When she and Jeanne opened it to release the girl, she stared at them as if they might be apparitions invoked by her prayer. Martine was kneeling in front of a small crucifix. Her eyes were bruised, red-rimmed, her nose pinched. Her mouth opened, at first to make no sound and then only a whispered query.

'Madame?'

Marguerite helped her up, and feeling her solidity, the girl threw her arms first around her, then around Jeanne.

'My deliverers,' she murmured, then in a movement which Marguerite could only read as guilt, crossed herself quickly.

They met no one, either on the stairs or in the hall or in the darkened corridor which led past the priest's study. In the church, people were beginning to gather for the afternoon mass and they slipped out the side door to make their way round to the waiting carriage.

It was only as Georges was helping Martine up the steps, that Père François emerged from the church. He was breathing heavily. He watched Martine's receding figure with open-mouthed disbelief. Like some Jeremiah, he raised an admonitory fist in the air. Then his face seemed to cave in on itself and crumble, leaving only a shrunken old man in a cassock.

'Yvette,' he wailed, his arms now stretched before him like a supplicant's. 'Yvette. No, you mustn't. You mustn't go.'

Martine hesitated. For a moment, it was as if the voice of the pitiful old man calling for her from the wide arched doors of the church, might pull her back into her imprisonment. Her body strained towards her jailor. Her eyes grew too big for her face. They yearned towards the priest with a feverishness which looked very like love, a kind of uncanny love. And indeed, there was the same intensity in the old priest's face, a father in more than name, perhaps, losing a daughter, whom he had held in a tortuous captivity which was also a closeness.

Marguerite shook away her fascination, climbed in quickly with Jeanne, blocked the man's view, and ordered Georges to hurry.

Throughout the journey homewards, Martine wept soundlessly and clung to Marguerite's hand, as if to let go would condemn her to an inferno reserved for the most atrocious of sinners.

At last, when they had reached the château, the girl seemed to shake herself internally. 'I am sorry, Madame. So sorry for the trouble I have caused. So very sorry.'

'Don't worry about it, Martine. You're safe and you're forgiven. We don't need to talk about it now. You need rest. A bath, sleep. Some food, perhaps.'

At the mention of food, Martine's hand flew to her mouth. A retching she tried to hide overtook her.

'Didn't he let you eat?' Marguerite whispered. She put her arm round the girl and drew her close. Her shoulders were as thin as a child's.

'He's right, Madame. I've been so bad. So many sins. Penance. I had to do penance. I'm dirty. So dirty. That's why I can't find Yvette. That's why she went off.' She was whimpering, a beaten animal, forced into a litany.

'Hush.' Marguerite tiptilted Martine's face and brought the restless vagueness of her eyes into focus. 'You're not bad, Martine. Whatever you might have done can probably be remedied. Everyone makes mistakes. It doesn't make them bad or dirty. Père François may not be the best judge of what mistakes are. He's very old now. In his dotage.'

The girl focussed for a moment, then fell back into her haunted emptiness. It was as if she'd been drugged. Or hypnotized. Hypnotized in the way the famous Charcot had hypnotized his hysterics. Marguerite recognized the look.

She patted the girl's thin hand. 'Rest now, Martine. You're safe. Safe.' She paused, then hurried on. 'He thought you were your sister, didn't he, Martine? He thought you were Yvette. She must have confessed to him. Confessed something he thought very bad. But you're not your sister, as responsible as your love for her might make you feel. Do you understand that, my dear?'

Over the next days, the account that emerged of Martine's kidnapping, made Marguerite rage. Old Père François had put the poor young woman through purgatory. Somewhere in her trajectory, Yvette must have confessed to him her rape by Napoleon Marchand and was therefore doomed in the old man's jaundiced view, through no act of her own. Taking Martine for her sister, her never-to-be-expiated penance was to fast and pray, to wear a hair-shirt and to flagellate herself before the priest's eyes before bedtime.

All this had eaten away not only at the girl's body but begun to tug at her mind. She had taken on the priest's estimate of herself, had lost her bearings, and had become, in some measure, a poor, frail, battered thing.

After an initial visit from Dr. Labrousse, who was tentative towards Marguerite and tender with Martine, Marguerite urged the girl into health with the only tools she knew: rest, good food, fresh air, and plenty of conversation. There was also time with little Gabriel, who was the only person regularly able to draw Martine's smile.

As for Marguerite's assurance that she was now almost certain they would soon find Yvette, Martine paid it little attention. She didn't want to think. Or maybe she needed to put some distance between the young woman Père François had conjured up for her as her sister and the Yvette she remembered.

Marguerite, too, needed the breathing space. Another matter had urgently to be contended with, much as she might secretly like to delay it. Madame Germaine had come good with an address for Louise Bertin, who now went by her stepfather's name of Limbour.

Marguerite stared at the piece of paper with the Blois address and wondered what impact meeting the woman Olivier had bedded would have on her future. Louise Limbour. Little Gabriel's mother.

_ 27 _

The morning dawned clear and with a warm, tantalizing breeze which sang of spring. Marguerite took it as a good sign, though she wasn't yet certain what good might mean in the present circumstance. She dressed simply— a small high-piled hat, a striped skirt with a lace-trimmed bodice, her auburn cloak with its black trim—and had already climbed into the carriage, when she saw Paul Villemardi racing towards her. He opened the door.

'May I accompany you, Madame? I'm told you're going to Blois. I have an errand to run. And Olivier said I might be of some assistance to you.'

'Did he?'

Olivier, it seemed, wanted his spies with her.

Villemardi climbed in beside her before she could think of a suitable excuse.

'I can see from her face that Madame would rather I minded my own business today. I promise to be as silent as Madame wishes. And to leave her quite alone when she so desires.' He turned an infectious grin on her. His eyes twinkled beneath the unruly fringe of hair.

He was making himself irresistible, Marguerite thought. There was little point resisting. She returned his smile, but refused the offer of conversation.

On the terraces, a caped Celeste was maneuvering little Gabriel's pram through the doors of the house which Armand held open for them. She wondered if Louise would want to come and visit her child. What might she feel about another woman taking her place as the boy's mother?'

The more Marguerite focussed on it, the odder her position in relation to the child became.

The adoption of a foundling, with its origins unknown to all, would have been a simple matter. But here, she was being asked to take on the role of stepmother to her husband's child, yet the child's real mother wasn't dead and would soon be known to her. She didn't want to dislike her. With painful honesty, Marguerite realized she did not even really want to meet her. But she had to know how the young woman felt about giving up Gabriel. And somehow a letter wouldn't be enough. Or maybe she was, after all, more curious than she liked to admit, even to herself.

Marguerite tried to imagine exactly how Louise had gone about abandoning the babe. Had she watched and waited for Olivier to turn up, and made certain he had the basket in hand before running off? Had the day had fleeting clouds like these creating shadows on the hills? How and when had she let Olivier know the child was his? Could the girl write? Had there been a go-between, someone in the house who knew that Olivier was growing attached to the child? All these questions and others coursed through her mind while they rattled towards Blois.

She watched Villemardi covertly. At first she had thought he was the girl's seducer. But no, no, he must have been the go-between. That's why he was here with her now on this lengthy trek to the royal city. Of course. Her glimmering but constant sense that she was somehow at the centre of an invisible cabal came to the forefront of her mind.

In profile, the sculptor's face had a feline aspect. She was surprised she hadn't noticed it before. What she had been aware of were his fine features, their delicacy atop that solid, peasant's body. She stared at him. It came to her like a shock of ice water on a hot day that she had got things all wrong. Because Villemardi had been so seductive, so beguiling towards her, it had deflected her. She had failed to take on board that it was he who was—or at least had been—Olivier's lover. Of course. It made complete sense. Villemardi had been Olivier's lover until Père Benoit arrived on the scene with his rather different ideas. That was why the sculptor had such animosity for the curé; and why Olivier was so torn about sending him away. She had been utterly blind.

Had she failed to pick up the cues because she simply didn't want to see them? She had no more wanted to identify the sculptor's bond to her husband than Olivier had wanted to recognize her in the smutty-faced Antoine. Surfaces, anticipation, habit—all had played their part.

'So Monsieur Villemardi, you feel Louise would talk to me more easily with you there?' Marguerite now forced a conversation.

He shrugged. Gave her the benefit of his velvet eyes. 'Olivier thinks so. And who am I to question Olivier's assumptions? I'm a mere bit player in his grand design.'

'Come, come, Monsieur Villemardi. I have never known you to be quite so self-effacing.'

'Then you don't know me well,' he said, suddenly rude. A moment later, he was contrite. 'Forgive me. Perhaps I'm looking forward to this interview even less than you are. It brings back a painful period.'

She didn't question him further. It felt tactless.

The historic town of Blois, home to French Kings and Dukes of Orleans and their murderous royal intrigues, rose with frayed majesty on its hill overlooking the Loire. The grand river of the region was a commercial artery as busy as the Seine, and noisier. Steam boats hooted, jostled with barges and fishing skiffs. All manner of building material, not to mention the seasonal riches of the valleys—apples and pears, asparagus and artichoke, melons and pumpkins and wine—made their way up and down river stopping at any of the many points between Orleans and Angers and further afield.

Her father had rarely taken her the distance of Blois and as a result she hardly knew the town, but she still remembered the high stone walls of the cloister on its outskirts and the massive spiky towers of St Nicholas, which seemed to puncture the clouds in their dramatic ascent towards the heavens.

The streets at the base of the town were narrow and gloomy with the weight of their houses huddled beneath the hill-top grandness of the castle. A square of brick and stone opened before them. The traces of the morning market were still in evidence. Farmers and hawkers emptied their stalls. Old, bonneted women, large woven baskets at their feet, gossiped in the pale sunshine. A knife-sharpener shouted his services. At far end of the square a gaggle of children gathered to watch what, from their gawking, could only be a procession.

It was as Georges stopped the carriage and opened the door to her that Marguerite took in that this was no procession of the usual kind. Moving slowly up the incline of the square was a woman on a broad-backed mare. She too was large, her garments of a maroon red somewhat tattered and spattered with mud. She moved regally, like a queen, her body echoing the rhythm of the mare in slower motion. Her face was covered with a heavy veil of what might have been fishnetting. It only partly obscured the milk chocolate of her skin, the deep, dramatic eyes, the brilliant red of the lips.

Leading the horse by a rope, as carefully as if he had in tow the Virgin and her unborn child, was a P'tit Ours transformed by his charge. His eyes were fixed directly in front of him. There was no shuffling. His clogs hit the ground with a steady, almost military gait. His shoulders were proudly high. When he glanced up at the woman it was with an expression which brimmed with love. Was it that which made him oblivious to the sporadic taunts of the children? Marguerite could now hear them clearly as she and Villemardi approached. They too stopped to watch the spectacle of this odd couple's steady progress.

For a fleeting second, Marguerite felt Amandine Septembre's eyes fall on her. The woman raised her hand in a half wave, as if she recognized her. And then they had moved past.

'I wonder where they're going,' she murmured.

'To the pier, I imagine. To take a boat somewhere.' Paul Villemardi urged her forward, 'According to Georges, we have to go down this way.'

Marguerite turned to catch a last glimpse of the fugitive couple. She now noticed that in his left hand, P'tit Ours held a strongbox. She was tempted to race after them and forget about Louise. But she forced herself to stay on course. She recognized the wish to avoid murky matters which implicated her more nearly.

The heat and clanging of their destination reached them even before they had glimpsed it. The old stone forge was tucked into the bottom of a narrow, sloping street the coachman had preferred not to enter. A horse was tethered to the ring beside its open half door. Through it, they could see a burly, aproned man, his face gleaming with perspiration. In his hands, he held a large hammer which he aimed rhythmically at the glowing metal of the horseshoe he was working. Sparks flew upward.

Marguerite restrained Villemardi until the smith had finished this stage of his work.

'Monsieur Limbour?' Villemardi then addressed the man.

There was an answering grunt, but the smith didn't turn towards them. Instead they heard the hiss of molten iron in water as he lowered the shoe into a barrel.

'We're looking for Louise.'

'Louise!' The man veered round, anger in his heavy face. 'You're not going to find her here, are you?'

His tone and face changed as he took them in. Marguerite was half ashamed of her finery in these workmanly surroundings.

The man made a small gesture of the head which could have been taken as a bow. 'You'll not find her here in the middle of the day,' he said, his voice barely audible now.

'Where will we find her, Monsieur?' Marguerite used her most gracious tone.

The man met her eyes briefly. 'She's working with the chocolates. If she's not up to worse.'

'Chocolates?'

Villemardi tapped her arm and gestured her away, thanking the blacksmith as he did so.

'Poulain's. She must have got work at Poulain's chocolate factory, La Villette.'

'Is it far?'

Villemardi shook his head. 'Quicker with the carriage though.'

As they emerged into the small square, they all but collided with P'tit Ours and his charge coming from the opposite direction. The youth's lopsided face took on a frightened look as he recognized her. But Amandine Septembre maintained her regal calm and addressed her from behind her veil.

'Do you know where we might find a blacksmith, Madame?'

Her voice had a music all of its own. It took Marguerite a moment to separate out the individual words and then she turned to point behind her.

'Right at the end,' she said and paused, before rushing on. 'Has your horse lost a shoe?

Amandine Septembre shook her head. 'No Madame. I have lost a key. A key to my strongbox.'

P'tit Ours yanked the horse along.

Marguerite swallowed hard. Again she wanted to race after the two, interrogate them. But she couldn't. Not now. Instead she called, 'Be careful that the smithy doesn't singe any papers.'

A throaty laugh came from Amandine. 'That's a good warning, Madame. I thank you.'

'Do come and see me if you encounter any problems. Do . . .' Her voice bounced off stone walls and came back to her.

Villemardi was looking at her strangely. She returned his gaze, head on.

'Yes, Monsieur Villemardi. We have strange ways in Paris. You said so yourself.'

He chuckled, a little too familiar. 'Don't worry. I won't report back to Olivier.'

The chocolate factory was a long narrow stone building set round a courtyard and back from the street. Smoke sprouted from its many chimneys. Its side sported the familiar blue Poulain sign with its majestic, sprawling P. All the posters she had seen advertising the chocolate maker's products, all that repetition of 'goutez et comparez,' 'taste and compare' over the years now leapt into Marguerite's mind. Yet she had never taken on board that the factory was in Blois and from the extent of it, a major employer.

A man stopped their progress as soon as they opened the door. Wafts of rich, bitter fumes came in his wake.

No they couldn't see Louise Limbour, he told them emphatically. Out of the question. She wouldn't be finished for another two hours.

It took all of Marguerite's authority, her insistence on talking to Monsieur Poulain himself, if necessary, to convince him that the young woman had to be called away from her vat, whatever the loss of steam time. Marguerite even offered to pay for her time.

When she was finally ushered through to them from the heat of a side door, Louise Limbour looked frail and fearful, not at all the buoyant young vamp gossip had led Marguerite to expect. Nor in her large, ungainly blue worksmock, was she the nymph of Villemardi's stonework. Was this what the loss of baby Gabriel had done to the girl?

With a flourish of hauteur which she saw frightened the girl even more, Marguerite asked the foreman if they could be shown to a room. They had a private matter to discuss.

Louise Limbour trembled visibly. Her pretty face had an unhealthy pallor, despite the heat. When she took in Villemardi's presence, she touched a delicate hand to the golden loaf of her pinned up hair, then looked down at the floor as if it had produced Monsieur Rama's serpent to turn her to stone.

The foreman ushered them into a tiny airless cubicle. Marguerite, in the hope that it would reassure her, pointed Louise to the only chair. The girl sat at its very edge.

'You don't know me, Louise, except as the absent Comtesse de Landois, I imagine. But I'd like you to believe that I intend you no harm. There is a delicate issue between us.'

The girl looked up at her with a start, intelligence glimmering in her blue eyes, colour mounting into her cheeks.

'The matter of a child.'

'A child?' she echoed.

'Yes, Louise,' Villemardi intervened. 'It's a little late to play the innocent prude. Madame is a saint and wants to adopt your bastard. So no games now. Just tell her everything.'

'Monsieur Villemardi,' Marguerite cut him off. 'You'll wait for me in the carriage, please. I want to speak to Mlle Limbour in private. Thank you.'

She stared down the startled face he turned to her. 'Right away, Monsieur.'

She waited for him to go, then smiled at Louise. 'These matters are better discussed between women. Madame Germaine tells me you want to work with her to become a midwife.'

The girl nodded, once. Then the fearful look came over her again.

'I can help you to do that. But first I need to know about the baby. The baby you left by the Loir.'

'No, Madame, no.' The girl protested.

Marguerite was surprised.

'So you didn't leave your baby by the river?'

'I have no baby. I have no baby.' Louise burst into tears. They flooded down her face and seemed to suffocate her. She started to hiccough violently.

'You have no baby?' Marguerite repeated. 'No baby that you took to the river and waited for Monsieur le Comte to pick up? No baby that was the result of an encounter between you and Monsieur le Comte?'

The girl shook her head so hard that the pinned-up hair tumbled. But the crying didn't cease. The sobs had taken her over, as vehement as spasms. They wracked her shoulders, contorted her delicate face.

Marguerite put an arm around her, but the tears didn't abate. She felt helpless. This utter denial was the one response she hadn't expected. She gave the girl her handkerchief and tried again.

'You had a baby, Louise. You had a baby by the Count. You couldn't keep the poor mite, because he was illegitimate. I understand. I understand the scandal it would have caused. Your inability to find work, because of it. I promise I won't publicize the fact. I just need to know. Need to know, if I am to be the baby's adoptive mother. You could even come back and live with us Louise. I wouldn't mind. I would be quite happy for you to take on the care of the child, if that's what you wanted. Your relation to him could remain a secret. Only we would know. I'm sure Monsieur le Comte would agree to that. You understand?'

Through all this the girl only sobbed more and more fiercely. Now and again, she shook her head, and repeated almost incoherently. 'No child. I have no child. No child.'

At last Marguerite realized she couldn't break through the girl's resistance. Some fear so powerful had taken her over, that she could only deny the fact of Gabriel. It was possible she even believed she had never had him. She had heard of cases like that. At the Salpetrière with its terrible complement of sufferers—people driven mad by the agony of their lives.

'Perhaps you'd like to talk to Madame Germaine about it all,' Marguerite said when she could think of no other approach.

The girl raised haunted, red-rimmed eyes to look at her. 'It's not my child,' she repeated. It came out like a mumbled response in a catechism lesson. The sobs shook her again.

Between them, Marguerite thought she heard her say, 'My stepfather will kill me. Kill me. He'll send me back to the sisters.'

With that the girl rushed from the room, leaving Marguerite to stare at the empty space which had so briefly held her adamant fragility.

_ 28 _

Marguerite sat alone in front of the blazing fire in her upstairs rooms. It was evening. She had wanted to be alone to think and had taken her supper here. But her thoughts moved obsessively in only one direction. She watched the flames coalesce into Louise's face, leap at her heaving shoulders, splutter out her repeated denials, echo the wail of her sobs.

An expectant Olivier had baulked when she said she was tired and needed to be alone. But in the battle between curiosity and contrition which played itself out on his face, the latter had won a temporary victory. He didn't press her. She knew he would talk to Villemardi to get news of the meeting with Louise.

To Villemardi in the carriage home, all she had said, was, 'Louise insists she had no child.'

The sculptor had made no reply. He barely spoke to her. He was still smarting at the brusque manner in which she had ordered him to leave. She, in turn, was angry at the high-handed, insulting way he had addressed the young woman. As if when she wasn't his model, she was less than a servant—an inanimate, earthenware container, first for seed, then for the babe. She wondered if it was his presence that had utterly skewered the interview.

Only later did it come to her that Paul Villemardi might feel a burning jealousy towards the Louise with whom Olivier had created a child. Had she already suspected what had come clear to her on the way to Blois, she would never have allowed him to come with her.

But that aside, could Louise be telling the truth? Or was she lying out of a fear of the consequences? Lying because her stepfather would kill her if he found out she had given birth to a child. Lying because she could lose her job, would have to leave everything that was familiar?

She had also made a mistake, Marguerite acknowledged. She had forgotten how frightened Louise would be of her. She should have sent Madame Germaine to prepare the ground.

The girl's thin face formed itself out of the flames again. Could anyone that transparently frail have so recently given birth to a child as healthy as little Gabriel? A child who had been left to the wintry elements and survived?

As the hours of contemplation passed, Marguerite veered between distrusting Olivier's assertions and doubting the girl's veracity. Her husband was wrong. The girl had had no child. But Gabriel was there. He existed. If not Louise, someone else had given birth to him and brought him to Olivier's attention.

Marguerite paced, paused in front of the mirror where the face returned to her looked like a stranger's. Her eyes were vast, lifeless, shadowed, the skin too pale, the cheekbones too prominent, the hair disheveled. Had she been weeping, without realizing it? She must take care or havoc would invade and sweep her away.

She sipped tea which had grown cold. She bit into a piece of chocolate. Had this come from the factory in which Louise worked? She stared into the flames, felt tears gather in her eyes and saw the walls and courtyard of the factory take shape.

A moment later, they had given way to the walls they had passed on the outskirts of Blois. Great high walls in the grey ugliness of the plain which stretched beneath the hill town. Walls which contained the convent of the Sisters of the Blessed Virgin.

The place had beckoned to her, and she had asked Georges to stop the carriage. But no amount of pounding at the door brought any response. Perhaps it was already too late for entry. As they drove away, she had imagined Olivier going there to deposit infant Gabriel in his basket. She had understood how he hadn't been able to push the mite through the bleak stone wall. She asked Villemardi to describe that day, but his terse answers brought no new information.

Well into the small hours, Marguerite sat in front of the fire and considered. She found herself wishing for Rafael's presence. With his demotic,

American spirit, perhaps he would be better placed to understand Louise and Yvette and Martine who had been conditioned to keep her at a distance whatever her intentions. He would be better placed, as well, to confront that strange couple she had seen in the streets of Blois. She wondered where Amandine Septembre and that awkward P'tit Ours, who had led her horse so nobly along the streets of Blois, had gone. If she wished them well out of the way of the turbulence they had so far managed to avoid, she still wanted some of the answers the majestic daughter of the murdering old reprobate might be able to provide.

Morning came sooner than Marguerite might have wanted. It came with a great torrent of distress from Jeanne, whose knock on the door she still locked rudely penetrated her cloistered dreams. There was an unwelcome pounding of rain against the window to provide a counterpoint.

'I'm sorry, Madame. So sorry. But that ghastly woman, she insisted. I thought she might hit Madame Solange. She wouldn't go away. She shouted and screamed. We had no choice.'

'Slowly Jeanne. Who are you talking about?'

'That fat woman with the hairy lip. All those ringlets. I'm sure they're a wig. Terrible dress, too. Flounces and ribbons everywhere. Pelletier or . . . I don't remember. We had no choice, Madame.'

'Tellier,' Marguerite interpreted for her. So the police hadn't arrested the woman yet. What were they waiting for? She searched for lucidity through the residue of dreams. 'Yes, Madame Tellier. It will do her no harm to calm herself and wait. So help me with my toilette, Jeanne. I fear I've been letting myself go a little.'

When she came into the small sitting room where Madame Tellier had been directed, the woman was prodding the logs in the fireplace. She was swathed in a long black coat and a vast boat of a black hat which shouted mourning. The logs must have taken Marguerite's place in her imagination, for when she heard Marguerite's greeting she turned and lunged the poker in her direction.

'What did you do with them? I saw you. Saw you prowling. Stealing. You're just a thief in good clothes. A worm.'

The spew of words was the only greeting Marguerite was to get. Madame Tellier's eyes were as hot and accusing as her face was red. They sent a threatening electrical charge through the room, as dangerous as the poker.

'Calm yourself, Madame.' Marguerite took a step backwards, then stood her ground. 'I have no idea what you're referring to. I should also remind you that you're in my house and to accuse me of theft is not only a lie but a base insult.'

'Don't start on me with your hoity toity ways. You know very well what I'm talking about. My father's papers. His will. They were in his desk. I saw you there. Saw you pilfering, filching. What have you done with it all?'

She shook the poker at Marguerite.

Marguerite eyes sought sanctuary in the painting above the fireplace where her mother presided with her regal stance.

'If you stopped to think for a moment, Madame, you would know that Monsieur Marchand probably lodged his will with his notary. I recommend you go to him. Right now. And leave my house.'

She stood aside and with a sweep of the arm showed the woman the door.

'It's not that easy. Not that easy.' The woman hissed. She waved the poker again and it caught at an ashtray which clattered to the floor. She took another menacing step towards Marguerite. 'Napoleon Marchand had little time for notaries. And I know he kept his will close to his person. Very close. In his room. Kept all his papers about him. Money, too.' She was shouting now, her voice rising through the quiet of the house like a trumpet.

It came to Marguerite that at any moment the woman might make good her fury and plunge the poker into her. She had had the same sense with old Napoleon, her father—minds gone awry and at the mercy of wild passions. They were immune to reason.

'I have nothing more to say to you, Madame.' Marguerite backed towards the door. 'This interview is over.'

The woman started to laugh. A loud guffaw of malevolence. 'You think that lover of yours, that Labrousse can help you out of this. Vouch for you in the courts. Well you're wrong. Quite wrong. He's had his comeuppance, the scoundrel. No more bribing for him. No more extra fees here and there. Not for shutting up that Yvette you're so interested in either. Or for providing a little sleeping powder for my poor father now and again. No more pretending he's interested in my daughters. Too good for him. Both of them.'

'I think, Madame,' a deep male voice, followed by a stentorian cough, startled them both. 'I think Madame, if my wife has taken a lover it can be no business whatsoever of yours. Nor is Dr. Labrousse of any interest to me. My men will see you out. Though if you prefer to wait for the constables, you can do so in the stables. With the other animals.'

Olivier snapped his fingers and two men appeared simultaneously at the door. Georges took the poker from Madame Tellier's hand. A man on either side of her, the surprised but still protesting woman was dragged from the house.

She shouted behind her. 'You'll be hearing from me. Don't think you've got away with it. No one robs a Tellier.'

Marguerite sank into an armchair and breathed deeply.

'If you will insist on keeping such low company, Marguerite, I don't know what you expect.' Olivier shook his head in distaste.

'Has it not occurred to you that I keep this company because you asked me to come here?'

'Hardly for Madame Tellier's sake.'

It was Marguerite's turn to see red.

'If you're speaking to me like this because you believe that lunatic woman's accusations, you have no cause.'

'I'm speaking to you like this because you behave in such a way that permits this lunatic woman to make such accusations. What you do behind closed doors is your concern alone. What you do in public is also mine.'

'And what you've done in *private* has become mine.'

The accusation leapt to Marguerite's lips before she could stop herself. Now that it was out she had no particular regrets. 'I suppose that Villemardi has told you that the girl you so assiduously bedded refuses to acknowledge that she is Gabriel's mother. If she is.'

Olivier looked down at his feet. They were well shod in soft brown leather. When he met her eyes again, his face no longer wore its arrogant condemnation. 'Paul told me,' he said softly. 'I don't know why she denies it.'

'What you need to tell me is how you became convinced that Gabriel was hers. And yours.'

He eased himself into a chair. She could see from the workings of his face that he had so long assumed it all as given—whatever the time scale of his confessions to her—that it was no longer easy for him to reconstruct how what he had assumed as truth had become so.

'The curé told me,' he said at last.

'You mean Louise confessed to him. He broke the confidence of the confessional and told you.'

Olivier nodded once abruptly. His attention was now all for the flames.

Marguerite brought him back. 'Did he also tell you that Louise knew the babe was here with us?'

Olivier considered. It took him time. She knew he was going through his many meetings with the curé, sifting them. It reminded her that she hadn't seen the man in the house since that Mass, the day of Napoleon Marchand's death. Was that to do with Olivier or with her?

'He intimated,' Olivier replied at last. 'I'm not sure he said it directly. So it's just possible she doesn't know. Which is why she couldn't be honest with you.'

He gave a little sigh of what seemed to be relief.

'I don't think it's as simple as that, Olivier. But nevermind for now. I must have some coffee. Then I'm going out. I'll need Georges all day.'

Madame Tellier's words about Labrousse had just come back to her. What could the demented woman have meant? And why was it she was still free to charge about the countryside? The old adage must still hold true that what was labelled madness in the poor was considered mere eccentricity in the rich. Had the investigating magistrate failed to find anything incriminating in the family houses and changed his mind about arrest? Or did he and the local police feel it safe Madame Tellier be free until they had amassed sufficient evidence against her? Given the barely contained violence she had long sensed in the woman, she feared they would be proved horribly wrong.

Fearing she might already be too late, Marguerite pushed open the door of Dr. Labrousse's consulting room after only the most cursory of knocks.

Her dire expectations subsided. There was no body slumped over the desk. The doctor was sitting up, filling out what looked like a complicated dossier. She didn't immediately notice the spectacled magistrate at his side.

'Dr. Labrousse. Thank goodness I find you upright. You're quite well?'

'Shouldn't I be?'

'Madame Tellier frightened me with vile warnings. I thought I might find you . . .' she hesitated, '. . . ill.'

'No. No. I'm fine.' He smiled, his beard moving with his lips. 'Just a little tired. I haven't seen Madame Tellier. Though her daughter dropped round at about five yesterday. And how is everyone at La Rochambert?'

'At five o'clock yesterday, you said?'

'Yes, to see how I was doing. To weep over grandpa. To talk about details of the funeral. He's been embalmed and is lying in state in the Tellier house, apparently.'

Marguerite had a sudden vision of Madame Tellier, hair loosened, shuddering tears, bent over her father's corpse for hours on end, begging him to reveal the location of his will.

'Laure also brought me some stew from her mother. Madame Tellier is convinced that I'll prefer her housekeeper's rabbit stew to all else.'

'And do you? You ate it?' Marguerite asked carefully. Had her fears about the frenzied woman been all wrong?

'In fact I didn't. I was dining with Monsieur Tournevau, the chemist, so I left the ragout in the larder.'

'I . . . I suspect we should look at it.'

Labrousse gazed at her as if she had suffered a fit of lunacy and he would like to prescribe a bromide.

'I don't think I understand you.'

'I understand you, Madame.' The magistrate, Maitre Narbonne, interrupted, his nose twitching. 'That madwoman probably put poison in the stew. So you wouldn't be able to stand up in court and say that her father had been helped to his end, Docteur.'

'That's exactly what I suspect, Maitre.'

Docteur Labrousse brought the cloth covered dish out of the larder, set it on the kitchen table and carefully unwrapped it. But for a slight scum that had formed at the top, the dish looked innocuous enough. But a moment after being uncovered, it emitted a pungent smell which tugged at their nostrils. Marguerite put a handkerchief to her nose.

Carefully, Docteur Labrousse dipped his finger into the sauce and brought a smidgen to his tongue. He screwed up his face, which had turned white and coughed with instant revulsion.

'Bitter. Strychnine, I'll wager.' He poured some water from the jug and rinsed out his mouth

'I imagine the taste is more in evidence since yesterday. She uses it on her rats, no doubt. And I've become one of them. Lucky you came to warn me, Madame. I was planning to make a meal of it this evening.'

He disappeared out the door with the dish in hand.

The magistrate called him back. 'No, no, don't empty all of it. It's the first substantial evidence we have.'

'You're right.' The doctor wrapped the dish up again. 'Though a small quantity should do us. This will be a putrid mess before we get it to court. In fact you should bring her in for questioning again straight away, and feed it to her.' His laugh was as sour as the stew.

'When will that be?'

He glanced at his pocket-watch. 'I'll have someone go and fetch her now. Little came from our prior interviews as you've probably gathered. She just cried all the way through. Nor did my men find anything in their search of Monsieur Marchand's house. She kept at them like a snapping terrier the whole time. And there were thousands of papers stashed in every available space. Scribbled records of purchases, sales, bills of lading. We'd need another importer on the premises, if we were to prove fraud. Particularly now that the plaintiff, Xavier Marchand, is dead.'

'But you still have the brother's notebook which details the fraud?'

He nodded.

'What about her house?'

He squirmed a little. 'We haven't managed access yet. We agreed to wait until after tomorrow, when the old man will be buried.'

'Given the tricks she seems disposed to play, Maitre, I think you had better have her carefully watched until then.'

'How did you come to know about all this, Madame?' The Magistrate suddenly returned her suspicion.

'Madame Tellier came to me first thing this morning—to accuse me of stealing her father's will. Other documents, too. Threatened me. If I had your authority, Maitre, I would have locked her up days ago. But I must leave you. There are some others Madame Tellier might threaten. Time may not be on their side.'

'Where? Who?' Labrousse towered over her, his narrow face gaunter than ever. 'I'll come with you. We'll bring the constable.'

'No, no. Not immediately in any case. It might scare away the truth forever.' She considered for a moment. 'But why not come after me in about an hour. It may all be a wild goose chase, but it may not.'

'Where are you heading?'

Marguerite told them.

'I doubt that is wise, Madame.' Labrousse intervened. 'You must let me come along.'

Marguerite shook her head. For all his free-thinking intelligence, the doctor she estimated would be as intrusive as Paul Villemardi in the interview she had now to undertake.

_ 29 _

The manor lay beyond the forest on the other side of La Rochambert. A high, ivy-clad brick wall masked its existence so that coming to it, even from the road, the whole establishment looked like nothing so much as a dark extension of the wood overgrown with parasites and creepers.

Apart from her unfortunate trek on the day that she had discovered Danuta the Dancer's body, it was Olivier's aerial photographs which had alerted her to the secretive presence of the house. A further foray in the library through her father's old military maps of the region had shown a network of tunnels, one of which joined the house with Napoleon Marchand's.

'The Emperor,' Auguste, the strongman, had called him. It was the name Danuta had given old Marchand. And she had evidently blackmailed her Napoleon after she had witnessed the death of Xavier Marchand, the Emperor's brother, in the house they had called Beaumont.

These old walls seemed to lift the murderous family with its colonial extensions and rampant illegitimacies out of the register of the contemporary. The history of the valleys had been shadowed by pernicious royal intrigues. Now they found their echo in a local tyrant who had grown fat on far-flung interests. She had blundered into a war of succession between rival sisters, each laying claim to a legacy which had grown large through corruption and the labour of others. All she wanted to do now was to prevent more blood being spilled in passion and greed.

At last, two chestnut trees appeared to mark a break in the wall. Between them was a muddy, rutted drive, half covered with last year's mouldy leaves and overgrown with the creeper which had spread everywhere. Napoleon Marchand had evidently not thought it worthwhile looking after this property.

When the carriage lurched wildly, she told Georges to stop and wait. She would continue on foot. Surprise might be essential if she was to find anyone at home.

The grounds of the house were in disarray and had been left untended for what seemed like years. The outhouses she came upon were tumbling. An old wagon stood in front of the stables and from their depths, she heard the furtive trampling of a horse's hooves on hay. She peered in and recognized the large mare on which Amandine Septembre had ridden through Blois. There were no other animals, carts or carriages visible.

A sigh of relief escaped her. Madame Tellier wasn't here. She had come in time.

She made her way across the undergrowth towards the house. It was a prepossessing Restoration structure. But its stucco was crumbling. The tiles on the roof were in need of repair. Flaking shutters drooped on loose hinges and rattled in the wind.

With no warning, her feet lost hold of the ground and tripped over some obstacle. Her heel caught on her dress. She barely put out a hand in time to stop a head-first plunge.

A body lay splayed on the ground. It didn't move. A man's body in work-a-day clothes. She lifted herself up gingerly and held her breath. His back was to her, his neck at an angle which suggested it had snapped, his cap at a little distance from his head. She recoiled, then forced herself to turn him over. The blood on his face was black. The mouth moved. She stepped backwards in revulsion. Maggots. He must have been here for some days.

She recognized the face in its distorted remains. It was the old servant. Hercule. The one who had looked after Amandine Septembre. The one who had thrown stones back at the children. The one who was missing on the day of Napoleon Marchand's fall. She covered his face with his cap.

She had come too late. Too late to warn. No, no, that didn't make sense. This wasn't a fresh death. But why Hercule?

The large wooden door of the house stood half open. She didn't know whether to pull the bell cord or to step in. Out of propriety, she decided on the first, though it was unlikely that the bell would be heard any further than the hall or the servants' quarters.

After a moment, she allowed herself to push the door open. A smell of fried onions and decay rose to her nostrils. She stopped in her tracks.

Emerging from a door to the back of the yellowing mirrors of the hall was Amandine Septembre. The woman gave Marguerite a dazzling smile.

'Oh happy. So happy you could come.'

She sailed across the room towards her, her frayed dress billowing, and curtsied grandly. 'Madame is kind. I told P'tit Ours you would come. I knew. I didn't think he would find you so soon.'

Marguerite worked to accustom herself to the island rhythms of her voice.

'P'tit Ours?'

'Yes. P'tit Ours. My protector. That's what I like to call him. He fetched you quick. Is he here? With your carriage?'

'No, no, I came alone.' Marguerite slowly took all this in. It was odd that she had been sent for. Maybe the woman practiced those magic arts Marguerite didn't believe in. Voodoo. She had read accounts of it.

'He'll follow later then. He'll bring food. Come. Come. I have nothing to offer. Only rum which ladies do not drink and chestnuts and jams I found in the pantry along with the mice and the spiders. And yesterday's bread and cheese. Come. P'tit Ours is a good eater. Everything else is finished.'

P'tit Ours, her protector. Was it he who had protected her from gnarled old Hercule?

The woman lifted her skirts and led Marguerite up the stairs into a sizeable drawing room which wore a quantity of framed oils. Admirals, generals, a judge presided over dust and derelict grandeur. There seemed to be a charred hole in his brow. A bullet hole, Marguerite thought, adjusting her gloves with renewed nervousness.

On a long rectangular table lay an array of papers. To the right stood the strong-box Marguerite had seen P'tit Ours carrying in Blois. It was open.

'Did my protector explain? I am not a good reader. He is not a reader at all. We have these papers. None of them is my pass from Martinique, which I had hoped P'tit Ours had fetched. I have lost that or my protector couldn't find it at Napoleon Marchand's house. But on one of these papers I read my name. I can read my name, at least. I am Amandine Septembre.' She stretched out a hand.

Marguerite proffered hers. 'Marguerite de Landois,' she murmured.

'Good. Now we know each other.' Amandine waved her to a chair. 'I knew you would help. You came. You came to the other house. I saw you. I sent you a note. The bad Hercule and my father decided I should not go out. As if Amandine were a slave. There are no more slaves, Madame. Not since 1848 on my island. I have learned that. But my father is not so good to me.'

She looked away. Looked out towards the door as if Napoleon might come through it. Her smile had vanished. Her lips trembled. 'Not so good as Uncle Xavier promised. He said it was his sacred mission to bring us together. And since Papa wouldn't come to my beautiful Martinique, I was to come to him. But my father, he drinks too much. All the men they drink. I think it kills them. P'tit Ours, he tells me, my father is dead. Now Amandine Septembre only wants the little that is hers to help her go home to her island. I do not want to stay here. No. Never. You will help, Madame, yes?'

Marguerite nodded. 'I will do my best.'

Amandine reached for a sheaf of papers. 'You see here, and here again, there is my name. I think it is a will.' Her broad index finger slowly underlined the word, '*testament*' as she pronounced it slowly.

Marguerite studied the papers. This was indeed Napoleon Marchand's will. She couldn't take in its complexities now, but it seemed he had overwritten the name Amandine in two places and scratched out the name beneath.

She held the paper up to the light and under the scratching out she could see the name of Estelle Tellier. There were other scratchings-out, too. Marguerite read quickly. From a brief glance it seemed that old Napoleon had changed round his bequests to the two daughters, so that what had originally gone in the favour of one now went to the other. The advantage was all Amandine's.

She was pursued by the thought that, for all her ostensible innocence, the woman might just have executed this overwriting herself.
There was a simple way of finding out.

Briefly Marguerite explained what she had read, then asked if Amandine had a pen and paper on which she could write a note authorizing
Marguerite to take the documents to the notary and magistrate.

Amandine stared at her from eyes round with concern.

'Ah, Madame. We must search the house for ink and paper. Perhaps
in my Papa's old room. There is a desk. Let us go and see. But Madame,
Amandine can only sign. She cannot write well. Her maman didn't teach
her. Or Uncle Xavier. Poor Uncle Xavier. He so wanted to come home.
And now he is home for good. He died here, I think. In this house. I heard
something, you know. In my sleep. Screaming. A body falling down stairs.'
Tears flooded her eyes. She shrugged them away and motioned Marguerite
down the hall.

'Do you have any idea where your old servant, Hercule, might be, Mlle
Septembre?' Marguerite asked as the woman strode ahead in front of her.

'Hercule? No, I don't. And I don't want to know, Madame. He was
less than kind to Amandine. Less than kind. To tell you the truth, Madame,
since I have arrived in your country, my country too, few have been kind
to Amandine. Uncle sometimes, P'tit Ours and yourself. That is all. Is it
to ask so much for a little kindness? Kindness from one's kin? Even in the
village where we met, the children, they had no manners . . . Amandine
will be very happy to go back to Fort de France. Very happy to have
warm sunshine and flowers and the blue of the sea.'

She gave Marguerite her own warming smile, then ushered her into
a room which housed a vast four-poster bed, complete with dusty muslin,
and a shapely desk. In the drawer of the desk, they found a pen, but no
ink well and no paper.

Disappointment turned down Amandine's lips. Perspiration gathered
at her brow. 'There are many rooms. We can try the others.'

'Or we can take all this back to my home. To La Rochambert. We
will find everything we need there.'

'Amandine is not dressed to visit a lady, Madame. Another day, perhaps. And I must wait for P'tit Ours. I will give you the papers and you

will take them with you. You will write what you need to write and then bring it to me to sign. Uncle Xavier did the same.'

'I would rather you came with me, Amandine. It would be better. And we can find you some good clothes, I'm sure. We might even meet up with P'tit Ours on the way.'

Marguerite had a renewed urge to hurry. There was no guile in this woman. At least not the kind which would find its way into forging documents.

'You think so? You will really have a gown for me?' She looked sceptically at Marguerite's slenderness, the close-fitting dress, the rows of buttons up to the ruffled neck.

They had reached the drawing room again and Marguerite started to assemble the papers. 'I'm sure we'll be able to adjust something for you.' She bent for the strong box to put all the papers in, but Amandine stopped her.

'No, if we take this, P'tit Ours may think I have gone. We will leave it for him. There is money here. Money for our journey. We will only take the papers. That's all we need, don't you think?'

Marguerite nodded. She folded the documents best she could into her pocket, when a noise made her turn.

At the door of the room, filling its frame with her girth stood Madame Tellier. Her eyes darted like nervous beetles, then seized with hatred on Amandine, on Marguerite, on the papers she had been folding into her jacket, on the strong-box in full evidence on the table behind.

'You. You with her! Both of you.'

The woman's face took on a cold, watchful stillness. Time seemed to stop.

Marguerite was reminded of a wounded heron her father had found by the river. Its wing was broken. He had put a splint in it, a slow painstaking process, while she had held the bird still. During the entire operation, the heron had stared at them from its yellow predator's eyes, cold and deep and still, waiting, watching for the kill.

'I knew you had them. I knew it.'

'Madame Tellier,' Marguerite tried to break the mesmeric hold of the woman's eyes. I don't know if you've met Amandine Septembre. I believe she's your half-sister. Your father names her as his daughter in his will.'

'I have no sister.' The woman's voice was low, icy. It throbbed with undisguised venom. 'That woman is no more my sister than an ass is the sister of a thoroughbred. You will give me my father's papers. Now. Bring them to me. Right here.'

'Ah no.' Amandine Septembre spoke for the first time. 'No, no. These papers bear Amandine's name. Papa Napoleon put Amandine's name there. They stay with me. I have worked for them. I have come a long way with Uncle Xavier.'

'You will bring the papers to me,' Madame Tellier repeated. 'Or you will meet the same fate as that traitor, Xavier.' She lashed out with her booted foot, making her skirts and petticoats swing. Her hand disappeared into the folds of her dress and re-emerged with a gun. A pistol with a long, shining barrel. Marguerite had no doubt at all that it was loaded.

She reached for the strongbox and was about to ferry it to Madame Tellier, when Amandine placed herself directly in front of her, whether to stop her or protect her wasn't clear.

'No, Sister. I said, no. The papers stay with me. We are sisters. We will share what there is.'

Gunfire exploded into the stillness of the room. With a moan, Amandine staggered to the floor. Marguerite knelt down beside her, touched the blood that was oozing from her shoulder.

What happened next was almost too quick for her senses. She heard a roar, like that of a wounded animal trampling through the undergrowth. Then a shot from Madame Tellier's gun. The bullet ricocheted off the wall. Madame Tellier fell heavily to the ground. On top of her sprawled a giant figure, kicking, punching, wrestling with her.

P'tit Ours.

He was bellowing, howling. His face was contorted with pain. 'Amandine, Amandine. Darling Amandine. You killed her. Killed Amandine.'

With each strangled syllable, he kicked the supine figure beneath him, until with a superhuman lunge, Madame Tellier turned over and fired once more. Fired directly at the youth's head.

With a gasp of surprise, he grasped her shoulders and butted her head against the floor.

'No,' Marguerite was shouting, had been shouting throughout. 'No, no, no, no.' She rushed forward, pulled the gun from the woman's hands. It came easily. Madame Tellier had the full weight of a prostrate P'tit Ours on her, his poor head punctured, bleeding. Bleeding across the now unconscious woman who had taken his life.

An unearthly wail rose from behind Marguerite, first soft then growing louder and louder. She turned to see Amandine on her knees, clutching her arm. The blood seeped from it, carmine. She struggled towards P'tit Ours. She stared at his poor broken form with an expression which denied the terrible irreversibility of death. Calling his name. Calling him, 'My Protector.'

Sobs shook her. Her dress trailed the floor and made it into a soft bed. Somehow, she lifted P'tit Ours and cradled him gently in her lap. She rocked him like a child, a large overgrown child who had died for her.

Marguerite, watching their blood mingle, found she was crying too. The pity of it. The pity.

_ 30 _

The days passed. La Rochambert, on its little hill overlooking river and valleys, had taken on the aura of a sanatorium. Madame Germaine had moved in, sent by Docteur Labrousse to help in the care of Amandine Septembre whom Marguerite had insisted would convalesce better under her watchful eye. Faced with this more immediate charge, the elderly woman had not yet gone to seek out Louise Limbour, who was much in Marguerite's thoughts.

Amandine's wound—after Dr. Labrousse had pried the bullet from her shoulder to the sound of her heart-rending screams—was healing well. Her soul, it was clear, would take longer. All her best hopes had been shattered, the last one disappearing with P'tit Ours to whom she had grown attached with the kind of strong bond that links strays and outcasts. She wept for him. She mourned. She repeated over and over that he had died for her.

Papa Napoleon had warned her that her sister could kill. She hadn't believed him. She was stupid. Unworthy. She too deserved to be behind bars like Estelle. She rocked herself and an invisible P'tit Ours in the comfortable bath chair Marguerite had had moved into the music room for her. She stared out the window as if the strength of her gaze might provoke the forlorn winter landscape to transform itself into the bluest of seas on which P'tit Ours would come sailing.

Only Marguerite's piano playing or Martine's tears seemed to stir her from her sadness. At the first, she would break into a deep hum and provide a strange harmony to the music. Marguerite encouraged her to sing. She had a wonderful throaty voice which could rise and fall in waves of throbbing sound. Martine, too, came to life with Amandine's singing. Marguerite watched the two women, initially suspicious of each other, grow closer and closer with the passage of the days. She had a wish that the closeness might outlast convalescence. Martine needed a strong friend and Amandine, it was clear, thrived when she had someone to look after.

That became increasingly clear when baby Gabriel was wheeled into the room, initially to listen to the music the women made. Amandine's song grew firmer in his presence, took on a note of rapture. She was never so happy as when the babe nestled against her, rocked by her crooning voice. He, in turn, would give up any grumbling or plaint as soon as Amandine's arms folded round him and the voice thrust its way into his tremulous body.

As her physical strength returned, Amandine also began to exchange herbal remedies with Madame Germaine, the two of them pitting their native lore against each other and sometimes bursting into paroxysms of laughter.

Marguerite had already assured the woman, that unless Napoleon Marchand was in great debt, she stood to find herself in possession of a tidy sum once probate was over. In the meantime, should she wish to travel home, Marguerite would be more than willing to advance her passage.

She had handed the will and all the other papers in Amandine and P'tit Ours's possession over to the police, though she had had a good look at them first herself. Only one thing disturbed her. The warring half-sisters apart, there was a third beneficiary to old Napoleon's estate. And this one only, wore a collective and altogether holy name.

The convent rose from the mist on the plane like an ancient fortress that had turned its back on the world and its ways. Its wooden door, faced by grillwork, opened to reveal a wizened, apple-cheeked woman in a severe grey habit and wimple. She was small and round and she gazed up at Marguerite from bright blue eyes, her forehead crinkling in friendly interrogation.

'I am Marguerite de Landois.'

The interrogation didn't leave the woman's face.

'The Reverend Mother has given permission for me to make a brief retreat behind your walls.'

'Oh. I see. Come in, my dear. But I'm afraid no one's told me anything about it. Nothing at all. And the Reverend Mother and the holy sisters are at prayer now. You've come in the back door, you know.' She took Marguerite's bag and scrutinized her with sudden canniness. 'Never you mind. You can stay out here with me. I've been tending the grounds. That's why I heard you ring. But no one told me. No one told me to expect you. They don't ever tell me much.'

They were in a tidy, formal garden, backing onto the grey stone of the convent. Even from here, the structure looked uninhabited, the restricted windows blinded by shutters. The garden was more appealing, its pebbled lanes edged with evergreen shrubs. Everything was preternaturally quiet.

In front of them at the end of one of the garden's lanes, stood a grotto, its sides overgrown with vine. A niche at its centre held a painted statue of the Virgin Mary, all blue and gold and with a pretty, girlish face. Beneath her on the ground, a fountain bubbled water. For a moment, she was reminded of the alcove of a shrine in Napoleon Marchand's house. It seemed more likely that she had stepped into a re-creation of the scene at Lourdes. Had a local shepherdess or milkmaid experienced visions here, too?

A magpie startled her, thrashing brilliant wings as it flew from the grotto.

The sister laughed. She set up a chatting which completely belied the inhospitable air of the buildings.

'I'm responsible for the gardens. A lowly occupation, but it suits me. Not all that busy this time of year, except through here. Always things to do in here. Next month, I'll be in the kitchen garden.'

They had passed through a gate, beside which she had deposited Marguerite's bag. Marguerite was startled to find herself in a cemetery, overcrowded with tombstones, inscribed wall plaques, and an assortment of crosses, many of them plain and wooden. The sister knelt down beside a tiny, freshly dug-over grave. A bucket stood to her side. She lifted bulbs and prodded them into the soft, turned ground, patting the earth above them flat with the heel of her broad hand.

'Poor little mite. Didn't have much of a chance. Almost dead by the time he came to us. So many of them are. We baptize them as soon as they arrive, of course.' She looked around her at the jumble of graves with their unadorned markers, then turned to dart a quick look at Marguerite's waist. 'I'm so sorry, So sorry.' She crossed herself quickly. 'Still . . . He's with Jesus now. And the ones who are born here fare better. Really.'

She tried a reassuring smile which didn't quite work and it was only then that Marguerite took in exactly what she was saying.

She flushed a little. Didn't quite know how to disabuse the sister, who must be a lay sister, she now thought. But it didn't really matter that the woman might think she had come here to hide a pregnancy. She lowered her voice.

'I believe you had a young woman here called Louise Limbour.'

'I wouldn't know, Madame. I can't know. Everyone's given new names when they come here. Our special saints names. For the day we arrive. As if we were baptized again. At that very moment. The Reverend Mother insists. That way there's never any problem about gossip or . . . but weren't you told?'

The old woman was suddenly in some confusion. She raised herself a little unsteadily from knees that had started to ache.

'Let me help you.' Marguerite took her arm. 'No. I wasn't told. But I won't be staying all that long, so perhaps there's no need,'

'I see, my dear. I see. I wasn't sure . . . but I thought you might be one of the . . . one of the poor mothers. They often come through the back door. Well, then . . .' She smiled and bent again to pick up her bucket and small spade. 'Let's walk back. They'll be out of chapel soon.'

'It's wise of the Reverend Mother,' Marguerite offered.

'Yes. Yes. She's a wise woman. She herself took the name of Saint Helena. Her feast day is on August 18. Saint Helena was Constantine's mother. She built churches, you know. And she's the patron saint of divorces and difficult marriages. Are you married, my dear?'

She searched Marguerite's gloved hand for evidence of a ring.

Marguerite nodded hastily. There was a simpleness to the woman, yet she cut to the quick.

'Perhaps you've come to the right place.'

'Perhaps. And you. 'When did you first come to the Sisters of the Blessed Virgin?'

The woman chuckled. 'Longer ago than you were born, I imagine. I came with the Reverend Mother. She wasn't a Reverend Mother then, of course. Oh no. But she was always clever. And she's made a difference to this place. It's grown. Flourished. Yes, she's made real changes.'

The old features grew blurred. There was a tremor in the apple cheek. It made the papery wrinkles prominent. 'I didn't have the real vocation. I talk far too much. But there's a lot I can do for them. There they are. Look. I'll take you to the Reverend Mother.' She darted ahead of Marguerite, as if the sight of her superior were a signal to quell words.

Bells had started to ring. Coming out of the chapel with its two court-yard buttresses was a double file of women. They were all in grey. They walked to a common rhythm, slow, contemplative, the large crosses over their bosoms swinging. Their eyes were lowered to the ground. Their hands were clasped in front of them. There was no chatting or stray move-ment. Whatever personal nightmares or doubts might plague them, for now they were as one, almost emanations of the church from which they streamed. Only their headdresses differed. It was hard to say precisely how from this distance, but the youngest seemed to be wearing pure white.

The dim, austere corridors with their rounded arches had swallowed them by the time Marguerite and her guide came in. The gloom stretched into an unpeopled infinity. They walked briskly, their shoes echoing on stone, disturbing the hush. A loggia overlooking an inner courtyard brought light and then there was a turn, another corridor, and the Sister stopped. With a little sigh, she knocked at a door.

'Come,' the voice was firm, yet melodious.

'Reverend Mother. Your guest has arrived. Madame Marguerite de Landois.'

'Thank you, Sister Constance.'

It was the first time Marguerite had heard the pleasant old woman's name and she repeated it now as she made her own thanks.

Sister Constance hurried away. In her hurry, Marguerite caught a wish to avoid the Reverend Mother who now faced her.

She was a tall, prepossessing woman, herself a little like a Gothic cathedral, with a sharply angled face where the grooves ran deep. Her coif was stiff with starch and impeccably placed, so that it flowed out over the lines of her fine-woven habit. She had the grandeur of some Spanish patrician and the pride. It was there in the bony hand that she thrust in Marguerite's direction, in the grandly prominent ring with which she had married herself to Christ. Marguerite bowed her head and made a gesture of touching her lips to it. She murmured a respectful, 'Ma mère.'

'Welcome to our order, Madame la Comtesse. I hope your stay replenishes you. I don't know if Sister Constance explained the rules.'

She motioned Marguerite to a chair in front of her desk and sat down herself. The room had been tastefully furnished, spare but with touches which gave it an aspect of wealth and grace—the polished mahogany of desk and chairs, a small glazed bookcase, a fine oil showing a Virgin and Child. Mother Hélène picked up a rosary of thick beads and played it through her fingers. Behind her, windows of stained glass split a sudden beam of sunlight and lodged a rainbow of shards across the opposite wall where a great heaving Christ rested on a stout cross.

'We lead a simple life here, Madame la Comtesse. You may even find it austere. We congregate in the chapel for the hours. Mass is held at None, when I trust you will join us. The sisters break their fast after the office, though there is an earlier meal after Terce for our lay sisters and guests. When they're not engaged in duties, the sisters follow the rule of silence from Compline until None and into the dinner afterwards.'

'I see,' Marguerite murmured.

'Your letter said you wanted to help out in the nursery. Sister Agnes will direct you. The nursery is in the east wing. We ask the women who have sought refuge here and who will soon be mothers to help out as well. You might say it's a kind of training.'

Her smile was so brief, Marguerite wasn't certain she had seen it. It left a faint curve in the line of her mouth which gave her face a mundanity, even a fleeting wickedness.

'Now is there anything in particular you want to ask of me, Madame?' Anything that is troubling you that has sent you to us?'

'I felt I needed a period of quiet and contemplation, ma mère.' Marguerite could say it without dissembling. 'It has been a fraught time.'

'If you want to share this with me, my child, then I am at your disposal. I cannot offer you absolution, but I can offer relief in other ways. Otherwise Father Hippolyte comes to us daily to take our confessions.'

'Thank you, ma mère.' Marguerite lowered her eyes. It was best not to let herself run away with questions to the Prioress until she had been here a little longer. She had to feel her way.

On the desk, she noticed an old leather-bound breviary, its edges frayed with use. There was a name embossed in gold at its base. She read it upside down, only half taking in the swirl of letters as she listened to the Reverend Mother.

'Good. You will want to be quiet now, after your journey. One of our novices, Sister Beatrice, will see you to your room.'

Marguerite stared at the woman. Could she have read the name correctly?

Mère Hélène rang a little gold bell on her desk and a moment later a woman, wimpled in white, swept into the room from a side door.

Marguerite stepped back. She arranged her expression and thanked the Reverend Mother. It was now difficult to take her eyes away from the novice's face.

The skin was fair, the features delicate, the forehead high, the eyes glowed blue beneath the lashes half-lowered in perpetual modesty. The likeness, even without a visible aureole of hair, even with this lacerating thinness of cheek and hand, was uncanny. It had to be her. She hadn't anticipated meeting her so soon. Her pulse set up a triumphal beating. She was alive. Yvette was alive. She hadn't wholly dared to count on it before.

'Do not expect Sister Beatrice to respond to your questions, Madame la Comtesse. She is under the rule of silence.'

Marguerite gave a little nod of thanks and followed the novice into the corridor.

She could only see her profile, but she studied it covertly as they walked back through the arcade and up a flight of stairs. The girl she assumed was Yvette wore an expression which was quite different from her sister's. There was a containment to her, a quietude even in the fingers which calmly counted the beads of her penitence. The face was longer too, now that she looked at her more closely, the chin stronger. Yes, she would be less vulnerable than her younger sister to the slings and arrows of everyday fortune. Might even welcome their pain as something to overcome, something to signal her marriage to the greatest of sufferers. Martine had intimated that, she now remembered. She had conveyed it as a buried secret.

But there were shadows under the girl's eyes, her nose was pinched. Her hands shook slightly. The passionate austerity was taking its toll. It would be a delicate task to urge the girl into speech. This mixture of fragility and elation was not something Marguerite had confronted before.

The room under the eaves was chill. The bare, whitewashed walls wore only a single medallion-like picture of the virgin and child. This hung above the narrow bed. An oak table held a pitcher and a bowl. There was a plain chair with a woven cane seat. On it lay a prayer book. The window looked out on the courtyard, at the far end of which stood the buttressed chapel. The door sported two hooks on its back. On one of them hung the grey cloak and the mantle which would now be her daily apparel.

The young woman she would have to think of as Sister Beatrice stood by, whether waiting for an instruction or waiting to be dismissed was unclear.

Marguerite smiled at her.

'You're very familiar to me, Sister Beatrice. You're very like your sister. She has been searching for you everywhere. She's been in some distress, you know. She'll want to come and see you, now that I've found you.'

The girl stared at her in shock. Tears leapt into her eyes. She shook her head. Her lips clenched as if to force away speech. Before Marguerite could say any more, she had fled the room, leaving Marguerite to wonder at her reaction.

She washed the dusty traces of the journey from her face and tried to take in the solid, if silent, fact of Yvette's presence. Had her response of flight meant that she didn't want to be found. And why not? Was it mere coincidence that had led the girl to take refuge in a convent which bore some link to the name she was now certain she hadn't dreamt on the cover of the Reverend Mother's breviary? Marchand.

Barely had she had time to consider this, when the Reverend Mother appeared at her door. Were Sister Beatrice's sudden departure and her proud superior's arrival related? Marguerite smoothed the habit she had only just finished slipping over her head. The Prioress had a gleam in her eye, as she looked at her. She couldn't be certain whether it intimated humour or malice at her new modesty.

'I thought we might have a little time together before mass, Madame la Comtesse. We could take a stroll, if you like. I'll show you the grounds. We have a library, too, for the more studious sisters. It contains a fine illuminated volume of St. Augustine, and some early and beautiful editions of the church fathers . . . Oh yes, we have had our bequests over the years. All this may serve to comfort you during your stay.'

Marguerite followed the woman dutifully. Despite her walking stick, the old Prioress was nimble, her carriage erect as they moved down the stairs and into the gardens.

Only then did she address Marguerite again. The intimacy of the question took her by surprise. As did the mother superior's knowledge.

'Has your husband's decision to run for public office distressed you, Madame? Oh yes, yes. News travels, even across these thick walls. The Bishop sometimes visits . . .'

Marguerite measured her reply. 'It has a little if I am honest. It was not something I expected. But that is not what has brought me here.' She side-stepped the woman's questions. Walking next to her like this, and looking straight ahead rather than at her, the Reverend Mother lost a little of her frightening aura. She had the feeling she was simply another woman, one who wanted to pry into her private life. It was not something Marguerite acquiesced to easily.

'No, ma mère . . .' She stumbled over the words as well as over what to say. She had never thought to call anyone mother again, couldn't remember doing so in the past. Why did the church take on these family names, mother, father, sister, brother? Why did they want to displace or replace an existing family? Was this a better one? Or worse? Was it useful to be turned into a child again?

At least, mothers and fathers apart, the sisters were all equals, equal before Christ. A democracy of faith within a strict hierarchy of rule.

The thoughts raced through her as she talked.

'No, what has distressed me . . . But I doubt that events of this kind should make their way into your sanctity . . .' She had leapt haphazardly and landed on an answer which bore a partial truth.

'Speak, my child.'

'Very well, what has distressed me is a murder I witnessed. A killing. Of a young, rather simple-minded man, who was no less worthy of life for that. He was killed by the woman his mother worked for. The circumstances were tragic.'

'I see.' There was a long pause, then a slow, resonant utterance. 'Remember, death is a beginning, my child.'

Marguerite said nothing. They had reached the maze at the centre of the formal gardens. It was darker in here. The blue green of the high, trimmed evergreen hedge swallowed the light. The silence felt more intense.

'You do not feel it this way,' the Reverend Mother said at last. 'Perhaps by the time you leave us . . . I will do my best for you.'

'Thank you, Reverend Mother.'

'Were these people related to you in any way?'

'No, ma mère. I only knew them a little. The youth was called P'tit Ours. Though his real name was Eustache Molineuf.'

Even in the shadow of the hedge, the woman's piercing glance seemed to bruise her cheek.

'You have heard of him?'

'No, no. Though the family name means something. Perhaps one of his relatives came to us for one reason or another.'

'Madame Molineuf works for Madame Tellier, who was the perpetrator of the brutal act. A difficult family.'

The mother superior looked straight ahead. Her long, thin fingers worked her rosary. The beads gave off a distinct clack. Their sound and the woman's expression prevented Marguerite from pressing her questions.

It was clear, however, that she somehow knew the family. She must have heard of Madame Tellier from Martine's sister.

'We will pray for all their souls. Prayer can help, my daughter. Believe me.' Intense eyes flashed at her to bring the point home.

They walked in silence for a few minutes. Marguerite was about to try a delicate question about young Sister Beatrice when another figure appeared in the maze. Reverend Mother called her to their side.

'This is Madame's first day here, Sister Agnes. I would like you to show her the nursery and then accompany her to mass. You can point out the delivery rooms on the way. I want you to see those, Madame. We have recently refurbished them to the highest standards.'

The path took them through a warren of corridors and small court-yards, through massed arches and airy loggias. She wondered if she would ever be able to replicate the route on her own, though at one point she did realize they must just have crossed what was the front drive of the convent and the point at which she should have entered. Somehow, she had chosen the hidden door which the fallen mothers used, the door near the place where the orphan children were left, rather than this grander entrance.

Sister Agnes, who smiled and gestured, but didn't speak, gave her a glimpse into an infirmary which contained three high beds, masks for oxygen, an assortment of polished instruments neatly laid out on a rolling table. A lone figure was mopping the floor. From a half open door, came murmurs and a low mewling cry.

'Anne has just been delivered of a girl,' the woman with the mop announced. 'Sister Constance is with her.'

Sister Agnes nodded sagely, and whisked Marguerite away. At last, past storerooms and a laundry where a number of sisters scrubbed and ironed, they arrived in a long rectangular room, ranked by cots and cra-dles and a few narrow beds. The white-wash was fresh, the shutters half closed. One of the cradles and two of the cots had children in them. They were asleep, as quiet as if they had taken in the rule of silence with their first breath.

Next door, there was a schoolroom. A dozen or so toddlers sat on benches on one side of the room. Slightly larger children were two at a table on the other side. Their hands were neatly crossed in front of them. It took Marguerite a moment to realize there were no boys amongst them. The girls wore long dresses, a fall of grey beneath scrubbed faces and rigidly held-back hair. There were pictures of saints on the walls and they were all listening to a story about Saint Anthony which a burly sister recounted. The robed and wimpled storyteller walked and gestured like a competent actor, so that the girls' eyes hardly strayed when they entered.

Two women looked on. From the swing of their protruding robes, she realized they must be expectant mothers who had come here to seek shelter. The grey habit of the convent had a way, at first glance, of wiping out all distinctions.

A second room, all but replicated the scene in the first, although there were fewer children here and they were all boys. There was also a blackboard with the alphabet written on it and the numbers 1-10. In the corner, a nun tapped a threatening ruler over her palm, as if the quiet boys might at any moment burst into unruliness without the menace of punishment. Beyond this room, a courtyard was visible through the windows, a place for recess.

The tolling of bells erupted like an alarm. The children rose from their seats as one, even the smallest of them, and lined up behind the sisters. Sister Agnes motioned Marguerite into the line. Within moments, the queue was marching silently towards the chapel. A single straggler was prodded into the procession with minimal fuss.

The voices rang out clear and pure and high even before they had entered the chapel. After the whitewashed walls and plain stone of the rest of the convent, its interior was a cornucopia of riches. Carved stone pillars, adorned arches, warm wood, sumptuously painted Stations of the Cross, all tantalized the eye and gleamed mysteriously under a brightly starred indigo canopy of Italianate inspiration. Striated light flowed through an ornate rose window, picking out sacral objects for illumination.

Marguerite slipped into what she hoped was an inconspicuous place near the back. Her height permitted her to see over the heads of much of the congregation to the richly dressed and gilded altar. Behind it, the image of the blessed virgin and her plump child wore the imprint of a

Master. She wondered for a moment at the wealth of the convent and then felt her eyes drawn to that known face in the choir of voices. Sister Beatrice, who had become everyone's sister but her own, had a voice that seemed to rise in plenitude above the others. Her mouth was a perfect circle. Her eyes were raised to an invisible sphere. Her chest heaved with the exuberance of her musical praise.

Then, as if pulled downwards by a terrible weight, everything about the girl drained away and fell: her eyes lost their lustre, her colour dimmed, her lips sagged. She held on to the rail in front of her so as not to topple.

Marguerite looked round for the cause of this sudden transformation. Was it the thin, hawk-nosed priest who had just come up the blood red carpet of the chancel steps. Or the mother superior, who moved behind him with the slow grandeur of a ship of state that would stop for no obstacle in its path?

_ 31 _

The routines and rituals of the convent had their own mesmerizing logic. Under the Mother Superior's intractable rule, any interest in the noisy outside world was efficiently shut out, unless it penetrated in the form of a penitent woman or an abandoned child. Whatever her intentions, Marguerite's retreat became the very one she had told Olivier she needed. The similarity of each day, the strict order of the hours, the ringing of bells, the stately procession to chapel, the frugal meals eaten in silence with only the drone of a lesson in Latin for accompaniment, all this made one lose one's sense of time, except as a passage. Though only three days had passed, she felt she had been here for a very long time. Passions had grown distant. La Rochambert had become a misty figment on a receding horizon.

Perhaps that was why she had discovered so little. Twice after mass, as she filed out past her, Sister Beatrice had raised eyes of fearful despair toward her, but then walked on as if that look meant nothing. The girl had made no attempt of her own to see her. And Marguerite had been unable to find her outside the chapel. She melted away, swallowed by the endless corridors, the sway of look-alike grey.

Despite all this, something made Marguerite feel that the girl was in need, that she would welcome contact with her sister. Simply asking under the Reverend Mother's vigilant, all-seeing eye was out of the question. Terrestrial power in the convent lay too firmly in the woman's gnarled, ringed hands.

Nor had Marguerite been able to learn anything about Louise Limbour and the babe she had given birth to from the silent sisters in the infirmary.

There seemed to be no way of unbuttoning the secrets held by these smiling, tight-lipped women. She had asked. She had looked for some kind of registry in which births must be recorded. She had drawn a blank.

For the rest, she had put in her allotted hours with the children in the nursery, had walked in the gardens, had even read her breviary and tried to waken her dormant Latin. At table, she had wished that a prayer could produce a miracle of palatable loaves and fishes in the convent's kitchens. And that was it.

Today, she had determined would be different. The Mother Superior had asked to see her. She wouldn't waste the opportunity. She would put her questions directly, if need be.

The library in which they were to meet was in the west wing. It occupied a mid-sized room with arched and deeply alcoved windows which had been fitted with reading desks. Two tables took up the centre of the room. The rest of the space was crowded with books. Their spines gleamed with leather and embossed, gold lettering.

The Reverend Mother looked toward her from the central table she occupied. There was a yellowing tome in front of her. Her walking stick rested by her side. In her hand she held spectacles on a gold wand. She put these down swiftly and closed the volume she had been studying.

'You are early.'

'Am I? I hope not too early.' Marguerite went towards her, She read the title of the book on the table. '*Malleus Maleficarum*?' The words spilled from her on the tide of her surprise.

The Prioress stared at her with a cold reptilian eye. 'You know it? That surprises me, Madame la Comtesse.'

'Does it? A doctor of my acquaintance used to quote from the book at length. *The Hammer of Witches*. He was emphatic in his understanding the characteristics attributed by the Benedictine monks to their supposed witches, when they weren't invented, as the signs and symptoms of what today would be diagnosed as a nervous illness. Those women were no more possessed of the devil than you or I. I doubt they had special powers either, or a wish to do evil, to steal husbands or babies. When the madness wasn't in their accusers' eyes, they were just poor, sad and sick women.'

The Mother Superior frowned at Marguerite, her haughty face bellowing the disapproval she didn't speak.

From one of the alcoves came a sob and the sound of robes stirring.

Marguerite had talked too much, the result of all these days of silence. She shouldn't have spoken so critically. If the woman and her nuns believed in witches so be it. Maybe belief was simply a state of mind and could extend and extend into credulity. Now, she would send her away.

But it was someone else the Reverend Mother addressed. 'You will leave us, Sister Beatrice. Quickly, now.'

Marguerite put a protesting hand out as the girl she hadn't noticed suddenly appeared from the depths of an alcove and brushed past her towards the door. 'Oh no, no. Please stay. It was in part about Sister Beatrice that I wished to speak to you, ma mère. You see her sister is pining for her. She hasn't known for months where to find her.'

'Sister?' The woman's voice cut like a razor.

'Yes, Yes. They need to see each other, ma mère. Her sister is desolate. She had no idea . . .'

The older woman's face was hard with displeasure. It moved between the flared nostrils and the eyes like kindling. At any moment, it might burst into consuming flame.

'Is this true, Beatrice?'

The girl nodded once. Her eyes looked bruised.

'Does she know?'

She shrugged. The plea in her eyes extended to Marguerite. She could not determine whether the girl wanted her to stop her persistence or to carry on. She also noticed a scrape across the girl's upper lip, red and jagged, as if she had grazed against an abrasive surface—or someone had taken a file to her.

'Go now, Beatrice. Quickly. Quickly. We will contend with the meaning of these lies later.'

As Beatrice pulled the door behind her, the Mother Superior rose to her full height and turned to Marguerite. The look on the woman's face sent a cold fear through her. The Reverend Mother's eyes held a Medusa-like stare, a monomaniac's singleness of passion and purpose which would annihilate all obstacles.

'Sister Beatrice can neither leave the convent nor entertain visitors. Her devotion and obedience must be total if she is to be accepted into our order. I am sorry she saw you here. Your words will distract her devotions.'

She ushered Marguerite towards the door, then changed her mind, as if she were suddenly aware that this woman would be less obedient than her novice. She needed to hold her back at least as long as it took Beatrice to vanish.

'I suspect, Madame, that you have come here with an ulterior motive. That is not conducive to a proper retreat. I now see that it would be best if you curtailed your stay. I shall arrange for a carriage for you, tomorrow at dawn.'

'But ma mère, surely this is altogether contrary to the charity you . . .'

A loud knock at the door cut off Marguerite's words. It opened on a sister Marguerite didn't recognize. She was out of breath. 'Ma mère, ma mère. A messenger has arrived. From Maitre Artaud. In Tours. There is a big document. You must come quickly. He is waiting for a response.'

'Our meeting is over Madame.' The Mother Superior brought a watch from the folds of her habit and glanced at it. 'You will make no further attempt to speak to Sister Beatrice. I have your word.'

Marguerite said nothing. She watched the woman sweep from the room. Maitre Artaud. She knew that name. Napoleon Marchand's notary. Her mind flew, faster than her feet. Of course. That name on the breviary. She hadn't understood. And now the will, signalling that here was the missing third party.

The afternoon still held a little brightness. She walked slowly through the quiet gardens at the back of the convent. High above the walls, clouds raced in a milk-blue sky, creating shadows on the paths.

An odd, ungainly one slipped out from behind what she thought of as the Virgin's grotto. It took her a moment to realize that the shape was not shadow but substance. A cassocked man and a woman cloaked in grey were walking swiftly away from her. She only recognized the man from the brown of his habit, its belted waist. By the time the couple had reached the back gate and were through it to the outside, she had recognized the woman, too. Louise. Louise Bertin, now Limbour. So she had guessed rightly about the connection.

Rushing away from the grotto in the opposite direction, she now made out the rolling gait of Sister Constance. She hadn't seen the gardener for some days. She called out to her.

The woman looked round, a little furtively. Marguerite caught up.

'So you know Frère Michel?' Marguerite smiled at her, wishing her into ease. 'Such a good soul.'

The woman was nervous about something, her kind, wrinkled face rigid with the effort of holding it in.

'I know him a little.' The woman stammered.

'Yes. A fine man. And Louise, or at least the young woman I recognize by that name. You're acquainted with her, too? She worked at my house, you know.'

'Janine?'

'So that was the name she took here. Yes, Janine. She lost her child, did she? Poor girl. I wish she'd come to me.'

'So you knew about it, Madame? She was desolate. Even Sister Beatrice couldn't console her.'

Marguerite noticed the woman's eyes were filled with tears. 'The two became friends here, did they?'

'Yes, Madame.'

'And Beatrice's child . . . the child she had by Napoleon Marchand, what became of that babe?'

'You know him, too?' The old sister's face suddenly collapsed. Tears poured from her eyes. 'I've just learned. Just learned he's died. Mère Hélène will . . .'

'Will what? Of course, I'd forgotten. She's his sister isn't she? Agathe Marchand. Yes, yes. Though it was all before my time.'

They had reached the cemetery at the edge of the gardens. Sister Constance nodded through her tears, then slipped behind the gate. Marguerite followed.

'Is that why Sister Beatrice came to her?'

'Ah no, Madame, how could you think that? How could you?' The woman burbled through her tears.

'Do sit, Sister Constance.' Marguerite led the old woman to a stone bench at the edge of the cemetery. 'I understand your sorrow. Has it been long since you saw Napoleon Marchand?'

'Over fifty years, Madame. Over fifty.' The woman rocked a little then crossed herself. 'She was quite right. She never let him in here. Even though he sent money. He was not to be forgiven. Never. She had told him that. Even back then, Agathe was a woman of principle.'

'So the rumours were right. She came here to have his child.'

'Still-born.' The sob tore out of her, as fresh as if the dead infant lay in her arms now.

'I'm so sorry. How dreadful. And she never forgave him that either?'

'Never. Christian mercy, she said back then, doesn't extend to the devil.'

'And so he didn't send Beatrice to her?'

'No, Madame. She came. Came because she wanted to be one of us. Only later did we discover she was pregnant. She was so thin. Poor little thing.'

Constance crossed herself again, then rose. She took up a little spade which had been leaning against a tombstone. Like an automaton, she began to dig.

'So the baby Napoleon Marchand fathered lies buried here, too?'

Sister Constance responded with the heave of another spadeful of earth. It hit the earth with the force of a dead body.

Marguerite's conjecture had been wrong.

'How dreadful. But we should tell Sister Beatrice. About Napoleon Marchand's death, I mean. It may make a difference to her. The girl does not seem well to me. '

The woman flung her shovel down and gripped Marguerite's arm with surprising strength.

'Please Madame, please. Don't say anything to her. Don't say anything to anyone. Certainly not to her.' The clear blue eyes in the wizened face gripped as strongly as the fingers. 'It will end up by harming her. Please. It's better she doesn't know.'

'I don't understand.'

'No, my dear, no. You can't understand. But everything gets back to her. To Agathe. To Mère Hélène, I mean Then she takes her vengeance.

She doesn't mean anything bad. But she can't help it. Can't. Not where he's concerned. Please, my dear.'

The woman seemed to be in the clutch of a terrible fear. 'She has fits you know. Every anniversary of the death, she has fits. Awful to behold. They think it's holy. Our sainted mother. Visions, too. The Virgin comes to her. Pregnant with the saving of the world. But I know. I know it's to do with the child. The birth. The shock of it. She arches in the same way. Possessed by a ghost. That's why we couldn't allow it. Couldn't allow Sister Beatrice. She sees herself in her. We were afraid.'

The woman's eyes darted round the graves. She murmured what must have been a prayer.

'No, Beatrice mustn't mention his name. No. Not even in confession. It reminds her. Makes her violent. She orders more and greater mortifications to exorcise the demon of Napoleon. And the child doesn't understand. Doesn't know. She thinks everyone is good. She blurts out everything to her. If only she hadn't mentioned him to start with.'

Marguerite stared at the crumpled mouth which had uttered words she couldn't quite grasp.

'You mean she punishes Beatrice for being like herself. For being with that old reprobate.'

Sister Constance nodded, then sunk down on the bench beside her again.

'She loved her piety, her sweetness. At first. Then she found out about Napoleon and the pregnancy. It's better now that old Père François has gone at last . . . he was a horror. The penances! The mortifications in the name of purifying the body, ridding it of the devil of the flesh. In the name of our dear Lord. They would egg each other on, the two of them. I don't understand her anymore. I don't. Please. You mustn't say anything to Beatrice.'

Marguerite patted the old gnarled hand and wondered at the blistering passions Napoleon Marchand had unleashed.

The sun had slipped from the sky and dusk gathered them in a damp cold. The shadows took over. And still they sat there, the old woman weeping. The ivy on the older graves grew luminous. Somewhere a dog had set up a howling.

'And the mortification goes on?' Marguerite asked at last, 'Even now that the greatest of punishments has been undergone and the child is dead? It can't have been very long ago.'

Sister Constance stared at her. 'That was it, you see. That's what so frightened me. Beatrice's baby was due around the time of the anniversary. The anniversary that induces Mère Hélène's holy fits.'

'So you worried she would damage the child?' Marguerite said it because it came into her head. She only saw how right she had been when the old woman gasped and recoiled.

'You understand,' she murmured. 'I had to do it.'

Marguerite held her breath. 'Do what exactly.'

The old woman hid her face in her hands. 'Spirit it away. I had to. Frère Michel helped. I've known him forever. He was a friend back then, he knew them both. Napoleon and Agathe. And me. I looked after her. I always have.'

She kicked at the damp earth with the toe of her boot. It was a man's boot, made for heavy wear. Damp earth gathered on its soles in clumps.

'Beatrice must have been in terrible anguish.'

'She was. When she woke. I had given her a powder to make her sleep, you see. Mother Superior, too. But Beatrice accepted the babe's death. Took it as the just punishment for her sins. I dug a hole and buried an empty coffin, while Frère Michel spirited the mite away. All in the space of one night and morning.'

Sister Constance's eyes glimmered a clear, triumphant blue. She had ripped a child away from the certain punishments that would attend its life within the precincts of her superior's power. They were punishments which would bring about its early death.

'That was good of you,' Marguerite murmured. 'And where did Frère Michel take the child?'

She asked, although she already knew the answer. She had seen the girl not so very long ago, drifting out of the convent walls. Beatrice's friend, Louise. She and Frère Michel must have come to warn the woman that someone was looking for the infant's parents. A someone who was herself.

The hard, bright sliver of a moon had already risen in the sky when they heard the tread on the pebbled path. Sister Constance urged her further into the shadows of the small graveyard. They stopped behind the largest of its tombs, a mausoleum, thick with ivy which obliterated their presence. But they could see clearly enough.

The person who came through the gate was girlishly slender and wore a glistening white veil. She stopped by the tiny grave Constance had packed with bulbs and knelt, crossing herself, her lips moving in silent prayer. Even in the glimmering starlight, the pure and delicate lines of the profile were easily distinguishable.

Tears rose in Marguerite's eyes and spilled over. She had to go and speak to the girl, assuage her with the news that her child wasn't dead. But Constance held her back, her grip fierce.

She understood why a moment later. An imposing figure swept into the graveyard, her walking stick tapping out her hurry. She breathed hard as she looked round. Her face beneath the elaborate wimple was stretched so tight over her prominent bones, it resembled a skull. A birdlike swoop brought her to where the girl knelt.

She prodded her with her stick, her great cross swinging with her anger.

'I told you. I told you never to come here. I warned you. This is rank disobedience. You must distance yourself from the sewer if you're to reach the skies. He's dead. Dead. The bastard's dead. We will have no more bastards. Dead, I tell you. Both the father and his filthy bastard.'

The words grew into a shriek which flew above the walls of the cemetery to rebound through the evening air. Marguerite felt her blood running cold. Beatrice was trembling like a frightened animal hypnotized by her predator.

She bent towards the ground to accept her punishment as the Mother Superior's stick rose high into the air.

Marguerite lunged towards that gaunt, hooded face and held the arm upright until she shook the stick from it. Inside her head there was screaming, a loud railing against this infernal abuse of power. She had to remind herself that the prioress was only an old woman, whatever the strength her punitive hatred gave her and the holy aura she found for it.

'Sister Constance.' Marguerite's tone was as cold and clear as the night with its icy moon. 'Take Beatrice to her room, pack her bag and have her meet me by the front doors. Order a carriage to ferry us.'

The Prioress was shaking. Her voice was thunderous when it came. 'How dare you? What gives you the right?'

'I dare, Mademoiselle Marchand. That's enough.'

The use of her family name in front of the girl seemed to rob the woman of some of her power.

'Beatrice, I think will dare, too, when she hears what Sister Constance will tell her. It will be her choice. Go now.' She gestured towards the girl and Sister Constance.

When they were a good distance away, she released the staying hand she had kept on the Prioress' wrist.

'It's time to put that old ghost to sleep, Mademoiselle Marchand. Your brother and his dead child have prowled through you and these precincts long enough.'

There was no carriage to take them that night. They left at dawn instead. Beatrice, who had knelt in the chapel with Sister Constance by her side for the length of the hours, was now once again Mademoiselle Branquart in an old suit of striped serge, her pale, shorn hair peeking like duck's down from the bounds of her hat.

Without her nun's habit, the young woman looked even more vulnerable. The veins stood out in her high forehead. Her wrists free of folds to hide in were bird-like. There was a slightly clumsy angularity to her movements. Nor had she spoken to Marguerite yet. It wasn't clear whether shock had gripped her after the revelations of her strange kinship with the mother superior and the truth about her child. Or whether she had simply not yet regained the habit of speech.

In the carriage, which she had determined should take them first to Blois, Marguerite quietly gave the girl her version of events. She told her that because the Reverend Mother was the sister of the very Monsieur Marchand, now dead, who had played such havoc with the course of both their lives, she had been over-ardent, indeed excessive in her relations with Beatrice. Sister Constance had been worried about the fate of her child under the Reverend Mother's aegis. She was also worried for her. Thus, it was best for her to leave the closed world of the order, where the Reverend Mother yielded too much power.

She said no more than that. She realized, that whatever her knowledge of the events which had shaped Yvette's life, she really knew nothing of this troubled young creature. She had never heard her speak. Until now, she had rarely given a thought to how much the sound of a person's voice played into her sense of their character.

On her instructions, the carriage took them first to Blois. They got out in the market square which thrummed with morning activity. Fruit and vegetables grew into piles and pyramids before their eyes. Servants and housewives bustled and bargained. Chickens squawked in their cages. The cheeses competed with goggle-eyed fish in filling the morning air with musty scents and stronger reeks. After the austerity of the convent, with its punishing prioress, this sensuous abundance had a thrilling everydayness about it. She would have liked to saunter, to shop, to buy and taste, to bask in the ordinary.

Yvette-Beatrice had a frightened air about her, as if the assault on the senses was more than the thinness of her skin could permit.

Marguerite hurried her across the square and downhill towards the Blacksmith's forge. They had all but reached it, when a woman walking briskly in the opposite direction lifted her eyes from the cobblestones to stop and stare at them.

'Beatrice? Beatrice . . . is it you? You've come out!' Louise Limbour flung her arms around her friend. Tears and words poured out together.

'I'm so glad. I'm so glad. But has she told you?' Louise's eyes darted up towards Marguerite and gave her a look which was both scathing and fearful. 'I had to, Beatrice, I had to give him away. I couldn't keep him, not at my stepfather's. I would have had to explain how I had met you, then everything would have come out and he would have killed me. Or burnt me. Branded me with his pokers. So I couldn't, couldn't keep the babe. But he's safe. I'm certain of that. I gave him to the curé, to Père Benoit.'

Louise paused to look round her, adjusted her bonnet, then urged a confused Beatrice up the street, further away from the blacksmith's shop.

'I don't know what you're talking about,' Beatrice's voice cracked with bewilderment and disuse. It was a thin reed of a voice, like the girl herself.

Louise looked round her once more, cast her eyes up the windows of the narrow street. She wound her arm through her friend's and hurried her into the hubbub of the market square.

Marguerite followed quickly. She needed to hear every word of this.

'Your baby. Frère Michel brought him to me. A bonny little thing. But I couldn't keep him. I gave him to the curé.'

'You gave him to the curé,' Beatrice echoed.

'Yes. I took him to the church. I wish you'd been there with me. I told him. Told him everything. Almost like a confession, but without the box. I begged for mercy. For both of us. I told him that the baby had been born to a friend of mine and his father was this rich man called Marchand, and that Père Benoit might take the babe to him, or find another suitable home.'

'What?' Beatrice grabbed at Louise's arm and made her stop.

'Yes, I thought that would be for the best. I know the curé, you see. I knew him from a post I had.' She stole a look at Marguerite, as if to estimate her intelligence. It was a look that again spoke of independence and a certain effrontery. It was the look she had imagined in the Louise she had been told about, who was not the crying woman she had met in the chocolate factory.

'Yes, I took him to the curé and I told him everything. But I don't think he believed me, you know. He thought I was lying. Cause he lies all the time himself.'

'Lying?'

'Yes,' Louise suddenly giggled. Her voice took on a lilt of scoffing triumph. 'He thought I'd made up all that stuff about you and that the child was really mine. And his. He patted my hand in that way he has and I could see . . . could see exactly what he was thinking. It was his. He thought I was covering up for both of us. Serves him right.'

She laughed again and this time Marguerite joined her. She could imagine the curé's preening look.

The two young women stared at her.

'No, I really don't mind that you've been to bed with Père Benoit, if you didn't mind, Louise.'

Louise looked a little put out. 'Only now and again. And I was hardly in a position to mind.'

They had turned another corner and were walking downhill now. Respectable, clustered houses pushed in on them with the pressure of ears attuned to scandal. Louise lowered her voice.

'You won't tell anyone, will you? Please. And it wasn't my doing. Père Benoit has ways of being persuasive. He ruts like any other man. Never mind the cassock.'

Marguerite smiled. She hadn't considered that. Though she had wondered whether the piece of black cloth she had found in the woods might indeed have come from a cassock. There were ways in which she was more naïve than this slip of a young woman who had been to a different school of life.

'Don't worry, Louise. I won't talk.'

'So my baby is alive. Alive and in the hands of a curé.' Beatrice's face wore all the traces of someone who could make no sense of a world turned topsy turvy.

'I didn't want to say anything to contradict the curé. He's so vain. I knew he'd find the best possible home for your poor tyke if he thought it was his. I knew Marchand meant less than nothing to you. Worse than nothing. A blot. And the curé, it seems, had set his sights even higher.'

She shot a glance at Marguerite and started walking very quickly. Nothing was said until the river appeared before them, a vast artery, yellowy-grey in the morning light.

The girl stopped abruptly.

Along the river, workers were moving towards their places of employ. But Louise's eyes were fixed on the clean water spewing out of the gutter, the rag that forced its direction. 'I didn't know he was going to choose your home. I didn't, Madame. Believe me. Not until you said. It was only twice with Monsieur. He wasn't really interested in me. It was only because you were always away.'

Marguerite nodded.

A barge hooted its passage. Fishermen heaved their catch onto the shore. A burly man in a bowler held up a pair of scales. A cat scooted past her, miaowling his passage to her skirts, only to wind his way downhill.

'So you put the babe in a basket and took him to the river on Père Benoit's instructions,' Marguerite said softly.

'Non, Madame. Non. I would never have done that. I wouldn't be stupid enough to put a living child into the river. I just left him with Père Benoit. He promised to take care of everything. Everything. The next I heard was from you. That you had discovered a child. My child. You wouldn't listen to the truth.'

'I see. I am listening now. I hear you clearly, Louise. Thank you.'

The curé, it seemed, had ordered things in her husband's life for far too long. He would have to go now. But it was best that Olivier, himself, saw to that.

Beatrice was clutching at her friend's sleeve. Her voice a plea. 'I don't understand. Where is my baby? Where is he? Why didn't they tell me. Why didn't Mother Superior tell me?'

'They thought she would kill him,' Louise was blunt. 'I tried to tell you that she was too hard on you. All those beatings and scourgings, it wasn't right. All you did was fall prey to a man. Jesus was kind to Magdalene. There wasn't the need for all that. She's mad. Spent too long inside.'

Louise kissed her friend on both cheeks and told her to come back and visit soon. There were plenty of jobs in the factory if she wanted one. Then with a sudden shyness, she curtsied briefly towards Marguerite and rushed away.

Marguerite watched her, grateful for the clearer rendition of the state of things than she herself would have been able to offer.

_ 32 _

They had all come to see her off, to kiss her good-bye. To hug, to thank, even just to wave. It made her loathe to leave. But the sky was so blue, and inviting, and the wind beckoned. Its gusts were strong, flapping at the ends of the linen they had draped over the long outdoor tables, so that a parting toast could be raised to her, though it was still early morning.

There was Olivier, a little languid, but himself again in his yellow cravatte and checked frock coat. He had returned to the vagaries of his own uncertain conscience, rather than the one awoken in him by the insidious and ambitious curé who had played to his vanity with controlling lies. The sculptor Villemardi was at his side. Both of them were talking, laughing, eyes and hands alight, wondering when she would come for more sittings, so that her likeness could become more like, wondering about a little sorti to Paris to see the latest work, wondering about a new crop for the far fields.

There were the sisters. Yvette, with her cropped head, was still painfully thin, as if the punishing regime imposed by the Order had taken up a permanent residence in her mind, as if her body were still sullied, a marionette separate from her being except when pain united them. Still, she occasionally held Gabriel with a rapt expression. And Martine's joy at finding her Yvette again was so great that Marguerite hoped it would breach her sister's impermeability, which was both a strength and a kind of visceral loneliness. It reminded her that the girls themselves were orphans, left motherless, too soon. This had been one of the things that had initially drawn her to Martine.

The babe wasn't motherless. In fact he had now acquired several mothers, not to mention two godparents. He had been baptized as Gabriel Olivier Branquart by the Bishop himself, whom Olivier had called in to lodge a plaint in his ear against their altogether unsatisfactory curé. Père Benoit had been quickly removed to unknown climes to avoid scandal.

In the role of Godfather, Olivier re-discovered himself. He also discovered Amandine Septembre, who had won the hearts of everyone around her. She was holding Gabriel in her capacious arms now. The babe was staring at her with that gurgling and placid amazement which was always and ever his response to her voice, sung or spoken. It evidently tickled him in some deep region. Or maybe it was simply her vitality which brimmed and billowed, inviting them all to come close.

Amandine had a plan for the sisters and herself. They were family, after all, she told them with her deep laugh—wasn't Gabriel in fact her half brother, which made Yvette a kind of aunt and her sister another kind. And as the eldest she had to look after them. She would be a rich woman soon enough, after that mischief maker's will came good. And his partner, that miniscule Monsieur Tellier she had finally met seemed right enough. He was happier than all the rest of them to have his erstwhile wife put away. He wanted Amandine to carry on with the Caribbean side of the business. She knew it well, but with her uncle gone she needed help. The sisters would help her. Hadn't their family been in the trade, too? Or if Yvette preferred, she could train to teach. They would be well off by the standards of Martinique. Which meant that no one would think twice about Gabriel's dead father.

Marguerite had applauded the plan and told them that until their departure, they would have a home in La Rochambert. They could all keep Olivier company. She was needed back in Paris.

She looked round at the gathered crowd and met Dr. Labrousse's eyes. He was talking to Madame Germaine and Martine, who was gazing wistfully at the returned-again, older sister she so plainly adored. Marguerite had a hunch about the doctor. She wouldn't be surprised if he too one day set sail after the girls. As for dear Mr. Rama, who was bowing to Yvette and asking after her health, he and his entourage had been busy repainting their wagons and preparing for a spring foray further south.

Marguerite smiled at them all as her pilot urged her into the basket of the great balloon. It was Olivier's present to her. A flight to Tours, or near enough, from where she would take the train to Paris.

She stepped into the small wicker space, skirted the brazier, helped take in the ropes and sandbags despite her pilot's admonition, and waved as they were unmoored. She waved to Madame Solange and her husband, to plump Armand and to Celeste, the wet-nurse. Waved to all of them. She tried to keep her smile intact as the basket leapt and swung into the air, taking her stomach with it. She gripped the ropes and hung on. They were growing smaller and smaller, children all of them.

The wind streamed across her face, her hair fluttered loose from its pins and hat. Her hands grew cold. The wonder of it began.

The trees seen from their webbed tops down looked like giant sway-ing creatures tied to the ground by sticks and longing to be set free. There was a green sheen to the earth, as if the colours of spring grew denser from above. Cows lolled as small as toys and La Rochambert began to take on the air of a dazzling white and perfectly carved play house for some doll-mad girl and her indulgent father.

Yes, Olivier had chosen her present well. She had been complaining of her sense that she had come to La Rochambert to enter some strange, hoary clime far from this new twentieth century, a space where medieval tortures and consciences abetted by ideas of sanctity were still at their destructive work and no one seemed to notice. A place where families were allowed to abuse and women were mistreated; where the enlightenment had never taken place and the Republic might as well never have been born. All that, plus the murder of innocents. How could such a world still exist in the twentieth century?

Olivier had grinned his old world-weary grin and said he wouldn't be all that surprised if it went on existing for quite a while. But if she was bent on change, she might like to run for office on a different ticket than the one he had aspired to.

She was a woman, she reminded him. She couldn't even vote.

He was sorry about that, he said. But he was grateful that she had saved him from his own political ambitions, and rid him of the sombre emi-nence who had provoked them. As thanks, he would fly her out of here at the first opportunity.

She hadn't taken his words literally.

Now she was floating like a soaring bird, then rushing on a gust of wind. She clutched at the edge of the basket. Below her, she recognized the ivy-clad house that she had first noticed in Olivier's photographs, Beaumont, where P'tit Ours had bravely met his end defending his Amandine.

She said her goodbyes to him, too, and watched the distant roll of the land, the forest where she had found the body of Danuta the Dancer and been felled by Auguste, the strongman. The bulge of the hills was so minimal from here that perspectives were flattened, trees grew into hedges, the river into a strip of waving ribbon on patched, irregularly woven cloth. Suddenly she recognized Blois and at its edge, the cluster of buildings where the sisters lived out their walled lives.

She let her eyes roam the horizon. She felt free up here. Light. Yes, she was flying. In this third month of the new century, Marguerite de Landois was flying. The world dipped and rushed toward her, then tilted and rushed away. Deep in her pocket, she fingered the letter from the other side of the ocean. It was a letter that made her spirits soar and billow and float. Soon, she might just follow them out over the Atlantic.

LISA APPIGNANESI is the
bestselling author of seven novels
and ten works of non-fiction.
Raised in Montreal, she now lives
in London. One of her mysteries,
The Dead of Winter, was shortlisted
for the prestigious Arthur Ellis Award.
Losing the Dead, her memoir about
growing up in Montreal, was shortlisted
for the inaugural Charles E. Taylor
Prize and her most recent novel
The Memory Man won the 2005
Issac Frischwasser Award
For Holocaust Literature.